LOST

REBECCA GUY

Rebecca Guy

Copyrighted Material

This book is entirely a work of fiction, all names, characters and incidents portrayed are the work of the author's imagination. Any resemblance to actual persons, living or dead, events or localities is entirely coincidental.

Copyright © 2022 by Rebecca Guy.

ISBN: 978-1-913241-06-3

Rebecca Guy asserts the moral right to be identified as the author of this work.

All rights reserved.

No part of this book may be reproduced in any form or by any electronic or mechanical means, including information storage and retrieval systems, without written permission from the author, except for the use of brief quotations in a book review.

Cover photo © Shutterstock

Copyrighted Material

Want access to exclusive behind the scenes content and extra's?

Want to be the first to hear about promotions, discounts, forthcoming titles and competitions?

Get all this and more by signing up to my mailing list - It's free and I never spam!

Details of the current freebie at the end of the book.

Follow on: Instagram, Facebook, Goodreads, and Pinterest

www.rebeccaguy.co.uk

ALSO BY REBECCA GUY

Ruin

Shattered

Haunted

ABOUT AUTHOR

Rebecca Guy was first introduced to all things paranormal at the tender age of ten when she received Hans Holzer's 'Ghosts-True Encounters with the World Beyond' from Father Christmas. She tortured herself with the stories late into every night, after which she was too terrified to sleep. Thanks Santa. The trauma started a love affair with all things horror and supernatural and she now like to write her own novels to torture herself and others with until they can't sleep. After all, sharing is caring. Rebecca was born and raised in Staffordshire. She still lives there with her three children and a beagle called Rosie.

f facebook.com/rebeccaguyauthor

instagram.com/rebeccaguyauthor

g goodreads.com/author/show/19771021.Rebecca_Guy

p pinterest.com/rebeccaguyauthor

For Dawn, whose enthusiasm and dedication ensure that my writing journey must continue, with love and thanks and many more enjoyable reads to come!

CHAPTER ONE

A̲PRIL

'Y̲OU LOOK LIKE HELL, Mac.'

Mac Macauley looked up at his older brother; the *only* person from whom he would take such a statement. Tom gazed at him across the table, his eyes narrowed and scrutinizing. Finally, seeming to accept Mac's state of hell, he gave a small nod and flipped open the paper. Mac felt his stomach sink.

'Want me to make you feel worse?' Tom said, eyebrows raised over the paper's edge.

'Sure, why not?' Mac said with a sigh, leaning back into the chair and bringing a hand up to scratch the back of his head.

Tom placed the paper - 'The Times' of all things - down onto the table between them, spinning the writing to face Mac. He placed a finger on the article as if it didn't already have a screaming headline that may as well be emblazoned in red and roaring with flames.

HAS THE MIND MAN LOST HIS MIND?

> After another embarrassing send-off, you have to wonder if the guy who says you can have it all, Mac Macauley, really has lost it all. The motivational sensation who once filled the Royal Albert Hall with his astoundingly fool proof plan to hack the mind, and access the subconscious to create the perfect life, regardless of circumstance, once again left us with a lack lustre feel at his latest talk in Islington yesterday. Seemingly a theme after the loss of his wife six months ago, the media mind-hacker can't seem to get it together, forcing us to wonder if there really is a mind-hack after all, or whether his framework is built on less solid foundations when faced with real tragedy...

No. Not today.

Mac dragged his eyes away from the article and back to Tom's, hoping his brother wouldn't see the thud of his heart under his worn jumper.

'It's a good point,' he said with a shrug as he reached for his cigarettes from his jacket pocket. He pulled one free and put it between his lips.

'What?' he said, catching Tom's frown.

'Sula hated that. You'd given up.'

'For all the good it did me. Sula's dead.' His heart gave a small jolt. A lot less of a shock at saying the words out loud now than he'd had in the beginning. The effects of true love and companionship already fading.

No, not fading. *Suppressed.* He closed his eyes.

'What happened?' Tom said gently.

Mac opened his eyes, confused.

'The talk?' Tom gestured to the paper, which accused innocently from the tabletop. Ignoring Tom's disapproving look, Mac lit the cigarette as he thought.

What happened? That's a good question, Mac. What the hell happened?

He'd lost it. That's what happened, just as the paper said. Lost his wife, lost his life. And now his career was busy getting lost, too. Why not? When life shit on you, it really took a dump, and then it added some more to the pile for good measure.

'You read the article,' he said with a mirthless laugh. 'I lost my wife. Lost her, like we were strolling around Sainsbury's, and she wandered down the wrong aisle. Like an odd sock, she just got...' he threw his hands in the air, '...lost. As if she can be found. Like she'll just turn back up with a smile and say 'gotcha! Had you going for a minute there, didn't I?'

Tom raised his hands. 'Okay, okay. I get it, and I know it hurts. Listen, Mac, maybe it's time for a break, you know?'

Mac took a drag of his cigarette, his face flushing under a week and a half of dark stubble. Heck, the one thing he hadn't lost was the ability to grow a beard. How about that?

'Why would I need a break?'

Tom's mouth bobbed open as he fished for the right words to say. 'Well, you haven't stopped, Mac. All the booked engagements, all the talks, the shows, the interviews. You've just kept steamrollering right through.'

'That's how we get through these things, right? We carry on, Tom, because there's nothing else to fucking do is there? What do I have left? You think I want a mini break in the Maldives? Work. My work is all I have. I want to help people-'

'You're wrecking it, Mac. You need a break. You can't keep going-'

'I *have* to keep going, I have no choice. It's okay for you, Tom. You're not in the public eye. There's no escape for me. Ever since Sula died, people with cameras have been camped on my lawn. My fucking lawn, Tom. And do you know why? Not because they care, not because they want to wish me well, oh no, because they want to see me collapse. They want me to crumble. They want pictures of me looking wasted and beaten. They want to be there to capture it all, to laugh, to write their stupid stories. Because they want headlines like this-' he waved a hand at the paper, which fluttered and crackled under the force of the air thrown at it. 'This sells, Tom. It sells.'

Tom was nodding. 'Yes-' he said, as Mac barrelled right on over him.

'Tragedy sells, shock sells, bereavement sells, falling apart sells. No one wants to listen to the good news anymore. They're all baying for blood. My wife died, Tom, she *died*, and they love it, they...' Mac felt his voice quiver, felt the depth of emotion cut him short, and felt the hot tears threaten to burst forth. He jabbed his thumbs into his eyes, removing them before they arrived.

Mac heard the scrape of a chair and felt a hand squeeze his shoulder.

'Yes,' Tom said, closer to him now, 'that's exactly what they want, because they don't know you. They don't care. It's so easy to de-humanise these days. So easy to tear people apart on social media, in the paper, on the news. But Mac, you're giving them exactly what they want.'

Mac looked into the crow-lined eyes of his brother. His best friend. He cared, Mac knew that, could see the depth of emotion running behind his eyes too. He had known and loved Sula like a sister, as had Tom's wife - who was still here. Flesh and blood.

A stab of unfairness ran through him at the aneurysm that had taken his perfectly healthy wife with a ferocious disregard for the lack of her years.

Tom placed a hand on his arm.

'Look at you, Mac. Have you looked in the mirror? Seen your clothes, your hair, your face? When did you last have a shower? You have to stop because you're giving them fuel. Your career will be over if you keep going. Is that what you want?'

'No, of course not. Being able to help people reach their potential isn't a career, Tom, it's a calling. I have to do this. There are people that need my help...'

'You are one of them,' Tom said. 'Take a break. In six months, a year, you'll be-'

'A year?' Mac spluttered. 'I can't take a year off. Don't be ridiculous.'

'Call it development. You've barely had time for yourself for the last ten years. Read up, learn, look at new theories, rejig the framework. Think of it as a working break. One where you don't need to take a shower and look the part. One where you don't need to worry about getting lost when giving a talk because you think you see her in the audience. Take books, get researching, write a whole new fucking formula, but take a break, Mac, please. We're worried about you.'

Mac swallowed. Tom was forgetting the one problem with his little theory.

'Tom, the other reason I can't take a break is a little more obvious. They won't let me. Wherever I go, Whatever I do at the moment, they're there. Always. Sometimes just one, sometimes a dozen. Do you think I'm going to get off the plane in Gibraltar to find not one person has discovered where I'm going and on what flight? To find not one of them has followed me? I'm stuck. From all angles. I've tried to ask for privacy, I've tried the 'leave me alone', it's not working.'

'Because you look like hell when you're asking. You look broken. It's what they want.'

'So, what's the solution, Tom, because from where I am, it seems you're enjoying this discussion a little too much. Pointing out how dirty and slovenly I am-'

'No, Mac. No. That's not it. Not at all. And yes, I do have a solution. One that I think will work. Just hear me out.'

'I'm all ears.'

'Good,' Tom said, then he took a breath. 'Do you ever watch Bear Grylls?'

CHAPTER TWO

AUGUST

THE OLD FOUR-BY-FOUR TRUCK bounced its way slowly down the dirt track. Pines sheltered either side of the unkempt mountain road which Tom had said ran on for three long miles right out into the desolate Scottish wilderness. Five miles per hour was all he could manage, or risk wrecking the truck's suspension, which gave Mac a lot of time to think. Time to think about what he was doing and whether he had made the right choice, time to wonder if he was capable, time to wonder if he was mad. Beck certainly told him he was a 'Creep' from the radio, which cut out with every bump of the road.

It had taken four long months to get to this point, much to Tom's disgust, but things had to be taken care of. When it looked as though Mac would never take up the offer of the small, isolated cabin on Loch Spiorad, Tom had offered him a million to go and stay the year – 'call it loss of earnings, but please, for the love of God, stay the damn year!'

Eventually, despite starting to feel stronger and more himself, Mac had decided he would go. A year wasn't the end of the world, and anyway, he had social media. A few Facebook and Instagram lives would keep his name out there, and he could record and upload some more videos with a loch-side setting. A few ideas had begun to take seed until Tom shattered his thoughts.

'There's no internet,' he stated, 'and we're taking your phone.'

'My phone?' Mac had said, wide eyed, 'Oh, I don't think so.'

'You'll get another, with limited contacts and limited data per month. They can trace you, Mac. I don't need a horde of media splashing my secluded cabin across the news along with a picture of you in that god awful jumper with a ten-day shadow across your chin. You can have it back afterward. Here.'

He had thrust a new phone into Mac's hand and held out his other hand for Mac's phone, which he had given up reluctantly after seeing the problem with taking it along with him.

No ties, Tom had said. None. He was to use Tom's truck and the new phone. Off media grid. Off GPS. Gone. Completely.

And so, he had been hustled into Tom's house at 3am after leaving through the back door of his own house with a single bag and his golden retriever, Rolo. After stumbling through a small track flanked by trees and out onto a neighbouring street he was collected by Tom, who screeched off so loud it was a wonder no-one had seen him go. At Tom's house, he was to put his bag in the truck and leave. The directions were written on a piece of notepaper for fear of voice recording giving the game away. Tom was very thorough, and very paranoid, but two hours later, humming along to the radio, alone on the road, Mac had to admit it seemed like the perfect getaway.

The sun had been high in the summer sky as he found the small turning for the lane that lead to the three-mile track. Little used, Tom had said, and Mac thought that was an understatement. It barely existed at all. Even now, he wasn't sure this was the right way, or if it was a vehicle track at all. If the instructions hadn't marked waypoints along the route that Tom had set up for his own guidance, he would have tried to turn around long before now.

But here he was, with all his worldly possessions for the next year, bumping down a track that would have done better as an off-road test course, and thinking how Sula would have laughed that he would even consider coming to a place like this with his limited physical skills.

'Who you think you are?' she would smile, her mocking voice in lilted Italian. 'Some great explorer, huh? Ralph Fiennes? You have trouble with can of baked beans, tato!'

Tato had been a term of endearment she had told him long ago, but even now he wasn't sure she hadn't been calling him a potato for all these years. She had howled with laughter when he pressed her, shoulder length tight black curls falling back from an oval face which lifted to the sky, and the biggest brown eyes he had ever seen filling with tears of laughter at his serious question. Laughter had been her go to emotion. She could find humour in the solemnest of situations, lightening the atmosphere, and lifting people up with her along the way.

He should know. Depression had dragged him way down when he had met her. He owed her his life.

But now he could give her nothing.

A familiar pain worked its way into his heart, and a moan escaped his lips. Hot warmth pressed against the back of the hand resting on the gear stick; and then it was gone, leaving a cold wetness in its place. Mac blinked back tears and looked over to the passenger seat to see Rolo grinning at him, tongue lolling out of his mouth as he panted in the heat of the midday sun. Mac couldn't help but grin back. Then he let out a chuckle and rest an elbow out of the truck's open window.

'All right, all right. I know, I'll stop.'

Rolo grinned out of the windscreen, wind ruffling his gleaming golden fur as he licked his lips, sniffed the air, and returned to his grin. Mac reached over to give him an affectionate scratch behind his ear, silky fur leaning into his hand.

'I need to stop. I'm the mind guy, right? I know how this works. I have to stop dwelling and move forward. There is no future in the past. I need to wrap the memories, reset the thermostat, and head off on a different course. She's not coming home. It's been ten months. Did you know that?'

He glanced at Rolo, who cocked his head at him, tongue retreating into his mouth in question.

'Oh yeah, believe it, buddy, ten long months. How did it come to this? In ten months, my life has been picked up, shaken upside down and placed back onto its head. I nearly ruined everything, you know that?'

Rolo cocked his head to the other side in further question and gave a small bark.

'Oh, I did. I saw her everywhere. I *see* her everywhere, in everything I do, or say, and everywhere I go. I need to change this path, buddy, or I'll end up right back where I was twenty years ago.'

Rolo lost interest and went back to grinning at the windscreen.

'That was a bad place, a really, really bad place,' Mac whispered, more to himself than the dog now. 'The more I think about this, the more I know Tom was right. I do need it. I just didn't want to deal with my feelings. I didn't want to think about life moving on without her. Hell, I *don't* want to think about it, I really don't, but maybe it's time. There has to be a time to put this to bed, doesn't there? What do you think, buddy?'

Rolo gave a small whine and placed his head out of the passenger window, his fur blowing comically back from his face as he snapped at the breeze. Mac grinned and turned his attention to the track. He was beginning to wonder just how much longer they'd have to bounce around in here in the heat of the day, when he caught a glimpse of something shining through the trees.

'That's water, Rolo, I'm almost certain. It can't be too much further.'

He turned the truck slowly past the large trunk of a pine tree and almost laughed with relief. Ahead of them was the glint of the loch, and a little further ahead he saw the trees open up and the mountains which rolled around them.

Finally, the cabin can't be too much further now.

Mac's back and legs rejoiced, and he gave a sigh of satisfaction as they turned a corner out into the open. A small wooden cabin came into view, nestled right next to the loch ahead of them. The truck slowed to a stop as Mac surveyed their surroundings with a low whistle.

'Pretty damn perfect, eh, Rolo? Welcome to your luxury abode for the coming year.'

CHAPTER THREE

THE TRUCK SHUDDERED TO a stop between the cabin and a small open-sided structure that housed a wood pile. There wasn't much of it left now. Tom had told him he would need to start chopping soon to stockpile before winter. Mac had thought that he would just pop somewhere and pick up pre-chopped wood, but the drive down that track was enough to make him change his mind in an instant.

He threw open the door and stepped out into the warmth, stretching his back, as Rolo snuck by him and jumped down to sniff and mark his new territory. The trees were thinner here, the forest fizzling out before the shore, and ahead of him stretched the loch. A deep, silent, dark blue, that snaked between the immense mountains.

'Glad Tom threw in the kayak for us,' Mac said, as Rolo sniffed around the woodpile and then ran to the loch edge to lap the water greedily.

Mac shut the door, listening to the pop and ping of the cooling engine as he took in the small one-and-a-half story cabin. Paint was peeling from the central red door - one of the list of jobs that Mac was to complete before the summer was over - but other than that it looked in good shape. Two small windows flanked the doorway before the roof rose up and back, almost comically large in relation to the cabin itself. A small roof light was the only indication of the mezzanine floor that was concealed inside.

At the left side of the wooden structure, where a patch of trees had been cleared long ago, was a small patch of earth with a long-forgotten greenhouse, a shed, and some leftover chicken wire. To the right was a small pier that lead out from a wooden deck right over the water.

Quaint, Mac thought, almost idyllic; but certainly but not for the faint of heart, Tom had said. A lover of getting down and dirty in nature, and a philosopher of self-sufficiency, Tom had acquired the cabin a little over four years ago to satisfy his craving for getting 'out into the sticks' alone, and for bonding with his only son, Josh. From here, Mac could see why. There was nothing around him but mountains, water, and trees. No other buildings, no structures, no people. The only life here other than Mac and Rolo, was nature itself.

Tom had been strict in his instructions, if Mac didn't want to drive down the three mile track every couple of days in summer, or die a long, slow, painful death in winter when the track was snow covered and there was no way out, he would need to be stringent and self-sufficient.

Wood had to be chopped; the log burner would need to be on almost constantly in winter as the only source of heat in the cabin. Running water and filtered drinking water were available, but hot water had to be boiled. The only luxury was a generator which provided electricity for lights, a cooker, a fridge, a freezer, and a shower. Fruit and veg were to be replaced, seeds sown and nurtured, if he planned to tend the vegetable area - which he didn't. Tom had said the cabin was stocked with plenty of long-life tins and packets, and a freshly stocked freezer to boot, Mac was sure that would suffice. If not the nearest village was twelve miles away. If he had to replenish anything, he would just need to do it well before winter.

The vast amount of work that it would take just to survive here hit Mac as he stared at the cabin. He wobbled. He thought about getting back into the car and sodding Tom's promise that this would sort him out. This was Tom's idea of what he needed because this was Tom all over, but it was certainly not Mac. Not by a long shot.

There was a series of splashes and Mac turned to see Rolo chasing a large grey heron from the water.

'Oi!' Mac shouted, 'Leave, Rolo. Leave it alone!'

The heron flew off as the dog shot Mac a wounded look.

'You can get your fun without getting into fights. I need you here with me, okay?'

The dog lolloped back to him, stopping to shake the water from his wet fur.

'Thanks.' Mac said, wiping at his wet jeans. 'Shall we go inside and take a look at our new digs before unpacking our very sparse life from the truck?'

Rolo shook again and ran to the small red door, tail wagging furiously as if he was visiting somewhere he knew. Mac followed with a laugh and placed the key in the lock.

The dog ran in first and set about sniffing as Mac let out a breath between his lips in surprise. The door opened into a cosy living area that belied the outside dimensions of the cabin. To the left sat a snug settee and a chair, and against the wall was the log burner, a bookshelf, and games cupboard. A small window overlooked what Mac knew would be the vegetable garden. To the right was a small kitchen area with a sink and small electric hob, oven and grill, a white melamine dining table for two, and a fridge complete with magnetic letters and numbers - Ignore them, Tom had said, Josh and I leave each other messages if we go on solo missions out. Mac grinned and brought his gaze to the small window which looked out over the fishing pier to the loch.

'Pretty nice,' Mac said, turning away from the kitchen.

Ahead ran a small flight of open-backed wooden stairs that lead to a railed mezzanine floor which Mac knew housed two single beds, just visible from his position at the doorway. Beyond the stairs was a small corridor.

Mac walked past the stairs to investigate. A small window sat at the end of the corridor looking out onto the trees, but it did nothing to let in the light. It was much darker at this end of the cabin. A door on his left lead to a small storeroom which held torches, candles, kindling, fire lighters, and rope, alongside extra bedding, towels, and masses of tinned and packet food on its shelves. Against one wall stood a chest freezer which Tom had rammed full of fresh and frozen food just the week before.

Enough to feed five of us for the next six years, thought Mac with a grin. *Typical Tom and Meg.*

He turned to the door opposite the store which held the small bathroom. There was a composting toilet, with a small bucket of sawdust and a scoop next to it, a sink, and bath with shower. Mac thanked the lord that at least he wouldn't have to shower outside or bath in the loch. He peered out of the corridor's small end window to see the large, continuous run generator that powered the entire cabin. It had cost Tom a packet, but after having a diesel generator out here and getting stuck one year, he vowed to have something much more reliable, and much less of a pain in the ass, whatever the cost. Tom said that it would be good to see him through the winter, although he had given him a number to call should there be any trouble. And of course, he had Tom's number too, just in case.

In case of what, Mac hadn't dared to ask.

Tom had checked the cabin and fired up the generator only last week to let the fridge cool for his arrival. There was nothing to do there, and looking at the hulking thing outside, Mac was glad. He wouldn't know where to start. He walked back to the brighter area of the cabin and switched on the low wattage kettle to boil the water for a hot drink. He was leaning back against the worktop, Rolo busy licking at something unseen stuck to the floor next to the log burner, when he noticed it.

He frowned.

A piano. A full-sized upright piano. Right behind the sofa, under the mezzanine floor. It's dark wood combined with the darkness from the floor above had concealed it from view.

Mac blinked. There was something very wrong with this picture. Tom didn't play the piano, and neither did Josh. There would be no reason to have a piano here, unless...

Rolling his eyes with a sigh, Mac pulled out his new phone and dialled Tom's number. The kettle boiled, and he poured water into the cup, leaving it to brew as the phone rang out. He turned his back on the instrument and stared out of the cabin window at the pier.

What the hell are they doing? trying to kill me?

CHAPTER FOUR

'D AD, PHONE'S RINGING.' JOSH called from the front door, holding the mobile aloft as though it would magically transport from his hand to Tom's down the driveway.

'Right, give me a sec, who is it?' he said, grunting as he lifted the wheel back onto the axle shaft, and picked up a nut from the floor. He twisted it onto the thread and secured another to keep the wheel stable.

'Dunno.'

'Looking at the screen too much for you in this bright light?' Tom said. He watched as Josh sloped down to the car, dishevelled hair falling over black eyeliner ringed eyes which squinted into the sun. Today he wore a black t-shirt and jeans with more holes than a block of Braemar cheese.

'Hah. Funny,' Josh said, thrusting the phone at Tom as he wiped a hand on his jeans. He took the mobile, turning it to look at the screen.

Mac.

'Thanks,' he said, swiping to answer as Josh sloped back up the driveway with the nonchalance that all teenagers seemed to possess when they got to the grunting stage. Josh grunted on cue and flicked a hand toward him for good measure.

'Mac, how are you, buddy? You found it okay?'

'I know what you're doing, Tom. I get it. This was all pre-planned, huh? So, who had the big idea?... Meg?'

Tom frowned and stood, stretching his legs. He opened his mouth to reply, but couldn't wrap his head around what Mac had said.

'What?'

Mac chuckled down the line. 'I said, who had the big idea? Get Mac out here, cut him off from the world and give him a piano so he can heal while he's there. I can see right through the both of you, you know. I've known you for too long, don't play coy.'

Tom stared at the house across the street, with it's neat lawn, and sports car in the driveway. As he watched, Mrs Turney stepped out of the front door and placed a newspaper in the bin, lifting a hand in greeting, before she turned to go back inside.

Tom raised a hand in return.

'None of this was planned, Mac, I have no idea what you're talking about. You needed a break, and I have a cabin sitting empty, perfectly situated away from everyone and everything. I'm sorry I didn't think of it sooner to be honest, but...'

'So you play the piano now then, too?'

Mac's voice was croaky, and then he let out a breath and Tom knew he was smoking. He grit his teeth and forced his attention back onto his brother.

'I have never had any inclination to play the piano, little bro. That is your forte. You're the musical one in the family, and I really don't mind handing you that cap. Wear it with pride.'

'Oh, I will, and that's great, but then why is there a piano sitting in your cabin a million miles away from anywhere. A cabin only you come to?'

Tom frowned and turned to lean his back against the car.

The sun was hot today; the sky cloudless, and he was obviously becoming dehydrated in the burning sun. Why else would he be having a conversation about a piano being in his cabin? He wiped perspiration from his brow.

'Um... I really don't-' He started, bending to pick up a rag to clean a spot of dirt that had clung to the paint in the last two hours. He hadn't missed a spot. He never missed a spot. The BMW X5 gleamed on all occasions.

'I'll tell you why,' Mac said, humour in his tone, 'because you had it transported here to get me playing again. It worked to get me out of a funk before, and now you think it will help me again. The thing is, Tom, I'm never playing again. I quit piano. I can't play, not...' his voice caught and Tom stopped wiping. '...not without her,' he finished.

Tom placed the rag on the bonnet of the car and swallowed hard at the emotion in his brother's voice, which brought his own emotions to the fore without warning.

'Mac, listen,' he said. 'I don't know what you think I've done, planned, worked out, or what. I don't play the piano, I don't own a piano, and I certainly don't have one in my cabin. Did you follow the instructions? Are you sure you're at the right place?'

Even as he asked, he knew it was futile. There were no other cabins for miles around, as far as he knew.

'I am at the right cabin. I followed the instructions carefully, and the key fit the lock like a glove. You do have a piano in your cabin.' Mac said, emotion erased and sounding like himself again.

'Mac, I'm confused. I really don't... what the hell would I do with a piano?'

'That's what I want to know, but it's here. Look.'

Tom waited as there was a scuffle and a faint click, and then the phone pinged. A message. Pulling the phone from his ear, he opened it and saw his sofa. Same chequered blanket thrown over the back, the wooden underneath of the mezzanine floor behind. It was his cabin, but Mac was right, behind the sofa sat a dark mahogany upright piano. Tom pinched the photo closer, further away, closer again. It had to be a trick of the light, surely. He scratched his head as his lip curled up.

There is a piano. Who the hell has been in my cabin?

'So, am I at the right place or not?' Mac said.

'Uh-huh.' Tom replied.

'Right, so, now we've confirmed that I am here, we can drop the pretence.' Mac huffed a breath and Tom was lost for words.

How is there a piano in the cabin?

Then Mac was back. Softer now.

'Listen, I'm not mad. I do appreciate all you're doing to help me, and yes, you're right, I was messing things up. I get that now. But I'm the mind guy, right? If I can't sort myself out, who the hell can? You didn't need to do this. I won't play again, Tom. I can't. Thank you, but no.'

'Okay.' Tom said, his mind whirring with questions. It must have been Meg... but how had Meg gone all that way with a goddamn piano by herself? 'Okay, fine. If you don't want to play, of course you don't have to. I'm not sure how it even got there. I'm as flummoxed as you, buddy, really. Ignore it if you don't want to use it.'

Mac slurped. It sounded like he was having a drink, something Tom could do with, and maybe a chat with Meg while he was at it.

'Yeah, I will,' Mac said. 'Thank Meg anyway, if it was her. I'm going to unpack my stuff now. That'll probably take me most of the afternoon.'

Tom smiled at the irony in Mac's voice.

'Well, take it easy. I don't want my cabin filled with your junk when I'm next there. How do you like the place, anyway?'

'It's good.' Mac said, 'It's nice. I can't believe I knew nothing about it before.'

Tom snorted air from his nose.

'If I'd have told you, you'd have been up there too... not that I begrudge that, but so would your admiring fans, and the lunatics with the cameras who insist on following you about. Before long, you'd have been holding breathing and neuro-hacking retreats, my poor track having been tarmacked and turned into a duel carriageway!'

Mac laughed softly on the other end of the line. 'Yeah, I get it,' he said. 'It's okay, and thank you for letting me use it now, and for helping me get away. No-one followed me here today, so I guess I'm actually alone for the first time in a good many years.'

Tom smiled, but his heart gave a small flip. He only hoped that Mac could cope with the lack of people.

'I'm not sure you'll be thanking me in a couple of weeks, and certainly not when the snow comes down. Your mind will play havoc for a while. Make sure you chop enough wood to keep the place warm over winter. There is a stack of logs at the back of the log store that should see you through. You'll just need to chop them down. Put them in the store and use the tarp to cover them, keep them dry.'

'Okay, where's the tarp? In the shed?'

'It should be over the wood already?'

'Nope, the wood isn't covered,' Mac said.

Tom clenched his jaw and had a sudden urge to check whether Meg had sent the piano, or whether there was someone up there after all. The tarp was secured with rope through hooks and eyes and weighted with bricks. There was no way it had blown away, surely. In all the years he had been up there, he had never once lost the tarp.

'Check the shed then,' he said, keeping his voice light. Mac didn't need to know, 'there'll be a spare.'

'Right.'

'There should be some veg ready outside, too. Check the seeds. Any ground you clear feel free to replant.'

'Hmmm.' Mac replied and Tom knew he was struggling with the concept of not only gardening, but survival gardening.

'You can't go wrong, I plant through tarp to stop the weeds, the veg looked fairly neat last week, if you want to check what something is I've put an app on the phone, just scan it and it'll tell you. Or just send me a picture.'

'Got it.' Mac said, and Tom very much doubted that he had at all.

'Okay, well, there's sawdust at the side of the shed for the toilet. When the bucket gets low, just refill it, saves you getting caught short with a smell. The water is pumped and filtered directly from the loch, so there should be no trouble there unless the pipe freezes. I've insulated and buried it deep, but it still freezes up occasionally. You can take water from the loch in that instance. It's fresh water. Just use the sterilising tablets to purify it before drinking. They're in the back store. What else?' Tom tried to think of all the things he took for granted as knowing how to do. 'Ah, the genny. It shouldn't give you any trouble, but there is a small backup supply of fuel if you need it. Call the number I gave you if there's any trouble, or you have to use that fuel. It'll only keep you going a couple of days. There are candles in the store if you need them. There's also a small camp stove and an extra bottle of gas to cook with should that happen. Obviously, the fridge and shower won't work, and the freezer food will quickly become obsolete. Just keep food cold outside, especially if it's snowing, and don't have a shower unless you're into cold water.'

'Right.' Mac said, and Tom realised he was wasting his breath. There was no way that Mac could take all of this in - which is where Meg was a godsend. She had typed a folder of things to know and do, and the processes, together with Tom over the last few months. He had dropped it there early last week with the food...

Last week, Tom. Last week when there hadn't been a piano behind the damn sofa.

Tom swallowed.

'Anyway,' he said. 'there is a yellow folder in the store with instructions and tips, and obviously I'm at the other end of the phone. Anytime. Especially if you need to talk, or there is anything untoward, right?'

Especially if someone turns up that shouldn't be there.

'Yep, sure. Don't worry Tom, it's all in hand. I'll be fine, really.'

Tom sighed, hoping he was right.

'Like I said, give it a couple of weeks before being so sure. Loch Spiorad will test you, Mac. It's hard, but it's rewarding. You'll certainly get to know yourself out there. Hopefully, you can grieve in peace and get things back into perspective at the very least.'

'I aim to. Things are already coming into perspective, even just from the drive here.'

Tom ran a hand over his face.

'Okay, buddy, call if you need anything, yeah?'

'Will do. Bye, Tom, and thanks again.'

'No worries, I'm here if you need me. Take care, Mac.'

'I will, speak soon,' he said.

Tom suddenly wondered if he had done the right thing sending Mac to the cabin. For the first time since his idea, he realised that not only may it heal him, but it may also break him. At worst, it could drive him insane and quite possibly kill him.

'Oh Mac! I forgot to say...'

Tom listened as the phone cut off the connection between the brothers.

'If you can't hack it, get out before the winter, or you'll be stuck for months,' he finished to himself.

Shit. I'll message him later.

Flinging the cloth over the car's wing mirror, Tom went to find a drink. After that, he would find the next most pressing thing... his wife.

CHAPTER FIVE

M AC THREW HIS TRAVEL bag onto the sofa and opened the zip. He pulled out his toiletries and took them to the bathroom, placing them in the tiny cupboard under the sink. There was a small oval mirror just above, mottled with brown spots of damp. Mac tried not to look, caught a glimpse of himself, and looked back with a sigh.

Mac, buddy, you look like a hot mess. No wonder the tabloids were having a field day.

He ran a hand over his half-grown beard, now flecked with grey like his dark hair. He noted the shadows under his eyes, the new lines in his forehead and around his mouth, and a new, longer line that started at the corner of his eye and crawled down his right cheek each time he smiled. He tested it out, pulling his mouth back into a smile and then setting it straight, using his fingers to massage out the crease. He cursed the face cream that had cost him a fortune, and a promise of eternal youth, but which obviously did nothing for the effects of grief.

Sula would say it was a laughter line...

Mac stopped poking his cheekbone and stared into his own grey eyes. She would. They had laughed at all of their respective lines as they had appeared.

'These are laughter lines,' she had said once, climbing onto his lap and pointing to the crow's feet around his eyes. 'This one is a worry line,' she continued, with her own frown as she had pointed to a small line creasing his forehead - that particular line was deeper now, and a few more had joined it for good measure. 'This one,' she said, lifting his jumper before he could stop her, 'is a 'get the hell in shape, Mac' line!' She had pointed at the crease of folded skin above his 'spare tyre', and, oh, she had laughed at that. Long and loud, until Mac had finally joined in with her.

The next day he began to jog, and then run, and then bike, then hike, then kayak. For the next year, Sula scolded that Mac was either at work or on the move. He was never still, always active. The only time she got to spend with him was when they were having sex. Not long after that she had appeared in the kitchen in leggings and Nikes, and placed a new water bottle down on the countertop.

'What you can't beat, you join.' She had said with a flash of perfect white teeth. And so, they had moved together. Mac had never felt healthier, and he thought Sula had been the same.

No accounting for what life thought; or indeed death.

In the bathroom, Mac pushed the thought away. He huffed a breath and lift the same green jumper that Tom had scolded him for wearing and not throwing out. Sula's favourite on him. His belly sat flat and firm, with the ripple of muscle sitting just under the skin. A stomach and chest that even a younger man would have been proud of. One that had cost him blood, sweat, tears, and near-death experiences on a daily basis in the early days as he had pushed himself to get into shape. He gave the taut skin a pat for good measure.

Not lost it all yet, bud, you've still got something.

The face in the mirror grinned, and then blanched as Rolo gave a series of harsh barks outside. Pushing off the small sink, Mac half jogged to the open cabin door and peered outside to greet whoever was here.

Then he kicked himself. There was no-one. Tom said he had never had a single visitor in all the time he and Josh had ever been out here.

Outside the day was still and warm, the sun still mid-afternoon high. Basking in the warmth after the cool of the cabin, Mac called Rolo, and found the dog barking into the trees just off the track, facing back out into the wood.

'Rolo!' he yelled, 'There's no-one here, boy, come on.'

He pat his thigh with a slap, but still the dog barked with no pause.

Probably a wildcat, or deer, or something.

'Going to have to get used to them. We're here for a good while yet,' he shouted, placing his hands on his hips to watch.

There was no movement in the woods, just darkness, but still the retriever barked. Mac sighed.

'Christ on a cross, Rolo, it's nature. Get a grip!'

He walked to the dog, and placed a hand on the back of his neck. Rolo was immediately quiet, but Mac felt the tension flooding the dog's body. His hackles were up, his fur standing on end at the base of his neck and tail. He glanced at Mac with a whine.

'What is it?' he said, squatting beside the dog to squint into the trees. Rolo's barking had ceased, but growls rumbled through his body, despite Mac's hand on his back. It was so out of character for the dog that Mac felt his heart thumping under his jumper as a ripple of unease crossed his chest.

He has my attention, so now what's up?

The heat of the day beat down on the back of Mac's neck. There was no wind. No noise. The forest was still and dark. The smell of dry pine and dirt filled his nostrils.

'There's nothing here,' Mac whispered, half to himself, as Rolo stared into the darkness.

And then there was a rustle and Mac flinched as Rolo gave a long series of barks. A small brown pheasant shot out of the bracken and tore up the track on stubby legs. Rolo lunged and tried to give chase, but Mac had a hand on his collar, pulling the dog straight back. Rolo strained, and finally gave up.

'Come here,' Mac said, feeling a little wired as his heart pumped. Rolo turned and sat almost on top of Mac's feet, staring up as Mac pointed down at him. 'No. You can't chase the wildlife. You'll scare it to death. It was here before you. You're a guest, remember?'

Rolo cocked his head to one side, looking a little less grumpy. Mac stooped down and placed his hands into the golden fur around the dog's neck, massaging with his fingers as his heartbeat slowed.

'Stop pouting,' he said. 'You're hot, and I have an idea. How about we set up the kayak and take a paddle down the loch?'

Rolo stood and shook, shaking Mac's hands out of his fur, and picking up a swift pant as he looked up at him.

'Well?' Mac said, standing up. 'What are you waiting for? Go on!'

He stood, swinging a hand toward the truck where the kayak sat in its bright orange bag in the rear of the covered flatbed. Rolo jogged forward, and Mac, satisfied that he had forgotten the bird, strode after him, wiping sweat from his brow.

Almost had a heart attack over the damn wildlife, he thought, shaking his head with a grin. In fact, it was almost comical just how unnerved he'd been. Tom would have a field day if he knew.

I'm in for a whole heap of mind shit, eh, Tom? Lets start the ball rolling the first hour in with a simple growl and a pheasant. In my defence Rolo never growls, it was a little weird.

At the truck Mac shook his head, opened the tailgate and dragged the kayak bag toward him. The oars clattered out with it, and as he stooped to pick them up, he realised that Rolo had gone again. He glanced back to find the dog staring out into the woods, his body stiff and alert, although mercifully quiet this time.

Shit, Rolo, you can quit this bloody game.

'Rolo!' he called, sliding the straps of the kayak bag onto his back and grabbing the oars and the pump. The dog turned and ran toward him, and Mac turned back to the loch and the small pier with a breath of relief.

Pumping up the two-man kayak and getting it into the water was easy. Getting Rolo in was always a little harder. He had accompanied Mac on his boating trips since he was a puppy, but 6 years later he still had to find a way to get in that didn't look like he was skating on ice - all legs, teeth, and tail. He tumbled in and Mac followed, grabbing the oars, and screwing them together. Pushing an end at the wooden post of the small pier, the boat moved away, and Mac began to paddle.

The water was calm, barely a ripple besides the one the boat cut through the deep blue water, and the paddling was easy. Rolo set up his post at the front of the boat, his legs and paws draped over the front like a wet towel. Occasionally he sniffed or lapped at the water, mostly he stared out in front like he belonged on the crest of a pirate ship.

When the cabin became just a dot in the distance behind, and a bend swung the water to the right in front, Mac lay the paddles in the boat and sat listening to the quiet. The loch was serene and majestic. The mountains rose either side of the water like forest infested giants, and higher up there were open patches of grass and scree. All he could hear was the odd call of a sheep, a caw of a crow, the rustle of the water, and then... nothing.

No wonder Tom kept this place to himself. It's perfect. So peaceful.

Mac took the straps out from the seat and lay it flat. He lay back, the top of his shoulders and head lying on the raised back of the boat, in much the same position as Rolo was spread at the front. He arranged his legs so that they missed the dog and settled back, trailing his hands in the quiet water, enjoying the sheer cold seeping up his arms.

I could swim every morning, he thought, pushing down his anxiety at the close confines of the cabin, and the intense feeling that he had nowhere to complete his daily run except back down the dirt track. It was an illusion; he knew. There was more walking, hiking, and running territory here than he'd ever had at home—and besides, neither icy water, nor swimming, had ever really been his thing.

Maybe I'll give it a go anyway. Tom will be proud.

His face stretched sideways, and he realised that he was smiling. Involuntarily. With the sheer joy of just being here and being present. Something he hadn't done for months, since Sula.

Tom, you may just have done me the biggest favour. I reckon this place may heal me yet.

His smile widened as he closed his eyes and felt the heat of the sun on his face.

CHAPTER SIX

M AC SOBBED SO HARD he thought his heart would come right out of his chest. Darkness had fallen, and the lack of things to do - television, books, his phone with his personal emails, messages and games, his laptop - had brought his thoughts fully to the fore tonight. With no distractions, he wandered a little too far toward Sula, and hadn't been able to pull himself back. She had swamped him with emotion, and he had given in, losing the fight on the sofa. Rolo had curled up at the other end, his nose on Mac's thigh watching intently. Mac rubbed his head but couldn't console the dog, and couldn't console himself.

Earlier, he had pulled the boat up next to the pier, and tugged it clear of the water. With the sun dipping, they had had a dinner of sausage and egg sandwiches. Minus the bread and egg for Rolo, who had only wanted the sausage.

'Picky,' Mac had scolded, as Rolo had downed his three sausages in one gulp, even with their heat.

Then he had opened a can of beer, and sat on the pier looking out over the loch. He was there when thoughts of Sula and how much she would love it here came flooding his way, pounding at the door of his conscious. By the time he had decided to pack up and go in, she was fully inside him, ripping apart his mind and heart with all that she had been and done. He had managed to get inside through blurry tears before really letting go. He wasn't sure he had cried this hard since she had gone, and there was no stopping the flow.

'Get your game on, tato.' Sula said, blowing a kiss from the other end of the corridor. Mac made an exaggerated catching motion and deftly blew her one back. She pretended to miss it, and made a show of trying to find it. Mac raised an eyebrow and tapped a finger on his watch.

It's time.

Sula dropped to the floor, cotton skirt fanning around her, found the missed kiss and planted it on her lips with a smile that would have melted snow. Mac smiled back and placed a hand on the stage door in front of him.

'Tato! Don't forget to breathe.'

Mac frowned and glanced back toward where Sula had been. Now she was gone, and the corridor empty, but that was okay, he knew she would be rushing to her seat in the audience. She was the biggest ambassador of his show. Her show, really. All of his drive, his knowledge, and his passion for helping people had been driven to fruition through her, and her complete faith that he had something special to share. She was the real brains behind the setup. He adored the facts and the science, and he loved putting the framework together, but he was a showman, a speaker, a teacher. Sula was the organiser, the director, the nuts and bolts behind the scenes. Together they were the 'A-team'; indestructible, and had been for many years. They travelled, worked, ate, and slept together, and not always harmoniously. Sula had a hot head and a hot heart, Mac had never met a woman as passionate as his wife. She had a passion for understanding, a passion for learning, a passion for listening, a passion for eating, a passion for music, a passion for life. If Sula had an acronym, that would be it – passion.

Mac heard the audio announce his arrival on stage, and heard the thunder of applause from the stadium. He turned back to the stage door and pushed.

The crowd cheered, all twenty thousand of them. The noise was almost a roar. Mac liked to see the audience, but the lights in this auditorium were too bright, the stadium too big for individual connection. A mass of black stretched beyond the lights as he thanked the audience and held up his hands for silence.

The claps and whistles trailed off and there was an air of expectation in the stillness.

'Ladies and gentlemen, good evening and welcome. Are you ready for a mind altering, life changing experience?' Mac let the shouts and cheers die away before continuing. 'My name is Mac Macauley, and we're here tonight to...'

He trailed off. His mind suddenly empty.

What the hell was he doing here? What had these people come to see? Frowning, he cleared his throat and looked for Sula in the audience. She was good at prompting, but her seat was empty.

Think Mac, what are you talking about tonight?

His mind was blank. He could have been talking about fishing or life-saving surgery for all he knew, there was nothing firing in his brain. He cleared his throat.

'Try again,' Sula said in his mind, 'sometimes the act will give you prompts, yes?'

Mac tried again. 'Sorry about that, ladies and gentlemen, I lost where I was going there. I'll start again! We're here tonight to... to... er...'

It's not working.

Mac swallowed hard. The lights suddenly seemed too bright, too hot, and under his suit jacket, the temperature seemed stifling. Sweat trickled down his chest, and he pursed his lips, tasting the salty liquid gathered on his top lip.

'Erm, one moment, please,' he stammered, turning to grab the glass of water from a small round table by the curtain at the back of the stage. He took three big gulps, biding his time. The audience began to shift, and he knew they were getting restless. Mac tried to think, but there was nothing to give away what he should say, no name of the show behind him, the screen was unusually blank.

He turned to Sula's front row seat and was relieved to see her there. He tried to catch her eye, willed her to give him a sign, but she sat passively, staring past him.

The audience was murmuring now, a buzzing that started in the auditorium and ended in his head, in his brain. Mac shook his head, the buzz turning into a whine. The lights seemed to merge and change colour, and then two Sula's were coming across the aisle that ran between the chairs and the stage. They merged, and then broke apart again.

'Breathe, tato. I told you, breathe,' she screamed.

A cloth was in her hand. She lunged it at him, and it landed across his face. Warm. Wet.

'Breathe! Breathe, Mac!'

He closed his eyes and wiped a hand across his face as another warm splat landed.

'No, I am... don't...'

He pushed at the cloth, grabbing at Sula's furry hand.

Furry?

Mac opened his eyes. The auditorium was dark, no lights, no audience, no stage, no Sula. He sat up with a gasp, pulling back from Rolo's wet kisses, and hitting something soft. He realised it was a sofa, but not his. Rolo jumped up next to him, placing his head in Mac's lap with a whine as it came back to him.

The cabin. I'm at Tom's cabin!

'All right,' he said, stroking Rolo's head as the cabin furniture came into dark focus, 'It's all right, just a dream.'

His head began the dull pounding of a headache, and his bladder called. He pushed the dog off to take a leak, checking his watch for the time as he came back down the corridor. He had the second jolt of the night.

3.06am.

'Shit! I must have fallen asleep right there on the sofa.'

He rubbed at his head and reached into his travel bag by the stairs for some paracetamol. Popping two and swallowing them with water. He rummaged for his sleeping pills, couldn't find them, and decided it was almost morning anyway. He climbed the stairs to the comfortable bed waiting at the top, and fully clothed, he lowered himself between the cool sheets. There was a clicking on the stairs and a weight landed on the bottom of the bed.

'No bed, Rolo,' he murmured, as his eyes closed and sleep took him for the second time that night.

CHAPTER SEVEN

M AC OPENED HIS EYES to bright sunlight which dappled from the roof light above. He rolled onto his back, looking up at the cloudless blue sky through the treetops that loomed overhead. Another fine day was in store, he didn't need a weather app to tell him that.

What also struck him was that it didn't look much like early morning sun, and that he had slept almost soundlessly without sleeping pills for the first time in months. Not only that, but he felt awake - alive - and he couldn't remember the last time he had felt like that, either. Usually, it was a slog to get up and get dressed, always pushing himself to do the things he knew he had to, so that he could relax into the ridiculous stupor that involved watching trivial nothingness on television.

This morning his head was clear, and his mind bright. Refreshed, he stretched and climbed out of bed, changed, and went downstairs. After letting Rolo out to do his business, he washed and got breakfast, and then he ate out on the pier overlooking the loch. It was already hot, any early morning mist had been burned off by the time he arrived out there.

He was eating his breakfast when the familiar nagging began to eat at him - he should be doing something.

Checking messages, checking emails, checking his calendar, meetings. Anything. Even knowing that there was nothing much he *had* to do here at all. Placing the finished bowl of cereal back inside by the sink, he found his phone lying by the kettle. There was a message from Tom sent over three hours ago. Mac pressed the screen to open it.

Good morning! Hope your first night went well. Forgot to tell you yesterday about the emergency code. If you get stuck at any point or need emergency assistance, there's a number written in the front of the yellow book. They will have to send a helicopter to you. There is a flare gun in the store, which will alert them to where you are if you've been out walking or are away from the cabin. Store the number in the phone so you have it with you at all times, and take the gun when you go out. You never know when trouble may strike. Better safe than sorry! Ring if you need anything.

The yellow folder. I should probably go through it, see exactly what needs doing around here.

Feeling better that he was 'doing' something, Mac spent the next hour going through the book. He checked the storeroom for all the things it mentioned - spare candles, rope, pipe, food, and the flare gun. He stored the emergency number in his phone and pulled the spare tarp out to cover the wood. Then he went outside to find Rolo, who was digging a hole by the vegetable patch, something long in his mouth that was about to meet a soily grave.

In the heat of the midday sun - something he would think about in future - Mac spent an hour chopping one of the large logs behind the wood store into sixteen rudimentary logs ready for the wood burner. Something that he clearly needed to practice if his logs were going to sit as neatly in the store as Tom's did along the bottom. For now, he had made a start. He had burned off some energy, and parched didn't begin to describe the way he felt. It was after 1.30pm when he finally got a drink and thought about lunch.

The afternoon he spent unpacking the rest of his bag. He kicked himself that his sleeping pills didn't come to light, and realised that he must have forgotten them in the rush to leave. He stuffed his shoes under the bed, arranged his books ready to add to a shelf in the bookcase, and folded his clothes neatly in the small dresser. After Folding down the bag and placing it under the bed out of the way, he grabbed the pile of books and took them downstairs, moving some of Tom's books, and claiming a shelf for himself.

Then he stood, twiddling his thumbs, nervous energy pouring from him at the lack of anything more to do.

Come on Mac, this place will be hell if you don't learn to relax. Just do nothing, don't fight it. Relax.

He stood for a while, sat on the sofa, shifted, bit his lip, stood again, and then he left the cabin, calling Rolo as he went to the pier and pulled the kayak out onto the water. The dog scramble-jumped inside as Mac began to paddle, pulling backwards today. Strong, sure strokes taking the boat quickly away from the shore and the cabin, and into the centre of the deep loch. When he was far enough out that he felt himself relax he laid the oars down and stared at the beauty around him, natural and unspoilt. Wild and green. Rolling, sweeping and open.

It was a far cry from the centre of London where he had lived his whole life. If London were to have a colour Mac would paint it deep red and grey: prestige and poverty over concrete and brick; bustling, confident and commanding, edges, angles, and symmetry. In London everyone was always going somewhere, always doing something, and usually in a hurry- he should know, he had been one of them, a part of the beating heart that was England's capital city. London had it's own beat, it's own symphony, it's own *hum*. There was always a noise to be heard. the roar of traffic, the chatter of people, the buzz of machinery, a siren, a shout, a bang, but out here...

Out here everything is still. Still, and quiet, and slow. There's no hum. That's why you can't relax, Mac, you need a new beat.

He closed his eyes and listened to the sounds of the Loch, the sun warm on his face. The birds sang, the loch rippled and lapped, leaves rustled gently in the trees, a sheep bleated from the mountainside. Mac listened intently but that was pretty much it, apart from the growling.

growling?

Mac opened his eyes to find Rolo standing in front of him, his hackles raised as he stared at the shoreline where the cabin sat. A low rumble seemed to vibrate through the boat as the growls rippled through him.

Twice in as many days? I don't think Rolo has ever growled in his life!

'Rolo, how can you live in a city, with all of it's noises and smells and not raise an eyebrow, and yet you come out here and growl at nature?' He leaned to put a hand on the dog's back but Rolo didn't flinch. He simply stared and growled. Every nerve seemed to be alert and on edge. Mac felt that same unease swirl in his chest.

'What the hell is bothering you out there?' he said, leaning close to the dog to squint at the cabin. As far as he could tell there was no movement. The cabin sat quaint, heat shimmering from it's roof in the warmth of the day. 'There's nothing there, Rolo, seriously.'

Rolo continued to growl and with a huff of nervous frustration Mac finally grabbed the oars and turned the dog away. He paddled further out, forward this time, and with the cabin out of view, Rolo finally got the hint, calmed, and flopped back over the front of the boat as though nothing had happened.

With a frown, Mac looked back toward the cabin and scoured the woodland, but there was no movement, and nothing to see.

So what was he growling at then? Surely not another pheasant from all the way out here.

He let his eyes linger. The cabin looked as quaint as it had yesterday, perfect under the cloudless summer sky.

There was no reason to think that anything was wrong, or out of place, and yet, under his t-shirt, for reasons he couldn't quite put his finger on, Mac's heart continued to bump wildly.

CHAPTER EIGHT

SEPTEMBER

THE DAYS HAD BEGUN to take on their own routine. It wasn't one Mac was particularly fond of, but there it was. It was how it went, and there seemed little point in fighting it. There wasn't much else to occupy his time, anyway.

The days started bright. Late for Mac, the earliest he had risen was 8.40am, which was unheard of in his world of shows and talks. The marvellous mind guy, Mac Macauley, had risen way earlier, back then. Then, the day had always begun just before 5am, with the dawn song Sula had said, but Mac had always been a morning person. He could complete and gather some of his best work and ideas before 8am.

Waking at 5am had always been easy with Sula around. His driving force for getting things done. He had always been bright in the morning, but this changed when Sula went.

Tom had said back then that Mac should slow down. Give himself time, let himself feel the grief. But Mac, of all people, knew the importance of pretence. He knew how to trick the brain, how anything visualised in that goldmine that was a human's imagination could be perceived as real, and with the right consistent action and belief it could eventually become real. And so, he had carried on as though Sula were still there; getting up early, going through his morning routine, giving thanks, asking for guidance, priming himself for the day ahead, noting the important tasks to complete, and writing his goals for the day.

It was a routine Sula had helped to instil at the beginning, and he knew it worked because it had worked on him. That was why it was part of the framework he offered to help others overcome their own barriers and limitations - whatever they were going through. That was what he preached, and Sula's death had seemed the perfect time to check its validity again.

The problem was that instead of the ease and confidence with which he had flown through his days before, the sense of satisfaction, and belonging. The calm clarity that comes with knowing what your calling is, and knowing that you are fulfilling it to the best of your ability. Instead of that fullness, after Sula his days felt empty and lack lustre, celebrations half hearted, findings half researched, show material half finished, having no one to share them with. Still, he knew the mind - it was easily tricked, that was routed in science - and so he had carried on. Unfeeling, suppressing any negative emotions, and corking the lid on tight. A smile on the outside, a volcano building on the inside.

Eventually, the volcano would diminish, right? Except that it hadn't. It had built and built, and the more that he had tried to let Sula go, the more she had filled his mind. The more she had taken over his days, his work, his shows, until Tom had thrust the paper at him and told him to take a break.

Out here in the cabin, with nothing to fill his days, that volcano finally blew.

His bright mornings, full of hope, had eventually turned into lunches of irritation that he should be doing something. Afternoons, he had taken his frustration out on the kayak or by walking the small deer tracks around the area. Tired and hungry when he returned each evening, emotion swamped over him. He spent dinner in a quiet self-sorrow, and eventually turned in on the sofa with a plan to read, to take his mind off the numbness. Tears had followed not long after, and each night he had sobbed himself to sleep on the chair, only rising in the early morning to go up to bed, and wake late morning with a renewed sense of hope, revived and refreshed to start the entire process again.

His routine, his wonderful framework, had crumbled. Not just slowed, but stopped completely. He had failed. They were right. His mind was lost. If *he* couldn't get through this using his own set of 'proven methods', then how could anyone else be expected to?

All the books, all the science. It had all failed in the magnitude of emotion that came with losing someone you love. Tricking the mind was easy, tricking emotion was impossible. Which meant everything he had done, all he had worked tirelessly to learn and teach, had been a lie. It had been possible for some who were already on their way up, impossible for most who came to him, or his shows, with a multitude of problems that they had to move before even starting on their potential.

Just push through, keep going, keep writing, keep working at it, he had said. It was imperative to break through the barrier and start to climb the mountain for the mind to believe it, and before people could start living as they intended.

But it didn't work, and he realised now that it had only worked for him in the beginning because he had already been on the way up. He had already met Sula. She had been by his side. He'd had someone to work for, to get better for, to champion him. Lots of his followers had no one and nothing - much like he had now - and far more dire circumstances.

Mac plopped down onto the sofa with a frown, the last of his tea sloshing inside the cup as the blow hit him hard. Everything he preached. All that he taught. The people that depended on him, and that needed him, and *trusted* him.

It didn't work. He felt his face flush.

It's all a lie.

He blinked at the bookcase, lined with books on the mind and the universe, brain science and the power of gratitude.

Useless, all of them.

All of it.

He couldn't help anyone. Who the hell had he thought he was? And if the framework of his own life had gone, what more was there?

What's the point?

There was a small clatter in the kitchen and Mac turned to look. Rolo, who had taken to lying at the foot of the stairs tonight, in the cool, also raised his head. When there was nothing else to hear Mac went back to his thoughts.

Only Rolo noticed the fridge magnets that had let go of their hold and fell onto the floor. Now that their dance had stopped he watched a while longer, and then lowered his head, and went back to his nap.

CHAPTER NINE

OCTOBER

THE WIND WOKE MAC early with a mournful moan around the cabin, which creaked and groaned under the strain of each gust. The trees bent in the half light of the roof window. Scattered leaves swirled over the glass, tapping and skidding up and over the roof. Mac half wondered where they had come from in this dense evergreen forest. He watched what looked like a sycamore leaf hit the glass with a plop, flattening into its full gory before flying off again. He stared at the place it had been, tracing the invisible edges with his eyes.

The days were getting easier now, there were longer periods without the ache and loneliness of his new life. Or maybe it was just that sleeping longer made the less tolerable hours shorter.

He pondered that for a while and realised that the waking hours really weren't so bad anymore. Sula and the memories were always with him, but there was less crying. Less time to cry.

He was finding more to do in those hours. He had chopped most of the wood, replenishing the store to full capacity, he had hiked a few the mountains, bagged two munro's from around the loch, watched a herd of red deer that liked to come down to graze now the weather was getting cooler, and sailed the lake to the bend too many times to count. He also swam most days - if you could call it swimming - most of his swims comprised him doing three strokes of front crawl before the cold brought him out again.

It felt more like home here now though - a lifestyle, a heartbeat. The place felt all at once both wild and insular, like nothing beyond the cabin, mountains, and loch existed. There was himself, Rolo, and the elements, which was good for letting the emotional wild man out without judgement, but awkward when he wanted an intellectual conversation. Especially when his only companion found it acceptable to turn upside down mid speech, let everything he had hang free, and express his interest with a heavy snore.

Balls to the human mind, eh, Rolo? he had said last night, eliciting a chuckle that had made the dog open one eye warily. Rolo *had* wagged his tail lightly. Not all bad then.

Watching the leaves and the trees blow, Mac put his hands behind his head and closed his eyes.

I should get up.

Just a few more minutes.

Rolo jumped off the bed with a whine, and Mac opened an eye.

'Toilet in ten.' Mac murmured, closing his eyes again.

The bed dipped and warm breath fell on his cheek, followed by whiskers that tickled as the dog sniffed. Mac played dead. Rolo could wait. It was early yet. The bed rose again as the dog's paws hit the floor, and Rolo gave another whine. Mac opened an eye to see him lying at the top of the stairs, facing down.

Good, if he hasn't gone to the door, I'm safe. He can hold it.

Mac closed his eyes again and let his mind drift, while listening to the soft whine of the dog and the creak of the cabin under the pressure of the wind outside.

He was in Tom's garage, checking out his brother's latest set of wheels with an ice-cold beer, when Rolo gave a volley of loud barks. Not pulled, so much as thrown out of sleep, Mac jumped out of bed, his heart banging in his ears. He tried to get his bearings as Rolo took off down the stairs, barking furiously.

'Rolo,' he croaked. 'Hey! It's just wind. Quit it, will you?'

Rolo took no notice and Mac grabbed the nearest thing to hand, a white trainer, and flung it down the stairs, where it hit the side of the bookcase with a soft thud. Rolo flinched looked to Mac with disdain, his volley of barks broken.

Mac shrugged. 'I told you to shut the hell up. I meant it.'

Rolo whined and barked again, this time at Mac.

'I'm coming,' he grumbled, descending the wooden stairs slowly, as he peered through the small windows to see if anything had been damaged. Across the vegetable patch, out of the front window to the truck, and out of the kitchen window to the loch. Everything seemed in order.

Stepping into the living area, Mac put a hand on the retriever's back. The dog was tense, hackles raised, and he was growling softly...again. Not at the door to the outside, but back inside, toward the rear of the cabin.

Mac turned to look down the corridor, which was dark in the early morning light, especially with today's weather.

'It's just the wind, buddy, will you quit this nonsense, there's nothing there.'

Rolo whined and continued to stare. Raising his eyebrows, Mac huffed a sigh, walked under the mezzanine floor and flicked a light switch. The corridor illuminated, showing its wooden emptiness. Mac looked back at Rolo, hands out in question.

'Nothing here.' he said, coming back into the living room. The dog jumped up at Mac for an ear rub, seemingly calm again, hackles back down. He sniffed unashamedly at something on Mac's t-shirt and then dropped back down and headed to the door, claws ticking on wood.

'Oh, I see, it was all a ploy to get me out of bed, eh?' he opened the door, and the dog ran out to relieve himself up the wood store. 'Next time try a lick not a bark, I almost had a heart attack.'

A gust of wind battered Mac in the doorway, spilling leaves with it. He shuddered. The temperature had dropped at least 10 degrees from yesterday, autumn kicking in with force after he had been thinking there would be an Indian summer.

No such luck, Maccie boy.

Rolo ran back inside, skidding around the leaves which kicked up in his own breeze. He barked and jumped at them, playing statues, until another moved, then he barked and jumped again. With a yawn Mac moved to the kitchen to flick the kettle switch, sending the dog jumping onto the sofa, leaping off, tearing around his legs before running back onto the sofa and starting the whole lap over again in playful wind driven frenzy.

'Jeez, Rolo, cut it out. This place is too small for your games.'

Kettle on, Mac went to the toilet, splashed water on his face, and brushed his teeth before looking into the mirror.

'A little less dark round the eyes, I think. Rest is what Dr Tom ordered and rest is exactly what I'm getting. I may take a picture and send it to him.'

From the corner of his eye something looked wrong in this small room, and a glance at the bath told him what it was. The shower curtain was pulled across the tub. Mac frowned and pushed out his lips. He had had a few showers here now, and he had never left the curtain closed... he thought.

Or did I?

He took a step to the bath, reached a hand around the curtain, and pulled it back with one swift movement.

'Hmm,' he murmured, looking into the empty bath. 'Mac the mind guy. I do believe you are going just a tiny bit mad.'

Grinning at himself in the mirror as he passed, Mac left the bathroom and continued to make his tea, before sitting with it at the small dining table, his hands cupped around the warm mug. He looked out of first one window, and then the next, taking the time to watch the shadows from each perspective. The wind roared, the tarp flapped, the shed door rattled, the cabin creaked. As long as the roof didn't blow off, they looked set to have an indoor day. An icy breeze ran around his feet, making him shudder. He eyed the log burner.

'I guess it may finally be time to fire you up,' he said.

Rolo lay by the door, watching Mac's vigil. He thumped his tail as Mac put his cup in the sink and came to him, dropping a hand to his head.

'Okay,' Mac said, 'I'm going to get wood, it's a dangerous operation but one of us has to do it... and then I'm going to get the yellow folder to help light a fire which doesn't burn the place down. I hope. Want to come?'

He opened the door wide, realising for the first time since he had got here that he never locked it.

No-one here anyway.

Rolo raised his head but remained on the door mat facing the kitchen, or was it the corridor he was still guarding?

'Suit yourself,' Mac said, pulling a coat over the t-shirt and jogging bottoms he had slept in, and slipping his feet into his shoes. 'If I'm not back in two minutes, call for help.'

Mac shut the door behind him, and the dog placed his head back on his paws, his gaze trained on the kitchen area.

On the fridge door, the magnetic letters parted and slowly reordered themselves. Rolo picked his head up from his paws with a whine, continuing to watch until they were still again. The dog couldn't read, but if he could, he would have seen the word now neatly spelled on the door.

LYE.

CHAPTER TEN

O UTSIDE MAC HUNCHED OVER, half-jogged to the wood store, and untied one of the top strings. The tarp snatched from his hands with a sharp snap, catching him across the cheek.

'Aaah.' he gasped, his hand coming up to his face to check the wound. No blood, no damage.

'Bloody wind.' he muttered, taking six logs from the top of the pile and hunch-jogging back to the cabin. He stacked the logs by the door and went back twice to fetch more. Keeping a pile by the fire would save him from having to be out in the cold and wet if he ran out. The beauty of forethought. He grinned as he re-tied the tarp, picked up a few of the stacked logs, flung open the cabin door, and nearly fell headlong over Rolo.

'What the-' he began.

The logs fell from his arms as the dog skittered behind the stairs, claws scrabbling on the wooden floor like a cartoon. All action, but no movement.

'Rolo, you nut, why in the hell were you right behind the door?'

Rolo at least had the dignity to look sheepish as Mac piled the logs on the hearth and finished retrieving the rest. His head was down as he eyed Mac, tail thumping lightly.

'It's okay, no harm done, at least you didn't lose a leg.' Mac said, and immediately thought of Sula patching his bloody arm after a solo mountain biking accident.

Mac had full on panicked. There was so much blood he had thrown up on the side of the road, staggered a few steps, then his legs had given out and he sank to the floor. He had called her from his position in the gutter, nose to nose with a cigarette packet and an old condom, thinking that these may be the last two things on earth he ever saw. Sula had been calm as Mac lay dying.

'I'm sure it's not so bad, tato. Where are you?'

Mac rasped, his gaping mouth dribbling saliva onto the tarmac in a long stream. 'I'm... on the road... in a gutter.' he managed before closing his eyes.

Sula was quiet for only a beat.

'Right, I can be at the road in five. Left or right gutter?'

'I... I'm not sure, please hurry.'

Sula huffed a laugh. 'Mac, it is impossible to find one road in a million...'

Sula's voice had trailed off as a car engine pulled up, idling next to him. Mac stayed still. Sula was coming, no need for any interjection. And then rough hands pulled his shoulder, turning him onto his back. Mac yelled, Sula shouted, and the man yelled louder.

'Fucking Christ mate, I thought you were dead!'

Mac, dribble now stringing onto his cheek, looked at the man above him, who had one hand on his hip, the other on his chest.

'What is it?' Sula said. 'Is it trouble?'

'You've done your arm a good 'un mate, needs a wipe, you want some help? I can give you a lift somewhere. That your bike?'

The man strode off to pick up the bike as Mac stared after him, watching him bring it back as Sula asked him a million and one questions from the other end of the phone.

He loved her, but god, he didn't need to have to think so hard when his last breaths were near.

'Sula?' he said.

'What is going on, Mac?'

The man lifted the boot lid and threw the bike inside before turning back to Mac.

'You'll need a new wheel, proper bent that one, mate. Looks like a stone age replica. Come on, let's get you home.'

The man laughed heartily and stooped next to him. Mac thrust the phone at his face.

'What's this?' the man said, putting the phone next to his ear. 'Want me to call someone for you? Oh, hello, darlin."

Mac watched the man's Dr Martin boot as he answered Sula's questions.

'Right. Right. Yeah. Okay darlin', no problem. I gotcha. Nah, it's just a scratch. I'll bring him back. We're only a mile or so from there.'

Mac curled his lip. A scratch indeed. Sula would see soon enough there was no need for the man to play it down to save her feelings. Mac attempted a glance at his mangled, blood covered arm, but quickly looked away as the man ended the call and gave the phone back.

'Come on then mate, Let's get you home. Can you get up?'

The man reached down and hooked a hand under Mac's armpit. His bad arm. He screeched and the man let go, jumping back.

'Fuck, shit, fuck. I thought you'd just cut it. Is it broke? Fuck! Can you move it?'

Mac tried. It felt okay, just sore around the broken skin on his forearm.

'It's okay,' he said, 'just be careful, please.'

The man hoisted him up again, and Mac had trouble getting his legs together enough to hold him. He held the car, panting as he stood, testing his limbs one by one. Nothing seemed out of place other than his arm.

'Your legs okay?' the man said, and Mac gave a nod. 'Good, let's get you home.'

Less than a minute later they were at the front door of the house, and Sula was running out to meet him. He collapsed in her arms, being careful of his injured one, as the man placed his bike on the front lawn.

'Thank you.' Sula said with a wave as the man left.

'Wait...' Mac said, catching his breath. 'No... I didn't get his name. That man saved my life, and I didn't get his name.'

Sula blinked at him.

'Mac, you are not dying, tato. You have-' Sula pulled out of his grasp to inspect his arm. 'You have a, how you say? Little hurt? It bleed a little, it's true. But it's a little hurt, Mac.'

Mac blinked at her and finally plucked up the courage to look at his arm. A thick red welt ran from elbow to wrist. It was no longer bleeding, no longer even felt painful other than the sting.

'A graze?' he said, flabbergasted. 'I swear, baby, it was more than this. There was so much blood. I thought I was a goner. It's a bloody graze? It can't be.'

'It can. Unless you have superpower. You heal quick?'

Mac looked at her, saw the play of a smile around her mouth and felt his shoulders relax as the grin reached his lips too.

'Shall we go give it a wipe?'

Now that the wound didn't really hurt, there was nothing less in the world that he wanted to do, but he nodded his head and they turned to go inside, Sula linking her arm in his good one.

'Looks like your bike fared worse than you, tato. No harm done. At least you didn't lose an arm!'

In the cabin, Mac found himself sitting on the sofa facing the fire, a small smile on his face as the memory flooded back.

'I was such a wimp back then,' he said to Rolo, who was sniffing around the kitchen looking for scraps. 'Come on, let's go for a walk.'

Rolo's head came up, and he stood to attention, long curly ears up as far as they went before flopping back down against his face. He stared at Mac.

'Yep, you heard right. Let's wrap up and go for a walk. What do you say?'

Rolo ran to him, jumping up his legs excitedly in bound after bound like his back legs were springs. Mac laughed and pushed him down. The dog had been out umpteen times, had the run of the forest if he liked. There were no restrictions here like back at home where a fence kept him inside and away from the delicious smells that caught his attention, and still he was this excited for a walk.

Mac grabbed his phone from the kitchen side, pulled on his coat, and headed out the door with Rolo dancing on his heels like he had just been released from a thirty-year captivity.

CHAPTER ELEVEN

T HEY WERE DEEP IN the forest following one of the deer tracks, keeping the loch in view on the right to keep their bearings, when the phone rang. Mac pulled it from his pocket and saw Tom's face smiling at him from the screen. With a smile to match, Mac answered the call.

'What's up buddy?'

'Mac?'

'Yeah, who the hell else have you given a phone to and sent off into the wilderness all alone?'

Tom laughed. 'If I had more than one cabin, I'd make it into a little business. How are you doing out there?'

'Good,' Mac said, panting as the incline rose ahead of him. He pushed on, following Rolo, who was having no trouble with the hill, having two legs and two back springs to run with. Mac saw his yellow tail disappear into the trees ahead of him.

'Good? That's it?' Tom said.

'Well,' Mac said, stopping at a boulder to sit and take a rest, 'I'm climbing the north bank right now, we're about halfway up... Rolo, back here, boy.'

'You're what? Climbing? Didn't take you long to get to grips with seclusion and nature, did it?'

Mac laughed as Rolo came lolloping back.

'Well, I told you I was into hiking, biking, and stuff before. You just didn't listen, obviously.'

'I did,' Tom said. 'I just thought you meant on a small scale. You know, hill walking, a bike ride around the block.' he laughed at his own joke, although Mac heard the truth in what he said.

Tom had always been the active brother. He had been into water sports, hiking, climbing, swimming, and biking for too many years to count now, and had won the local and regional triathlons four times each. He quit the year he won both within four months of each other –to give someone else a chance he said. After that he had turned to swimming, with a new goal to swim the English Channel. That one he hadn't accomplished yet, but he had tried to get Mac into cold water swimming alongside him while he practiced. More for keeping an eye on him than for partnering, Mac supposed, as Sula had only recently passed at that point. Mac had found no relief in the chilly water either way, and refused after one session, insisting on watching from the bank instead.

'I've been swimming and kayaking too.' Mac said, 'It's great out here… and man, just to not have a camera shoved in my face is amazing. It's so peaceful. You may never get me out.'

Tom paused on the other end of the line.

'I am talking to Mac Macauley here, right?'

Mac chuckled.

'I filled the wood store with chopped logs, lit the log burner with no trouble and checked out the generator just in case. No problems yet.'

Mac waited for Tom to process what he'd said. The other end of the line was silent, until Tom finally began to chuckle.

'I'm impressed, buddy. I really am. What did you do with my little brother?'

Maybe you don't know me as well as you think you do.

The thought flit in and out of Mac's mind so fast there was barely time to register that it had been there. He laughed along with Tom as he took in the view across the loch. It was mercifully sheltered where he sat, the north face of this mountain and the tall pines protecting him from the worst of the southerly gale. Across the loch, the trees were bending and swaying precariously on the mountain, and down below small waves surged their way forward in bursts of spray that forced their way up onto shore, the grey loch water tumultuous and unforgiving.

'So how are Meg and the kids?' Mac said.

'They're good. Beth spends her days covered in glitter, Josh covered in eyeliner, and Amy, well, heaven knows what Amy is up to. She's still out most of the time.'

'Is she still with that boy, who was it, Jason?' Mac said with a smile. Across the loch there was a moment of stillness before a large gust of wind battered the mountain with a noise that boomed as it pulled through the trees.

'No, there have been five so far since-'

'Five?!' Mac shook his head in surprise, cutting Tom off.

'Five, the new one is Franco, I believe, although we've yet to meet him.' Tom replied.

'Bloody hell, last I remember, my niece was just sixteen!'

'She'd correct you there, almost seventeen. And besides, sixteen is the new twenty-six, you know.'

Tom huffed a laugh and Mac was suddenly glad that he didn't have a teenage daughter.

'We keep an eye on her as much as we can. She's not a bad kid, and quite homely, really. I can't imagine she's up to much that we don't know about.'

Mac raised his eyebrows and laughed as he pulled the packet of cigarettes from his pocket and put one to his lips.

'It's the quiet ones you have to watch,' he said as he was lighting it.

'Yeah, thanks for that. As long as she's not smoking, I'm happy.'

Mac pulled on his cigarette with a grin.

'Really? There's a lot worse out there that teenagers are doing all the time. I've been witness to some really fucked up people trying to get themselves together. Sexual abuse, mental abuse, physical abuse, never mind the drugs and alcohol which you already-'

'Yeah, yeah, I know, and it does worry me. I just don't think she's the type. That's all I was getting at.'

Right, sure you were.

'Tom, listen, you really don't need to worry about me, okay.' Tom was silent. 'I'm going to be fine, really.'

'Fine with a habit. Cancer got all our grandparents, mom, and dad. What are the odds? They're already stacked against us. We need to keep in shape, buddy. That means not poisoning our bodies with something as harmful as the old cancer sticks.'

'I don't have a habit. I've only had two since I've been here, and once I finish this pack it's voila smoking, or drive twelve miles for another pack.'

'Desperate people have done worse for an addiction.'

'I know, but they're not me. I've seen and heard as much as you have. I won't go there, I promise.'

Mac looked back across the loch. Tom had seen addiction from all angles, he worked with addicts every day. He had started with psychology and become a psychologist. First with the NHS, then going private, and then setting up his own practice. When the job had worn him down enough, he quit to work with addicted teens, and now ran a clinic working to get kids off the junk they plied into themselves trying to keep up with their peers.

Mac's thoughts trailed off as movement caught his eye across on the other mountain. He watched and waited. His eyes fixed on the area right at the top where he thought he had seen activity. There was movement again, but not solid, more like a swirl. A mist he supposed. With each gust of wind, it was gone, with each stillness it came back.

Mist wouldn't disappear like that. What the heck is it?

'Mac, are you still there, bud?'

Mac had been staring so intently at the mountain that Tom's voice made him physically jump.

'Yeah, think I lost you for a second there,' he lied. 'What did you say?'

'I said, I can't understand what the hell you possibly get from a smoke, anyway? It must...'

Smoke, Mac thought.

Smoke. It's smoke!

'Nothing, Tom.' he said stubbing the small cigarette end out on the rock. He wet his fingers and pinched the end so that it cooled too much to cause a fire... but someone obviously has a fire going over on the other side of the loch. 'I'm throwing the pack when I get back. You're right. It was silly to start again. I'm over it, last one just gone.'

'Mac...' Tom started.

'No, Tom, really. You're right. They're gone. I promise you.'

'Well, I suppose I'm happy about that.'

'Good. Tom, is this area used for hiking a lot? I mean, is it a well-known route or just off a trail?'

'What?'

'Do many hikers use this place, these mountains?'

Tom seemed to take forever to answer as he wrapped his head around the change of subject. A sign of age, Mac thought, as he waited.

'Hikers? I suppose it's free hiking country, there may be a few. It's not near any major walking trails though, and if you're out climbing today, you've seen the tracks you have to follow. Deer tracks. There are no paths, really.'

'So no-one comes up here - except you and Josh, obviously.'

'I can't answer that Mac, I don't know. What I do know is that in all the years we've been going there, we've never seen a soul up on the mountains. And we've traversed much of the area in one way or another over the years.'

Mac nodded, although Tom couldn't see him anyway, so he didn't know what the hell for. He squinted at the mountaintop. It was smoke; he was sure of it. Which must mean other campers. Maybe he would have some company tonight if they came down to the cabin. Whether it would be the sort of company he wanted was another matter altogether.

'Mac? Why do you ask?'

'No reason. I just wondered how alone I actually am here.'

'Totally. Absolutely. Completely. Mac, I promise you there is no-one around to spy on you or sneak pictures to the press out there. No one.'

'Okay, I hear you.'

'But Mac, I'll warn you now the mind can play some terrible tricks when you're all alone. It can imagine all sorts of ghoulies, believe me. When I've been up there alone-'

Mac spluttered a laugh, cutting Tom off. 'Yeah, Tom. You know who you're talking to, right? I'm well aware of the way the mind works. I've studied it to the nth degree. I study it every day.'

Mac heard Tom heave a sigh.

'I know you know. But knowing and experiencing are two different things. You know how the mind works in theory-'

'I've also been down there. I've been in the depths of depression, Tom. I've experienced. That's why I can help others down there. I understand the way it works.'

Or I could, before I thought it was a crock, anyway.

'I know that Mac, and I don't want to argue with you, but loneliness and isolation aren't the same. This is a new experience. I'm just saying it will get hard.'

'And you think I won't cope? So why push to get me here?'

Mac stood, shook out his legs and climbed onto the small boulder to see if he could see any more. He was less interested in some argument with Tom, than finding out where that fire had come from. He craned his neck, but the source was just too far away.

'I know you'll cope. Of course you will, but don't think it isn't hard, okay?'

'Because you think I've had it easy here so far?'

'Well, you don't seem to have struggled yet.'

Mac sighed and climbed down from the rock.

'Okay, so it's going to get harder. Anything else you think I should know?'

'Mac, please don't-'

'Maybe I should write a daily diary and email it to you so that you can check my mental wellbeing?'

'No, Mac, of course that's unnecessary. I wouldn't be human if I didn't worry about you out there, that's all.'

Mac raised his eyebrows and looked at Rolo, who was sitting up now that Mac had moved. He ushered him forward, and upward. If they got higher, maybe they could see the source of the fire.

'Good, because I wasn't intending to do it anyway,' Mac said. 'I'm a grown adult, and you are my brother, Tom, not my doctor, or anyone else's doctor, for that matter. I will be fine. Trust me.'

Mac heard Tom push out a long breath.

'Well, let's keep in touch then. A call with an update once a week, and I promise I won't worry. Okay?'

Mac stepped back into the cover of the pines and followed Rolo through the trees.

'Sounds like a plan,' he said. 'I'm going to carry on my hike now. I'll call you next Friday unless I hear from you first.'

'Okay,' Tom said, 'You can call me anytime, not just Friday.'

'I know. Take care, Tom.'

'You too, Mac. Be careful.'

Mac cut the connection before he realised what Tom had said.

Be careful? He just told me there's nothing and no-one out here.

A glance back through the trees toward the loch revealed the white swirl of smoke - just a strip but visible all the same. I guess we find out if that's true then, he thought, urging Rolo ahead.

The tree line thinned as they climbed higher and finally, they reached grass and scrub. It was easier to see, easier to climb, but each time Mac looked over to the other side of the loch, the mountain concealed where the smoke was coming from.

Just below a patch of scree, Mac flopped onto the grass in frustration. It was windier the nearer the top he climbed, which was beginning to feel precarious, and he wanted a drink but hadn't thought they would be out long enough to need one. When he looked how far they had climbed right up to the higher parts of the terrain, he kicked himself.

He was almost at eye level with the crest of the smaller mountain across the loch, which had kept him going, kept him climbing, but now the bend of the loch was in view and behind it the mountain fell away before another rose. The smoke fell behind the mountain with it, or maybe it had always been there, but Mac would need to hike three times as far as he already had to get around the bend of the loch, and even then, he still may not be able to see. The only thing to do right now was to go back to the cabin and keep an eye out. If he could see the smoke from there, then he could climb that side tomorrow if the wind had stilled a little by then.

Rolo lolloped over, tongue hanging from the side of his mouth. He put a paw on Mac's knee.

'Ready to go?'

The retriever cocked his head, and Mac removed his paw to stand again.

He stretched his back, felt the ache in his calves, and started back the way they had come. His mouth felt full of sawdust, and he suddenly knew it was going to be a very long walk home.

CHAPTER TWELVE

T OM PLACED THE PHONE on the counter with a smile.

'All good?' Meg said, serving spaghetti from the colander onto plates ready for their family dinner. The children were older now, Beth was ten, Josh thirteen, and Amy sixteen, but Meg still insisted that they eat together every evening. Their days could vary wildly with where they were, and what they were doing, but dinner time stood at 5pm sharp. If you couldn't attend, there'd better be a damned good reason for not doing so.

'Fantastic,' Tom answered, grabbing a string of spaghetti, and placing it into his mouth before his wife could do anything about it. He chewed as she gave him a sharp look.

'Dinner is ready. You couldn't wait until it made it to the table?'

There was a flash of red at the kitchen door, and Meg was immediately on it. She missed nothing.

'Get here, young lady,' she shouted, her Scottish accent thick. There was a sigh and a blonde head popped itself around the doorway. Amy was as different from Josh as night and day. She was fair skinned with white-blonde locks to Josh's thick dark hair and olive skin. To confuse matters, Beth was a redhead, with freckled skin and blue eyes. Tom often wondered what the hell was up with his gene pool. He had been waiting anxiously to see if Mac had children, whether he would have the same kind of mix. Unfortunately, Sula had lost their only baby at seven weeks, just a short year before she followed on. Now it was looking increasingly unlikely that Tom would ever find out.

At least Amy's eyes were the same as Beth's. It had to count for something, he thought, looking at his oldest daughter.

'I know I'm late,' she said, although in reality she was barely five minutes past the hour. Then she glanced at the spoon in her mother's hand. 'You're late too, so it's only fair,' she finished.

'Never a better job,' Meg said, pulling open a kitchen drawer. 'Get the table laid, I'm bringing it through now.'

Amy rolled her eyes but came in to collect the table mats, knives and forks, salt and pepper, and a large container of Parmesan cheese. Balancing it all in a teetering tower, she disappeared from the kitchen and into the dining room.

'So?' Meg said, going back to the spaghetti. 'How's our Mac?'

'He's good. Doing way better than I thought he would, to be honest. He sounds brighter than he has in a long time. I think he's enjoying it.'

'I'm not surprised at all.'

Tom frowned at his wife's back, marvelling that she seemed to have gauged Mac far better than he had. 'You're not?'

Meg threw a glance over her shoulder at him as she moved the colander to the sink.

'Well, of course not. Good Scottish air would do anyone good. It should be a natural therapy. You and Josh always love it up there too, don't you?'

Tom smiled. 'We certainly do,' he said, omitting the thought that he would enjoy any kind of desolate mountain wilderness pretty much anywhere.

Sorry Scotland.

'Is he coping with the log burner and such? I presume he's having to light it now?'

'It certainly seems like he has everything covered.'

Meg finished spooning the bolognaise meat into a dish and turned to look at him, red curls ringed with sweat hanging down her freckled face, she used her wrist to push one aside exposing a ruddy cheek.

'Then you can relax now, can't you.'

'Yeah, I suppose,' he said, following her to the dining room with the plates.

She went back for the dish, calling to Josh and Beth as she went. Amy sat at the table, busy in phone-land, head down, fingers tapping.

'You don't sound so sure,' she said as the others sat down and began to serve themselves. Tom and Meg sat back. The children always went first at dinner time, something Meg had never had the privilege of when she was growing up. Her father had to eat first and, being a selfish brute - her words - there was never much left for Meg or her five sisters. She had promised herself that her children would never feel unworthy, or ever go hungry.

Tom looked at Meg's satisfied smile as food disappeared onto three plates. Regardless of the children, his wife always put others before herself. She was the kind of woman who would go the extra mile with gifts, something personal, and would almost always get it right. Which was why it wouldn't have been out of character for her to have the piano delivered, but as yet, she hadn't admitted to the plan.

Meg looked back at him, eyebrows raised, a small smile on her lips.

'I am,' Tom said, 'It's just, well... you know the whole-'

'Ach, don't start with the blessed piano thing again. It's there because it's a blessing. Mac saying that he won't play only reinforces the fact that he will. It was meant to be, don't question it.'

'I think I want to question who has been in my cabin, piano or no piano,' Tom murmured.

'I thought Uncle Mac was at the cabin.' Josh said, kohl-lined eyes just visible under his hair.

'He is, but the piano was there before him, and now your dad thinks he had an intruder who brought a piano along for the ride,' Meg paused, glancing at Josh, 'Heck, I suppose if I'd got to lug a piano all that way, I may leave it in the cabin at the other end too.'

'There's a piano at the cabin?' Josh wrinkled his nose and looked at his dad. 'What-'

'Oh, don't you start,' Meg cut in.

'What a lovely idea,' Beth said dreamily. 'Now uncle Mac can play again. I used to love to listen to him play.'

'Exactly,' Meg said. 'It's a lovely idea. If he plays again, what's the harm. It's there. Let's just leave it. You're giving me a headache.'

Tom smiled to himself. If he knew his wife at all, then he would think she had just made a confession. It had to be Meg, and if it was, then so be it, and he would relax. Tom smiled and leaned to kiss his wife's temple.

'It is a lovely idea,' he said, 'very thoughtful.'

Meg bat him away with a fork and narrowed her eyes at him before breaking into a smile.

There was a beat of harmonious silence, the sounds of a family enjoying their food, and then Amy piped up.

'Mom, dad? I was wondering... would it be okay if I went to Switzerland with Franco next month?' she said brightly.

The harmony was lost, and the piano forgotten in the fray.

CHAPTER THIRTEEN

Rain beat at the window, long streaks running down the glass in the growing gloom. It was half-past six and Mac had just finished a tin of spaghetti and sausages with toast for his dinner. What had taken a couple of hours to climb up had taken nearly three to descend. They had run out of path and had to backtrack too many times to count coming down. Exhausted, thirsty, blisters on his heels, and a throbbing headache to boot, Mac thought that being able to see the dot of the cabin in the distance was torture beyond comprehension. So close, yet so far. In the end, it had been keeping the cabin in his blurred vision that had got him back. After gulping a pint of water, he had removed his shoes and decided to make tea before he sat down and wasn't able to move again.

Now, with his empty plate before him, full bellied, warm and comfortable, he had completely seized up.

He decided he would investigate the mountain on the southern side of the loch tomorrow and see if he could see where the fire had been. He made a plan of when he would start, what he would take to eat and drink, and plasters for his heels. It didn't really matter who was out there, of course, free country after all, but it gave him something else to think about while he was here. The wood had been chopped, the rest of the cabin was in order, all except for the 'vegetable garden', which Mac had no interest in right now. All he had left to think about was himself, Rolo, and Sula.

Unfortunately, Sula still took up the majority of his time.

He sniffed and stared out at the darkness outside, at the water sliding down the pane of glass, and waited for the familiar tears to well as they usually did during the evening's here when he wasn't busy.

It was the evenings that hurt the most, when he felt the most loss. Evenings with Sula had been fun, even when they were travelling and he was doing shows, or the popular three-day events - which let's face it, was more often than not - they had always set a time to be 'home'. Even if home was a hotel room, even if they had been together all day, even if they were in different cities. Each evening was a ritual. To come together, to wind down, to get back to what mattered after the rush of their respective days.

Sula travelled with Mac as much as she could, and as she worked alongside him - she helped build the company and the brand, booked events, sorted his diary, sorted links, files, worksheets, landing pages, even answered emails, and everything else that came with running a business both on and offline these days - she would be with him most of the time. The times that she couldn't travel with him, she stayed at home, and they came together via Skype, Zoom or WhatsApp video calling where they would chat, laugh, and play games until late into the night.

7pm was their time. It was an unspoken and never broken agreement. All events were at an end by 4pm and they would be home alone by 7pm. This usually gave Mac enough time to mill around and speak to people after the event, which was the other bit of the job he loved - getting real stories from real people. Listening and understanding what worked for them, what their thoughts were, and getting ideas for where to go next. It was a heavy price to miss the opportunity when a show ran late, but getting together with Sula was priceless.

Evenings would always start with food. Sula was a wonderful cook and would use her skill where she could, but hotel rooms would usually be room service, and video call nights they would often get a takeout and eat together over video. Sometimes they went out, mostly they dressed down and spent the time together alone.

Mac smiled out of the window at the loch, lost in thought.

Sula would have lots to say about his dinner of spaghetti and sausages and what was in the tin. He remembered the last time she had caught him opening a tin of tomato spaghetti during one of their video chats. Even from five hundred miles away, she had forced him to bin the contents and go to the shop, where she had talked him through the ingredients he was to buy and watched as he made his own pasta and tomato sauce.

'Much better,' she said with a relieved smile, 'tins are crap, Mac. It's much better to do yourself, no?'

Mac had to admit it had been delicious, although the preparing and cooking had annoyed him at the time, especially when his lovely tin of heat-up spaghetti stared at him forlornly from the top of the bin every time he had thrown something away. But this dinner filled him with far more goodness, Sula said.

After dinner was games time, but no consoles allowed. This was purely games of the physical variety. They played everything from Yahtzee to Monopoly, Backgammon to Cluedo, Scrabble to Othello, Twister to The Game of Life. The older original games were the best and sometimes a game of Monopoly could lose them hours. When they were online, they played charades and Pictionary, or a game Sula could never remember the name of, where you had to stick a card on your head and ask questions to discover which it was. This game usually ended with tears as Sula laughed so much, she often ended up without the card on her head and had to replace it. Mac found it hilarious that she never knew it was gone for a few seconds, and then she made a show of scrabbling around to replace it. Mac never cheated himself, but he had no idea how many times Sula had used the tactic to look at her card. By the number of times she just pipped him to the post with her correct answer, Mac would say many. He didn't begrudge her. It was a joy to see her laugh, and a pleasure to watch her.

Quiet time came after the games, where they sat with a bottle of wine between them. If they were on a video call, they had to have the same wine, Sula insisted, so that they were having the same experience. They could chat, get anything they wanted off their minds - strictly no arguments. Late chats were for listening without judgement, although judgement often came the next morning, anyway. It was delayed torture. But mostly they read - or Sula read - while Mac surfed the net looking for interesting articles, new findings, and new ideas. Mostly, though, he watched her.

He watched the way she would frown when the book got intense, pages moving faster under her fingers. She had an e-reader only under duress. Sula loved the smell of a book. Mac had no idea what he was supposed to make of that.

He watched the way she would bite her lip, smile, wipe a tear from her cheek, even laugh out loud as she entered the book's private world. When they were through reading, or Sula at least, Mac would cuddle her close as she told him what she had read, all about the characters, what they were up to, where they lived, whether they had made the right decision. It was as if she had a thousand friends in a thousand different places, but this also went against their quiet night sometimes. One book had made Sula cry so hard she had physically thrown the book at the wall.

'Stupid man!' she had yelled, 'he's stupid, why he do that? Why, Mac?'

Mac had only shrugged and let her rant. He didn't know this man, had no idea of his actions. Most of all, he was fictional. Mac really couldn't see why it mattered so much, but it did to Sula. The moment she started a book, she was involved. Period. Cuddles at this point usually drifted into something far more animal and they had sometimes retired to bed, sometimes they never made it before instinct took over, and the bed was for afterward.

Rolo whined and Mac was back in the cabin again. He blinked in surprise, feeling the warmth of the lone tear roll down his cheek. Rolo was scratching at something by the sink, partially blocked by the table.

'What have you found?' Mac said with false lightness, wiping the tear away and ducking to look past the table. He winced as his back complained and stood instead. His calves hurt, but that was less of an ordeal than his back right now.

Rolo was busy scratching at the letters on the fridge. Some of them tumbled to the floor of the cabin under his paws.

Mac stooped carefully to pick them up.

'You writing me a message? I knew I should have called you Lassie,' he chuckled.

He moved Rolo away from the fridge with a hand, and placed the magnets back on the door. Rolo whined and immediately began to drag them back off, and Mac sat back, scratching his head.

'Rolo, they're just plastic letters. What did they ever do for you to take such a dislike to them?'

When they had all fallen to the floor, Rolo sat and glanced at Mac, tongue lolling from the side of his mouth. Mac stared back and Rolo gave a small bark, more of a yip.

Mac nodded and rose to get a sandwich bag from the drawer.

'Okay, you win. We'll leave them off for whatever your dodgy doggy reasons are.'

He scrubbed Rolo's head and placed the letters and numbers into the bag. He put the bag on the kitchen countertop and vowed to move them to the back store later, when his bones and muscles weren't quite so shot.

It would save picking them up each time Rolo knocked them off.

Washing his dish in the sink, he looked out of the window at the loch.

'Nearly black out there now, the nights are finally drawing in.' he said, as wind battered the cabin, blasting rain at the window. Mac decided he wasn't too fond of the dark and the weather combined. 'I wonder if there's a light outside.'

He and Rolo went to look. Thirty seconds later they were back inside, having concluded that there was no light outside, and that it was bloody cold.

Back inside, Mac decided the tears weren't going to make an appearance tonight at all.

A rare, blessed night.

He doubled checked his emotions, just to make sure. When he still felt okay, he threw some logs onto the fire and lit it. The instant heat blocked the cold that was creeping over the cabin now that night was falling. He picked a book from the bookshelf and sat on the sofa in front of the roaring fire.

'I suppose it's time to see what the world of the mind has to teach us, eh?' he said as Rolo shook the water from his fur and jumped up onto the sofa. 'Looks like a night in for us either way,'

He glanced back at the rain-streaked window as a gust of wind battered the cabin, elongating the streaks and whipping them sideways.

Looks like we could be in for a good many up here.

And even though he drank very little, the desire for a pub right now with people, music, and atmosphere, was intense. He didn't read more than a line before he got out his Bluetooth speaker, loaded Linkin Park onto Spotify, and put the book down to play a game on his phone.

Anything to detract from the noise of the wind and the shadows behind the curtain-less windows.

CHAPTER FOURTEEN

M AC OPENED HIS EYES to darkness. There was a ringing in the cabin. Half asleep, he scrambled for his phone, which he found had powered off during the night. With a tut, he put the phone back on the small chest of drawers next to the bed and settled back onto the pillow, pulling the covers up around him.

Must have rung itself flat. Oh well.

He drifted, half in the world of sleep when the ringing came again. Only it wasn't a ringing really, it was more a...

A low hum?

Mac frowned and propped himself up on his elbows. The sound died away as he listened. It was certainly more of a hum, he thought, a low sound, like a vibration. It almost felt *familiar*. The wind blew outside, not as forceful as the day before had been, but still gusty. As it pushed against the window, the low hum came again. For a second Mac wondered if he was going mad, it was such a low sound it could have come from his own head, but then Rolo lifted his head, too, from the bottom of the bed.

All was quiet again, but then so was the wind for now.

'You know what?' Mac said to Rolo. 'It's probably the straps on the tarp under the pull of the wind.'

He patted the dog's head and settled back down into the covers again. The wind blew and the vibration gently hummed. With Mac's hand on his head, Rolo settled back down and closed his eyes, and Mac realised why he thought he knew the sound.

Sounds like a low D, possibly octave one?

It was Mac's last amused thought as he drifted back to sleep.

'I don't get it.' Mac said, 'It's too hard.'

Sula laughed and dropped onto the piano stool beside him, shuffling him off the other side. He raised his eyebrows and stood. All the better. Now he didn't have to play.

'No, it's simple.' Sula pressed the keys with her right hand, lowering and raising her voice with them. 'This one is high, higher, higher, higher, higher.' She tucked her chin into her chest with a frown and placed her left hand on the keys. 'This one is low, lower, lower, lower, lower.'

Mac gave her a look of disdain.

'I know that,' he said.

Sula looked at him, eyebrows up, mouth in a smile of delight. 'Ah, see. Not so much a beginner after all, huh, Zac? You can be learned.'

'Taught,' he grumbled. 'It's Mac.'

'Mano destra.' She flapped her right hand at him, ignoring his pout. 'We learn right first, see?'

Mac waved his right hand back, dragging his lips into a mirthless smile.

'Ah, molto bene, you know right, this is good, Zac. Now, you play.'

Sula moved from the stool and motioned for Mac to sit back down. He rolled his eyes as he slumped onto the small stool waiting for the next instruction, and was shocked when he felt firm hands, one on his chest, the other at his back. They pushed together to force his back upright.

'Sit up, shoulders back,' Sula mimicked, thrusting her ample bosom toward his face. Mac reddened, but Sula didn't seem to notice. 'To play, we need to breathe. Like life, the breath is most important. Don't forget to breathe.'

Mac awoke to sunshine. He frowned and glanced at his watch - 9.08am. He lay back down, amused to see another large sycamore leaf plastered to his roof window.

In a forest full of pines. This place is goofy.

He watched until the leaf ripped off in a small gust and then sat up, his back and thighs moaning as he swung them out of bed.

'Ooohh, crap,' he said, rubbing at his back. Rolo jumped off the bed, shook, and stretched. 'I really don't think we'll be hiking anywhere today. You'll have to make do with taking yourself out.'

Rolo watched as Mac held onto the head of the bed with one hand and straightened himself to stand.

'Ow, bloody hell. That's ridiculous. It hasn't been that long since I last exercised. Shit.'

He shook his legs out and completed some neck and shoulder rolls before attempting the stairs.

It was before Sula died, Mac, that was when you last exercised.

He took himself by surprise and stood a minute to see if the voice was right. It was.

'Wow, Mac, that's lame,' he said to the cabin. 'That's over ten months since you did any serious exercise? I can't believe it.'

You know what else? You've been busy shooting down your own framework, and what is one of the top steps?

'Self-care and physical exercise,' Mac mumbled as he sat back down on the bed. 'Mac, you bloody idiot. You've been carrying on thinking you're the mind guy, you can get through it, but you haven't even been following your own fucking plan, have you?'

Because it's lies, it's all shit, Mac.

His heart gave a lurch at his own criticism.

'But you don't know that, do you,' he whispered, 'because you've helped people to help themselves through it, but you've never been in a position to have to help yourself. And that's where you've been going wrong. That's why everything went to hell. You've been too focused on helping others when you should have been helping yourself.'

And you know it works. You had shows booked a year in advance because you've helped people. You've got sterling reviews and accolades in the industry because you've helped people. Your team could have booked longer than a year ahead, but you didn't like to commit.

Mac felt a twinge of fear. By the time this little break was over, there would be nothing booked. All of his shows had been cancelled. He was officially out of work, and now he wondered which was worse; committing, or letting go completely.

He thought of the rush of the shows, sometimes in two different countries a day. The rushing about would be one thing he wouldn't miss. He had been on the brink of exhaustion when Sula died, working almost twenty out of twenty-four hours every day, seven days a week. Lots of their special evenings together had been fraught, Mac not able to concentrate because of things he wanted to complete, and deadlines he had to meet. He had often snuck back out of bed to work, leaving Sula asleep. He had thought she was unaware, but they had had their last major argument about that very thing, and how hard he was pushing - the day before she died.

Mac suddenly found himself looking down on his own life. The rush before Sula's death that had consumed every waking hour for the two years previous. Sula's death and the rush to push harder, to block the pain, and then the inevitable backlash that comes with ignoring the pain and not taking care of yourself.

This happened for a reason.

Mac blinked. As if anything quite so dramatic had to happen for him to stop and get off the industry wheel, and yet he knew it was true. He wouldn't have stopped. People needed him.

But you couldn't help them; you weren't helping. You were too preoccupied. You were giving too much of yourself.

Mac thought of the well-known quote that said, 'When the airplane is about to crash, always put on your own oxygen mask before taking care of others.' and he suddenly felt the beauty of how true the statement was. He couldn't help anyone the way he had been. He had to take care of himself, and this was an intervention to make him stop and take notice. For the first time since Sula's death, he felt real, emotional gratitude.

'Thank you,' he whispered.

Mac didn't believe in God, he wasn't religious, but he fully believed in something that worked behind the scenes, something he could only think of as the universe, and right now it felt as though the universe had his back. It had been busy having his back, even when he didn't know it.

So, you do believe in your framework?

Of course I do, he thought. I just lost my way a little. Mac squinted. He suddenly had an idea of just what he could do while he was taking some time out in this cabin.

He may have nothing left now, but nothing was a good place to start. If he had nothing, he had nothing to lose. He decided to write a new framework. This one he would test on himself first, and he would record every bit he could so that he would remember how it felt.

He painfully dressed and made his way downstairs. At the bottom, his thighs and calves didn't hurt quite as much as they had at the top, and he knew he was already winning the day.

CHAPTER FIFTEEN

'CAMERA ON, TEST, TEST, test.' Mac said into the phone lens. He hadn't ever used a phone camera as a video before, but he would start now. There was nothing else pressing to learn.

He flipped the phone over and saw the file in the gallery. He pressed play... and decided he could do with a shave before starting over. He was hairier than an Afghan hound. He could also do with changing Sula's favourite jumper, too. The green had faded, and it had an actual hole in the right shoulder where he had snagged it on a nail getting down from the loft a few months back. It was hanging off him, ragged with washing and wearing day after day.

Mac grinned. 'Time for a new Mac, and a new jumper.'

He lay the phone on the sofa and went into the bathroom to shave, pausing in the doorway to frown at the shower curtain, which was pulled across the bath again.

Was it Rolo? Could he be pulling it across? It wasn't like he hadn't pulled magnetic letters off the fridge in his spare time, too.

Mac had to give the retriever props for his weirdness... but then he thought. He had never actually seen Rolo enter the corridor toward the store, or the bathroom, at all. Not since they had been here. He often made it to the mezzanine floor and the stairs but came no further.

Or maybe he does when you're not looking.

Mac pulled the shower curtain back and shaved, then he went upstairs to get a new jumper.

Feeling more presentable, he went back downstairs and grabbed the phone. He decided to record from the sofa. Standing didn't matter, surroundings didn't matter, presentation didn't matter. Either way, he wanted this to be real. As real as it got. Holding the phone in front of him seemed too close. There was too much of him in shot without a selfie stick, at least, but the phone didn't stand anywhere else.

In the end, he opted for leaning it against some books in the bookcase, angled toward the sofa. He flicked the camera to face forward so that he could see himself, see how he looked in-shot. And then he turned the phone around, checking and hoping that the angle was the same. He didn't want to watch himself; he'd had his fill of position checks and face angles. Then he pressed record and went to sit down on the sofa.

He crossed his legs, looked at the camera, and dried up.

What was I even going to say? Where do I start?

Mac scratched the back of his head and thought.

At the beginning of the end. Simple.

He looked back at the camera and began with the end.

'Hi, I'm Mac Macauley. Yeah, that guy, you know, the mind guy who lost his mind. A wise man once said, 'when things go wrong, don't go with them.' Guess what? I went. I went with it all the way to the bottom. Then I tied it around my neck and let it keep me down there.'

Mac huffed a breath. He was getting into the swing now. He was just going to be honest. It wasn't like anyone would see this: it was personal, research, healing. Who knew if he would even carry it on, but he'd go with it for now.

'I think it's pretty much public knowledge that I lost my beautiful wife and business partner almost twelve months ago. Since then, I've been stuck at rock bottom. I've thought I was beyond help, lost to traverse the rapids by myself, but then I realised I'm the mind guy!' he tapped his temple. 'The bloody mind guy! This is exactly what I do. So, armed with my own book,' Mac held a copy of his latest book next to his face, hoping it was in shot. He didn't want to say the name. This wasn't a plug, it was personal. It was serious. 'I'm on a journey to follow my own strategies, theories and exercises - and possibly find some new ones - to help me deal with my issues, limiting beliefs, mindset and grief. I hope it works, because I realised it doesn't matter how many people rave about my system and how it's helped them, I have never actually tested it on myself. It doesn't matter how much I preach. I don't actually KNOW.'

'Now it's time to find out because it is in my blood to help people to be their best, to understand their potential. If I can't help myself, then I need new strategies because I really want to be able to help YOU. The journey will be raw, real, and completely honest. This is day one of Mac Macauley's Mind Adventures. I'll be back soon with more diary entries, and quite probably cabin fever.'

He held up a hand with a grin and then moved to turn the camera off.

'Mac Macauley's Mind Adventures!' Mac laughed to himself. 'Sweet. I've got a good feeling about this. Recording may just help, and maybe I'll go public with it later too.'

CHAPTER SIXTEEN

TOM FELT THE CRAMP grab his left side and scrunch it into a hard ball. Pain shot into his stomach with every breath he breathed. He set his teeth and tried to push through, but the pain became debilitating, so he stopped to tread water. He could see Josh looking bored on the spectator chairs through the blue of his goggles, and as the stitch began to ease, he waved a hand at his son.

'Two hundred and ten,' Josh shouted and placed his chin back in his hand.

Tom mentally calculated the mileage.

Three.

In just over an hour, which wasn't his best by a long shot. If he was going to complete the twenty-one-mile channel, which couldn't take place in a swimming pool, he was going to need to up his game.

For now, the game was over. He had to be at work in fifty-five minutes.

He swam to the side and got out, taking his goggles off and rubbing his eyes as Josh came down to the spectator railing. They were the only people in the pool this morning, so Tom shouted to him.

'You're free to go, Josh. Go get ready for school, buddy. Thanks for that.'

Josh gave his father a sad grin.

'It was good, dad. It has been three days, don't be hard on yourself. You were near your best time.'

Not by enough, he thought, but he grinned at Josh anyway. 'I know, champ, I'm not too upset. I've just got to up my game.'

Josh grinned back. 'See you at home, dad,' he said.

'Thanks for this Josh, I appreciate you keeping time and count. I really do.'

'I appreciate not having to do it with you.' Josh said, referring to when Tom had first had the idea and began to free swim. He had tried to get Mac swimming, but when it was clear that Mac wasn't interested, he tried to get Josh involved instead, a kind of team pair just for the training, but Josh had hated it as much as Mac. Anything not to wet his hair and smudge the kohl around his eyes. He had offered to get up early and keep length count, though, after Tom had forgotten to click each length on his watch as he swam. To be fair, it was a lot less hassle not having to think about it, anyway.

Josh stuck up his hand and left through the spectator's exit, leaving Tom alone on the side of the pool. Standing, he shook out his goggles, and ran a hand through his hair. The lifeguard got down off his chair and walked toward him.

'Good swim, Mr Macauley,' he said.

Tom gave a small smile as the young boy walked past, and wondered if there was ever a chance that little strip of wind could rescue him if he got into trouble.

'Thanks son,' he said, and headed for the changing rooms.

As he changed, he thought about how far he had slipped in the three days he had taken off.

Two hundred and ten lengths in seventy minutes equated to around twenty seconds per length. Last Wednesday he had managed to keep an even fifteen seconds with not much fuss, completing two hundred and thirty lengths in just fifty minutes.

Too long Tom, it's too long.

With a huff, he packed his bag and pushed off the bench, leaving the leisure centre with not quite as much enthusiasm as the last few weeks. He was getting into the car when the phone rang. He threw his bag onto the back seat before answering. It was most probably Meg.

'Yeah?

'Tom Macauley?'

'Speaking,' Tom said, not recognising the voice, and not really caring for a sales call this early in the morning.

'The Tom Macauley, of Better Young Lives?'

Tom frowned. Whoever this was, where the heck had they got his personal number from?

'Yeah, that's right, but this isn't the work-'

There was a huff on the line cutting him off, and then the connection went dead. Tom rolled his eyes. Probably one of the gang at work winding him up. He got in the car and pulled out of the parking space, turning the vehicle toward the exit.

As he braked at the junction, he glanced into the rear-view mirror. Behind him, a man-sized figure dressed entirely in black stood at the edge of the building, stuffing something into a pocket. Tom narrowed his eyes to watch. Were they putting a phone away? Had it been them that called? There was a moment where Tom and the figure seemed to be staring at each other, although Tom couldn't say for certain – he couldn't see a face under the hood – it was simply a hunch. Tom continued to watch, and when he didn't move the car out of the clear junction the figure moved first, adjusting their hood, putting their head down, and hurrying away. Tom's chest lurched. A lone figure wasn't completely out of the ordinary here, but something was tugging at Tom's radar, his instincts kicking in.

Shit, they found me?

Tom swallowed hard, put his foot down, and left the car park, the tyres squealing his exit.

CHAPTER SEVENTEEN

NOVEMBER

A FEW DAYS LATER the there was a break in the weather that not only saw the wind and rainfall drop but also the temperature. Mac, bundled in his hat, scarf, and gloves was outside taking advantage of the dry weather to cut more wood to replenish what he had used over the last couple of weeks. Which was a lot. Almost half.

Going to be tough to keep on top of this in the winter months he thought, thanking Tom for the foresight to have enough large logs piled at the back of the store that he wouldn't have to worry about cutting down any trees. He also hoped that he wouldn't have to bother with the vegetable patch, but if his calculations were correct, the storeroom food should last all winter.

This morning he had stood at the patch, identifying cauliflower and cabbage. The rest he knew nothing about, and what in the hell he would do with a goddamn cauliflower out here he had no idea. So, he left it... and chopped wood - which was something he could cope with.

Rolo was scuffling with something down by the loch as Mac chopped. He turned his attention to the dog, who seemed to be busy digging to the underworld next to the pier. Mac stared.

'Rolo! Enough!'

The dog carried on digging with no sign that he had heard. Mac set the axe down into the chopping stump with a thunk and strode to the pier edge.

'Oi, buddy! Enough.'

He put a hand on the dog's head, and he finally stopped digging to look up at Mac. The hole was about five inches already, the earth soft around it.

'Jeez Rolo, what on earth are you...?'

Mac trailed off as movement caught his eye. Just above the mountain, to the right, was a small pillar of smoke. Not wanting to go chasing after something that was no longer there, he had decided to put the fire mystery to bed until he ever saw it again - if he ever saw it again. He hadn't thought he would, half thought he had imagined the whole thing in the swirling storminess of that day, but now here it was. Smooth and tall, plain as day. Thin tendrils curling around themselves gently in the light breeze.

Mac moved onto the pier and stared at the mountain. Rolo came to sit at his feet importantly.

It's the same place, isn't it? Is someone camping in this weather? Why haven't they moved on by now?

The questions came quick and fast, and Mac looked at his watch. 11.15am. He kicked a foot at the pier, causing Rolo to startle and look at him accusingly. Mac took no notice.

Fuck, why couldn't I have seen this earlier? No way I'm hiking all the way up there now and getting back before dark.

But tomorrow it may be gone.

If they're still there now, maybe they're camping a while, they haven't moved on yet.

Why do you need to know?

There must be an easier way…

He crossed his arms with a heavy sigh of irritation… and then he almost fell off the pier with revelation.

The kayak!

'Rolo! We can take the boat.'

The dog turned to look at him, head cocked on one side, and then he shuffled forward to sit at his feet. Mac stooped, stroking the dog's head as he stared across the water.

'If we climb the mountain, it will take us a good three hours judging by the other side, and then we have to locate the fire, which seemed to be over the mountain last time.'

Rolo whined. His head tilted to the other side as he listened to Mac intently.

'It's too much of a trek from the time it is now, but if we go in the kayak, it only takes us fifty minutes to the bend. In under an hour, we can be investigating the back of the mountain, I think. And with just an hour's paddle back, we shouldn't need more than a drink with us.'

Rolo whined again.

'You're right, I do. You have a whole loch to drink from. What do you think?'

Rolo gave a sharp bark and jumped, putting his paws on Mac's shoulders, and panting hot, steamy, breath into his face. Mac pushed him down with a laugh.

'Let's get going then,' he said.

Mac filled a bottle with water from the kitchen after picking the letters and numbers up from the floor again, and placing them back on the kitchen side. The sandwich bag had gone to who knew where, but he could deal with that later.

Outside, he pushed the bottle of water under the straps at the back end of the boat to hold it secure, and then dragged the kayak into the water and called Rolo. The dog fell into the boat from the pier, righted himself and propped his feet over the front, narrowly avoiding knocking the oars over the side. Mac arranged the phone so that it held itself upright in the straps at the front end of the boat - now between Rolo's legs. He pressed record, and pushed off the wood of the pier with the paddle.

'Time to explore,' he said to the camera.

He pulled the oars hard, long even strokes out into the centre of the loch, like a man on a mission.

Hell, he was a man on a mission.

The loch was smooth and glassy, a dark blue that seemed deep and mysterious, reflecting the mountains on either side in a perfect upside-down symmetry. Until the oars broke the effect, anyway. As he rowed, and Rolo navigated, his nose in the air to sniff new smells, Mac felt himself relax. It was cold, but he was building heat, and the views were beyond beautiful from here. He even positioned the camera to catch a perfect view of the cabin, and clicked to record a few stills. Maybe he would send them to Tom later.

At the bend, the loch turned to the right and opened into a long and narrow stretch of water. Keeping his eye on the smoke, he paddled until the first mountain did indeed dip away and another mountain rose. However, by luck or good fortune, Mac saw he had made the right decision to Kayak.

Not only was the smoke coming from behind the first mountain, but it was coming from a small, secluded valley *between* the mountains. A valley that he was looking straight at.

'Well, what do you know, Rolo? Not only would we not be halfway up the mountain yet if we had hiked, but by the time we had got to the top, I'd have been very pissed to see the fire in the bloody valley.'

Rolo turned to him, nose still sniffing the air.

Mac pulled closer to the edge of the loch until he found a small inlet between the trees. It wasn't quite big enough for the boat, which was just as well. If this place had seemed well used, Mac would have deflated the boat and carried it with him. As it was, he felt that this place was so secluded that the boat would be fine for an hour or two alone.

Just to be sure, after taking his bottle and his phone and putting them in his pockets, he unscrewed the oars and took the halves with him, too.

'If anyone takes the boat now, good luck to them. Unless they brought their own paddles, anyway. And if the owner of the fire turns out to be a psycho, we have a weapon. Two for the price of one.'

Rolo didn't answer. He was too busy sniffing ahead, and running off into the distance toward the smoke.

CHAPTER EIGHTEEN

Tom swung the X5 into the driveway and turned off the engine. He had been followed home, he was sure of it. His heart was pounding and he sat with his fingers gripping the wheel for some time before he began to calm and finally let go.

Then, behind him, an engine revved and a car pulled up at the bottom of the driveway.

Fuck, here we go.

Tom's heart ramped up again as he watched. He scanned the rear-view mirror, deciding to wait before getting out. Gripping the wheel again, he grit his teeth as he watched the car, which now sat silent and still.

Tom began to shake. He'd had a feeling that they would follow up, but it had been mere days since the call. Would they come for him this quickly?

There was movement in the car now. Shadows. He ducked his head down below the headrest and waited. A sheen of sweat had broken out over his forehead, and he closed his eyes, wiping it with his wrist.

There was a pounding on the window. A voice.

Tom yelled, eyes flying to open to meet his son's, whose hands were cupped on the driver's side window, nose scrunched. He yelled again, his heart doing a double flip, before finally calming with recognition.

'What the hell are you doing?' Josh said from the driveway.

Tom was about to tell Josh to get back in the house when another shadow fell over the passenger side of the car. He gave a yelp and turned to see Amy peering through the window at him with a look of amusement. She raised a hand to the side as the car tooted its horn and drove away. Tom stared at her.

'Franco? he said.

'What?' she mouthed. Her hands spread apart in question.

'I said was that... oh, never mind,' he said, opening the driver's door, and pushing Josh back up the drive.

'I said was that Franco?' he said to the now empty passenger side of the car. He caught a glimpse of Amy's dress as she floated through the front door. Josh stood with his hands in his pockets, staring after her. Tom turned to him.

'Was that-?'

'Franco.' Josh confirmed with a nod. 'What the hell was all that about, dad? Are you freebasing, or what? A car pulls up and you act all shady.'

Tom crossed his arms as he beeped the car locked.

'I was not acting shady.'

'You so were, dad, I've got you recorded.' Josh held aloft his phone. A still of Tom filled the screen, his eyes closed as he sat low in the front seat, the window edge of the door cutting his head in half right under the nose.'

Tom raised his eyebrows. 'Is there nothing sacred with you kids? I was thinking, okay?'

'What about?'

'Work stuff.'

'What stuff?'

'Work stuff.'

He motioned Josh toward the door, and they went inside. Tom peered up and down the street looking for unfamiliar cars before he closed the door. Josh laughed, equally deep and squeaky where his voice had finally broken last month, and Tom turned to see the camera aimed at him.

'Turn that bloody thing off, will you,' he said, arm outstretched to cover the camera lens as he moved past Josh and into the kitchen.

No Meg.

Josh ambled into the living area as Tom took the stairs two at a time and found Meg in the small bathroom. Her mouth opened in a small 'o' as he flung himself inside and shut the door with a quiet click.

'Good day, dear?' she said, hands covered in moisturising cream halfway to her face.

'I think they found me.' Tom whispered urgently.

Meg calmly placed her hands on her face and begun to massage without a word.

CHAPTER NINETEEN

M AC HAD IT ALL wrong, he thought, as they walked down a dirt path that was a lot wider and more well used than any of the tracks around the cabin.

Tom said there was no-one around here for miles, though?

But then, he supposed this inlet probably was a couple of miles from the cabin by water. By road, it may be a good ten. So, who was the keeper of the campfire? He soon found out when he was turned a little off course from the fire and hit a dry-stone wall with a small wooden gate.

There were no signs, no throughways, no bridle paths, no indication of any sort that this was a public right of way.

So, it's private property then. A house!

He felt a small pang of regret that the fire didn't belong to some mysterious and friendly camper. He could have camped on the cabin grounds and he and Mac could have whiled away the winter together. Who knew, if they got on well enough, he may have invited him to stay inside the cabin. But now the owner of the fire had a house. Bricks and mortar. There was no way the offer of camping on the cabin grounds would stand.

Maybe I could camp on his grounds. The company would be nice, I wouldn't need to tell Tom... Ah, but I don't have a tent. Shit.

Something dropped next to him with a hard thud and a plop. He swung toward the sound.

An apple.

Mac raised an eyebrow. If he had been standing just slightly to the left, he could have been nursing a bump and discovering gravity just like Sir Isaac Newton - except that gravity had already been discovered, he would only have the bump. He chuckled and then Sula's voice resounded in his head, along with her throaty laughter.

'Do you want an apple, Mac?'

It caught him off guard so much that he spluttered laughter. Rolo stopped sniffing to watch him.

It had been one of the many jokes that had been thrown at him amongst his team back at home. Mac loved apples. They were his favourite fruit. Any would do, and in any form, although his favourites were Braeburn and one of those always made it into his pocket each day as a snack, usually courtesy of Sula. Unfortunately, it made for some mick taking. *Do you want your apple, Mac?* Someone would say, holding up the apple? *Yeah, go on then,* he'd reply... and promptly get a MacBook delivered to his table from one of the surrounding team. They'd hoot with laughter before giving up the apple for him to eat.

A similar grim joke came in the form of Mark Morrison.

It was a running joke for someone to shout, 'Mac's returned!' each time Mac entered a room. The whole team would then burst into a tuneful rendition of 'Return of the Mack.'

Mac smiled at the memory. He had worked too hard, burned himself out, especially toward the end, but his team was top class. There was no better bunch of people that he would ever work with. There had been some tough times at the end, especially after Sula, but there had also been many phenomenal times along their journey together, and always, always, they had his back. Even when he had been busy botching shows for the last six months before the cabin.

Mac perched himself against the wall as he thought, Rolo in his peripheral vision, sniffing something exciting in the weeds at the side of the path.

He wondered where his team would be when he returned, whether they would keep the company rolling over for him or move on. They had no obligations, and with Mac gone and no way to contact him, there was only so much they could do with backlist material. Even that depended on the state his reputation was in, and what the media had said about his absence and cancelled shows. He shook his head.

You really blew it Mac, you're such an idiot.

He sniffed, blew out a breath, and made himself a promise. He wouldn't go back to the frantic life he used to live anyway, not now that he had stopped. When he thought about it, he had travelled to one-hundred-and-sixty-eight countries in the year before Sula had died, and they were the ones he had counted before losing count. But he realised that for all his travelling he had seen extraordinarily little of the world, almost nothing of the countries that he had been in. He hadn't the time to stop at a French patisserie and sit with a pastry, enjoying the scenery and the language. He was shuttled from the plane to a hotel room, was on stage within a few small hours, and either back on a plane to somewhere else, or straight to bed to be on a plane first thing the next morning. It was too much. It was no way to live. Sula had moaned at him constantly over the last two years, right up until she had died, but it was only now that he saw it.

Whichever way he looked at how things had turned out, he was exactly where he needed to be right now; taking a break, and catching his thoughts as to what he may want the future to look like.

Not like it had been, that's for sure!

But did he still have the same drive to help people get over their biggest barrier - their own mind?

Absolutely, he thought, with no pause. The thought filled him with pleasure and satisfaction. The desire could only be described as a hunger. An all-encompassing hunger that ate every second he thought he wasn't doing anything toward it. Even standing here, reminiscing, he had the urge to paddle back to the cabin, work on an exercise with himself, record a video diary about his thoughts, and pick up an unread book on the subject that just wouldn't leave him be.

He decided that when he made his comeback - which he would - he would contact each and every one of his old team in person. If they wanted back in, great, if not he would thank them for their time and their loyalty over the last ten years, anyway. That was all he could do, but he trusted enough to know that things happened for a reason. Most people, Tom included, had a problem for every solution, but Mac never worked that way anymore. Every problem was an opportunity, and the biggest one was staring him in the face. He had to pick himself up, get to work, but this time his way, and that involved taking the time needed to sort himself and his life out first.

If only I had had the opportunity when Sula was here.

But he knew the world didn't work that way. Knew better than anyone that sometimes we need a jolt, something to shake us out of our funk. He was only at this crossroads because of Sula's death.

I'm sorry you had to go for me to realise it, baby. I truly am. I love you so much. I know at the end you weren't truly convinced, but you were the only one for me. I hope you're more content now, wherever you are.

There was a thud to his right, and he looked down at another apple through blurry eyes.

Apple, Mac?

He let a couple of tears fall before wiping his eyes with the thumb and forefinger of his right hand and shaking his head.

What the hell is up with you today? I thought we'd done with the tears.

He let them pass before wiping his eyes and looking down at the small green and red fruit. He imagined sinking his teeth into a fresh, crunchy apple and suddenly his mouth was watering. He blinked and sniffed.

I could have a bite, try it. It would be fresh if it had just fallen from the tree, right?

He picked it up and turned it over. The whole of the underside was rotten mush, brown and soggy.

'Yeuch.' he said, throwing it into the undergrowth. Rolo chased it.

'Leave it alone, you'll have bad guts all night and I won't be wiping your backside. You can sleep in the wood store.'

Rolo looked back at Mac with a grin on his face, tongue hanging out. His golden head was covered with dirt from his nose right up to and inside his ears. Mac couldn't help but grin back.

'Your call,' he said in a serious tone. 'And what the hell did you do to your face?'

The dog trotted over to sit at his feet, tail thumping against the ground as he looked up at Mac.

'Have you been burying apples, by any chance?'

Rolo grinned innocently.

'Don't give me that, if you've eaten any - wood store, I told you.'

Rolo sat up into a begging position on his back legs, front paws curled in the air.

'Nope, I don't take persuasion or negotiation. You're a bad dog.'

Rolo stood on his hind legs and Mac caught his front paws, resting them on his stomach. He gave his head a scrub, wiping the wet dirt off his face as much as he could. The dog's velvety golden fur was now a smudged brown. Mac held a hand under Rolo's jaw, bringing his face to the dog's.

'It's a good job you can't see yourself right now, you know that?'

Rolo's tongue flicked out of his mouth, catching Mac's face in a warm, wet dog lick. He pushed the dog down with a laugh and wiped his face with a hand.

'You got an apple, dude. I'm not pleased.'

He looked up into the branches of the small tree above him. It was late in the year so many of the apples had been picked or had fallen - or were falling, Mac thought. Such a waste when there's still a handful up there.

An idea brewed. Apple trees above him, a few apple's on the trees, all in a line, and a stone wall to climb onto, like the universe sent a pair of ladders. He peered over the top of the wall and moved around to get a good look at the garden behind it. The smoke still rose from beyond the brow of a hill, but he couldn't see anything that even looked like a house from here. Still, if he couldn't see a house, then no-one in a house could see him either.

So, it would be possible to claim a few apples for myself, wouldn't it? Would that be considered stealing?

He supposed it would.

He pondered that thought, and then scoured the wall for the best place to climb. He placed his foot on the indents between the stone, lifting himself up enough to use his upper body strength to get on top of the wall, where upright slabs of stone didn't lend themselves easily to being sat or stood on. For a moment, with no way back from a slip, Mac had thought his baby making days were over, but he had caught himself just in time and straddled the wall enough to be able to place his feet on top in a crouch.

From up here, he could finally see the house in the distance. Large with grey stone walls. There was also a man with grey hair and what looked like a dark wax jacket tending a fire in what looked like a large fire pit. Mac knew that his chances of being in and out of the tree quickly were slim to none. He looked up and saw an apple just above him, which may just be within reach if he stood fully. The man seemed involved with the fire. Mac couldn't see the problem with plucking the one apple. It was do-able.

Getting his balance, he arranged his feet at angles in front of him, like a high-wire walker, then he stood, his legs shaking until he could put his right hand out onto the tree for support. When he was steady, he looked at the man, who hadn't moved.

All good, Mac, just take it easy and we're in for a home run.

He pressed a finger to his lips, looking at Rolo, who stretched up the wall to stare at the strange antics of his master. Rolo wagged his tail, staying quiet.

With a final glance to the man, who was still focused on the fire, Mac turned his own focus to the apple. It was higher than he thought, and he readjusted his feet to stand on tiptoes. He touched the bottom of the apple, but it swung away from him. He waited for it to stop its dance before trying again, but his fingertips barely grazed it. He just wasn't quite high enough. He huffed a frustrated breath.

I cannot be this close to my first apple in months and lose the fight. It's right there, Mac, jump if you must.

Flitting his tongue between his lips, Mac bent his legs into a sort of half crouch, eyed the apple and launched himself up. His feet didn't leave the wall much, but it was enough. He had it. He grasped the apple with both hands, arms in the air, balanced now only by an apple stalk as leaves rained over him with a rustle.

I'll just pull it and jump, so I land in the bush next to Rolo.

He tugged the apple, but the stalk held firm. He shook it, twisted it, tugged again, but the apple was still holding on.

'Come on, you bugger,' he muttered, eyes on the green bottom. His arms ached, but there was no way he was letting this one go.

'Are you really apple scrumping?' a voice said.

A figure came into view below him, and Mac's heart flew into his chest just as the apple finally snapped away from the tree. His arms dropped, throwing him off balance. He wobbled for an impressive number of seconds before he fell, hitting the ground on the wrong side of the wall with an ungraceful thump, and an 'oof' of air.

CHAPTER TWENTY

'Y̲OU SHOULDN'T HAVE DONE it.' Meg said, rubbing the cream vigorously into her cheeks. 'I told you it would come back to haunt you, didn't I? Well, didn't I?'

Tom shrugged his shoulders.

'What do you expect us to have to do about it now, then?' she continued. 'It's your mess, Tom. It was yours then, and it's yours now. I'll not have any part of it. If you want to act like an eejit, I told you, do it on your time and sort out your own mess.'

'I don't know how to sort it. How was I supposed to know they would find us, they–'

'You.' Meg said pointedly, drying her hands and picking up the brush to run through her hair.

'Me,' Tom said, 'Okay me. They had no details. It wasn't an official visit, was it? What they did was wrong. What else could I do?'

'Sometimes you just leave well alone, Tom. Don't stick your beak where it isn't wanted.'

'I couldn't,' he said, looking down at his fingers; all smooth skin, and buffed nails. He picked at a piece of non-existent dirt.

'I know. It's one of your worst faults. Never could keep your nose out.'

'The situation back then was-'

'I know what it was.' Meg said, putting down the brush and turning to face him. She cupped a hand to his chin with a sad smile.

'It was the honourable thing to do,' he muttered, holding her hand with his own.

'No, Tom. No, it was a bloody stupid thing to do, and what of the mess that needs sorting now? I'm not moving, and I don't intend to run, from anyone - ever. So, you need to sort out who the hell this is and what they want from you to put a stop to it. Whatever it is-'

Tom stepped back with a shake of his head.

'Absolutely not. Do you know what they were doing with those drugs?'

'I'm not interested in their affairs. I know about enough about people who deal with drugs in any form to know that they will happily gut you like a fish. I want my husband in-tact. The kids need their father. If you leave me alone, Tom, I shall be so damn angry with you. Give the damn people what they want.'

Tom huffed a breath and clenched his jaw.

'Well? We have a lot of money, Tom. They want money, give them money. Do they want money?'

Tom shook his head with a frown.

'Well, what do they want?'

'How would I know?' Tom said, exasperated. 'Blood, probably.'

Meg didn't flinch. She turned to wash her hands, looking at him in the mirror.

'Tosh. I don't know anyone who cannot be persuaded with money. Why would they want blood over money? I don't know, what are they, vampires?'

'Of the worst sort.' Tom said with a sigh.

Meg flicked the towel at him, catching him across the wrist.

'Ow!' he stared at her, and she stared right back. He swallowed hard.

'What do they want from you, Tom?' she repeated.

Tom shrugged. 'I seriously don't know.'

'Have you spoken to them?'

'No!' he said, looking at her like she was mad. Why the hell would he speak to them? They'd just as well cut out his tongue. 'I don't-'

'Then how do you know they want anything?'

Tom shut his mouth, and then opened it again. 'It's obvious.'

'Is it? How do you know it's them?'

'Who the hell else would it be?' Tom could see his face getting red in the mirror, his nose a big red beacon, always the first thing to go when he got angry. He focused on his wife, who was looking a lot calmer than he felt. 'Someone I don't know watches me at the pool, and calls my phone? My personal phone? More than once, now.'

'And you didn't speak to them?'

'They didn't say anything, so I disconnected the call,' he said, exasperated. Why wasn't she getting how serious this was?

'It could be any number of people, Tom. It could be bloody Curry's about the washing machine delivery.'

'They said nothing!'

'You put the bloody phone down on them, that's why.'

'I don't think Curry's make silent phone calls as part of their customer service,' he said, his voice raising.

'How long did you give them to speak? You put the phone down on your own daughter yesterday because she didn't speak quickly enough!'

'Her number didn't come up, I thought it was *them*,' he said.

'But none of *them* have ever spoken to you! Do you know how silly you sound, Tom?'

'I just... I...'

'You what, Tom?' Meg was getting angry now too.

'I have a feeling.'

'Ah, well I don't do feeling Tom, I do man at the door demanding money. I do 'I've spoken to said man, and he wants a million pounds.' You're running scared from one silent phone call. Is that the truth of it?'

'Five.' he said, gritting his teeth and running a hand through his hair.

'Okay,' Meg said. Her face softened and Tom thought she was finally getting the seriousness, and then she added, 'One unknown silent phone call, three from Curry's and one from your own bloody daughter. Get a bloody grip, Tom, for pity's sake!'

Meg slapped the towel onto the towel rail.

'When you've spoken to them, and you have a ransom amount, let me know. Because they *will* want money, Tom. If they're coming after you still, all these years later, then they've not mended their ways, have they? So, number one, the whole thing was pointless. They probably have more drugs in their car glove box now than they ever had in that house. Number two, they're criminals, which means, number three, they have one brain cell between them, and that teeny tiny brain cell knows only one thing - money. I guarantee it.'

Tom pushed out a breath.

She could have a point. What the hell are you running from when you don't even know who these people are? Negotiate Tom, you're a fucking businessman!

'The other thing is,' Meg went on, 'You don't even know what they've found, because you've not spoken to them, whoever they are.'

'Yes, Okay, you're right, I agree.' Tom nodded his head. He could always trust Meg to put things into perspective, however hard he didn't want to look.

'So, you'll speak to them next time? Yes?'

He nodded his head again. 'Absolutely. Yes, I'll speak to them and find out.'

Meg stared at him, eyes narrowed, and then she planted a kiss on his mouth.

'I love you, Tom,' she said as she left the bathroom and walked to the stairs.

'I love you, too,' he said.

She looked at him, one hand on the banister of the stairs.

'But if Curry's call me saying they've been trying to get you, so help me, I'll wrap that bloody washing machine around your head. I mean it, Tom.'

Tom had no words to respond. He watched his wife disappear down the stairs, checked his nose had returned to normal colour, and followed her down.

CHAPTER TWENTY-ONE

ROLO WAS BARKING FRANTICALLY from the other side of the wall, and from his position on the floor, Mac saw his head pop up and down like a jack-in-the-box over the top. If he hadn't lost the ability to speak, and his eyesight was working properly, he may have found it funny - but winded, he could do nothing but gasp for breath. He rolled from his back onto his front, the blurry figure now standing before him. He tried to raise himself enough to explain what he had been doing, but only made it as far as his knees. Somehow, the apple was still clutched in his hand.

He blinked, trying to clear his vision. He saw the skirt first, one of the long hippie sort Sula loved to wear, and then the long cardigan pulled around her slim frame, held by her hands as her arms folded across her chest. Her face looked fresh and young, a smattering of freckles and pale blue eyes, her golden blonde hair tied up in a messy bun behind her.

She raised an eyebrow, managing to look both sweet and disappointed at the same time.

'If my da had found you, mister, you'd have been missing a few teeth to eat that apple with right now. You're lucky you only get me to deal with.'

Mac felt a sense of comfort and familiarity, which set him at ease. Meg - the girl's manner reminded him of Meg.

Not the girl herself, of course. She's much younger and more pleasing to the eye than Meg. Just the manner. Just the accent.

Mac grinned at her, wondering why he was talking himself in circles, while not knowing how to respond to what she'd said.

You could say sorry?

'I don't know why that's funny. You were stealing, mister.' She said, pointing a finger at him and then using it to tuck a loose tendril of hair behind her ear.

Mac got himself together at the word stealing. He felt himself redden and held a hand palm out to her.

'No, no, I wasn't,' he said. 'I... I can explain.'

'Sure, mister.' the girl said, a slight grin playing around her full lips. 'I'd like to hear you explain how you're not stealing, with an apple from my da's land in your hand, now. An apple I saw you pick, with my own eyes.'

Mac looked from the girl to the apple, juicy, green, and perfect. His mouth watered.

I can't lose this damn apple now.

'The evidence is in plain sight, for all to see.'

'Where?' Mac said. He threw the apple back over his shoulder as hard as he could and, with a surge of satisfaction, saw it sail over the wall near to where he had been standing before he had picked the damn thing. It landed with a thud and Rolo stopped barking instantly.

Mac closed his eyes as the sound of the dog's chewing and crunching filled the silence. Mac huffed a breath.

'Thanks, Rolo, as much as I admire your skills for hiding evidence, I really wanted that damn apple,' he muttered.

The woman hooted a laugh and stood on tiptoe to peer over the wall.

'Is this your dog?' she said, turning to Mac. 'he's a clever boy isn't he,' she looked back over the wall. 'Yes you are, what a clever boy. I couldn't have planned a better punishment myself. Aw, you're so cute, and so clever, yes you are.'

Mac scrunched up his nose. A little bit of his lunch arrived in the back of his throat.

'You'll give him a big head. He's not so clever. He'll give himself bad guts later.'

The girl spun to grin at him, before half jogging to the gate and opening it so that Rolo could come through. He ran to Mac, sniffing and licking his face like they had been apart for days, not minutes. The sweet smell of apple only rubbed salt into Mac's already open wound.

'Get off,' he said, pushing the dog down and scrambling to his feet.

Rolo went straight back to the woman, who happily scrubbed at his ears. 'You're a good boy, and do you know what your da got just then. That is called Karma. What goes around comes around. That's what he gets for stealing, isn't it? Aye, it is. Apple kisses.'

Mac pouted as Rolo flaunted himself at her, tongue flicking at her face, before dropping to the floor and rolling onto his back. She scrubbed at his belly and his eyes closed in pleasure.

'And what do you get? You get the apple and a belly rub because you're such a good boy, aren't you?'

'If you don't want me to lose my lunch on your dad's lawn, maybe you'll allow me to apologise, and we'll get out of your hair.' Mac said.

'He's only jealous,' she said to Rolo. 'See how the poor sportsmanship comes out. What your da doesn't know is that all the apples are past their best now and that one he picked was probably half rotten. You saved him, didn't you? Aye, you did.' She scrubbed harder and Rolo squirmed in pleasure. 'That's why you get the bad guts, Rolo, karma. As I said. You were too hasty.'

Mac watched the woman who was sitting on her knees scrubbing at Rolo's Stomach. A huge smile spread across her delicate features.

Was that true? He knew it was past apple season, but he had no idea about growing or gardening. He frowned as the woman looked up at him.

'If you wanted an apple that badly, you could have just asked. We have buckets full of them stashed in the outbuildings.'

'Fresh?'

'Oh, Aye. These are all picked and stored for freshness. Ma makes so many things out of apple she could probably fill a six-hundred-page cookbook and go on to volume two.'

The woman laughed and Mac grinned, her laughter infectious.

'But...' he gestured to the tree, 'I stole one.'

The woman laughed again and got to her feet. Rolo bounced to his own feet and walked off to sniff and scent the wall.

Marking his territory. Guess he found a girl he likes.

'Listen, mister-'

'Mac. My name's Mac,' he said.

The girl held out a hand, and he grasped it. She shook it firmly, hand warm and skin soft.

'Mac, I'm Madeline. Maddie for short. Pleased to meet you and your dog, Rolo. Very charming! To answer your question, you were apple scrumping, aye, but the dog ate your catch. Karma. He ate the rotten apple, karma for him and for you, who will have to clean his mess. Double karma. My job here is done.'

Mac shut his mouth.

'So, that's it... You're not going to...?'

'What, get my da to knock your teeth out? Not today, but only because I like your dog. Come, I'll get you some apples to take if you like.'

Mac thought all his ships had come in at once as he followed her over the grass. He opened his mouth to call Rolo, but the dog ran past and was already galloping right to her side. She scrubbed his head before turning to Mac.

'Come on, it's a-ways to the house,' she said, 'do you want these apples or not?'

And Mac found himself running to catch up with her as eagerly as Rolo had.

CHAPTER TWENTY-TWO

THE HOUSE WAS LARGE and imposing, with grey stone and rounded third story dormers. In fact, there were many windows under the dormer's too, lined up symmetrically along the first and second stories beneath. Too many, Mac thought, as they walked across the grass.

'It's huge,' he murmured.

'Aye, far too big,' Maddie told him with a smile. 'My brother set up business in the front section of the house, a few years ago now, before he moved away. Ma and da had the room, and he paid them rent. It's the only good use the space has ever been put to.'

'Ah, so now it's-'

'Just a big old, dusty, drafty, cold, uninviting house that's far too large for ma and da, but they won't be moved. After my brother left, I told them to sell up, to downsize a little, take some of the load off, but they wouldn't hear of it.'

'Family heritage?'

'Naw, not at all. A bit of pride, perhaps. I grew up here, but my parents moved here when my brother was two years old. They brought it after a lottery win would you believe?'

Mac felt his jaw drop.

'A lottery win?'

'Aye, it were only two-hundred-and-fifty grand, but that was enough for them to put down a substantial deposit. It's a running joke now, they won the money on a Saturday and had it spent on this place two days later. Everyone was telling them what to do with it, where to put it, where to save it, what to invest in, what start up to do - although da already worked for himself. Everyone thought they were mad and that they'd lose the place within a year, but they didn't know that it was already a go-er, anyway. Ma and da just had to raise a small deposit to secure it - and bam, lottery win. They thought it was hilarious to tell everyone they'd blown the lot.'

'So, did they blow it, or were they joking?'

'Aye, they did, but as da said, money off one of the biggest debts you'll ever have to pay was worth its weight. They managed to get a much smaller mortgage with that chunk of money off, which made day to day living easier. So much easier, in fact, that I came along just a year later!'

Mac let out a surprised laugh. 'That easy, huh?'

She turned to him, her eyes twinkling with mischief.

'Aye, it all went downhill from there.'

'I bet.'

She laughed.

'So, you've always lived here, too?' he asked.

'No, I haven't. Honestly, Mac, have you tried living with your parents at thirty-three?'

Mac shook his head, studying her girlish profile and slight frame. She was older than she appeared. He wouldn't have put her past twenty-three.

'It's a bloody nightmare, don't go there. No, I left when I was seventeen to travel the world.'

Mac tried to keep his mouth closed, tried to hide his surprise, and take back his stereotypical assumptions. Country girl, farm hand, still at home, maybe a boyfriend, but no plans to leave, possibly waiting to take over the family estate...

How wrong can you get?

'Wow, so how far did you get?' he managed without squeaking too much.

Maddie turned to him, her face full of light and excitement.

'Everywhere,' she said, checking them off on her fingers. 'Australia, New Zealand, Indonesia, Thailand, China, Japan, India, Africa, Egypt, Turkey, all over Europe, the USA, Canada, and South America. I used to work and sleep where I found the means to do so. It was a great introduction to culture, meeting genuine families within those countries, and it really opened my eyes. I used to move on when I'd saved the money to do so, sleeper trains and boats mainly, although there were a couple of planes and lots of hitchhiking. I was on the road for almost twelve years in the end.'

Mac almost reeled with surprise. He found himself impressed with not only the strength of Maddie's ability to follow her dreams with no money, but also the belief and ingenuity that it would come when needed. He knew that was how it worked, it was exactly what he taught to millions every year, but he rarely met anyone so unknowingly competent at it. His own life of travel had been so similar in volume, and yet his experience had been so different. His travel was all secure and paid for. Limousines, luxury hotels and fine suits.

No hitchhiking for Mac 'the mind guy' Macauley.

He felt an elbow in his ribs and looked back to Maddie.

'What?'

'I said, have you ever travelled?'

'Yeah,' he said.

She jogged ahead and turned back to face him, walking backward now, Rolo circling her legs.

'Where to, bozo?'

Bozo?

Mac grinned. 'All of the above.' he said.

Maddie halted, it was her turn for her mouth to drop open with unconcealed surprise. Mac stopped walking to save bumping into her.

'Seriously?'

'Seriously.' Mac said. 'Add a good many more onto that list, too. Pretty much scaled most of the world.'

Maddie stepped forward and grabbed his arms.

'No way! We have to exchange notes. I'm a little stuck at the moment, but I'd like to get back to it someday. Anywhere you say is worth my while going, I'll go.'

Mac smiled down at her.

'I'm afraid I can't tell you much about anywhere I've been, really.'

For the first time since Maddie had spoken to him at the wall, a shadow fell over her face, and a frown creased between her eyes, the only tell-tale sign of her age.

'Why not?'

Mac shrugged his shoulders. 'Long story, but the shortened version is that I was working, and as such, I didn't really have time to see anything.'

Maddie looked flummoxed.

'So, you went all over the world to work and saw *nothing*?'

'Pretty much.'

'That's so sad, Mac. Did you ever go to Rio?'

Mac nodded his head. 'Five times.'

'Ever see Christ the Redeemer up close?'

'Nope.'

She fired more attractions at him, and he shook his head at each one.

'No? What about the Great Wall? A gondola ride in Venice? The Colosseum? Pompeii? Neuschwanstein Castle? Petra? The pyramids? Machu Picchu? The Eiffel tower?-'

'Ah, woah. Stop. Yep. The Eiffel tower. I can check that one off. Only because there was a rare free day in France. We travelled three hours there, queued two to get the elevator up, decided to take the stairs instead, checked out the view for five squashed minutes, and travelled three hours back to the hotel, too pooped to care. Does that count?'

Maddie shook her head.

'Absolutely not. You need to visit the tower out of season and get up there at sunrise or sunset when most of the tourists are in bed.'

'Well, I didn't have that window of opportunity, I'm afraid.'

'Doesn't sound like you have much opportunity. Who the hell travels all over the world and sees nothing?'

'Me.'

Maddie frowned at him.

'What the hell do you do? Because I wouldn't take that job for ten million pounds.'

'Just an events speaker,' he said. 'Nothing special.'

And you do it for a measly six million Mac, and how would ten have made life any better anyway?

Maddie studied him and finally turned to walk next to him again.

'See,' she said, 'I knew there was a reason you fell out of that tree. I have to educate you on the world and tell you some of the best places to see and things to do, and Mac?'

'Hmm?'

'I should jack that job in if I were you. What a waste of time and effort. Hell, what a waste of life!'

They reached an outbuilding, and Maddie stepped into a dark barn and pulled the lid of a large barrel. She pulled a bag from the wall and filled it with apples for him before shutting the lid and coming out to shut the door.

'Here.' She said, holding the bag out toward him.

'Thank you,' he said, peering into the bag. He felt his face stretch into a grin. 'These are perfect. I owe you one. Especially after being so nice when I was trying to steal from you.'

Maddie waved a hand his way with a grin.

'It's no bother,' she said with a smile. 'It's nice to see an unfamiliar face around here, gets a little lonely at this end of this track sometimes.'

He smiled and looked at her. She looked down and kicked the grass with the toe of a white pump.

'Don't you have a car to get out sometimes? How can you possibly be stuck here lonely?'

'Of course, but I'd have to go miles. I can go to the end of the garden and get the scenery alone. There's no need to waste the fuel for that. Anyway, it's best I just stay put for a while.'

Mac frowned, waiting for more, but she shook her head.

'It's a long and complicated story,' she said with a half-grin.

Mac nodded his head, intrigued. 'We all have them.'

'Aye, so shall we go the front way out to your car?'

'My car?' Mac said, the change of direction muddling his thoughts.

'You must have come down here in a car, bozo, unless you hiked for three days? Is that why you wanted the apples, huh?' Maddie crossed her arms over her chest with a grin.

'No, no. I came by boat, not a car. From the loch.'

Maddie raised her eyebrows.

'A boat? From the loch? That's the last place I'd expect anyone to come from. Mac, you are a strange man indeed. Where's the boat and how far did you paddle? The nearest village is over ten miles!'

Mac flicked a thumb over his shoulder. 'Back by the apples,' he said. 'and it wasn't that far, really.'

I hope it's still there.

'Okay, well, the gate has a simple thumb latch. I was helping da with the fire when I saw you. He'll be wondering where I am. Let yourself out.'

'Okay,' Mac said, and turned to go, 'well, thank you for these,' he held the bag up.

'No problem.' she said, hand over her eyes to shield them from the lowering sun. 'I'd advise you not to try anymore apple scrumping, you're liable to get shot or knocked out round here. If you want any more, just come back through the gate to the house and ask for me. We have loads. You don't need to lose a kneecap.'

Mac nodded his head as she turned with a wave and strode away leaving Mac to turn towards the gate.

'Oh, and Mac?' she called.

He turned back to her.

'Jack the job in. Anything that sucks all of your life away is just not worth it, however much it pays.'

CHAPTER TWENTY-THREE

M AC PULLED THE OARS hard, each stroke strong and sure, the boat cutting smoothly through the calm water. It was colder now, mid-afternoon, and they were already losing the light. As they rounded the bend of the loch, the cabin came into view. A tiny pinprick at the head of the lake, backlit by the lowering sun. Mac squinted his eyes against the glare.

'Going to be a nice evening, huh, Rolo?' he said to the dog, who was in his usual position over the front of the boat. Rolo banged his tail but kept his eyes ahead.

Mac stopped talking, the water rippling and splashing each time a paddle dug into the water, and propelled the boat forward. The birds were singing over each other in the trees, somehow managing to be a chorus of peace and tranquillity. A cool breeze rattled through the treetops and whistled past his ears, but he couldn't drown out Maddie's voice.

What a waste of life.

Mac frowned and pulled harder.

The more he gave himself space to think, the more he felt inclined to agree, which only made him kick himself harder. He had spent the last ten years trying to educate people against exactly that. Wasting their lives and their potential. But in dedicating his life to that cause, he had also given away his chance of living his own dream life with the woman he loved.

And she told you, Mac. She tried to tell you, but you couldn't see it.

No, I was trying to help everyone else. All those people who don't know what they can do, all those ideas, those dreams, going to waste.

But in helping them, you managed to lose your own dreams, your own life.

'No,' Mac said aloud.

Rolo swung his head from the front of the boat to look at him with a small whine.

'I didn't,' he said to the dog. Rolo looked at him a while longer, thumped his tail, and turned back to the front of the boat, losing interest. Mac looked out at the loch, his words going to waste, but he went on anyway. 'I've had a good life, smashed all of my own dreams and got to help millions in the process. I won't sit here and criticize my life and all of the good fortune I've found.'

What happened to taking Sula to Verona for a surprise break? Remember all the people you told. Did you get there Mac? Did you do it?

'I couldn't,' he said through gritted teeth.' We got to Rome, though. She liked that.'

Rolo swung to Mac again, decided he needed the company and turned to face him, lying in the bottom of the boat, eyebrows raised.

I bet she loved wandering the city by herself while you were busy. And she always wanted to go to Verona, remember?

'I was planning that. I didn't have time. Just a couple more years, that's all I needed. I was trying to find a gap in the schedule.'

Didn't have time! You have time, Mac, it was Sula that ran out of time. So faithful to you, she put all of your needs ahead of hers, and you weren't even fulfilling your own anyway.

'I'm lucky. I earned enough for us to have a nice life-'

Enough to fly to Verona for a romantic weekend, just the two of you. Pocket change.

'I was... working,' he whispered.

As she said.

With a roar of frustration, Mac stopped paddling and hurled the oars out across the loch. They landed a few feet away, bobbing gently on the water as Mac put his head into his hands and sobbed.

It's simple,' he told the crowd in the large conference room. About eight hundred tonight, a fairly select group. 'But that doesn't mean it's easy.'

There was a ripple of laughter. Mac looked at the audience before him - all of them smart, all ready to take on the world, all ready for change, all poised with pen and paper, all hanging onto his every word. Each of them ready for the secret that would transform their lives. He knew from experience that only one percent would take any action after the seminar was over. It was partly his lifeblood. They would pay to come year after year, some of them multiple times a year, paying him money to rinse and repeat until it sank in. For most, it would never sink in. For the ones who completed the tasks he gave them, however silly, some changed a little, most not at all. They were still writing their mantra's, affirmations, and gratitude journals years later, while their lives played out the same.

For the one percent who were serious, the results were astonishing. Mac had seen ordinary people complete amazing feats in amounts of time that would have made them laugh six months earlier. He had seen a young lady of twenty-four escape a well-known cult, when the day before the seminar she had been so terrified they would notice her gone that she had been on the brink of not attending at all. She never went back. She had been beaten, denied access to education and books, and sexually assaulted as a child for many years, but this twenty-four-year-old was ready. She was *desperate*.

She had sought Mac out after the seminar and he had given her extra information, extra ways to look at things. He had spent the time to go into depth, and she had listened. Not only that, but she had applied. She had taken action. A year later, she was a multi-millionaire fronting her own company, using her own experiences to help other women find a way out of cult lifestyles all over the world. Not just the Charles Manson kind either - for a lot of women, they simply wanted to get out of the ties of their religion or their marriages.

But it was the crisis she found herself in at the time that launched her, and it was a recurring theme Mac found. People in crisis, real, life-changing crisis, were usually the ones to step into their fear, because for them, staying the same or going backward was no longer an option.

Mac smiled around the room. All eyes were on him now, pensive, waiting for the magic formula. The framework to take them to superstar status in their industry.

'It's simple to take a seed and plant it,' he said to the audience. Some of them began to scribble, and he wondered if they were taking it in as they wrote, or whether it was passive listening. Real emotion was usually anchored to listening, and to following through, but genuine emotion wouldn't immediately pick up the pen just in case he said something worthwhile. 'But the time needed to take care of that seed, to water it, to protect it, to nurture it, through all seasons. That takes time, and skill, and patience.'

He waited, letting his voice reverberate around the room. When he had most of the room's attention again, he continued.

'How many of you have the patience to wait it out for as long as it takes? Because it takes time. And no-one knows how long your wait may be. It's personal to you and your journey. How many of you will go away and do the challenges for a few weeks before saying they don't work? How many will drop the whole thing because you don't have the time? How many of you will be here again next year with the same enthusiasm to change because nothing changed last year, and you're not sure why?'

Mac felt sweat trickle down the back of his shirt collar. The lights were at the wrong angle from the back. It seemed one hundred degrees of molten heat was pouring over him.

'I can tell you why,' he said, banging a fist on the podium. 'The seed you planted here, a similar weekend to this one? You didn't nourish it. You didn't take care of it. You let it die. And then you expect to reap the harvest from a dead seed? Not going to happen. If you don't put in the work, if you don't make the decisions, if you don't make that call, if you don't take the necessary ACTION, it will die. There will be no rewards, no harvest. Because you let it die. Life got in the way, excuses got in the way, and you let it die.'

Mac pursed his lips and shook his head, taking a drink of water from the podium stand. The room was silent, and he wondered how many of them it had hit.

'How many of you,' he said, 'have let seed after seed die without deciding to learn the skills to nurture it? The seed is a seed. It's the only one you've got, and you can't change the soil. Is it bad luck that it died? Absolutely not.

Every seed has the same fighting chance. For this seed to grow and flourish, only one thing needs to change. *You*.'

Mac looked at the crowd. No-one was writing now. All eyes were on him.

'So, what is your dream? Are you willing to give your life to nurture it? Because that's what it takes. That's *all* it takes.'

In the boat, Mac sniffed and wiped his eyes.

That's what it takes. Just your life.

God, I was an idiot, Sula, and if half of my audience listens to me, I'm leading them astray. Of course, dreams take time to build. That's a given, and routines are a given, but your whole life? Forever?

At some point there had to be a place to stop, a place to look around and smell the flowers you had grown, and enjoy the fruits of your labour.

Rolo picked his head up from Mac's knee where he had laid it as Mac had cried. He whined and Mac scrubbed his ears, feeling their perfect velvety softness, the small lugs in his fur.

'I gave my life for my dream, Rolo,' he whispered, looking across the lake to the cabin. 'I would have loved to see more places like this, to see the goddamn Eiffel Tower properly, Machu Picchu, Christ the Redeemer, from less than a few miles away. I had it all in my hands, boy. I was there, I was in charge, I agreed the schedule. I wanted to work. I neglected my wife for it. Ridiculous.'

Words from his own mentor flowed into his head. *We have to make mistakes to learn. There is no getting it right without first getting it wrong.*

But what a way to get it wrong. Did it really take this?

Mac shook his head. There wasn't a point in getting worked up again out here in the cold. The sun was dropping, the air was getting chilly, and Mac was already shivering.

Get it together, Mac. Learn and move on. This is done, suck it up.

It still hurt, though. His chest literally ached with the injustice of seeing his mistakes, having them pointed out by a stranger when his wife was dead. It was too late.

Mac located the paddles a few meters to the left. He steered the boat with his hands to reach them, cursing his stupidity for throwing them. Frozen hands were good to no-one. He grabbed the oars, wiped his hands on his jacket, and began to paddle back to the cabin.

'I have been telling people it's never too late. Never. How wrong was I? Of course it gets late. Time is short, Rolo. Very short for Sula. If I'd known what was coming, I would have made more time for her, but that's the lesson here. No-one knows the time left - even their own. My framework had a fatal flaw, huh? There needs to be more balance in the future. I need to make sure I get that over. There's more than one need in everybody's life. We don't need to give our life for one thing, we need to *change* ourselves, nurture what's important first and change the rest.'

Mac had changed gears, thinking fast. This was good stuff. The framework had to shift to be reworked into something better. Sula's life would not be in vain, of that he was certain.

'No way, baby, I get you now. I know, I know, you're rolling your eyes and telling me I'm *sei in ritardo*. Late. If I could take it back, I sincerely would. I just couldn't see it.'

Mac felt another tear fall and caught himself fast.

Get home before you fall apart, Mac.

He stopped paddling and wiped his tears with the sleeve of his coat before they froze to icicles on his face. Rolo shifted his head with a whine.

'I know, I'm sorry, boy, losing my head a bit here. I think I need some dinner. I don't know about you, but I'm starving.'

Rolo picked up his ears at the word dinner and climbed up, front paws on Mac's legs. He wagged his tail furiously, rocking the kayak. Mac pushed the dog off with a laugh. The light was dimming, and they were almost back.

CHAPTER TWENTY-FOUR

THE CABIN WAS FREEZING, and Mac's hands shook as he tried to light the fire. The more he tried to keep the match steady, the more his hand shook the flame out.

Rolo watched from the sofa, his breath clouding before him.

'If I can't get this fire lit, we may as well sleep in the bloody wood store, because it has to be warmer than this outside.'

Rolo grinned, his tongue lolling out, face half hidden by breath.

It had been dark when they had got back, and the night was dropping cold with surprising speed. Rolo had jumped off the kayak to wait as Mac dragged it up onto the shore with shaking limbs and rigid arms.

He hadn't been outside in the dark yet, and this place had to be the stuff of nightmares. The forest was imposing - too close. There were faces in the trees, unknown strangers mocking him from the shadows. He thought about all the films where hordes of unsuspecting and incompetent teens had gone to a cabin in the woods for a break, and ended up as fodder for some psycho slasher guy, hungry for blood. With the boat pulled high, and his heart thudding, he had run to the cabin like his heels were on fire, and locked the door behind Rolo. Not that it blocked the darkness outside when the cabin had so many windows and no curtains.

The fire seized hold and Mac almost sat on top of it, trying to get any amount of warmth into his icy body. He was so utterly cold, he vaguely wondered if he could have hypothermia.

'This needs rectifying,' he said to the dog. 'Curtains. This place need curtains. I'm sure it would keep the warmth in. I'll have to tell Tom. Maybe Meg can make some and send them over.'

Rolo shut his mouth and cocked his head. Like hell she will, he seemed to say, you'll end up making them yourself, Mac.

As the fire soothed his jitters and warmed him, Mac set the small speaker to play some of his old favourites, skipping over 'Highway to Hell', and rose to put the kettle on. Double warmth never hurt anyone.

'Fancy a brew, Rolo? Looks like it's just the two of us again tonight.'

The dog thumped his tail as Mac passed the foot of the stairs... and then he was falling. His legs literally slipping from under him. He went down with a bang and a curse, and places that he didn't know he had hurt falling out of the tree earlier, suddenly flared back to life.

'Shit,' he yelled, 'What in the hell?'

He grabbed the stair rail and pulled himself up, rubbing at his leg as he looked for what had knocked him off his feet.

It sat just past the stairs, small and discreet, but lethal enough. A puddle of water. From this angle, it glistened in the low lamplight. Mac touched his fingers to it.

Wet.

What did you expect?

He sniffed.

Water. Only water.

Rolo whined from the chair, looking decidedly guilty.

'You're clear. It's only water. Guess you were standing here when you came in, huh?'

Rolo stared back at him, his ears flat against his head as he looked up from under his eyebrows. Mac grinned.

'You're not in trouble, don't worry.'

He stepped around the water to get a cloth from the sink, aiming to clean the mess before making his drink. When he turned to clean the puddle, Rolo was sitting by the cabin door facing him, ears down, tail close around his legs. He stared at Mac, a low whine leaving his throat.

'What?' Mac said. 'I'm cleaning your mess, unless you'd like to do it.'

He held the cloth to the dog with a grin, but Rolo only stared and whined back. Mac felt the hair rise at the back of his neck.

'Okay, be weird,' he said, dropping to his knees and clearing up the water. 'There, all done,' he said. 'Wasn't so hard, was it?'

Mac turned to Rolo, who was busy staring past him, back toward the lit kitchen area.

'Oh, come on, this is getting more than a little spooky. Snap out of it will...'

Mac's voice trailed off as he followed the dog's line of sight. From here, he had a perfect view of the under counter fridge. A perfect view of the scramble of magnetic letters on the door. Letters that Mac had placed in the store at the back of the cabin only last night.

But the letters weren't the problem here. If the dog had wanted, he could have reached the bag from the store and brought them back out. With a little luck, he could have placed them back onto the fridge... possibly. What Rolo couldn't possibly have done was rearranged the letters into the perfectly aligned word that was now sitting in the middle of the door.

That would be too much of a coincidence because the word that sat in the middle of the fridge was very personal.

MAC.

CHAPTER TWENTY-FIVE

'Has anyone been down here?'

Tom hesitated, trying to digest the question. Had anyone been to the cabin in the middle of nowhere? The cabin that saw not a single soul from year to year as far as Tom knew, certainly he never saw a soul when he was up there four or five times a year, anyway. He lay back on the sofa, a premier league match on the television in front of him. He didn't support either team, but he liked to watch who was up and coming, anyway.

'Up there, Mac, and no. Not that I'm aware of. Why, what's going on?' he said, using the remote to turn the sound down as the team in red scored the first goal.

'Someone has been here. They know I'm here, Tom. Do you have someone checking up on me?'

Tom's stomach plunged through the floor at the urgency in Mac's voice, the hushed tones, like he was trying to keep quiet. Tom swung to an upright position, feet firmly on the floor, the match forgotten.

'What do you mean someone has been there? No-one has been there, Mac, no one knows the place exists. And I certainly don't have anyone checking up on you, that's for sure.'

'Are you absolutely sure? Because what has happened in this cabin today is freaking me right out.'

Tom felt his heartbeat slow, and he wiped a shaking hand over his brow with mild relief. The nights were drawing in. Up at the cabin it would be cold and dark, and lonely, and that was when Tom knew exactly what kind of games the mind could play when you were alone in a vast wilderness.

'Ah, I thought you were doing too well. It just kicked in late, huh?'

'What the hell are you talking about?' Mac said.

'Mac, calm down. Listen. When you're up there alone and it gets dark early, it can be quite something. I know because I've been there, your mind-'

'For fuck's sake, Tom, would you stop telling me about my goddamn mind? I am absolutely fine up here. I am telling you that someone has been here. Do you know who it is?'

Tom shut his mouth, shocked into silence. Mac was a laid-back character, not prone to raising his voice often, but although they hadn't spoken to each other for a few days now, Mac was almost full on yelling down the phone.'

'Well?' he shouted. 'Who the fuck has been in the cabin, Tom? I'm not into playing fucking games, and if this is the one you had in mind when you sent me up here, it's not funny.'

Tom was now standing, a frown etched into his forehead.

'I'm not playing games, Mac. I promise you. I'm just saying I understand that sometimes you go a little doo-lally up there and start to see ghouls down the corridor.'

'Ghouls?' Mac spat, 'can ghouls spell?'

Tom's frown deepened as Meg appeared in the living room doorway, wiping her hands on the tea towel. It was clear from her own frown that she had heard Tom's side of the conversation from the kitchen, where she had been washing the pots from dinner.

'What's wrong?' she mouthed.

Tom shrugged his shoulders at her.

'Mac, you're losing me. What has spelling got to do with someone being in the cabin?'

Meg finished wiping her hands, flung the tea towel over her shoulder and crossed her arms, watching him.

'Someone has rearranged the magnets on the fridge, Tom, someone has been in here and spelled something on the fucking fridge while I was out!'

Tom opened his mouth, and for one horrifying moment thought laughter may come spilling out. He shut it and swallowed quickly. Meg held her arms out wide now, her meaning clear - what is it?

Tom moved the phone away from his face, covering the microphone with his finger.

'Mac thinks someone has been in the cabin while he was out.'

Meg's mouth dropped open in surprise.

'Did he lock it? How would they get in? Did they take anything?' she whispered.

Tom's mouth twitched, and tears began to form in his eyes.

'Tom? Are you listening?' Mac said.

'Well?' Meg said at the same time from the doorway.

'Yes, Mac. I'm listening,' he said. 'I understand you're upset, but why in the hell would someone break into the cabin to play with the fridge magnets?'

Tom tried to conceal his mirth, but Mac detected it in his voice anyway, and Meg now had a hand comically over her mouth, making his bout of laughter ever more certain. His shoulders shook, and tears slid down his face as he tried to think of anything not funny - anything at all. The recent bomb in Beirut, the lost company earnings over the last six months, Auntie Maud dying just last month.

'I'm glad this amuses you, Tom, because it scares the fucking hell out of me! Who is dicking around outside this cabin when I'm out here alone? If you know, then spill, because it's not funny.'

Tom spluttered, a rasping sound emerging from his lips. Meg turned away, shoulders shaking silently. Tom wished she would go. The sight of her was making things worse.

'Mac, Mac, buddy, I'm sorry. I'm sorry. It's just... you have to see how ludicrous it sounds when you say it out loud?' some of the laughter escaped him fully now and he heard Mac huff on the other end of the line.

Get it together Tom, you moron.

'Mac? You know you're saying someone broke in to write a word on the fridge? There was nothing else taken or moved?' Giggles escaped Tom again and he wiped at his eyes. Meg let out a small howl in the doorway and disappeared back to the kitchen. Tom heard her laughing in Mac's silence.

'Mac?' he said. 'You still there?'

'I am.'

Tom felt the laughter dying down and took a breath, getting himself together.

'Okay, Mac. I'm sorry, bud. I just lost it, it sounded so funny-'

'I guess you had to be here.' Mac said, no trace of laughter in his voice.

Tom licked his lips.

'What happened, Mac? Maybe you'd better start from the beginning. It came across funny the way you said it, that's all. I'm not laughing at you.'

'I went out for around four hours, took a trip up the loch, arrived back just after 3.30pm. When I got in, I slipped on some water and saw the writing on the fridge. And yes, Tom I'd be inclined to agree with you that it's funny if - one, there had been someone else here. Two, I thought Rolo may have accidentally messed with them and inadvertently made a word. And three, if I hadn't bagged them up and put them into the storeroom this morning, because Rolo kept knocking them off.'

'Right,' Tom said

'And if I thought for one minute that Rolo was clever enough to get into the store, take the letters out of the bag, and rearrange them into a word on the fridge, then I would stupidly be in the wrong business, and I should get Rolo into the bloody circus.'

'Okay, Mac. Okay. I get you. I just want you to give this a serious think, because there is no one out there, Mac. I never see a soul, ever. The cabin has never been messed with when I get there. To me, it just sounds odd.'

'Odd?' Mac exploded, 'Odd? You're fucking right, it's odd. What would you like me to 'seriously think' about? Someone came into the cabin and wrote my name on the goddamn fridge. There's no other way to look at it, is there?'

Tom tried to shush Mac, to calm him, but the giggles were back.

'Okay,' Tom tried and more laughter escaped him.

'Okay.' Mac repeated. 'Thanks Tom. Good to know you have my back.'

Tom heard the connection cut off.

'No, Mac! Mac?'

He pressed redial and got the answerphone.

Shit.

Dropping back into the sofa behind him, he stared at the phone.

'What was it?' Meg said, appearing from the kitchen and sitting down beside him.

'I have no idea.' Tom said, 'he said someone was at the cabin when he was out. Nothing was taken, nothing moved. They just wrote his name on the fridge.'

Tom's voice ascended into a full-on squeak as he began to laugh again.

Meg tried to keep from grinning. Her mouth twitched as she spoke. 'Tom, you're so bad. I could hear Mac shouting from the doorway. He's having a hard time.'

Tom shut his mouth, opened it to speak, and shut it with a moan. Meg laughed at his face, and then they were laughing together.

'I mean,' Tom said, gasping for breath, 'who would take the trouble to break in just to write his name?'

'Someone who wants to give him a fright?' Meg said, wiping her own tears.

'There's no-one out there, Meg. Ever.'

'There must be. It can't be the dog now, can it? Are you sure you haven't let slip to one of the boys where he is?'

'No. No-one knows, I'm sure of it. It's probably just a coincidence. Mac really is losing his mind. It happens out there; he'll get through it. I'll give him a call tomorrow when he's calmer.'

'Hmm.' Meg said, her face suddenly furrowed.

'What are you thinking?'

'I'm wondering if you called that number back, or spoke to the guys who are 'after you'?'

'No. I have had no calls in the last couple of days. When they give me another silent one, I'll speak, like you said. Curry's rang me this morning, by the way.'

He grinned at Meg and elbowed her lightly in the ribs. She didn't smile.

'Meg?'

'I'm just wondering,' she said. 'These guys wouldn't have any beef with Mac, would they?'

'Mac? Why would they want Mac?'

'Just a thought. You've heard nothing, Mac's heard something.'

'They knew nothing about Mac. He wasn't mentioned.'

'Are you absolutely sure?'

'Positive, Sula was extra cautious.'

'You're sure? because maybe they can get back at you with more effect by hurting Mac first?'

'No,' Tom said, shaking his head, 'no...'

They didn't know. Couldn't know. He and Sula had checked in under a completely different name. How would they find out? And yet, Mac was a well-known figure. Google him and his life story practically spilled from the page... along with his wife. How hard would it be to find out, really?

Tom pressed a hand to his forehead. Suddenly, it didn't seem so funny anymore.

'Shit.'

'Likewise.' Meg replied. 'Sort it out, Tom, because Mac has been through enough.'

CHAPTER TWENTY-SIX

M AC STARED AT THE wood crackling in the log burner while snacking on a tub of Twiglets he had found in the storeroom that were just in date. The phone call had been a blessing in its way. Tom was an arsehole, but if anyone wanted to walk into the cabin and fuck around with the magnets now, Mac was so angry he thought he would be able to single-handedly rip their head off. He couldn't remember the last time he had been so furious. It was all good and well for Tom, in cosy suburbia, to tell him that no-one was around, but how could he be sure?

Mac mashed a Twiglet between his teeth, far too hard for the small crispy puff to withstand. His teeth crashed together with a satisfying click.

He had removed the magnets again, double bagged and top-shelved them in the storeroom. If it happened again, he would put them in the shed outside and leave. If there was anyone watching outside, then he wasn't about to play sitting duck. At worst, he could be murdered, and out here, no one would hear him scream. At best, pictures of him looking rough in this secluded location would hit the papers and the mob would turn up. He wouldn't play. Nope. In fact, he should just leave tomorrow.

He crunched another Twiglet, threw one to Rolo, and stared at the flames of the fire. He felt the anger subside, along with his resolve.

He didn't want to leave.

He couldn't say he had enjoyed all of his time here, but he had found the peace, and time to chill and explore exhilarating. The time just to be, to do as he pleased, dress as he pleased, cry as he pleased, to be as he pleased. With no expectations, and no repercussions.

I feel like I'm just finding myself again, after too long. I'm finding Mac, peeling back the mind guy to expose the man beneath. I'm not done here yet.

Another three Twiglets bit the dust, and he lay his head back against the top of the settee, closing his eyes.

Hands massaged through his hair. Small hands with a firm but tender touch, rubbing away all the tension, all the anger. He moaned.

'Keep going, baby,' he murmured.

'Just there?' she asked, rubbing her thumbs over his hairline and just down onto his forehead.

'All over. It's so good.'

Her soft laughter came from behind him, a smell of musky perfume. Firm delicate hands.

'You need to calm down, tato, everything is okay. It will all be okay, I promise.'

'I hope so, baby,' Mac opened his eyes to the cabin, the roof light shining stars across a dark sky above him.

Hands pressed and teased, a small moan left his mouth and his eyes half closed again in pleasure. It was so perfect here.

He flinched and his eyes flew open. Twiglets flew across the floor as he swung upright, spinning round to look at the back of the chair. He brought a hand to his head as he registered the piano and the empty space before it. Just enough to pull the stool out and play. His scalp tingled with massage after-glow, and he thought a trace of musk hung in the air. He swallowed.

'Sula?' he whispered. More goosebumps littered his body at the sound of his own voice in the quiet cabin, than at the thought of his dead wife massaging his head.

The cabin was still and dark, the effect of the massage wearing off, and Mac wondered if he had briefly fallen asleep.

'And felt her hands as you watched the cabin roof?'

Is that better or worse than your wife giving you a massage a year after she died?

He wasn't sure. Being alone here was liberating, but to have Sula here, in spirit or otherwise, would be better. There was just one problem... Mac didn't believe in ghosts.

'Shame,' he muttered with a small chuckle.

He lay his head back again, testing his reaction but no hands massaged now. The effect was over. Mac found himself vaguely disappointed.

Oh well, at least I have Twiglets to keep me company.

He grinned until he saw the empty box on the floor, Rolo licking his lips next to it.

'Are you kidding?' he said, his smile slipping.

Rolo had the decency to look guilty as Mac picked up the box and gave it a shake. Empty.

He spied a lone stick on the floor by the fire. Rolo also spied it, snapped it up, and crunched it while looking straight at into Mac's eyes. Mac felt his lip curl in disgust.

'Some friend you are. Dogs are loyal, are they? What happened to mine?'

Rolo cleaned his mouth and walked to Mac, lifting himself to put his front paws on his knee. Mac pushed them off, and the dog dropped back to the floor.

'I don't think so, buddy. First the apple, then the girl, now the Twiglets? Not only are you cramping my style and stealing my new friends, but you'd happily let me starve too?'

Rolo barked and jumped up to lick at his face. For the second time that day, the smell of something he had wanted to eat wafted from his dog's mouth.

'Good job I love you, animal. Your loyalty is wholly questionable.'

CHAPTER TWENTY-SEVEN

Daylight woke Mac the next morning, not only daylight but the sound of scratching. Mac lay listening to the intermittent noise, trying to figure out what creature it could be.

Scratch-scratch-scratch-scratch. Pause. Scratch-scratch-scratch-scratch. Pause.

A *mouse?*

He listened again.

Too big, possibly a rat. A pheasant? Maybe even a wildcat. A deer would make more of a thud, I suppose, and there are no bears in the UK.

There was a longer pause when Mac almost forgot about it entirely, lulled by the sunshine outside and the warmth of the bed. Then a new sound joined the noise.

Scratch-scratch-scratch-scratch. Pause. Whine.

Mac knew that whine, and it wasn't quite as exotic as a wild animal from the woods. He propped himself onto his elbows and checked the end of the bed. Rolo was gone.

Which means I have to get up.

With a sigh, he pushed back the covers and swung his legs out of bed with a stretch.

'I'm coming, hold your bladder,' he called to the dog as he stood, stuffing his feet into socks, and pulling a jumper over his t-shirt and jogging bottoms. He usually slept naked. Out here naked had found him shivering in a ball of ice more than once, and although it was sometimes more than warm when the fire was on, he didn't like to tempt fate by leaving it lit during the night.

He descended the stairs with a yawn and found Rolo sniffing at the piano under the stairs. Much closer to the corridor than he had ever been. Mac raised his eyebrows, one hand on the rail at the bottom of the stairs.

'Finally getting brave?'

Rolo quit his investigation and jogged to Mac before using him as a stretching post, paws almost at his shoulders. Mac hugged his arms around his dog and Rolo tried to pull away, licking at Mac's ear.

'Come on then, you got me up, out you go.'

He pushed the dog down and opened the cabin door where he waited, enjoying the sunshine, even as the cold made him shiver. The ground was wet and earthy, the air pine-forest fresh, something you certainly didn't get in London.

'Beautiful day.'

Rolo finished his business and ran around to the side of the cabin, toward the loch, out of sight.

'Rolo?'

The dog didn't reappear, so Mac shrugged, shut the door, and went to make a hot drink and some breakfast. He wouldn't go far.

After a breakfast of toast and jam, Mac decided to get the cabin in order. It was dropping colder, and he wanted to have things in check before the weather had a chance to trip him up. He spent the morning chopping more of the logs behind the wood store, filling both the store and the small storage area inside by the hearth. Then he checked the shed outside (mostly tools for the veg area) and watched the generator for a few minutes - which was as much as he ever wanted to do with it. Genny's were notoriously similar to a boiler - if they were needed in the cold, that was the time they would be most likely to pack up working. Today it seemed to be running fine, levels were still high, and there was spare fuel in the small shed should he need it, as Tom had said, along with five propane gas bottles.

Back inside, he found a cloth and set to work wiping down the surfaces, tidying what he had out, cleaning the kitchen sides and making his bed upstairs. Downstairs he checked the storeroom, checking the freezer and the food he had left on the shelves - plenty, and a good stash of beer that he hadn't seen when he arrived too. He grabbed four cans to stash in the fridge.

The only thing he couldn't do much about were the water pipes. If they were going to freeze, they would. Then he would use the sterilizing tablets for drinking water. If the power went out, the candles were at the front of the storeroom, just inside the door, along with the small camping stove and gas cannister.

And that's about it, all you can do. Here at the cabin, the living is easy!

With a chuckle to himself, he shut the door to the storeroom, and thought he may catch a beer and a smoke on the pier. He hadn't smoked in days, and maybe that's why he had been so eaten up and on edge. Maybe that's why he'd been hallucinating Sula's amazing head massage.

The shine of the water on the wooden floor caught his attention, the fall of light reflecting on its surface. Mac stood with his hand on the storeroom door handle, four bottles of beer nestled in the other hand. He paused.

More water? The roof must have a leak.

He walked to the small pool, which sat right in the middle of the corridor, just behind the stairs, and stooped beside it. Small, wet, definitely water. He glanced up at the ceiling, but of course, the mezzanine floor was above him.

Shit, if the roof is leaking the bed may be wet too.

He put the beer in the fridge before aiming for the stairs and finding the second pool where it had been the other day, just in front of the stairs. Where he thought Rolo had stood wet, but Rolo hadn't been standing here wet now.

With a sigh, he took the stairs two at a time and checked the bedroom area. Up here, all was dry, including the floor.

Strange.

'Oh well, at least the bed isn't wet.'

He went back down the stairs, and cleaned the puddles with a cloth, before taking a camp chair out onto the wooden pier. Back inside, he put a frozen pasty in the oven and grabbed his coat. It was cold outside now, probably even hat weather, but he would suck it up today. Pulling the coat around him, he grabbed a beer and went outside.

It was peaceful watching the loch, the shimmer of golden glow that fell across it as the sun dipped below the trees behind him, small ripples on the surface in the afternoon's calmness. He had dodged time like this at home, time to do nothing, to sit with his own thoughts, to listen to his own head. Out here there had been plenty of time to sit with himself, and plenty of tears to go with it, but today was different. There was an air of calm around him, peace, even a little joy at witnessing the wildlife that came and went as he drank. A deer on the mountain, the sheep, the birds.

He pulled the collar of his coat up around his neck and thought about how this perfect this place would be, shared with someone else. His thoughts drifted to Tom and why he never shared this place with Meg. It was a perfect little romantic getaway, and yet he always came up here alone, or with Josh.

Rolo padded round from the front of the cabin and put a paw up onto Mac's knee.

'Coming up?' he said, patting his legs. A little warmth shared would be pleasant right now, and Rolo had a lovely thick warm coat to dig his hands into. The dog jumped up onto his lap and curled himself across Mac's knees. The warmth was instant.

'You're like a hot water bottle,' he said, scrubbing the dogs' head, and noting the dirt on his ears. 'You been digging again?'

Rolo rolled an eye to look at Mac, thumped his tail, and then closed his eyes as Mac's hand massaged.

Feeling content, Mac's thoughts returned to his brother. A success in his own right. A little intense and driven. Too driven in Mac's opinion. Mac was the one who was a little more chilled, liked to take things a little easier, and yet, he thought, he had been the one rushing through life with no time for himself.

Tom was the one who wanted to achieve, wanted to win, wanted to grab whatever he could. Mac had his dream of teaching what he had learned to people who needed it. He wanted to help. That was it. He wasn't bothered about scaling Everest, about sailing the world, or about trekking the Antarctic. In fact, if he thought about it, it was Sula who had pushed the business. He had simply read, listened, learned, and spoken. She had booked, written, created, and pushed. For his own good, she said.

'If you go any slower, tato, you'll stop, and end life one millimetre from where you stand.'

Mac took a swig of beer and frowned.

And yet, when he had taken the bull by the horns, strived to reach more people, to make his work more streamlined, got involved, organised some events, took the pressure off her a little, she had moaned that he was working too hard. And he was, he knew that now. Maybe she had been disconcerted that all the striving hadn't been like him?

It wasn't, he thought. It's not.

I was on a rollercoaster. I couldn't stop until this put the brakes on for me. I was caught up in the fever of the shows, the adrenaline rush. I needed the high...didn't I?

And yet, sat on this chair in the middle of nowhere, freezing cold, with a filthy dog in his lap, he thought he would rather be here than anywhere else. It had been going wrong, he realised; his life and his marriage. It wasn't the same, and hadn't been the same for a few years. He had denied it to himself, and to Sula.

He was just busy.

We loved each other, we just lost each other a little, didn't we?

Looking back, there were a few trivial things that she had begun to do without him that she had never been interested in before. Such as, going away with her own friends, friends he didn't know, and wasn't even aware of. At the time he had been relieved that she was occupied, so that he could concentrate fully on his work, but sat here now he wondered who those friends were, and why they hadn't been at her funeral.

An uncomfortable feeling sat on his chest. Something about their last few years together didn't add up at all.

Quit Mac, or you'll talk yourself into things that can't be defended. She loved you, as much as you loved her.

Mac finished the last of the beer and pushed Rolo off to check the pasty.

In the kitchen, he stared at the oven. Cold and dark.

'What... I switched it on, didn't I?' he frowned at the appliance which sat unaffected by his stare. He turned the button, and the light glowed. The oven sprang to life.

'Fuck. You idiot.'

His stomach growled, adding insult to injury, and Mac pulled the bag of apples he had placed on the kitchen side toward him. He put in his hand and pulled one out, bringing it straight toward his mouth. He noticed the flash of white just before he took and bite and lowered the apple back down.

Paper.

He took a bite of the apple and unfolded the paper, flattening it on the countertop. At the top, Maddie had written her name and a telephone number. Underneath, she had written a small note.

Call if you need any more apples, or if you just fancy a chat!

Mac smiled, remembering the girl he had almost forgotten in the events of the last few days. She had promised to swap information of places around the world to see, hadn't she? Mac decided that he would make a list and when he was out of this cabin next year, he would travel... properly this time, in sections of downtime that people called *a holiday*. Something he'd never done. Maddie had called it a waste. He didn't intend to waste any more time.

CHAPTER TWENTY-EIGHT

DECEMBER

THREE WEEKS LATER THE rain had settled in, and the forest floor was awash with mud and pine needles. The trees were a sheet of darkness all day long, and the tops of the mountains disappeared in perpetual mist and cloud. A small river ran past the front door of the cabin and down to the loch. If it rained much more, Mac thought, it may rain in.

His anger with Tom was subsiding now that all had been quiet in the cabin - aside from Rolo's interest in the piano, and the puddles that appeared periodically in the corridor - but the fridge magnets were behaving, staying on their shelf in the storeroom, and Mac forgot the frenzied attack of nerves he had felt at seeing his name up on the fridge. He decided to ring his brother and ask if he should dig a trench further out to drain the rainwater away, or whether this was the norm, and it would continue to pass the cabin by.

He pulled out his phone to make the call and the slip of white paper came with it. Now more crinkled than it had originally been. He looked at the neat writing. Maddie.

The apples were gone, and even with the premise of more apples and chatting about travel, he hadn't gathered the courage to call. In his old life, he had spoken to people most of the day on the phone, but now he couldn't call one woman? This year was doing him in.

He knew what it was. Guilt. She had been an attractive girl; he had felt drawn to her, and that made him feel like he was tainting Sula's name and memory. He didn't need to chat with a woman, even if it was just a chat. He had his wife.

'But you don't, Mac,' he said aloud, slapping the paper onto the side, 'and apples and a chat would be good. Seeing another damn person would be good. You used to chat to hundreds of attractive women a week, and it never bothered you.'

The piano thrummed under the keyboard cover, a low note, just once. Its tone lingered and stretched in the silence of the cabin. Mac turned to stare at the instrument, dusty and untouched in the corner.

He waited for the note to die away, and stupidly, for another to play, but the cabin remained thankfully quiet.

Must be struggling in the extremes of the damp cold and the log burner heat, he thought, neither of which were good for it. At least it wasn't Sula's ghost!

With a mirthless huff that was half relief, he walked to the piano, and paused. His heart thumped as he reached down and lifted the cover from the keys. He stared, assessing the ivory pegs that had helped him out of his last hole. The first thing that had made him feel anything as he came back to life after a dark depression. The second thing to make him feel was the piano teacher. Sula. He had been feeling everything through the both of them ever since. Until the last year anyway. Then he had felt nothing again. Not as dark as last time, not as far down, he knew more now about the mind, about the way to keep buoyant. To keep the things that happened as circumstances and opportunities, not things that ruled his life and took everything from him.

And yet, here he was, in a cabin in the middle of nowhere, with nothing, like everything had been taken after all.

Not everything, he thought, looking at the piano.

He hesitated, and then ran his fingers over the keys. He pressed a few before he had time to think, and felt the hair raise at the back of his neck at the tone. He felt transported, like Sula would flounce in and tell him to sit. Today they would play Chopin, and you will feel, Mac. Feel the rhythm, feel the music, let it flow through you.

He tried a trill with his right hand, just six notes, ending with a dull thud on the D one octave above middle C.

Mac frowned and pressed the D again. No tone, just a thud.

Thud. Thud. Thud.

No Chopin for you for a while, Mac.

There was a knock at the cabin door.

Mac blinked, and Rolo stared, then they looked at each other, the question in their eyes the same. Did someone just knock on the door? Out here where no-one came?

The knocks came again, hard and fast, and Rolo finally sprang into action, barking at the door as Mac moved to open it.

On the step, or in the river, whichever way you wanted to look at it, was a very wet man, his feet getting wetter as he stood. Taller than Mac, lean and fit under thick waterproofs, and complete with backpack and walking pole.

'All right?' The man said, his Scottish accent thick, 'sorry to bother you. I was out walking and-'

The man was eclipsed by a torrent of rain so hard that Mac couldn't hear himself think, never mind the man talk. Besides, it was cold.

'Come in,' Mac shouted. 'Don't stand out in the rain.'

The man stepped inside, and Mac shut the door. The sound of the downpour wasn't much quieter inside, but at least it was warmer.

'Thank you.' The man shouted with a laugh. 'Missed a good drowning there alright. It was some fortune seeing the cabin!'

Mac grinned. Now that there was another person in his midst, he realised how much he had missed people in general, and hey, at least this one was male. Sula's memory was safe for now.

'Take your coat off. You can't go anywhere in this. Do you want a hot drink while you wait?'

'Aye, that would be great.' The man took off his backpack and coat and scanned his eyes around the small space. 'Nice place you've got here.'

He hung his coat over the stair rail where it dripped onto the floor to make another puddle that Mac would have to clean later.

What's one more to join the rest?

He placed some kitchen tissue underneath, and the man took a handful to wipe the coat and bag down and quell the drips. When they had finished, the man handed the kitchen roll to Mac and then offered his hand.

'Saul,' the man said with a grin. White teeth and tan under his sandy head of wavy hair suggested this was a well-travelled man, or one that tanned easily.

Maybe he can teach me places to go, and I won't have to call Maddie.

You'd still like the apples.

Mac's Stomach twisted at the thought of her. He would like to speak to her again, either way. That much he knew.

'Mac,' he said with a firm shake of his hand.

'Thanks for this. The weather caught me out. I'm usually a good judge, but this wasn't even on my radar.'

'How far have you come?' Mac said as he held up the coffee jar to him.

'Brilliant! White, one sugar,' Saul replied, bending to his backpack, 'about six miles north. Over the hill there. I hike a lot, but usually the weather isn't so hard on me. I ran out of water, that's why I knocked.'

'Ah, let me fill your bottle,' Mac said, taking it from Saul and filling it from the tap.

The man turned to put it into his bag as the kettle boiled and Mac poured water into the cups, giving them both a good stir. Rolo sniffed at Saul, checking him out as dogs do. He seemed happy enough with the company, and if Rolo was happy, then Mac would take it too.

'You're after my dogs, right?' Saul said with a laugh as he fussed Rolo's head. The dog's tail beat a tune against the stair rail.

'Here you go.' Mac said. 'Rolo, off.'

'You're a star.' Saul replied, pulling out one of the small plastic dining chairs. Mac shook his head and motioned over to the settees.

'Over there is warmer and a whole lot more comfortable. The cold comes in through the windows and you're already wet.'

'Well.' Saul said with an easy laugh. 'Not only did I find a convenient cabin, but also a chap with a conscience, too. Next you'll be offering me a beer on the side of the loch.'

Mac couldn't help but laugh. 'Not in this weather, although it's been so long since I had company right now, I don't think I'd turn it down if that's where you said you wanted to sit!'

'Really?' The man said, folding himself into the chair as Mac took the sofa, Rolo jumping up beside him. 'How long have you been out here? Is it your cabin?'

'No, it's not mine, it's my brother's. I've been here since August. Four exceptionally long, and yet very short, months.'

'Alone?' the man raised his eyebrows.

Mac nodded his head and took a slug of coffee that burned as it went down.

'When do you leave?'

'Next August-ish.'

Saul nearly spat his coffee onto the seat. 'August?!'

Mac nodded with a grin.

'I know. A long time, right. I'm going for doing the year. My brother thinks I'll be home before the snow, but I quite like the peace.'

Saul looked bemused.

'You going for a total loony-bin mind-fuck or what? There's nothing out here. No-one. Peace? This is more than peace. Peace is getting the bairns to bed at eight and watching whatever the hell you want on tv. This isn't peace, Mac, this is death.'

Mac nodded in agreement.

'It was, at first. You'd be amazed at what you can get used to. You can adapt to any situation with the right mindset. That's where my brother thinks I'll fall down, see?'

Saul leaned forward, elbows on his already dry waterproof trousers.

'Ah, I get you. This is a dare, right?' he sat back with a laugh. 'Let me guess. So, your brother is the all commando, superhero, sustainable living type, right?

He's into the outdoors. The hunting, the hiking, the fishing, the growing veg.' he gestured at the window by the side of Mac, where the pitiful-looking vegetables were now drowning. 'Does he have chicken's too?'

Mac shook his head, letting Saul carry on with his analysis.

'Not quite whole hog then, eh?' he grinned, showing his brilliant white teeth. 'So, you're the... what? City slicker he thinks has no skills and no willpower?'

Mac chuckled.

'You're actually not far off the mark. It's not the reason, but definitely the thinking. I do normally live in London, as does he. But Tom is up here four or five times a year for at least a couple of weeks to a month each time. Sometimes alone, sometimes with his son. He says it's his salvation. I don't really have time for this kind of thing. I'd love to do it, but I travel a lot for work. I think that's why he gets the impression I'll leave. He thinks I can't sit still.'

Saul shook the water that dripped from his shaggy blonde curls and took a sip of coffee.

'So, what are the stakes?'

'Huh?'

'What's he giving you if you stay?'

Mac huffed. 'A million, apparently. I doubt I'll ever see it even if I do last the year.'

Saul gave a low whistle.

'Well, that's reason enough, but perhaps a little far fetched. Does he not have it?'

'Ah, he has it all right, but it'll probably have been forgotten already.'

'I'd remind him if I were you, mate. Always hold a man to his word.' Saul chuckled, 'So if it's not a dare, but there's money involved, what's the deal?'

'My wife died.' Mac said. He looked down into his cup. He never knew which way the words would take him. Bawling into his cup may not be out of the question.

Saul sat back and scrunched his face into a grimace. He ran his free hand through his hair.

'Ah, man. I'm sorry. And here's me making a joke,' he shook his head.

'No, it's fine,' Mac said with a smile. 'It was actually just over a year ago now. I just wasn't coping so well with it at home. You know, work and stuff, so Tom suggested I just shut myself off out here for a bit. He didn't actually specify a year in concrete. As I said, he thinks I'll be home soon. Probably thought I already would have been by now.'

'So, if it's no biggie, then why are you still here? It gets rough out here in winter, you'll be properly cut off. I'd guess that you may not even make it back up the track in the truck even now with all the water.'

Mac let the thought settle, toyed with it a little to see if he felt unnerved by that thought. When nothing arose, he simply shrugged.

'I'm not intending to leave. Being here has helped me to sort through a lot of emotions already. I feel almost a hundred times better now than I did back in August. I want to see if I can fully deal with it before I go, so that I can start afresh at home in whatever way that may be, because she's not coming home. I wish she was, but she's not.'

He swallowed hard. Talking about Sula was another world to just thinking about her and crying alone.

Saul didn't flinch, and didn't gloss over it as men usually did in Mac's experience. There was no 'well, she's gone, man up buddy', or a slap on the shoulder and an 'I've got to go now'. He simply sat and rubbed a hand over his mouth in the silence that followed.

'That's tough, Mac. Real tough. She was a good one, eh?' he finally said. There was no sympathy on his face, no pity, just empathy. It gave Mac some courage to talk. If he cried, so be it. He didn't know this man, although he did like him, and he would like to share a beer beside the loch one day.

He gave a nod and pursed his lips.

'One of the best. I don't think there's another like her.'

'Aye, there is. Just don't rest until you find her. My ma had a saying,' Saul cleared his throat and made his voice an octave higher. 'Keep your standards high, and your troosers up. The girl of your dreams won't be found with her knickers aroond her ankles, and likewise she won't want to find you that way either.'

Mac looked at Saul and opened his mouth, then he thought better of it and shut it again. A grin played around Saul's mouth.

'You're having me on,' Mac said.

'No, true fact. I had that thrown at me from around eight years old, back when I didn't know what the hell I'd want to drop my trousers for. No girl would be seeing my wee winkie, and I certainly had no interest in what she had in her knickers.'

Mac laughed hard. He couldn't help it, and when Saul joined him, he laughed harder.

'That changed over the years,' Mac gasped.

'Oh, aye. From about fourteen, I had trouble keeping my trousers on, let alone up.'

They laughed again. Mac's jaw beginning to ache.

'I loved when girls had their knickers down, too. I had no idea what the hell ma was talking about. She was keeping me from gold, man. Pure gold. Why the hell would she do that? I just didn't get it.'

Mac clutched at his stomach where the muscles ached from the vigorous workout. He shifted on the settee, grabbing his side where a stitch had set in.

'Stop, please,' he said. 'I'll bust a gut at this rate.'

When their laughter had died down, Saul drank the last of his coffee.

'So, the moral of the story is. There's another Mac, there is, but she won't have her knickers down if you keep your trousers up.'

'I'm not sure I like it that way round?'

'That's what I said to ma.'

Mac spluttered another laugh.

'You didn't.'

'I did. Got whipped with the dishcloth and chased out of the kitchen. She told me to keep my filth to myself. I was thirty at the time.'

The laughter flowed again, until tears flowed from Mac's eyes, and he suddenly found himself sobbing. If Saul had asked, he wouldn't have known what to say he was crying about.

'I'm sorry,' he gulped, rubbing at his eyes, but the more he rubbed, the more the tears came.

Fortunately, Saul seemed to know already.

'Aw Mac, let it out you numpty. You have been holding back, haven't you? If you can't laugh without crying, you're not healed yet. I've seen this a lot in my practice.'

Mac nodded as the tears finally slowed and he looked up at Saul.

'I'm sorry all the same. I'll get myself together.'

'And while you do that, I'll make another drink, shall I?'

'That would be good.'

Mac gathered himself as he took on what Saul had said.

Practice?

'What do you do, Saul?' he said. 'You mentioned a practice?'

'Doctor. I studied psychology, became a psychologist initially, and practiced as a psychiatrist for eight years. Then I opened my own practice. I worked with a partner until a couple of years ago when his dodgy dealings got us shut down.'

Saul looked away and Mac saw the tension in his shoulders.

'What happened?'

Saul brought the cups over, handing one to Mac before sitting back down.

'Illegal substances. Let's leave it there. It saw us both in jail, myself for six months, my partner for two years. The practice was closed down and I doubt I'll be able to work in that field again now. At least not practicing alone.'

The weight of the frustration and anger poured from him as he clenched his jaw.

'I'm sorry about that,' Mac said.

'Me too,' Saul said, mustering a smile that didn't reach his eyes. 'These things happen for a reason, I suppose. I'm just blowed if I know what the hell that reason is right now.'

'How long have you been out?'

'A year last September. And whatever I do, I'll make sure I never go back there. It wasn't nice, and the way ma looks at me sometimes now... it doesn't sit well, you know?'

Mac nodded.

'It'll work out.'

'Aye. And for you too. It'll get better for both of us, just got to keep going forward and keep our minds out of the past.'

'Couldn't have put it better myself.'

They finished their coffee, chatting easily as the rain finally stopped and the sun showed its face just over the mountain behind.

'I'll be away then, 'Saul said. 'Hopefully, I'll get a good way before another drenching. Thank you, Mac, it's been nice to have a good old man-to-man chat with someone other than my da.'

Mac grinned.

'It has, and if you're not too far and you fancy that beer by the loch, don't hesitate. I'm always free up here. There's time to watch your own nails grow.'

Saul frowned as he pulled on his backpack.

'Funny saying. I've heard that somewhere...' He trailed off as Mac waited, and then he looked at Mac with surprise. 'Here. I heard that here before. There was a woman here. I had to bring her medication. Got to be two years ago now. She said the same thing.'

Mac frowned back at Saul.

'There are never any women up here. Tom keeps the place exclusively to himself, and his son, of course.'

'Definitely a woman, or an incredibly good looking, very busty man, anyway.'

'Must have been his wife then, I suppose.'

'Must have.' Saul said, heaving his backpack further up on his shoulders. 'Well good to meet you, Mac, maybe I'll see you around if I'm hiking sometime.'

He held out a hand and Mac grabbed it and gave it a squeeze before letting go.

'Please do. I've enjoyed the last hour, thank you.'

Saul stuck up his thumb and turned to hike off to the trees. Mac held up a hand in return as he watched the man squelch over the mud and disappear into the tree canopy. He smiled, feeling a little loneliness hit after the laughter of the last hour.

He turned to go back inside, and a thought hit him.

Saul said he'd heard the saying before... from a woman. Did Meg even know that saying?

He frowned and blinked.

She must have, because the only other woman who said it was Sula. And there was no way that she had been up here.

No way.

That was absurd because Sula had no knowledge of this cabin. Never had.

CHAPTER TWENTY-NINE

S ULA CLICKED HER FINGER along with the fast tempo of the metronome, tapping the beat at the side of his head. He didn't dare look at her. The piece was too fast; the finger work of both hands complex and far-reaching as it spanned the keyboard.

Mac felt his shoulders tense and a small irritating pain gather in the muscles between his shoulder blades. He began to sweat.

Bad news. You can't do it.

'Goood,' Sula drawled beside him, 'feel the music, feel the rhythm, *sentire*, Mac, that's it!'

His fingers obeyed, but his arms stiffened. He closed his eyes for just a fraction of a second, trying to feel, to relax himself... and lost his place in the music.

His fingers continued momentarily, automatically knowing the song he had played over and over, and then he froze. His mind went blank. His fingers stiffened and hovered over the keyboard as the tempo raged on.

For one horrid moment, Mac blinked at the alien instrument before him, knowing that he should know what it was, and what to do, but equally puzzled that his fingers had played the tune just a few seconds earlier. His mind went into a tailspin. Why was he sitting here at all? What was he doing? And then Sula laughed and placed a hand on his back.

'Well done, Mac, that was *bellisimo*. Wonderful!' She pressed a forefinger and thumb together into an O and pressed it to her lips.

Mac felt a trickle of sweat roll down his cheek.

'I didn't finish it,' he said, half annoyed with himself.

'There is no finish. This is no race. Music is not about the finish. It is a process. You played very well. Take a breath, take a pause, try again.'

Mac nodded, wiped sweat from his forehead and turned the music back to the beginning.

'Good, now we go again.'

Sula clicked the tempo and Mac began to count the beats, to find the rhythm in his head. He looked at the music and discovered he couldn't read a note. He didn't know what the symbols represented or how they related to the keys in front of him. He gaped as Sula clicked beside him.

'Take your time, come in when you're ready, 1-2-3, 1-2-3, 1-2-3...'

The clicks beside him got louder, faster. The notes swirled and merged into a mass of unknown language before him, and he began to panic. His shoulders tensed, and his mind felt wild. What was he doing here?

He shoved the stool back and stared at the piano, panting hard.

Sula stopped clicking and turned to look up at him, deep brown eyes pools of warmth and empathy.

'Okay. Is okay, Mac,' she said, holding her hands out to him.

'It's not. I don't know this. I can't... I can't read it. I don't know how to read it!'

He stumbled back away from the piano as though it had a disease that would eat more than his mind if he got too close. Sula walked after him, calm, smiling, and placed a hand on his wrist. Warm, soft, grounding.

'Come,' she said, leading him into an adjoining room of her small home. A room normally out of bounds. The studio in the conservatory was where lessons were held. Mac swallowed, thinking he may well be losing his mind. Why was everything so damn different today? What was going on?

'Sit,' she said, motioning to a chair and leaving the room. Mac did as he was told, and the world slowly began to right itself. His heartbeat slowed, and Sula came in with a glass of water.

'Here, Mac. Drink.'

Mac gulped the water unashamedly. He didn't think he had ever been so thirsty in his life. When the last of it was gone, he placed the cup onto the floor by the chair. Sula watched from another chair nearby. Her gaze was bright but soft and he felt his heart flip.

She was beautiful, and he must be her worst student ever.

She must despair, Mac, really.

He broke away from her gaze and stared down at his hands.

'Do you know what happened, Mac?'

Shame crawled up his neck, colouring his face. He knew if he looked up, she would see, so he stared at the floor and shook his head.

'Try to tell me,' she said softly.

He finally met her eyes, and she smiled.

'I don't know,' he mumbled. 'I couldn't see the music. I tensed up. It was too fast.'

He expected a raised eyebrow, ridicule, disappointment - oh Mac can't cope with the tempo - but instead she was nodding slowly, the smile still on her face.

'I know it,' she said. 'I have seen once. In one student. Music blindness. It is like, how you say? Everything bunches together, is too much, there is no flow? Yes?'

Mac nodded and swallowed hard.

'Music blindness. It's a good name. Yes, I couldn't see, couldn't think. I couldn't think what the piano was, or what I was supposed do with it? It was alien, I know that sounds silly.'

'Not at all, but you will need minutes to recover. You won't play for a little while. The tension will go, but perhaps not today. Then you will be good as new.'

Mac looked back at his hands. She was turfing him out for today, well at least he could go knowing how bad he was. That would save some pride.

'All the better for your ears, eh? I guess that means the lesson is over.'

'For today,' she said with a brisk nod. Then she rose and returned with her phone from the music studio. She ran a finger down the screen. 'I will see you on Wednesday, at six. Okay?'

Mac frowned. 'But that's only three days. I normally have a week?'

'I know, this is extra. Just once, until I say again, anyway.' She gave him a bright smile as she tapped into the screen. 'The cost is no problem.'

Mac watched her, bemused.

'Says you.' he said with a small chuckle, starting to feel a lot more himself again. The colours of the world muted back to their normal shades, no more of the psychedelic blue on the wall in the living room. He glanced at the other colours in the room, checking those out too.

Quite some mind-fuck, Mac, buddy, I'm glad someone else has been here, or I'd be seriously worried about your head.

He looked back at Sula to find her looking at him, unimpressed.

'It is no problem for you. These extras are only cost to me and my time.'

Mac stared at her.

'Oh, no. I can't put you through my playing twice a week without paying you for the pain.'

Sula's eyebrows almost reached her hairline.

'The pain? Mac, you are one of my best students. You are, how you say? Gifted? Yes, musically gifted. Your playing is magnificent. Truly a great thing to hear.'

Mac felt his mouth drop open.

'You're talking about someone else, right?'

'No, Mac. You do not know. You play Beethoven, Chopin, Bach. You play just one year, Mac. One. This is fantastic, you see?'

'You told me to. I thought it was normal.'

'I push you. You play beautiful. Not all my students are like this.'

'Oh,' Mac said. He felt himself colour and Sula laughed.

'It is wonderful, no?'

Mac smiled and shrugged.

'I enjoy playing. It gets me out of my head.'

'Ah, so different to when we first meet.' She put on a low voice in imitation. "I don't want to be here. I don't like to play. Let's get this over, huh?' Mac, *your* playing gets *me* out of *my* head.'

She laughed, throwing her head back, and Mac grinned, swept up by her enthusiasm. She caught his hands and pulled him up from the chair to kiss both of his cheeks before cupping his face in her palms.

'I think you are wonderful, Mac. Do not play before Wednesday. The piano does not exists before then. Okay?'

'Okay,' he said, his face still scrunched in her palms, and she laughed.

Mac woke on the settee, her laughter still ringing in his ears. The log burner was getting low. The warmth he felt on his legs was Rolo, who was snoring at the other end of the chair. He shifted to look at the time, 9.07pm, and let his arm fall back to the chair.

Fabulous, you've slept most of the afternoon and missed dinner.

Like there was a dinner time out here at all. In the days before clocks, humans had only been ruled the sunrise, sunset, and their growling stomachs. They didn't care for dinner at 6pm sharp like modern day man. Maybe they had it right.

We are so ruled by time, Mac thought, throwing an arm over his face. Everything we do is timed. Catch the train at 7.10am, get to work for 9am, Lunch break at 12.30pm, home at 5pm, And although there was no official time for sleep - hooray, the ultimate freedom - sleep was to be seven hours or more, for your health.

Ridiculous.

Mac grinned as his stomach growled.

Now, it's time for dinner.

Throwing together a ham sandwich, Mac ate at the table and stared at the piano, the dream fresh in his mind.

Memory, he thought. That had been a memory. It had really happened. Music blindness. More than once if he had been trying too hard. Sula had helped him to overcome the tension, which enabled him to relax and let his mind and body do the work that they were capable of - in more ways than one. The exhilaration of finally playing Chopin's Nocturne No.9 had filled them both with so much adrenalin that the rest of the lesson had been much more of a physical affair, although with just as much passion.

That was something never lacking, Mac thought with a smile. Although not as frequent toward the end, of course, but that was normal, wasn't it?

Finished with his sandwich, he put the plate in the sink and made his way to the piano. Lifting the lid, he stared at the keys, swallowed hard, and finally pulled the stool out.

He stared at it, deciding if he wanted to sit down. If he really wanted all of those memories to come flooding back again. He wanted to play, loved to play, but he knew he would never sit at a piano again without thinking of Sula, and that was too hard.

*It **had** been too hard. How does it feel now, Mac?*

Mac tested his emotions, surprised to find them fairly stable. Sula still just a pleasant memory in the background.

In a quick motion, he sat on the stool and placed his fingers on the keys.

Okay?

A little wobbly now, but nothing seemed about to spill over just yet. This was the closest he had got to playing a piano since Sula had died. Truth be told, for a good amount of time beforehand too, but after seemed more poignant.

He sat, hearing nothing but the blood in his ears, the beating of his heart. Poised to play. Poised to *feel*.

His breathing and heart rate slowed, but he couldn't bring himself to press the keys. It was as though as strong a force was pushing up from underneath as on top. Finally, with a shudder that started at his feet and ended at the top of his head, he shut the lid and sat staring at it.

From somewhere in the room, the faint scent of musk reached his nostrils.

No, it's your imagination Mac. That's all.

He rose from the stool and slid it gently underneath the keyboard.

The smell persisted, and as he stood, he caught a movement in the darkness of the corridor. Something, or someone, going into the bathroom. Mac rubbed at his face.

Imagination, Mac. Imagination. You're tired.

But he wasn't imagining Rolo's low growls.

'Rolo,' Mac started, but his own voice raised hairs on the back of his neck.

The dog was standing by the stairs, hackles raised all down his back, as he stared down the corridor.

Just go and look, Mac. I bet there's nothing there.

But look at Rolo, He's freaked.

By your energy. He felt the change in you, that's all.

He's a dog!

Go look and find out.

Mac thought there was nothing less that he wanted in all the world, but he stepped out from under the stairs and began to walk down the corridor.

'Hello?' he called. 'Is anyone there?'

He swallowed hard, his heart beating double time in his chest as he reached the bathroom door, which was almost closed.

Light fell through the crack in the doorway.

Did I leave it on?

The smell of musk was more potent now, and Mac finally found he wanted to cry.

'Sula?' he whispered.

He put out a hand to push open the door, which swung inward with a low creak.

Rolo gave a bark that sounded to Mac as though it were in another dimension as he stared at the bathtub.

The shower curtain was pulled across.

'Dear God, I don't want to pull open that curtain,' he whispered as he stepped toward it. The door creaked behind him, and he turned to see it swinging shut. His heart thumping in his ears, he heard a volley of barks from the corridor, and then a dripping from the bath.

He turned back toward the tub and reached for the curtain. The room spun and pulsed along with his heart. The smell of musk making him gag.

He felt steam as his hand reached forward, heard the splash of water.

'Sula?'

He pulled back the curtain as the door crashed open, and Rolo stood barking in the doorway. Mac swung his head to the dog, and then turned back to the bath tub, the shower curtain still in his hand.

It was dry and empty.

No sign of the steam. No water. No Sula.

CHAPTER THIRTY

'THE MIND IS A powerful thing, it can make all sorts of realities out of the very reality you're sitting in right now. In fact, the reality you are experiencing - which you call life - only exists in your mind. Your personality, your thoughts, your physiology, your perception, your imagination, what you focus on, your values, your internal thermostat and where it is programmed. All of this and more is exactly the reason your life is yours. No one else will ever see the world as you do, all realities are different.'

Mac strolled around the audience; a rare opportunity to get up close and personal.

This particular venue was at a hotel in Germany. A beautiful, ornate hotel, with polished floors and rich furnishings in greens, golds, and reds. The room was intimate, only seating five hundred, and all at round tables, in groups. This was a setting he could use, to get people involved, get them sharing their own stories, which was just as important as the information he would share with them. In this setting his audience would go home with new contacts and new friends, new theories, and new projects, and maybe an opportunity to collaborate or form a mastermind. They would help each other through the weeks and months ahead, when most people lost the fever, and enthusiasm dropped off until the next show.

In this room the stage was small, the screen behind it large and warm. The microphone was attached to Mac's jacket, which meant that he was free to roam from the front stage right up to his team at the back who were taking care of the recording, the music, the lights, the audience, refreshments, paperwork. The clockwork process of each show, and the precision timing of each segment, the pulling together of his team, always made Mac proud to be part of it. Everyone had a job, and everyone did their job, he rarely had trouble with staff. This was more a family than work.

The cameraman followed him around the room. Jake, an old friend, and his cameraman for the last six years, knew not to get in the way. To back off, and get the best shots unobtrusively. The main thing was Mac connecting with the audience right here, not the audience who may watch later at home. The atmosphere was to be captured as organically as possible and edited to reflect the true nature of the show.

Jake backed between a couple of tables as Mac reached the back of the room and turned to face the audience from the back doors.

'Perspective,' he said, 'is powerful component of the way we live our lives. The way we choose to look at anything that happens to us, and the way we extract what we need to complete the story we tell ourselves, is what determines our attitude and reaction to the event. For good, or bad. Perspective can be any reason to say 'see? I told you that would happen.' Or 'This always happens to me.' Or it can be a reason to support our own story by saying 'I'm always lucky,' or 'Opportunity just seems to fall in my lap.'

Mac smiled at a woman in a red dress who was hanging on his every word.

'I have a friend in Kentucky, who's always down at the bottom. He tries, but he just can't get himself off the ground. He has fantastic ideas, brilliant marketing campaigns, world class people to help him, but he just never seems to take off. He works hard, day and night. He meditates, practices gratitude, exercises, takes care of himself, does what he needs to each day. But on this particular day, he said to me, 'Mac, I don't know what's going on. I just can't get it together. Why can I never get past the ten thousand mark? This stuff is good, right?"

Mac shrugged with a smile. The lady smiled back.

'I had to admit it was. He had some quality ideas, but he also had some limiting beliefs and perspectives. A whole heap of them that were holding him back. Keeping him down. Some he didn't even know about. The thing with this guy was that he always THOUGHT that he was doomed to have bad luck, so much so, that he actively sought it. Every day. Every way he looked at it, his life was a negative misery. I remember one afternoon he called me.'

Mac began to walk back to the front of the room, a slow stroll, allowing the words to fall over the room around him.

'I said, 'how are you doing? How's the business? How's the family?' he said, 'oh, the business is great. I'm about to close a huge deal with a supermarket chain, got a meeting tomorrow, could be the most I've made to date.' I congratulated him, and he went on to say, 'oh that's not all. I got a call from my wife. She's expecting our first child.''

Mac smiled at the memory, coming to a halt in between the tables to allow Jake to move back before he continued.

'I was pleased for him. They'd been trying a while, you know. This wasn't small fry. It was big news. But the best was yet to come. The guy should have been ecstatic, and he was, until his last piece of news. 'Mac,' he said, 'none of it matters. I'm in the hospital. I was crossing the street at lunchtime and got hit by a truck. Typical, huh? Just my luck!"

Mac turned to look back at the audience from the front. None of them seemed to be breathing, all eyes were on him. He adjusted his jacket and moved back to the stage, climbing the stairs slowly, letting the silence envelop him, the anticipation building. At the podium he faced the rows of tables and shook his head.

'I said to him, 'I'm so sorry to hear that. Are you okay? Is there anything I can do?'. You know what he said?'

Mac looked at the concerned sea of faces. Some were now shaking their heads, most were still.

'He said 'Nah, I'm fucked. This always happens to me. Any good that comes my way is always tailed by something ten times worse. I'll probably lose the whole deal now. I'm just at my wit's end. Why does this keep happening to me?' I asked him if someone could take the deal on his behalf, and do you know what he said? He said, 'oh, it won't come to that. I go home in ten minutes. I'm just waiting for painkillers for my broken toes."

Mac raised his eyebrows and gave a brief 'look' to the audience. A chuckle rippled around the room.

'I said to him 'you broke your toes? There must be other damage, surely'. He said, 'no, other than that I'm fine, but by god I'm sick of looking at these hospital walls. They take so bloody long, I'm sure it's just me. Five people who came in after me have already been and gone."

The laughter swelled and Mac shrugged, letting it die down.

'So, this is a guy who had an invite to close a major deal, found he's finally going to be a father, gets run over by a truck and ONLY breaks his toes - and he calls that a bad day? Man, I'd like to share some of my bad days with him.'

Mac waited for the laughter to die down again, and took a sip from the bottle of water on the small podium next to him.

'The point is, that it doesn't matter what you threw at this guy, he would always see the worst. A different man would have called the day a success and laughed at the whole truck episode - a minor blip - but not this guy, no. Those broken toes were just another indication of how his life was prone to bad luck. It didn't matter what happened, he could only see the negative. There was no changing him. I'm afraid he's still the same now, there is no way of making him understand that his view is just that - his view. His perception, his reality, is exactly what he makes it, and in this case, if he had just chosen to look at things a little differently, he would have been counting his blessings, not cursing his toes.'

Amongst the laughter, a man shouted up from table three.

'Did he get the deal?'

Mac chuckled and threw the question back. 'What do you think?'

'No?' as the man shouted a sea of heads shook from side to side.

'Of course he didn't,' Mac smiled. 'On deal day, something just as dramatic happened. He just kept telling himself the same old story, and sitting in the same old loop. Perspective is huge. Never underestimate the power of learning to see multiple perspectives, and then choosing the brightest one to go about your day with. If your friend didn't call? Instead of 'she doesn't care about me', maybe she's busy with her sick toddler today, or out running errands for her elderly father, she'll call tomorrow. Perspective is simple but so powerful.

Perspective is the difference between the fly bumping against the windowpane to reach the great outdoors through the glass, and it turning one-hundred-and-eighty degrees and flying out of the open door. Take stock, take a real good look. How many windowpanes are you trying to break through right now? If you turned just a little, it could all seem vastly different.'

Nods from the audience now. Some pens beginning to scribble, some clapping, and a cheer. Mac only hoped they had got something from it. Something real and poignant, something to work on, to investigate.

'Reality is what you make of the world around you. That's all. Anything you think - is as real as you think it is, and anything you can imagine - can become your reality. Anything.'

Mac stared at the puddle on the floor of the corridor as he thought about what he used to say to his audience on a daily basis. Most of his knowledge was rooted in science, although it could sound like lunacy to the unaware. Right now, his own words were beginning to sound like lunacy to himself, although in a slightly different context. Still, if it stood for one thing, it stood for another, right?

'But I'm not imagining this, am I?'

He stared at the puddle, as Rolo sat by the door of the cabin watching him with fearful eyes. He looked up at the dog.

'I don't know, Rolo. I don't know what to make of any of this.'

The dog whined but made no move toward Mac, who turned his attention back to the wet patch on the floor. Cautiously, he stuck out a finger and placed it gently into the cool liquid. The substance clung to his finger as he pulled it out and held it in front of his face with a frown.

'I'm not sure what other perspectives there can be to what's happening here, or how my imagination could possibly turn a couple of pools of water into a couple of pools of blood.'

He broke out into a cold sweat as he brought the finger to his nose and sniffed. Copper found its way to his nostrils, mixed with the musk that had been in the bathroom. The hallway shifted in his vision, and he struggled to hold on to consciousness, pulling deep breaths as he placed his hand onto the floor and dropped to his backside. Spots ran before his eyes. He breathed, slow and deep, until the feeling passed.

Rolo whined from the doorway, and not wanting to go back to the bathroom, Mac struggled to his feet and threw up in the kitchen sink.

CHAPTER THIRTY-ONE

SULA SAT ON THE bed crying as Mac tried to comfort her. She shrugged off his touch and let out long, hard, gasping sobs. Mac sat next to her.

'What is it, baby? What can I do?'

Sula gasped, and her breath hitched.

'Why won't you talk to me, Mac? I need you to talk.'

'I'm right here. I'm talking, speak to me, I'm listening.'

Sula's head whipped up. Her red-rimmed eyes were ringed with dark circles that had never touched her velvety skin before. Her hair was wet and wild, dripping onto the sheets with a plip-plip-plip-plip.

Mac tried to scrub the sound from his brain, tried to concentrate, but the noise was too loud, and there was now a major puddle around her. It irritated Mac that he would have to sleep in this bed tonight while she got the dry one. He wanted to tell her, to shake her, but he didn't want to touch her either.

'Sula?'

She bowed her head back down, dark curls falling over her face as she wept, her shoulders shook, and Mac felt a stab of agonising sorrow that he couldn't help her. He wanted to, but she wasn't herself. He didn't know how to console her. When he could take her anguish no longer, he reached a shaking hand to her shoulder again. Cold radiated from her skin, he felt it even before he touched her, and ice crept down his own spine.

On the bed, the puddle was turning red. Blood.

Mac stared at it horrified as big bright globs of it fell from her hair - or was it from under her hair?

Another drip fell and landed in the water.

Plip.

Mac's hand began to shake just above his wife's ice-cold shoulder.

'Sula?' he whispered.

His hand was almost on her skin when she whipped up to face him. He recoiled in horror, and scrambled back away from her across the bed, and right off the edge. He stood facing the woman that had been his wife, gasping for breath, every fibre aching to scream and run, while feeling so frozen to the spot that he could have grown roots.

Sula stared at him, the pain on her face absolute. Blood streaked down her features and soaked into her dress. She slowly cocked her head to the side with a small, but audible creak, then she put up a bloody hand extending her finger and beckoning him forward.

Mac felt himself drawn forward, equally repulsed and inquisitive at the same time. His heart was threatening to break down his rib cage as he leaned into her, the copper smell of blood leaving a metallic taste in his mouth.

She smiled. Sula, yet not Sula. This thing wanted to eat him alive, he knew it, but leaned in anyway.

'Mac?' she whispered, blood spilling from between her lips to run down her chin.

Mac was tongue-tied, his eyes glued to the horror of her face. He couldn't speak a word. He nodded his head, and she beckoned him closer still.

'I need you to talk to me, Mac. I have a bobble in my mind. A FUCKING BOBBLE!'

Mac's mind scrambled for her meaning as she continued, their faces only inches apart now.

'Help me, Mac,' she moaned. 'There's too much blood. Help me catch it before it runs.'

Her face twisted and her hands shot out to grab his jumper at the shoulders, bunching it with bloody hands.

'ARE YOU LISTENING TO ME?' she screamed at him.

Mac nodded his head. He had never understood her less in his life, but if she would just let him go, he would figure it out. Anything for her to let him go.

'I... I need to talk. I'll talk to you.'

Sula relaxed her grip and Mac felt overwhelming relief flood his pores, and then her grip re-tightened and she pulled her horror mask a mere inch from his. Then she opened her bloody mouth and screamed, spraying blood into Mac's face. Mac clamped his hands to his ears, shut his eyes, and screamed with her.

There was a loud thump, and a bolt of pain shot through his right thigh. Mac forced an eye open to find himself on the mezzanine floor in the cabin. He lunged around to look at the bed, scooting backward until his spine dug into the cabin wall.

There was no Sula, no-one on the bed but Rolo, who looked up at Mac bleary eyed from the covers.

'Shit. Shit. Dream, Mac, it was just a dream. Was it a dream?'

In the early morning half-light, a frenzy of nerves ran through him. He put a hand to his face, which was wet. Sweat, not blood. No blood. Getting to his feet, he peered over the balcony to the ground floor. Nothing seemed out-of-place down there, although he knew the corridor would be the place that anything would be out of sorts.

Blood.

There had been blood there yesterday, hadn't there?

Mac closed his eyes and leaned on the barrier, head in his hands. How could there be blood in the corridor? There couldn't have been. He must have been seeing things. It had been water, just like every other time.

And the bathroom? Someone had been in the tub, he had felt the steam, and yet there had been no-one there, had there?

'Fuuuuck!' Mac screamed into the darkness, 'I don't know, I don't fucking know!'

Disturbed, Rolo bounced off the bed and pulled himself up next to Mac, his paws on top of the railing, tongue licking at Mac's hands and face. Mac pushed him gently away.

'What's going on, Rolo? I think I'm actually losing my mind. Am I losing my mind?'

The dog licked at his face frantically and Mac moved away, giving the dog a rub on the head, before pulling on a jumper and going down the stairs.

'Blood in the fucking hallway,' he mumbled to himself. 'As if there was blood in the fucking hallway. You've lost it Mac. Never mind a screw loose. You have ten fucking screws lost and ten more on the way out.'

An hour later Mac and Rolo were in the truck having thrown a few things together and deciding to leave the rest. He would come back up here with Tom to sort out and clean up at a later date. For now, they were going home.

Except it seemed they weren't.

The truck was four-wheel drive, but even the high-tech system that the truck had installed could barely cope with the boggy mud of the land after the rain. Back and forth, and back and forth. Mac was getting nowhere fast, and he knew once they were in the trees, there wouldn't be room to manoeuvre. Stuck would mean stuck.

In the end, it had been the tree that had done it. Large and solid, and right across the track, just inside the tree line. The high winds had obviously brought it down, and Mac knew he would need a chainsaw to get rid of it. He had seen one in the shed, but even if he chopped it up, it was clear that the truck wasn't getting through the mud anyway. They were stuck here.

Mac slammed his hands onto the steering wheel and crunched the truck into reverse. Ironically, the truck moved back the few hundred yards back to the cabin without faltering, in half of the time it had taken to get to the tree across the track.

As the truck idled, Mac cried with frustration. The one thing he had been sure about was that he didn't want to go back into the cabin, which sat next to him undisturbed by his outburst of activity. Deceptively innocent and friendly.

Mac and Rolo got back out of the truck and entered its jaws.

It seemed to Mac that it grinned as it let them inside.

Three hours later, Mac was sat in his chair on the pier, wrapped in a coat, scarf, hat, and gloves, and with a blanket over his knees. There was a beer in one hand, cigarette in the other - the last of only three cigarettes that he thought he may have more need for now.

Idiot.

He shivered and stared at the icy grey loch. The morning was chilly, heavy and grey, but mercifully dry. Dry, he could take. He couldn't sit in that cabin any longer than necessary. His nose ran and his glove scraped across his whiskered chin as he caught the drip with a tissue, blowing everything out, only for it to drip again with cold only a few minutes later.

You need a shave.

Mac chuckled aloud at his own admission.

A shave? If you think I'm going anywhere near that bathroom, you're sorely mistaken. At this point, I may even dig a hole and shit in the woods rather than go in there and find the damn shower curtain shut.

Dirt flew into the air at the side of the pier. Mac frowned and leaned forward to see Rolo digging at the hole he had begun weeks before by the side of the wooden platform.

'You digging back to England, buddy? When the escape tunnel is complete, I'll be right behind you.'

Rolo stopped digging to watch Mac, ears silky gold, nose black as soot, right up to his eyes.

'You may have more luck digging with your paws than with your nose, that's what the claws are for.'

He motioned, air digging with clawed hands. The dog ignored him and set back to work. Mac shrugged and stared out at the loch, wondering if he could get frostbite from sitting outside too long, and deciding to get another blanket. If the cabin was willing, maybe he could even get a hot drink before he came back out.

He stood, stamping out his cigarette, and stretched his cold, aching bones. He was pulling the blanket around his shoulders when Rolo came running onto the pier with something long and black hanging from his mouth. Something that glinted in the grey light as Rolo tossed it high. It landed with a low thunk on the wood and Mac frowned.

'Leave it, Rolo,' he said as the dog bound forward. Rolo looked at Mac dejected, the thing now wedged between his paws. Mac waved him away and picked up the dirty, wet item from the floor.

A necklace.

The string was black rope. It could belong to Josh. Mac thought he had seen him wear a similarly stringed necklace last time he had been over for dinner.

He took off a glove, and rubbed his thumb over the metal design which hung on the black string. He narrowed his eyes, looking at it more closely.

An eye. Egyptian. A symbol, just like the ones Sula loved. Sula wore one just like this that he had brought her from Egypt when she hadn't been able to travel with him. It had a blue sapphire in the centre, Mac remembered, and she had worn it almost continuously.

He scratched at the dirt, and rubbed the eye further. Blue appeared, right in the centre of the eye, the same as Sula's. Mac shuddered and his blood ran cold. His hands shook as Saul's words from the other day entered his mind.

I heard it here... definitely a woman...

Mac shook his head.

'No, not Sula,' he whispered. 'Lots of women must have had a similar style of necklace. This probably belongs to a hiker, that's all. Someone who swam off the pier, maybe.'

There's one way to find out for sure, isn't there?

Mac closed his eyes as he turned the necklace over and rubbed away the dirt on the back. The engraving was there, he felt it before he saw it, short and sweet with the lack of room. He swallowed hard as he opened his eyes. There was no mistaking whose necklace this was.

Sula, All my love, Mac.

Mac felt his legs buckle. He hit the deck of the pier with his knees, breath leaving his lungs as he placed a hand on the deck to stop him from falling further.

No.

But the engraving was there. Sula's necklace. Blurry vision fell on the tiny words as tears filled his eyes.

'Sula?' he said. 'No. There has to be another explanation.'

She's been here, Mac. To Tom's cabin. Why the hell would she be at Tom's cabin...and was Tom here with her?

Did he want to know the answer to that?

His head ached, and his stomach swirled.

What does this mean, Mac?

Something white landed on his glove, large, fluffy, and round. He watched as it disintegrated in front of him, and then he looked up to see snow falling softly and stealthily. No noise, just quiet calm, consuming the dark land all around him.

And in that quiet, calm, beauty of the natural landscape, Mac clutched the necklace to him and let out a roar.

CHAPTER THIRTY-TWO

'Have you called Mac, yet?' Meg said, as Tom tried to tie up the invoices on the screen in front of him. He switched the phone to his other hand, clamping it between his chin and shoulder so that he could reach for the papers in the pigeonhole just above the desk.

'Not yet, I haven't had time.'

'You know what I think, Tom Macauley?'

Tom let out a sigh as the paper slipped from his hands, some landing on the desk, the rest on the floor. He grit his teeth as he looked at it.

Not really, but I suppose you're going to tell me, anyway.

'What do you think, honey?' he said.

'I think you're running scared.'

Tom sat back in his chair, giving up on the paper and the invoices until Meg was off the phone.

'Scared of what?'

'Mac.'

Tom huffed a laugh. 'Why would I be scared of Mac?'

'His temper worried you. You're scared of what you'll find when you ring again.'

Tom swallowed. She had a point. There was no hiding anything when you lived with Meg, she should have been a detective, but he wasn't about to let her know that she was right either way.

'I'm not scared, Meg. I've just been busy.'

'Right. So, when you said you'd call him back after his call five days ago, did you do it?'

'Busy. As I am right now,' he said, gritting his teeth. She either didn't hear the insinuation, or blatantly ignored it.

'Have you heard from him at all?'

Tom felt guilt and a little worry creep up into his chest. He smothered it quickly. Mac would be fine.

'No.'

'Not even a message?'

'No.'

'And that doesn't worry you at all? Did you find out who was making the silent calls and what they wanted? Was it those men?'

'No, and I don't know. They haven't called back for me to find out.'

Meg was silent on the other end of the phone and Tom knew she was getting angry, but he was also getting angry. He had things to do, invoices to sort that were already a month late. It was a mess he shouldn't have to sort, but the secretary had left yesterday without a word other than she wouldn't be back, and she had been kind enough to leave the paperwork and computer systems in one hell of a mess. He didn't have time for this crap right now.

'Okay.' Meg said finally. 'I suppose I'll see you back here for dinner.'

'Meg!'

He waited for the click that said the call had been cut off, but it didn't come. He looked at the phone and saw she was still there.

'Meg? Listen, I'm up to my neck in crap here. I'm tetchy, and I'm sorry. I didn't mean to take it out on you.'

'So, you'll ring Mac? Check he's not gone out of his mind or been murdered. Please. For my sake, as much as his.'

'Yes.' Tom leaned his elbow on the table, bowing his head to scrub at his hair with his free hand. 'Yes. I promise I'll ring Mac.'

'And you'll ring me straight back?'

Tom looked at the paper strewn around him and rolled his eyes.

I didn't say I'd ring him right now, Meg, for crying out loud woman. Give a man a break.

'Yes,' he said, trying to conceal the sigh that escaped his lips. 'I'll give you a ring straight back.'

'Good, speak to you soon.'

There was silence, and Tom glanced at the screen to see she had gone. He slammed the phone on the desk as the door to the office opened.

'Trouble?' Rob said, two take-out coffees in a tray in one hand, the door handle in the other. He put the tray on the desk and Tom smiled up at the man, twenty years his junior, but one of the few members of staff he trusted implicitly. Tom had made him deputy CEO of the clinic last year, the youngest to date, but also the most switched on, and ready to see the slip-ups that Tom was about to make before he even knew that they were there. They made a good team, and Tom was glad the man had walked through the door asking for a job two summers ago.

'Only of the family kind,' he said, taking a cup and sipping at the hot liquid. 'Thanks.'

'Kids?'

'Meg. Mac, really I suppose.'

He leaned to pick up the papers, thankfully most of them still in order, and placed them under the pile on the table, before opening the desk drawer and searching through the accumulated crap.

'Here.' Rob said, throwing a packet of paracetamol onto Tom's desk. Tom grabbed them and held them high.

'Thanks. The strain shows that bad, huh?'

Rob laughed as he sat in his own chair, bringing the cardboard cup to his lips.

'You always need paracetamol where Mac is concerned. What's he been up to now?'

Tom swallowed two pills dry and placed the packet back in his drawer.

'Nothing is what he should have been up to. He's at the goddamn cabin - that goes no further.' He pointed a pen at Rob, who pulled an unseen zip across his lips. 'I think he's going bloody insane and, like I haven't got enough to deal with here, Meg thinks it's my job to keep him upright.'

Rob raised his dark eyebrows. 'He's old enough to look after himself, isn't he?'

'He bloody should be. There's too much going on here to focus on him properly. I don't know why I sent him to the place, he'd have been less hassle here.'

Rob sipped at his drink.

'Maybe he'll drive himself insane and end up in a lunatic asylum. Make things a little easier, eh?'

Tom half smiled, more guilt falling over him.

'He isn't really the problem. It's what he could find out, and what he would do with the information. It's me that's the problem.'

Rob pursed his lips with a nod.

'Overstepped the mark, man. I'm sorry.'

Tom let out a small chuckle.

'Don't worry about it. I could do with phoning Mac, though, just to make sure he's okay. I'll do that first, then phone Meg, then I'll come and sort out the shit that woman left us with.'

'Want me to do invoices?'

'No, you carry on with the promotional stuff for next week. I'll take care of it afterward. It shouldn't take long.

Outside, on the metal fire escape stairs, Tom pulled out his phone and called Mac's number, which went to voicemail. He tried again with the same response. He rang Meg and told her the news. She told him to keep trying or he would have to pay the cabin a visit. He had tried twice more before he noticed the figure below.

Black jeans, black coat, hood pulled close around his shadowy face. A face that appeared to be looking straight at him.

Tom's heart gave a jolt and seemed to lodge itself into his throat. There were a few seconds which seemed to stretch into hours as he stared at the man, and the man stared back.

Finally, in a move that gave Tom more chills than the Woman in Black movie had, the man lift a hand and pointed to him. His other hand went to his ear, and then Tom's phone began to ring.

CHAPTER THIRTY-THREE

M AC PACED THE LIVING area of the cabin, dialling Tom's number and cutting off at the last minute.

I don't want to know.

You need to know.

I don't want to.

His thumb hovered over the green phone icon again, and then there was a knock on the door that nearly sent him vaulting over the settee to hide.

Was this the cabin? Or...

He waited, the knocks came again. Three short, hard raps. Mac paused, halfway to answering, and halfway to hiding, before he caught himself.

Who do you expect, Mac? Sula? Dead and cold on the doorstep, come to collect her necklace? Answer the goddamn door!

Mac shook himself out of his funk and opened the door to a very welcome sight.

'I come bearing gifts!'

Saul held bottles of beer and a large pie up high in the air, while a Sainsbury's bag dangled from his wrist. Mac smothered a smile. Saul looked like a veritable yeti. His thick coat, scarf, hat, and gloves were covered in white like he had been sitting in the large flakes for the last hour. Only his eyes and his thick accent gave away his identity.

'Figured you could use the company,' Saul said. 'And to be honest, I could really do with getting out. Home is driving me insane with nowhere else to be... well, what do you think?' He held the bottles up for Mac to inspect.

Mac faked a frown and squinted at the bottles.

'Hmm, well, I only like the good stuff around here. Old Speckled Hen? Isn't that your dad's ale?'

Saul turned the bottles towards him and looked at the label, a smile on his face, no offence taken. Mac decided he liked this fellow a lot. He had good vibes, as Sula always said.

'Well, I'm afraid you don't get a choice out here. It's the old bird or nowt. Are you going to let me in? It's like bloody Antarctica out here.'

Mac laughed as he found his manners and stepped back from the doorway.

'Of course, come in, come in. I was only joking. The old bird is more than good enough. Give yourself a shake off first though, eh? Every time you come through my door, I have to mop the bloody floor.'

He took the bag, beer and pie from Saul and placed them on the small table. Saul ran a hand over each shoulder and shook his head before pulling off his hat and gloves and stepping inside. Mac shut the door behind him and took his coat.

'Ah, that's much better. That log burner really does the job in here, eh?' Saul smiled.

'It really does. For all it's just a wooden hut, it can get really hot with that thing on the go.' Mac extended a hand, offering the settee opposite the fire to Saul, whose lips carried a tinge of blue.

'Thank you,' he said, perching on the edge of the settee, and extending his own hands to the fire, with a rub.

'You on your way out?' he said, looking to Mac.

Mac looked down at his own coat, still zipped up from his time out on the pier before he had found the necklace.

The necklace. Sula's necklace...

He pushed the thought away and gave a small chuckle.

'I've been out. To the pier, just come in. Not far to go round here in this weather.'

Saul laughed. 'Aye, that's true. You must have just missed me outside. Today I came by boat. A much easier way of getting here than hiking six miles over a mountain. I've put the kayak up by yours next to the jetty. I hope you don't mind.'

Mac shook his head as he took off his coat and felt himself relax a little. It wasn't expected company, but it certainly wasn't unwelcome, especially right now.

'So, hot drink, or straight for the hard stuff?' Mac held up the beer.

'Ah well, what's the saying? Go hard or go home? Let's crack open the good stuff. The pie was a gift from ma, she doesn't like the thought of you being out here all by yourself. How this makes it better, I'm not sure. Either she thinks you have nothing to eat, or the pie is a disguise for an invisible force field that will protect you from intruders for miles around.'

'What is it?' Mac said, giving the pie a sniff. 'Apple?'

'Not only apple pie, this is ma's one and only special apple pie. I hope to god you like apples, because she stuffs the things in like sardines.'

Mac grinned as his stomach grumbled. It was after 3pm, and he had been so wound up that he had missed lunch. Now that he thought about it, he was starving.

'Love them. Do you want to share? I'm starving. It's been a while since I had a pie and pint night.'

'Aye, I bet. And this little place looks like a cosy inn. We can pretend we're out.' He suddenly sat up with a grin and spread his arms wide. 'Well, I suppose I am out!'

'You are,' Mac said, wishing to god he was the one out.

Cosy inn? More like a scare-fest in the forest. Enjoy your stay, one and all!

'Ma said to put it in the oven for twenty, on one-eighty, warm it up. There's cream or custard in the bag, too.'

Mac felt his mouth water as he turned the oven on, set the temperature to one-eighty, and put the pie inside.

'I may just be a little in love with your ma, Saul. She's amazing. How did she know I needed this right now?'

'She's a mother. Which means she's psychic, has ten pairs of hands, can run one hundred meters faster than Mo Farah, and has eyes in the back of her head.'

Mac wrinkled his nose as he used a bottle opener on two bottles. They were so cold; he wondered if they would be ice inside.

'I think I may have jumped the gun about being in love...' he said.

Saul laughed from the settee and sat back in the chair as Mac brought the beer over.

'I should reserve judgment for sure. She's not an easy woman to live with. Cheers!' he said, lifting the bottle high.

Mac lifted his own bottle to clink it with Saul's and took a swig.

'Just what the doctor ordered,' Mac said, relishing the bitter taste and ice-cold liquid that he felt travel all the way to his stomach.

'If the doctor ever works again.' Saul said, pursing his lips.

Mac sat on the chair, heat from the fire wrapping itself around him like a warm blanket.

'Nothing, still?'

Saul shook his head and took a sip of beer.

'I'm sick to death of going over the same job adverts, the same crappy commute, the same crappy pay. Have you ever wanted to turn back time so much that you may actually kill if you got the chance to do it?'

Mac sipped his beer and thought about the question. It took little answering.

'Yep. All the damn time.'

Saul wrinkled his nose.

'Sorry, man. I forgot about your wife.'

'Don't be. Your predicament is just as bad. We both have to keep going forward now, whichever way life wants to take us, and I don't know about you, but this is the only time in my life I've not had any clue where I'm headed. It concerns me that it's come to that.'

Saul leaned forward and narrowed his eyes at Mac.

'How'd you mean, it concerns you?'

'I should have my map. I should be ready and heading down a road that's been planned by now, not fannying around in the wilderness... literally.'

'That's a lot of pressure, Mac. No one has a road map to life.'

'They should at least know their destination. Would you plan a trip around the world without taking a map and having GPS?'

'Well, no. Of course not.'

'So why are so many people charging off through life on an unchartered course? It's getting many people nowhere. They're spinning in circles, trying to make a living while not having two pennies to rub together, always waiting for a weekend and their two holidays a year to enjoy themselves. Meanwhile, life carries on, hurtling toward death, with no care for whether you've lived it or not.'

Saul sipped his beer and stared at Mac. Mac half wondered whether the man would get his coat and say goodbye, never to be seen again. When Saul spoke, however, he was pleasantly surprised to find a curious and open-minded man.

'But there is no map or GPS to life, Mac, is there?'

'Right. But remember way back when there were no maps of the world? No maps of towns and cities? Most people didn't travel far, like most people don't really *live* today. But a handful of people did something about it, didn't they? They charted where they had been, charted the dead ends and the unpassable moors and bogs. They left a map that allows us to get where we need to be without the guesswork. If you want to go to Edinburgh? A sat nav will give you the quickest route, the scenic route, the route avoiding tolls. Just press and go, and you will never waste time stuck, lost, or turning from a dead end.'

Saul nodded slowly as he sipped from his bottle and pursed his lips in thought. Mac let him digest both the beer and the information, sipping his own beer as he waited.

'Okay,' Saul said. 'But how do you make a map for something so personal? If every life experience and life-course is different. If every person is different, and starts at a different place, how is the race one big fair and easy map for all of us? Surely there is no such thing as a map for living?'

'There isn't,' Mac replied, sitting forward in his chair. Words and explanations came to him easily here. He was completely in his comfort zone. He knew this science inside and out. He placed his elbows on his knees, fingers and thumbs forming a small triangle in front of his lap. 'So that is why people need to make their own.'

Saul blanched and laughed. 'But making our own is surely navigating without a map!'

'No, it's different. Bear with me here. So just imagine that there is a map, very personal to you, but the map isn't revealed to you right now. The map only gets revealed when you begin to travel.'

Saul narrowed his eyes again and swirled the last of his beer in the bottle. 'But how are we supposed to travel if we can't see the map or where we're going? You're not making a lot of sense, Mac.'

'We plan. And by making a plan, we can begin to head in the right direction. Once we start the journey, the way will be revealed bit by bit. We can travel faster by using bits of other people's maps. Others who have travelled to the destination we desire ahead of us.'

Saul said nothing. He looked at Mac intently.

'See, all we have to do is make a decision and take action, but the decision is really what holds people back. And why do we avoid decision, especially about the things that we really want in life?'

'Because we think they're not attainable?'

Mac nodded.

'Absolutely part of the reason, yes. But by not attainable, what are we really saying to ourselves? That we don't want to try? That can't be right because we just said we want it. That we can't get there? That can't be right either - we know that in almost all cases of starting on any journey there are people who have got there before us, the destination is more than possible. That we're not capable? But we can learn any skill we choose, and with consistent practice, and repetition, we can get good at it - and there is always something that we want to get good at if we think about it - but that's the point. Few people think about it, and therefore they never decide. They never start. They wander aimlessly into a mundane life of work, depression, disease and pills, wondering if this is all there is to life.'

Mac trailed off to sip at his beer.

'They're scared,' Saul said, the sort of wonder in his voice that Mac had heard many times over the years as people 'clicked' with what he was trying to say. 'It's fear that stops them.'

'Right,' Mac nodded. 'To make a big decision and commit to it is scary. Fear is the basis of all human life. A very primal and instinctive way of keeping us alive. The thing is, when we don't have to fear sabre-toothed tigers anymore, this system is of little value in modern life. There are three major things that are stopping anyone from having anything on earth they desire - and anything really is attainable for anybody - fear, belief, and decision. After that, there's a science to success because even with decision, and even with a plan, a goal without action will remain just a dream. Action and reflection are the final key points if you want to be pedantic.'

Saul put his beer down on the floor and waved a hand at Mac.

'Wait, wait, wait. You make it sound so easy, but I'm a trained psychiatrist. I've studied psychology and the nature, nurture assumptions, as I presume you have too. This isn't attainable for *everybody*, really, is it?'

'I didn't say it was easy. It is remarkably simple, but most people will find it excruciatingly hard. The mind is like a thermostat, you see, which is programmed and set when we're children. Set it at thirty degrees and your subconscious will work to keep you at thirty degrees in everything you do, to keep you safe. That is why most people never change. They can't, and they don't understand why, but it's subconscious. Now, the subconscious can be reprogrammed, and the thermostat can be changed. Most people hate change, hate to be uncomfortable, but if you want those things you desire, you have to follow the path that will reveal itself, regardless of the lies you tell yourself, regardless of the story you have been programmed to believe. You have to get comfortable with being uncomfortable. You must develop the right mindset, and the right physiology, to get out of your comfort zone every day. To challenge the subconscious, and to question what you think you know - even about yourself - until the new programming becomes the reality.'

Saul rubbed a hand over his mouth.

'This is your thing, right?'

'I've studied it for eighteen years. The results are evident-'

'No, no,' Saul said, holding a hand up. 'I mean this is what you genuinely believe.'

'It's what I absolutely know for certain works. I've seen it, watched the process in action, seen the heights people have reached with a small framework and a lot of belief and a desire to shift their paradigms.'

'Which is why you're so uncomfortable right now. But, Mac, you just said being uncomfortable is good. You may not know where you're going, but you *are* uncomfortable. I take it you really don't want to stay here, and I take it you always had a plan before?' Saul raised his eyebrows and Mac nodded his head. 'So, like you say, it's really quite simple. Make a plan and start walking.'

'It's not that...' Mac trailed off with a laugh at something he used to roll his eyes at when he spoke to people after his events.

'Simple. No!' Saul laughed with him. 'And I'm with you. It's really not so simple for me either. How the hell do we get out of this Mac?'

'We make a plan.' Mac said, and began to laugh. 'Right now, I'm charting the way to the next beer and to check some apple pie, with a little belief, I should make it in one piece.'

'My plan is to eat the pie and drink the beer you bring back for us.'

'Then I think we're good for tonight!'

Both men laughed as Mac got up and went to the kitchen.

CHAPTER THIRTY-FOUR

'DO YOU BELIEVE IN ghosts?' Mac asked Saul after their third beer and second slice of apple pie.

Relaxed, warm and fuzzy, his speculation and worry about being laughed out of the cabin at such talk was completely dispersed by alcohol. He needn't have worried, either Saul was just as fuzzy, or would have humoured him, anyway.

'Nope.' He said, leaning back to look at Mac, hands behind his head. 'You?'

Mac wrinkled his nose and looked out of the front window at the darkening sky. Some of the biggest flakes of snow that he had ever seen sailed steadily past the glass in the gloom. His stomach gave a small, uncomfortable jolt.

Nowhere to go now Mac, you're stuck buddy. Well and truly stuck with whatever is going on in here.

He thought of the necklace still in the pocket of his coat, the faint thrum of the piano, the fridge magnets, and the bathroom antics and patches of water... *blood*.

'I didn't,' he replied with an involuntary shudder.

'Now you do?'

'I don't know. I suppose I may just be going mad out here. Grief, probably. I don't know why I said that. Ignore me.'

A frown crossed Saul's face.

'Your wife?'

Mac huffed a laugh and looked down at his half empty bottle of beer.

'I don't know. Something seems to be... I don't know, trying to get my attention.'

'Here?'

Mac pushed out his lips with a self-conscious grin and then shook his head.

'I don't know. It's probably just my imagination, eh? Forget I said anything.'

Saul leaned forward to place his bottle on the floor and leaned his arms on his wide-spread knees. He glanced at the bottle before looking back up at Mac, his face serious.

'You're the mind guy, Mac. You know that you can imagine those sorts of things, right? We can all do that when we're grieving. Our senses are heightened. We're almost searching for that contact now they're no longer here. It's absolutely possible for you to be imagining it, but then, I don't know what you're imagining, do I?'

The mind guy. Why did that name always follow him around? He had never felt less in control of his mind than he did right now.

'Nothing, just noises. Things moved. Yeah, I know, I'm also tired. I could have moved things and forgotten, you know.'

You sure as hell didn't spell your own name on the fridge door though, Mac. Nor did you place blood puddles down the corridor.

A shiver ran through him. Saul didn't need to know specifics. He was just feeling out the conversation.

'Right. You miss her, and it's obvious how much after you broke down on me last time. I'll say you want her back more than you know yourself. Your subconscious is working to make that a reality for you.'

Mac chewed on his lip and nod his head.

If only that were true. Or was it? Could he be imagining this stuff? He vowed to check the bin bag he locked in the shed outside with the others – Tom's suggestion to keep predators away. If the bloodstained cloths weren't there, he would admit it was all in his imagination.

He did want her back here, that much he was absolutely certain of - he would give both legs for the privilege.

'What do you think?' Saul asked when Mac had been silent for some time with his thoughts.

'I think you're probably right. I mean, why the hell would she come out here, anyway? Surely she would haunt our London house.'

Saul picked up his bottle and emptied it with a wink and a large swallow.

'Unless it's not her...' he said, letting the sentence trail off into the quiet of the cabin.

The wood cracked in the burner.

That was a good point... although the smell of her perfume had been pretty intense, and somehow that didn't sit right. He somehow *knew* that if anything was amiss around here, it was most definitely Sula.

'I was joking, Mac, just joking.'

Mac lifted his head to meet Saul's amused eyes with his own. He forced a grin.

'You're a funny guy,' he said, rolling his eyes, and Saul laughed good-naturedly.

'I know,' he said. 'I've actually been pondering a question while I've been sitting here. With all you know about the mind, I think you may be able to help me figure out something that's been bugging me for years now.'

Mac relaxed back into the chair, glad for the change of conversation, especially if it was about his favourite subject.

'Sounds interesting. What is it?'

'How far do you think we can control what happens to us illness wise... with just our thoughts.'

Mac raised his eyebrows and blew out a breath.

'How far do you want to go? We can't prevent all illness, the body gets old, and things go wrong. But, our thoughts control everything, as far as I'm concerned. If we think we can, we can. If we think we can't, we can't – that goes for anything. So, I believe that similarly if we think, and believe, we're healthy and fit, we most usually are. Cells work to the thermostat, remember? But the belief has to be strong. Absolute. No doubt. That's why people with life-threatening tumours who 'just know' that they will get better, come back from the brink of death, and erase all traces of the disease. The medical world calls that a miracle. I call it the power of the mind.'

Saul was nodding along with Mac's words.

'That's what I've thought too, although no-one has ever been so certain that I've spoken to – that's mostly doctors, though, of course. It's all about the medicine in the medical industry, the plaster for the sore. My theory has always been that the body can and will heal itself. We don't need the sugar pills in most instances.

Mac felt his intrigue heighten.

'The pharmaceutical industry would disagree with you,' he said with a grin.

'So would anybody who shares any of the hundreds of billions of pounds they earn each year. The machine is so vast it won't be stopped.'

'I agree completely, and yet the placebo effect has been tested and confirmed over and over again. If people believe they have the right medication, most of the time they get well, even if they have a sugar and water placebo pill. All healing starts in the mind. In fact, I've seen a 'so-called' miracle with my own eyes.'

'you have?' Saul raised his eyebrows and leaned toward him as Mac continued.

'I went to a sermon in America with a friend I traveled with. He was deeply religious, I'm not, but he didn't want to go alone, so I agreed to go with him. At the sermon, we met a lady who had been confined to a wheelchair for twelve years after a farming accident. She had fallen and fractured her spine in three places. Doctors told her she would never walk again... but right there in front of us, she was healed - by 'the lord' of course.' Mac used his fingers as quotation marks. 'The preacher simply told her to get up, God meant for her to walk again today, and that she should rise. Rise she did, and as far as I know, she's still up. The chair gone from that moment forward. She would say it was the power of God. I would say it is the power of belief. Her faith was stronger than the words of any doctor. There are no limitations except those we impose on ourselves.'

Saul's mouth dropped open and he leaned closer.

'He told her to walk and she did?'

Mac smiled.

'Seems like a miracle doesn't it? But when I spoke to her afterward she had known 'God' would help her, she'd already done the hard work. Her faith was strong and she already fully believed she would prove the doctors wrong. She had dreamed about it for years, visualised it, thanked God for helping her, moved her legs through the pain and stiffness every day, getting them stronger, believing she would stand on them again, until one day... boom. Church. All of her work and her faith came together into one, and she rose from the chair.'

Saul was on the edge of his seat now, and Mac could feel him almost bursting with what he wanted to say. He knew his own stories could go on, so he kept this one short and allowed Saul to tell his own.

'That's amazing, Mac, bloody amazing. Not just what she did, but the whole wheelchair thing. Do you ever think you stumbled on someone's doorstep, in the most unlikely of places, for a reason?'

Mac felt a grin cross his lips.

'I know you've saved me from a very lonely winter with my ghosts.'

'And I know you could be a godsend for our family.'

Mac felt a small amount of guard go up.

'I don't know what you think I can do, Saul, but I'm not a doctor and I'm certainly not a preacher.'

'This doesn't need a doctor, and the bairn isn't religious.'

'A child?'

'Eight. Let me tell you a story now. Ezzie was the most wonderful little girl I've had the privilege to be acquainted with. Bright, sunny, happy, always cheerful, always positive, always smiling. I always said if I could bottle what she had and sell it to my patients, I'd be a multi-millionaire.'

He paused to huff a laugh as he watched the fire. Mac waited until he was ready to go on.

'One day last year, out in Italy, she was snatched from the street, literally from under her mother's nose.'

Mac's mouth dropped open, his attention fully on Saul.

'Holy shit,' he whispered, and Saul nodded his head and lifted his beer bottle.

'Get another. I'm going to need it.'

Mac took the bottle and brought the last two over to the chairs, thanking the lord that he had put six in the fridge. He really didn't fancy tackling the corridor down to the storeroom tonight. He handed one to Saul, who took a drink immediately.

'What happened?' Mac said.

'Her father happened. There had been an argument, a violent one, that had been brewing over the course of many months after he and her mother split up. He threatened all sorts over those months, but never followed through. Until Italy. He got her all the way to Africa before we managed to get her home, but even that was only through the help of a friend who saw how unhappy she was, how unfairly she was treated by her father, and how volatile her life in Africa was. He thought she would be better with her mother, and got in touch, thank god. This man managed to smuggle Ezzie back, risking his own life, for us and for her. We collected her at Rome airport and brought her straight home to my parents. It was bloody lucky I was out of jail back then. A real bit of luck that I thank God for every day... and I'm not religious either.'

Mac stared at Saul as the story unfolded.

There's a little more than losing a career and serving a jail term to this guy's life. His little girl was snatched and here I am, moaning about losing my wife, which was always inevitable at some point in life.

'So, we got Ezzie home, but she couldn't walk. She complained of pains in her legs, pains in her stomach, pains in her arms. She made us carry her everywhere - or sobbed so dejectedly that we felt guilty for not. We took her to doctors and to hospitals, paid for private scans and private tests, but they all found nothing wrong.'

'So she is physically able to walk?'

Saul looked at Mac, the pain in his eyes clear.

'The tests confirm she can walk. There's nothing at all wrong with her, and yet, she sits in that wheelchair, looking dejected all day long. She eight years old Mac. If there's nothing wrong, then she needs to get out of the damn chair and start to move forward. Why does she sit there?'

'PTSD?' Mac said.

'More than likely, but she won't talk about anything that happened in Africa, she clams up. A physical injury or disease I could cope with, but not being able to talk to her about her ordeal, and to help her get better - especially when I've practiced successfully as both a psychologist and a psychiatrist? That hurts like hell and it's the most frustrating thing I've ever had to deal with. I think that this last year has been harder than jail.'

Mac placed a hand over his mouth.

'I understand, Saul, I really do, but I don't know how I can help. What can I do?'

Saul shook his head.

'I don't know. All I really wanted was confirmation that she could be talking herself into this, and that it is completely possible to talk herself back out of that damn chair… and dance again, and smile, and laugh, and make fun of me like she used to. I guess I just need to keep working on her, working with her.'

'That's all you can do. If there's one thing I've learned from this business, it's that the mind will work just as hard against you as it will work for you. It all depends on where you put the focus. If she doesn't want to come out of that chair, for whatever reason that may be? Then she won't come out. Simple.'

'But not easy.'

Mac smiled.

'Exactly. Hard as hell.'

Saul raised his bottle to Mac.

'At least I know for certain that she *can* do this. There's nothing physically wrong, we know that, I just need to get inside her head and see what's going on. Thanks for that, Mac.'

'I wish I could do more. I have done nothing for you.'

'You've done more than enough. I'm more certain going forward, even if nothing is seeming to work, especially as her mother and my parents just treat her like this is how it has to be. They don't even want to try to get her out.'

'I'm sure that's not true.'

'It's not callous. They love her, and they care about her. They just don't realise that *she* is the key, not something external.'

Mac sipped his beer.

'I think you're right, and given the profession you're in, you're the perfect person to get her to open up.'

Saul huffed a breath and brought a hand to scratch the back of his head.

'But none of it is working!' he said, slapping his hand back to the settee.

'It needs time, that's all.'

'It's been a little under a year now. How much time does she need?'

'How long is a piece of string?'

Saul ran a hand over his brow. It was obvious to Mac that his frustration came from a place of love, but even so, he knew now better than anyone that these things couldn't be rushed.

'Listen, it's like me, isn't it? I finish grieving for my wife when I'm done. I don't know when that will be. And yes, it's frustrating, annoying, and darn emotional, and I don't want to keep crying forever, but I still have to wait it out. Nothing more I can do. I tried to keep working, I tried to suppress my grief in the beginning. I ended up quite possibly ruining my career. It can't be pushed. I understand that now.'

Saul nod his head.

'I know, I get it. It's just so bloody-'

'Frustrating.' They finished together.

They grinned at each other over their beer.

'What did you do, Mac? Before? What did you so eloquently ruin after your wife passed?'

Mac faltered. He didn't know how well he was known out here, and certainly Saul didn't seem to recognise him, but it would only take a google search and he would be back in the land of the living. Once people knew who he was, there was no getting away from the change that overcame them, and the way they treated him.

'I was a teacher,' he said. 'I taught about the mind and about opening up possibilities, and potential.'

Saul was nodding. He gestured toward Mac.

'About the life map that doesn't exist.'

'Right,' Mac said with a grin.

'Where did you teach?'

'Oh, all over. I travelled a fair amount to different establishments.'

Mac felt his heart step up a gear.

That's enough now, Saul. At the moment, I haven't really lied, and I don't want to get into that business.

Saul contemplated this with a frown, and Mac knew that he was weighing up the travel with teaching, which normally didn't go too well hand in hand unless it was unorthodox - as he supposed his teaching was.

Get him off the subject then.

'You said something about a lady last time.' Mac said quickly, registering his own words a split second after he spoke them, and mentally gritting his teeth.

Anything but that, Mac, you could have said anything at all. Why that?

Saul looked at him, his frown now disappearing into surprise.

'A lady?'

Mac's heart banged behind his ribs.

It's this or the job, Mac, which would you rather?

Mac pursed his lips and picked at a spot of apple that had dropped from the pie onto his jeans.

'Here,' he said. This train of conversation was better. 'You said there was a lady here before.'

'Aye, and you said there was only your brother.' Saul was nodding.

'I was thinking it could have been his wife, that's all. He obviously just didn't tell me. I was going to phone him, jibe him a little about being an old romantic, but I want to get my information right first.'

Saul finished his beer and leaned into his fleece pocket to bring out a packet of cigarettes. Mac felt something in him give at the sight of them. Whatever this man was about to say about the lady that was here, Mac thought he may well need a crutch.

'Is it a smoking kind of story?' he said.

Saul laughed. 'I was moving them from digging into my back. I don't like to presume I can smoke on other people's property, so I don't bother. You smoke?'

'I shouldn't,' Mac said. 'I used to an age ago when I was young. When I met my wife, I gave up. She hated it.'

'So now she's gone?'

'Back to my old tricks and habits, I suppose. We can smoke, as long as we take it outside. If I burned my brother's cabin down, he would more than murder me.'

'Shall we?' Saul said, rising and offering the packet to Mac.

Mac reached for his coat, and Saul shrugged on his own.

They stood outside the front door of the cabin, overlooking the truck, which was covered in a film of white, and lit only by the light from the cabin windows. The trees were dark, Snowy grey pathways leading off into who knows where before disappearing completely into the blackness. Mac gave a little shiver, half cold, half disturbed by how dark it got around here. At least the snow had slowed now.

'Shit,' Saul said with a shiver, zipping his coat up to his chin.

Mac turned to look at him as he stepped away from the porch and looked out toward the loch.

'I'm going to have fun getting back over there tonight.'

Mac joined him to look at the frozen edges of the water. The middle still appeared wet. He shook his head.

'No, you can't. You'll drown or freeze to death. I have a spare bed upstairs. It's a single don't worry, although if you're that bothered, you can sleep on the sofa, and I'll throw you some blankets.'

Saul looked at him, and then back to the boat.

'I should be okay, once the ice is out of the way-'

'I'm offering you a bed. Take it. You're lovely ma doesn't want to find her son floating in the loch tomorrow. And I'd quite like him to bring more apple pie, beer and ciggies.'

I'd also like it very much, not being alone in this damn cabin any longer than necessary. One less night alone would be an absolute bonus.

'I don't know what to say,' Saul said, turning to him.

'Yes is the only word you need. Your ma will thank me for it.'

Saul nodded his head, a relieved smile spreading across his face.

'Thanks, Mac. I didn't fancy freezing back across the water when I've just got toasty warm. I've had too many beers, too.'

'Too many to paddle a boat?'

'Too many to walk. I'm not usually a big drinker.'

Mac grinned as Saul offered him a cigarette and a light.

'Let you into a secret, neither am I. I haven't had a lads' night this lively since I was mid-twenties.'

Saul laughed, and Mac joined him, enjoying the acrid taste of the smoke as they puffed in companionable silence by the door.

'The lady was his wife. They both confirmed that when my partner saw them initially.' Saul said. 'I can't tell you why she was here, but it was nothing romantic.'

Mac turned to him, cigarette dangling from his lips. He had forgotten all about the conversation before they had stepped outside.

'It was Tom's wife? How did you meet her? Here? Similar to us, now?'

Saul shook his head, blowing smoke.

'No, that was strictly business. To tell you the truth, I didn't know about this little cabin until I had to come here. She called me, had to guide me along the lane to find the driveway.'

Mac found the whole setup weirdly wrong. How did he have absolutely no knowledge that Meg had been here?

And how did Meg guide him when Tom says she didn't come here? And Meg didn't even know the saying that Saul had said he'd heard before, did she? About watching nails growing?

Mac knew he had to bite the bullet.

'What did she look like?' Mac said, and Saul chuckled.

'You need help to remember what your brother's wife looks like?'

'I'm just thinking...'

'He maybe had an affair?' Saul interjected. 'Well, that would certainly explain the reason they were here.'

Mac felt his jaw drop. The cigarette fell, bumping off his coat, and landing on the floor.

Fuck! Tom had an affair?

No.

Tom had never had an affair. Mac had never met a couple more in love than Tom and Meg. And if Tom had an affair, then...

'Fuck, I didn't think of that, to be honest. But yeah, he did say his wife hadn't been here... and yet he turns up to you at your practice?'

Saul nod his head yes.

'If it was him, of course.'

Mac loosely described Tom, who to Mac sounded like every other man with fair hair in his forties. Saul agreed it could have been him until Mac mentioned the large BMW - yes, that was what they arrived in, Saul said. A Large dark blue one. Mac had felt his stomach drop through the floor.

'Right, and he turned up with a lady he called his wife?'

'That's pretty much how it went, aye.'

Mac swallowed hard. He was suddenly frozen. His skin felt solid like ice, as though he would crack and shatter if he moved.

What did she look like?' he repeated.

'Oh, that's easy, she was a beauty.' Saul said. 'I still remember her to this day, quite a presence, even though she wasn't particularly well when I saw her later. She was about your height, deep brown eyes, and almost back hair, really curly. So long.' He held a hand just below his shoulder.

Mac staggered back to the cabin wall, putting a hand out behind him to catch his weight. Saul didn't appear to notice.

'As I said, she wasn't too well, but she was dressed nice, floaty skirt, cute top, quirky necklace. It was quite warm back then.'

'Sula.' Mac said.

Saul turned to look at him with a frown.

'Sorry?'

'Sula. That was her name.'

Saul shook his head.

'No, buddy. Her name wasn't Sula, it was Nicky. He introduced them as Tom and Nicky Devlin. I remember it well. I was in the foyer with Sarah at the time. I have a good head for names.'

Mac felt bile rise in his stomach. He turned and staggered indoors, leaving Saul to put out his cigarette and follow him inside. Mac was holding onto the banister, one hand on the necklace in his coat pocket as Saul shut the door behind them.

'Mac? You okay?'

Mac pulled the necklace from his pocket and held it out to Saul. Saul grasped it in his fingers, looking at the small metal design in his hands. He frowned and looked back at Mac.

'What's this?'

'Found it by the pier today. I just wondered if you recognised it.'

'Well, it's the same sort of design the one the lady had on when I came here if that's what you mean. Similar, anyway. Other than that, I can't tell you anymore. If it was by the pier, she probably dropped it... or maybe lover boy ripped it off in a frenzied attack of passion, eh?'

Saul began to laugh and clipped Mac on the shoulder. Mac clenched his fists at his side as he felt the heat bring colour to his cheeks. Saul caught the look on Mac's face and fell silent.

'What's the matter?'

'The description you gave very closely matches my wife, Nicky or not, her name was Sula... and this was her necklace.'

Saul looked back down at the necklace and Mac saw the implications click together in Saul's mind, he almost heard the clunk of the pieces fitting together. 'Oh bugger. Mac, you know, this may not have been an affair at all. I was only joking-'

Mac lost patience, hitting a fist against the railing behind him.

'No? Then what the fuck was it? Why the hell else would Tom introduce her as Nicky and pass her off as his *wife*? And why the hell would she let him? What was going on?'

Saul held his hands up and took a step back.

'I don't know, Mac, calm down. You're not even sure this was your wife yet.'

'You said-'

'I didn't know her, Mac, how can I tell you for sure. It was also two years ago, before I was even in prison. A lot has happened since then.'

'You said you remembered. She had a presence. You were certain, remember?'

'Of course, but I'm not certain it was your wife now, am I?'

'But I am! Her bloody necklace is here, solid fucking metal with an engraving I had put on the back of it! And she was *here* with *him*? What the hell for if not... *that*!?'

'Mac, you don't know-'

Mac pushed off the banister, throwing his hands up at Saul.

'I do know! I have her necklace. Found here. She was here, whether this was your lady or another of his fancy women. She was here! What the hell was she here for?'

Saul shook his head, raised his hands against the force of Mac's words.

'You do know. You visited her here.'

'I... Mac... I don't want-'

Mac lunged forward, grabbing the bigger man by a twist in the front of his coat and forcing him back to the wall.

'You know! Tell me. Why was she here?'

'I can't.' Saul said, closing his eyes, and drawing his lips under his teeth. He was anticipating a punch, and at the sight of him Mac suddenly lost all fight. He'd never hit anyone. This was the closest he'd ever come.

'Please,' he choked. 'Please, I just need to know why she was here.'

Saul opened an eye, nodded his head, and pushed Mac's hands down away from his jacket gently.

'Mac, I understand, I really do. But you still don't know for certain that this was her. I can't go around giving medical information about whoever was here, it may have been nothing to do with Sula at that time, and it may cause unnecessary problems.'

Mac ground his teeth, his face hot and flushed, half ready to fly at Saul, half ready to break down into sobs. Unfortunately, the sobs seemed to be winning out again right now.

God, why are you such a pussy, Mac? This is stupid.

That's no way to talk to yourself, remember thoughts are things. Keep a check on your thoughts, Mac.

Go fuck yourself.

'I'm sorry,' Mac said to Saul, stepping back and trying to calm his breathing. 'I just...' He broke off with a gulp, pain reaching up into his chest from the pit of his stomach.

'Don't worry about it, I get it.'

'I didn't mean to...' he trailed off and brought his hands to his face.

Sula was here. I mean, I knew that anyway with the necklace, but Sula was here with Tom. **With Tom**. *Oh god, what was she doing? What should I do?*

Hands caught his elbows, and he brought his face away, aware that he had been speaking his thoughts aloud.

'Ring your brother,' Saul said. 'I know it doesn't get any harder than the implications of this, and I know he's the last person you want to speak to, but he's the only one with the information you need. The correct information. When you have that, go from there.'

Mac nodded as Saul took his hands away from Mac's arms.

'Yeah. But if it was her, if she was-,' a deep ache fired through his chest, he swallowed hard, 'if she was here with Tom, if it was her, you'll tell me why, won't you? If he won't?'

'Mac, I-'

Mac grabbed the sleeve of Saul's coat.

'You'll tell me, won't you? Please,' he begged. 'I need to know.'

Saul swallowed hard, his Adam's apple bobbing. He chewed on his lip and looked to the floor, and then to Mac's hand on his arm. Something in him seemed to shift as he looked back at Mac.

'I guess the patient's charter doesn't really stand if I'm no longer a practicing doctor and the patient is deceased,' he mumbled.

'So, you'll tell me? Everything you know. I want every detail.'

Saul seemed about to backtrack. He opened his mouth, closed it again, looked at Mac, and nodded slowly.

'Okay. If it was definitely her - confirmed - and your brother won't say, then I will tell you what I know.'

Mac dropped to his knees and sobbed. He felt Saul's presence kneel next to him and clap a hand to his back.

'In these situations, Mac, it's best to make that plan, set that goal. Even if I tell you what happened, there's nothing you can do about any of this now. Make that plan and walk forward,' he said softly.

Mac nearly choked on the laughter that bubbled up from his stomach, fighting for attention with the tears rolling down his cheeks.

'That's my line, you shit,' he guffawed.

Saul grinned through Mac's teary vision as he looked up at the bigger man.

'One I'm keeping in my inventory for times like this.'

Mac wiped his tears, more replaced them, and the ache in his chest deepened.

'Oh fuck, I'm in for a night of this. I'm sorry. You'll never come again. My drinking buddy is lost.'

'No chance. I'm enjoying the chats, and you may be able to help me with Ezzie. Let it out. It's good for you to address the emotion, feel it. Let it come, and then let it go.'

'Oh, stop being such a fucking psychologist!'

'Head barman suit you better? I'll grab us a drink or two if you like?'

'Make it several, you have to sit with this too.'

CHAPTER THIRTY-FIVE

MAC FELT A CLOUD hanging over him the next morning. After breakfast, Saul had left to make his way home, after asking if Mac wanted him there for the call to Tom. Mac didn't. He knew the answer already. It was too much of a coincidence for this not to be Sula. The question was, would Tom admit it, and would he tell the truth about why she was here with him?

An affair.

The words dragged heavy daggers through his stomach.

They had all been close - all four of them - but Mac would never have considered bedding his brother's wife. Meg was a sister to him, nothing more. He loved her to death, but the thought of her naked turned his stomach. Sula was different, though.

Sula was beautiful. She turned heads wherever she went, not least because she was no wallflower. Her loud, raucous laugh without a care for who was watching, and her enthusiasm, lust for life, and fun were infectious. Not only that, but she could be an incorrigible tease. If Mac had retained any kind of jealous streak, they wouldn't have lasted two minutes, never mind seventeen years. Sula enjoyed winding both men and women up. Putting them under her spell, she called it, but she had never been so full on with Tom, had she?

How do I know what she did when I wasn't there?

How does anyone? She didn't know what you were up to when you were away either, remember.

'But I wasn't *doing* anything!' Mac yelled. 'That's the difference. She *was*.'

Rolo whined at Mac's outburst.

'Okay, yes, I know. I *think* she was. I *hope* she wasn't.'

There was a steady drip, drip, drip, from the corridor. Outside, the air was cold and still. The snow had stopped falling early in the evening; the ground was still white. Mac closed his eyes.

'Fuck,' he muttered, 'I suppose it could be snow on the roof leaking in.'

Could be.

'Could be a puddle of water in the corridor.'

Could be.

A shudder ran through him. He grabbed his coat and strode out of the door and to the pier where they had broken the ice for Saul to sail home. Last night he hadn't given a toss about the noises, the puddles, the shower, but now he was alone again, the whole thing was exacerbated.

I don't want to be here.

'No choice Mac, suck it up and phone Tom, will you? Let's understand what the hell is going on here.'

He shook the snow off the chair on the deck and sat down in it, purposefully facing away from the cabin and its haunted, dark windows.

He pulled his phone from his pocket and stared at the screen.

Tom had called him yesterday. Many times.

Thirty-six, to be exact.

A brief flutter of fear found its way around Mac's ribs.

Were they okay? Had there been an accident?

Adrenaline pushing all thought out of his head, he dialled Tom's number and heard it ring.

CHAPTER THIRTY-SIX

Tom stared at Meg, who was standing in his office, arms folded as she leaned against his desk. Her backside pinched the very papers he was trying to sort to the wood, meaning she had his full attention until she decided she was done with him and left to go home.

He wanted her to go, wanted to sort the mess here. He didn't have time for this. But she sat anyway, glaring at him.

Stalemate.

Her angry frown was one he didn't see directed at him often. He felt a little like a rabbit caught in the headlights. He picked a pen from the desktop and tapped it against the wood of the desk.

'What do you want me to do, Meg?'

'Call him.'

'I have.'

'Again.'

'Okay, I will, but I just-'

'Now.'

Tom put the pen down. It took some restraint not to slap it onto the wood.

'Okay.' Tom pulled his phone out of his jeans pocket and placed it between them. 'He probably won't answer.'

'Well, call again.'

She folded her arms tighter, cheeks read, mouth a hard straight line, giving him no leeway.

'Meg-'

'And again, and again, and again. Until you have him. If you don't have him by this afternoon, pack your bags.'

Tom reeled back in surprise.

'My bags? Meg-' he cut off as his phone screen lit up and began to ring.

'Don't you dare answer that,' she said with a glare as he moved his hand toward it.

Tom looked down at the screen, his mouth curling into a smile. He picked it up, showing the screen to Meg.

'It's Mac,' he said, almost giddy with relief. Relief that not only was Mac alive and well enough to talk, but that Meg wasn't kicking him out of his home today either.

'Well, bloody answer it then!' Meg said, leaning to swipe the screen with her own finger and pressing the speaker phone button so that she could listen in.

'Mac!' Tom said, placing the phone back between him and Meg. 'Good to hear-'

'Tom? What's the matter? Are you okay? The kids? Meg?'

Tom glanced at Meg.

'Fine, we're all fine, Mac. Calm down. Everyone is good.'

'Good? So why the fifty thousand calls yesterday? God damn it, Tom, I thought someone had died!'

So why didn't you answer any of them?

'I was trying to see if you were okay after the last time we spoke. You didn't seem in the best frame of mind, and I was worried when you didn't answer any of my calls, that's all.'

'I'm absolutely fine. I was busy yesterday. I don't always keep my phone glued to me. I probably didn't hear it.'

Tom exchanged a glance with Meg and she gave a small smile, the relief coming off her palpable. Gliding on her relief, Tom gave a laugh.

'Busy? It must be bloody freezing up there by now. What the hell were you doing that you couldn't hear the phone in that small space?'

Tom heard Mac shuffle something, his voice far away, and then coming back loud.

'It's not so bad, it's rained mostly, the first snow fell yesterday but today is only just white over. I wasn't outside, anyway. I was having a drink with a friend. I didn't hear the phone over us talking.'

Megs' face fell, and Tom felt her apprehension. His alarm bells were already ringing at the back of his mind.

'Drinking? Beer?'

'Ale.'

'Where did you get Ale from?'

Tom shook the disbelief from his mind and looked at Meg with a frown. She held her hands out to him, palms up. He shrugged back.

'Saul brought it over with him. As I said, we were probably too loud; but that's not why-'

'Saul? Who is this person, and where the hell did he come from?'

'He was out walking and knocked the door for a drink a few days back. I think he lives around the loch somewhere because he was back last night with some beer.'

Tom slapped a hand to his forehead and brought his elbow to the table. He rubbed a hand over his face.

'Mac, there is no-one around the loch for bloody miles. A walker? How far had he walked?'

Mac shuffled again, the line becoming muffled and then clearing. He coughed. Tom felt his heart begin to bang.

'Six miles, I think. I can't remember now. What the hell does it matter, anyway?'

'Of course it matters! I've never had a single-'

'-person visit the cabin,' Mac finished for him. 'Never see a soul, Tom, I know. But I have. Get over it.'

Meg put a hand to her mouth and Tom knew that she had thought about what had just crossed his mind, too.

'Mac. You need to be careful out there, really. You don't know who the hell this guy is! What did he want?'

'Want? He came for a chat and a drink, Tom.'

'And that doesn't strike you as odd? Out there in the middle of nowhere?'

Tom heard Mac sigh.

'Tom, this isn't what-'

Tom slapped his hand on the desk. Meg jumped and closed her eyes.

'Mac. You are in the depths of the wilderness, there's no-one for miles. I haven't seen a soul in all the times

I've been up there, why would someone just be walking around there on the off chance now?'

'He was walking, Tom. He needed water. I filled his bottle, and we had a chat. The guy turns up to repay the favour with beer a few days later. What's the problem?'

'There's no-one around there to just pop back with beer to repay the favour!' Tom yelled. Meg placed a hand on his shoulder and squeezed.

'There obviously is! Maybe the vibes when you're here repel people for miles. I don't know Tom, but this is a very real man. I'm not going crazy and having imaginary drinks with the ghouls!'

Tom closed his eyes and swallowed hard. If he had got this, and Meg had clicked, why was Mac not catching on.

'Do I need to spell this out for you?'

Now there was a clatter from Mac's end. Tom winced and drew away even with the phone sitting on the desk.

'Spell it out, Tom, please fucking do. Then maybe I can get on to what I want. I'm sick to death of the games.'

Tom sucked a breath between his teeth, and Meg shook her head slowly. A warning. Don't bite back.

'This is not my game, Mac, it's yours.' Meg kicked at his shin. He held a hand up to her. 'Last month when you called, you said that the letters were being moved on the fridge. Your name, you said, and who had I sent to mess with you? Remember that?'

'So, this is the guy that-'

'Don't be an idiot, Mac. Listen to yourself. You said there was someone up there messing around, and then this guy turns up out of nowhere?'

'I'm pretty sure Saul didn't write my name on the fridge.'

'How can you possibly know? You need to be very careful out there, there's no-one around for miles. You think there's someone in the cabin when you're out, and now this man turns up out of the blue? It's a bit of a coincidence. One I'm not sure I like.'

Meg picked at the skin on her fingers, a worried look on her face. Tom knew why, but this wasn't those men. If the man he had seen on the fire escape yesterday had been one, then they were down here in London, not up in Scotland. After him, not Mac.

Ah, but there was only one down here, though...

Fuck.

'You're wrong,' Mac said.

Tom frowned, and Meg snapped her gaze back to him.

'You don't know-'

'There is somewhere around here. A house. Not too far from the cabin, with real live people in it.'

Tom felt the floor disappear from under his feet. A house? The chair seemed to scoot to the left, and he fell to his knees. Meg frowned at him hard.

'No, Mac,' he gasped.

'Yes, Tom. I was there, sailed around the loch and came upon the garden. The lady there was kind enough to take me inside and give me a bag of apples. It is not in my head. I had a very real bruise where I fell off the garden wall. I can reach the house within an hour of the cabin. Not so far.'

Tom struggled for words. Meg got off the table and began to pace.

Not that house. Was there any other house around there? Oh god no, He hasn't been to the clinic? It was too far, surely, a good ten miles by road.

A hot flush swept the back of his neck. Meg was mouthing something to him, but he couldn't make out what she was trying to say. His thoughts raced.

Why on earth did sending Mac to the cabin seem like such a good idea?

'So, there are people, Tom.'

'I've never sailed past the bend on the loch,' Tom murmured, more to himself than Mac.

'Well, now you know what's there... a house. People. You aren't so isolated, see?'

Tom licked his lips, which felt like they hadn't seen moisture in the last forty years.

'Mac, -' He began with a croak, but Mac cut him off.

'And this man, the one you think would be idiotic enough to doodle on my fridge? He's a fucking doctor, Tom. I think his IQ may extend above fridge magnets. He's a good bloke repaying a favour. That's it. I like him. I'm not four anymore, and you cannot tell me who I can and can't see out here.'

Tom thought he was going to throw up his lunch. The man was a doctor? What were the chances?

One here to get me, one there to get Mac... You're a stupid, stupid man, Tom.

He slapped a hand to his head, still on his knees, the room spinning uncontrollably.

'Mac?' he breathed.

Meg was now standing with her back to the door, as if she wanted it to open up and send her somewhere exotic. As if she wanted to be anywhere but here, listening to this. Her face was pure horror, both hands over her mouth as she issued a small moan.

Mac went on, barrelling right over any noise he may have heard his end.

'The other thing is, Tom, I want to know what the fuck my wife was doing at the cabin. Why was Sula out here?'

Meg slid down the door to her heels, her face ashen.

CHAPTER THIRTY-SEVEN

'Your wife?' Tom said, his voice sounding far away and hazy on the other end of the telephone. Mac seethed. He scraped his boot against the wood of the pier floor.

There was obvious guilt in that very question. As if he hadn't known Sula at all. Anger flared, and all thoughts of trying to extract the truth became a full on an accusation that Tom would have to admit to instead.

'Yes, my *wife*.' Mac spat. 'Surely you remember Sula? Dark-haired, beautiful, died last year. Left her fucking necklace at *your* cabin.'

There was silence from Tom's end, and Mac's anger crept up another notch. Surely, he must know that the silence said more than his words.

'No,' Tom said, finally. 'Sula has never been to the cabin, Mac. You must be mistaken-'

'Liar!' Mac screamed, grasping the phone so hard he felt his frozen fingers may snap right off.

'No, Mac. Calm down-'

Mac held the necklace in his other hand, string dangling from his fingers.

'I have Sula's necklace in my hand. Rolo dug it up from under the pier,' he yelled. 'How did it get here, Tom? The question is simple.'

Rolo was sitting a safe distance away, warily watching his master from the corner of the cabin. Mac saw his head cock to the side, regarding him. Mac pursed his lips as there was a thump from within the cabin.

Not a thump... a thrum. His heart leapt into his chest and began to thud.

Can this not wait until I've finished on the phone?

Mac turned his back to the cabin and walked out onto the pier as he waited for Tom's answer, which was taking far too long for a simple question.

When Tom answered, he was too composed, too trite, and Mac's guard immediately went up.

'Mac, why on earth would Sula's necklace be at the cabin? If you've found something the dog dug up, it was probably from bloody years ago, another owner ago.'

'It's Sula's,' Mac said through gritted teeth. 'I think I would know my own wife's necklace, and it has an engraving on the back. From me.'

There was a beat of silence, and then Tom sighed, long and loud.

From the cabin came a high D, long and resounding, as though someone had a foot on the pedal, lengthening the note. Mac closed his eyes.

'Mac, you can't have. Sula has never been to the cabin. I promise you. When would she have chance? you two were always jet setting around the world.'

'I'm looking at it. Do not take me for a fool, Tom. Why the fuck was my wife at this cabin?'

Mac's voice echoed off the surrounding mountains and bounced back to him over the water. Rolo turned tail and disappeared behind the cabin, out of sight.

'I don't know...' Tom stopped, and Mac almost heard the gears click into place. 'Ah, I remember! There was one time. She didn't stay, but yes, she was there. Meg brought her to pick me and Josh up. The truck had broken down. You were in Versailles if I remember rightly. Sula was with Meg. They came together.'

Mac swallowed. Every fibre screamed lies. Saul hadn't known what he was saying when he described Sula, and Tom's voice had a slight hitch when he spoke, which hadn't escaped Mac's attention.

But Saul also wouldn't have known Sula. He may well be describing someone else. Maybe. There was nothing concrete. Not really.

'Mac?' Tom said, quieter now. 'You're upset. The cabin plays games when you're there a long time. It messes with you, I've told you that before. If you have a necklace that is engraved and you think it's Sula's, then yes, it probably is. She has been up there. It's not completely out of the question. You need to come home, Mac. Can you get the truck out while the snow is light? Abandon everything and come back. We'll sort this here. I can explain.'

'No,' Mac said.

'Mac, please–'

'The truck gets stuck in the mud. I tried to come home yesterday. I'm staying.'

For better or worse.

Inside the cabin an E resonated, an octave above middle C. Mac winced.

'Then I'll come to you. I can either collect you, or stay with you, but Mac, you can't stay on there alone, and pl-'

'No,' Mac said with a loud swallow.

From the cabin, more notes were playing - a melody. A melody that not only pierced Mac's heart, but brought a moment of clarity, a moment of understanding.

Sula.

Goosebumps rose under his coat.

As Tom protested and begged in the background, Mac thought he may have the answer to the activity that seemed to plague him in the cabin - real or imagined.

The song played on behind him. Fur Elise. A simple song, one of Sula's favourites.

You have an amazing imagination, Mac, if that is in your head. Or maybe you're asleep, and it's all a dream.

'Mac? Are you still there?'

Mac pulled his attention back to Tom.

'Yes. No, I'm not coming home, and I want to be alone. I don't want you here Tom... and I don't believe you.'

'About what? Mac-'

'Sula. She was here. I don't know why, and I don't know what the hell you were playing at, but I'm going to find out.'

The music in the cabin was getting louder, the melody flowing smoothly, rising and falling with the rhythm of the music.

'Mac, I told you-'

'I don't care, Tom, don't come here. I need to be alone with this.'

'Mac, you don't understand! There's more to this than you realise. The man, the doctor, he's not to be trusted, he's the one who will tell you the lies. I don't want you hurt, Mac. I can't explain right now...'

No, that's just it Tom, you never can. Secrets and lies.

'Goodbye, Tom,' he said.

'Don't listen to him, he wants to hurt you-'

Mac pressed the end call button, and the phone lapsed into silence. He flicked the volume onto silent and leaned on the small rail of the pier.

In the cabin the melody played on, full and rich, the player lost in the music they played. If Mac walked in now, he was certain that Sula would be sitting on the stool, hands fluttering across the keys, as large as life.

His bottom lip quivered, and a lump of lead sat in his chest. He hitched a painful breath.

Right now, he wanted nothing more than his wife. Just her. To go into the cabin, to see her turn, and rise, to hold her in his arms and feel her hold him. He wanted to lay her by the fire and make love to her, to never let her go again.

The first tears fell, but Mac swiped them away.

Something was sore in the feeling now, something wrong... a wound had opened, raw and bloody. A wound that he wasn't sure he would be able to fix, especially if no-one would tell him the truth.

Saul had no reason not to.

But Tom had just said that Saul wanted to hurt him...

'Hang on,' He murmured, standing upright, one hand on the rail. 'If Tom never sees anyone here, then how does he know Saul is going to lie? How does he even know the man? Unless...

Unless he went to see him with Sula. Unless Tom and Nicky Devlin turned up at his practice and asked him for treatment of whatever kind. Unless Sula asked him to come to the cabin.

Because if Nicky Devlin wasn't Mac's wife, then there would be no reason for Saul to want, or need, to hurt Mac anyway, would there?

Mac's heart was beating so fast he felt dizzy.

Saul was a psychologist, so what were they talking through together, Tom and Nicky? Their relationship? His relationship? And why so far from home? Shedding guilt?

An affair.

The music in the cabin stopped, an eerie silence flowed onto the pier.

Mac wondered briefly if Meg knew. And then he leaned over the railing and lost what little he had eaten for breakfast.

CHAPTER THIRTY-EIGHT

'YOU LIED.' MEG SAID, her eyes not only full of hurt, but disappointment, as she sat on her heels at the door.

Tom looked back at the phone with a tight nod of his head.

'Why?'

'He can't know, can he? You said yourself the other night, he's been through enough. I couldn't tell him. I didn't want to, Meg.' He put his head in his hands, phone between his elbows on the desk, the screen now dark.

He felt her hands go to his shoulders. She increased pressure, digging her thumbs right into the muscles at the side of his neck, just where he liked it. He groaned, but she stopped and draped her arms over his shoulders, clasping her hands at his chest and resting her chin on his head.

'Don't stop,' he said.

'I'm not sure you deserve it, Tom Macauley.'

She took her hands from him and perched back on the side of the desk where she could see him. Tom almost squirmed. The only thing he hated more than lying to Mac was the look in his wife's eyes right now.

'I didn't know what else to do,' he whispered.

Meg pursed her lips with a nod.

'But there are a couple of men out there that possibly wish him harm, and maybe you, too. Have you sorted the phone calls? Do you know what they want? Or if it's even them.'

Tom worked his jaw.

'No.'

'No?' Meg said. 'So maybe we've got it all wrong, maybe they were just silent phone calls after all then, yes?' The relief in her voice was evident, but Tom frowned and licked his lips.

'No,' he said quietly.

'No?' Meg whispered.

Tom looked at his wife, the worry etched in the lines on her forehead, the dull fear in her eyes, the rhythmic biting at her bottom lip. He wished he could take it away, that he didn't have to tell her any developments, but she would be twice as thrilled about being lied to as she was about his lying to Mac.

'The doctor at the cabin was one of them, wasn't he?' she said.

Tom nodded and ran his hands over his head with a sigh.

'I think so. It's hard to say, but how many more doctors can there be out there in the wilderness? How many that know about Sula?'

'Are you sure they're out of jail, Tom? This isn't something completely unrelated?'

'One was out around eighteen months ago or so. I waited for the backlash, but it didn't come so I thought it was over, that was it. The other one served longer, I think. I don't know when he came out.'

'So how do you know-'

'Because I saw him!' Tom said. 'I've seen him. Watching. He's been at the baths, at the store, across the damn road here.'

'You're being stalked? Tom, that is not acceptable. Call the police.'

'There's been no other contact than the watching lately. There's no crime against standing in the street, is there?' He heaved a sigh and placed his head in his hands, elbows on the table. He looked up at her.

'There must be something they can do,' she said.

Tom shook his head. 'I have a horrible feeling I know why he may have gone quiet, too.'

'Why?'

'If the other one has Mac up at the cabin, then they've put two and two together and come up with four, haven't they? They know that Sula and I had false names, and they've found out that Sula was Mac's wife.'

To Tom's surprise, Meg began to chuckle. He looked at her, horrified.

'I don't see what's so funny.'

'I don't see what bloody difference that makes Tom, you were the one who shopped them. If they want to be pedantic, you and Sula. But not Mac. Not her husband. What the hell would they want with Mac?'

'To get at me? I don't know. Mac is easier to hurt. He's alone. I have people around me down here, don't I?'

'Mac didn't do anything to them, Tom.'

Tom creased his brow together.

'But Meg, you said the other night-'

'I know what I said,' she said, holding a hand up to him. 'But now that I've thought about it, it's a silly idea, isn't it? Why would they bother?'

'To get at me!' Tom shouted, prodding a finger at his chest.

'Why would they need Mac to get at you? If they're that crooked, they'll come for you, Tom. How in the hell would they know who Mac is anyway, and how would they know he was at the cabin?'

'It's not hard to find anything about Mac, is it? If he's told the good doctor who he is, and he's googled Mac, he's surely seen Sula with him. That's how Mac knows she's been to the cabin. He's starting to pick at me already.'

'Sula saw the doctor over two years ago now. I really don't think-'

'What?' Tom said, slapping his hands on the desk as the heat ran up into his cheeks. 'That they've forgotten the faces of the couple that did them over? I don't think so.'

Meg stared at him.

'Well, in that case, maybe you shouldn't have done it, Tom, eh?'

'I couldn't turn a blind eye-'

'Why not? Because you felt guilty? What you do here is almost as bad!'

'Shhh.' Tom grit his teeth and glanced at the door before looking back at Meg. 'It absolutely is not. What we do here is for the good of the teenagers we help. Look at all the thank you cards. Look at the children we've helped. Look at them.'

He waved a hand over to a cork noticeboard full of thank you cards and photographs.

'So if I rang the police now, you wouldn't go to jail too?'

'No!' Tom said. 'This is not the same.'

Meg got to her feet, her face beetroot, the same shade as Tom's felt.

'I say it is! You know nothing about the bairns they helped up there, and that was the issue. Bairns who have got themselves into a situation they need help to get out of.'

'I deal with children that have got themselves into drugs, and got themselves into a mess, Meg.'

'As did they,' she stormed back at him.

'I do not do backstreet abortions for twelve-year-olds!'

'They are in a mess, just the same. You heard one conversation, Tom. One. If anyone listened in up here, they could charge you with exactly the same, and with the drugs you supply to bairns too.'

'I do not-'

'And where are those bairns going now? The ones who can no longer get help because you shut that clinic down? What will happen to them now?'

Tom grabbed the pen pot off the table and threw it across the room. It hit the door with a crash, pens flying across the room. Meg didn't so much as flinch.

'Where would these bairns go if you weren't here under the guise of a well-to-do private clinic, Tom? Where would your bairns end up if I shut you down?'

Tom kicked over the chair and took a step toward Meg.

'Whose side are you on?' he spat through a clenched jaw.

'Yours, Tom-'

'Could have fooled me!'

'I am, but I can't pretend I know why you've gone so deep into the things you supply, either. You started this clinic as a way to help. Not as a way to underhandedly supply to children! As much as I know that you're not a bad person, Tom, I don't agree with it either.'

'You've never said anything about it before,' he said, his breath coming in bursts.

'I trust you,' she said. 'I trust that you know what you're doing and the reasons behind it. But I think the stupidest thing you ever did was to call the police on that day, Tom. The stupidest!'

Tom swallowed hard, his anger dissipating almost as quickly as it had arrived.

'I didn't know you felt like that,' he said.

She sighed heavily and stepped toward him, winding her hands around his back, and tilting her chin to look at him.

'Now you know,' she said. 'You know what I would like, right now?'

He shook his head.

'I would like you to sort out who the hell the stalker is, find out if the doctor is any danger to Mac. Pay them off, whatever it takes, and then, Tom, I'd like you to quit.'

Tom startled, and pulled away from her.

'What?'

'Quit. Close it down,' she said, hands now across her chest, arms folded tight. Her mouth was a thin line, her eyes serious.

'Here?' he whispered, and began to shake his head as she nodded hers. 'No, Meg. I've built this up from scratch. It's the clinic I always wanted it to be, right now-'

'It's immoral.'

'It's not. I promise you-'

'I want you to quit. And then I want to move away, far away.'

'No,' he said, his face as stern and serious as hers.

'Then I will shop you in, Tom.'

His mouth dropped open. He frowned as his heart thumped.

'You wouldn't.'

'Oh, I would. I'll give you two weeks to sort this mess and quit. In whatever way you see fit, but this clinic is not what, nor why, you started it up, Tom. Get out before I start thinking you're as bad as the crooks you put in jail.'

With that, Meg turned on her heel and left, slamming the door behind her.

Tom let out a breath as he staggered back against the desk.

This can't be happening. What the hell is going on with my life? Why is everyone against me? What we do here isn't that bad...

But even as he thought it, he knew the clinic had got out of control over the last two years. Profits were up, but not for the most legal of reasons. If Meg dialled the police, he could well be in the same position as those crooks in Scotland.

Worse still, if the watcher dialled the police... returning the favour.

Tom closed his eyes and dragged his hands down his face.

Then he picked up his phone, found the number the caller had used saved under silent call in his contacts, and pressed the dial icon.

CHAPTER THIRTY-NINE

M AC SMELLED COPPER.
Blood. So much blood.

It trailed up the corridor in three pools, and Mac felt his stomach churn and gurgle. He closed his eyes and placed a hand over his nose and mouth. When he opened his eyes, they were no longer there. He shook his head, frowning at the floor, but there were no pools of darkness.

You've gone insane, Mac. Doolally.

He blinked and narrowed his eyes, but the corridor was clear, right up to the bathroom door. Where his heart almost stopped.

The bathroom light was on, the door allowing just a slit of light around its edges.

The tap squeaked off and there was the ripple of water from the small room. The smell of musk now overpowered the smell of copper. Mac gagged, his head beginning to ache.

'Mac?'

Mac looked toward the bathroom, every nerve in his body beginning to thrum and light up, charging him with a nervous energy that he thought would have carried him for miles if he would just open the goddamn door and run.

RUN, MAC!

He turned to the door, breathing heavily, wiping the sweat from his head with a shaking hand.

'Mac?'

There was a sob, and a gentle weeping. The sound so melancholy and empty that Mac had to bite on his fist to keep himself from joining her.

'Sula... I can't... I...' He said, his voice raising goose bumps, every hair on his head feeling electrified and lifted.

'Mac?'

Mac moaned and leaned against the stairs. In the bathroom the weeping increased, sounding haunted and hollow.

Mac felt himself turn and walk slowly to the lit door, the corridor seemed never ending - the door always in sight, but never coming any nearer - and yet he reached it far too soon. Mac turned to stare at the wooden door, Sula's sobs emanating from behind.

He gasped for air. His lungs so empty he thought he would die if he didn't get oxygen, and yet the breath didn't want to go in, like there was a blockage in his throat.

'Mac?'

Mac felt the terror rise as tears streamed down his face.

'Sula, No... I don't want to... don't make me look.'

He gasped sobs of pure fear, joining her soft melancholy sobs from the other side of the door. He watched his own shaking hand - at least he thought it was his own

- reach forward and pushed the door. It opened with a long, drawn-out creak. Too heavy, too slow.

Shaking hard, and thinking his heart may give out at any moment, he looked inside the small room.

The dim light showed the shower curtain shut. A small pile of clothes sat next to the tub.

Red. They're stained, red. Blood, Mac, it's blood.

A small whimper escaped his mouth as he moved forward, keeping his eyes on the clothes and the curtain.

Giddy with fear, and yet unable to stop, he reached out a hand to open the curtain, but a small, fairer hand beat him to it. Long fingers appeared from around the vinyl plastic, and drew it slowly aside with a long screech.

The bathtub was full, the water a deep red. A pair of knees appeared as the curtain drew back.

'No, Sula,' Mac whispered and fell to his knees.

The curtain opened fully, and she sat, head almost on her knees, tears falling from her mascara painted eyes.

'Mac? Why won't you talk to me?'

Mac sat aghast, trying to catch his breath.

'I... I...'

'Mac?'

Mac could do no more than stare. His knees on the white tile of the cold floor. Before him Sula rose to a stand, beautiful olive skin perfect in its naked glory, a small thatch of hair between her legs the only imperfection to the smoothness.

'Mac?'

Mac stared as she stepped from the tub. The water that ran from her body ran clear, as though the bath had been filled not with blood, but with red food colouring.

Better, Mac. The red isn't blood, it's food colouring, that's all, see? And your dead wife isn't rising from the bath because this is all a dream, a horrible, masochistic dream. You'll wake in a minute, and all will be normal.

He wanted to close his eyes, but he was fixated on the sight of his naked wife before him. He couldn't look away.

Sula tilted her head, and tears dripped from the end of her nose onto the floor.

She looked so sad that Mac felt his own heart swell as she spoke again.

'Why won't you talk, Mac? It's me.'

Mac closed his eyes. When he opened them, she was squatting in front of him, the smell of musk and something dead mixing to form a stench unlike anything he had never known.

'Mac?'

'Sula?' he whispered. Her eyes were black. Not the usual deep brown; jet black, with no pupils. He struggled for breath, whimpering as he tried to scoot away from her.

'Talk to me Mac.'

Now she grinned at him, her jagged teeth, rotten, yellow, and broken. Not the straight, white, wide smile that Sula had worn in life. The stench that poured from her mouth made him gag and wretch, and he turned himself onto all fours, determined to get out of the bathroom, and out of the cabin.

A hand grabbed the waistband of his jeans, and he gasped at the ice cold feel of it.

'YOU WILL TALK TO ME!' she roared, dragging him back.

Behind him, the water sloshed and splashed, and red appeared on the floor, running around him - thick, warm and sticky. It covered his hands, his knees, his shoes. The metallic stench overpowering.

Mac held his red hands up before him.

Blood. A blood bath.

Panting, he looked back to the tub. Blood was now pouring over the sides in thick torrents, pooling around him, and leaking out into the corridor. His gaze landed on Sula, next to him. Her body now streaked with red, her face a mask of rage and anger.

'YOU. WILL. TALK. TO. ME!'

She grabbed his hair with a sticky red hand, and before he could make a sound, she smashed his head onto the tile floor with a sickening crack.

Mac felt his world go dark.

It was dark when he woke, still lying on the freezing tile floor of the small bathroom, his joints aching with cold. He lifted his head, and a bolt of pain ran through it. feeling his stomach shift and grumble, he crawled to the toilet just in time to lose the contents of it into the hole. He grabbed the wooden seat to pull himself up off the floor, anything to get out of the...

He looked around the pristine bathroom. Clean white floor, clean bath, the curtain pulled to the side as he had left it last time he had been in there. No blood, no trace of water, no clothes, no Sula. It was as though she had never been there at all.

'She probably hasn't. How many did you sink last night, Mac?'

He had to admit; after the chat with Tom he had lost count at eight before he passed out on the settee.

It was a dream. No, fuck that, it was a nightmare of epic proportions, probably brought on by the beer.

He staggered to his feet and looked at his face in the mirror. The stubble was becoming more of a fully-fledged beard that covered the lower half of his face since he had refused to shave, but the skin above was pale and sallow, his haunted eyes ringed with darkness.

He checked his head and found an egg-sized lump just above his temple. He touched it with a wince.

That's the last time you drink, buddy, you obviously fell. What if you'd died right here in the bathroom?

The fucking bathroom, of all places.

He shook his head and threw some sawdust down the toilet to cover last night's beer and dinner. From the doorway came a whine, and Mac turned to see Rolo staring at him, a pained look on his doggy features.

Mac stepped forward to stroke the dog's ears, but the dog shrank back, dodging his touch and disappearing back down the corridor to the living area. Mac peered round the door to see the dog watching him with uncertainty.

'Was I that bad? It's just me, Rolo.'

He moved from the room, using the wall for support as he made his way into the corridor. The floor was clear. Rolo bumped his tail half-heartedly.

'Yeah, see? Just me-'

There was a small rattle and a bump from the door opposite. The storeroom.

Mac hesitated.

'I don't need any more of your shit, Sula,' he said, although he didn't know how much of this shit was in his head, anyway.

The storeroom remained silent, and Mac reached across to push open the door, one hand still on the wall at the opposite side of the corridor.

In the middle of the floor was a small sandwich bag, and spilled from the bag in cheery colour were the magnetic fridge letters. Mac licked his lips.

Talk to me Mac. Why won't you talk to me?

Mac felt his mouth fall open.

Is this what you meant, Sula? It was you on the fridge?

Of course! Who the fuck else, Maccy boy? Coco the fucking clown?

Mac stooped to pick up the letters, putting them back into the bag.

'Okay, baby. I'll put them back. Let's see what the fuck you have to say, eh?'

He gave an odd chuckle that raised the hairs on his own arms as he took the letters and placed them back onto the fridge, muddling them into the middle in a bunch of colour.

He stared at them as Rolo gave another whine.

'I know, buddy,' he said to the dog, 'I'm going mad. I'm actually losing the plot. I've gone. An absolute fucking loon. The cabin *ate* me!'

He laughed as he strode to the settee, grabbed a cushion, and placed it on the floor in front of the fridge.

'Let's see what's so important, then. We've nowhere better to be. If you want to talk. Goddamn talk.'

He plopped down cross-legged on the cushion, folded his arms, and stared at the letters.

CHAPTER FORTY

SAUL MONTGOMERY WAS TRYING to keep calm back in the bedroom of his parents' house. Being home was a ball ache when he couldn't work, made a thousand times worse by the fact that his time as a doctor was effectively over. He rolled his finger over the wheel of the mouse, scrolling the screen downwards.

One of the conditions of coming home was to find himself a new career - or a new job at least, to tide him over until that career turned up. He scrolled past pages of uninspiring drivel, and jobs that ensured that he was stuck under the thumb of someone else's dream. It sucked, especially after being the owner of his own practice for all those years.

He could take a minor role, he supposed, stay in the medical field, but that would mean working from a hospital or clinic, under their policies and procedures. Before there had been no commute, no set hours, no shifts, private patients, and profits that went into his pocket.

The screen blurred in front of him, and he thumped a fist onto the table with a bang. Pens flicked into the air and landed with a clatter next to his fist.

I was helping them. I was fucking helping them. That's what you get. Use your power for good, they said. Help people who need it. Plenty of those around here. Plenty that came. I didn't think they'd do the dirty across me.

I was fucking helping. That's the thanks I get.

He put his head in his hands, elbows on the desk, and rubbed his hands over his hair and down his face. The jobs on the screen blurred into one mesh of un-inspirational letters.

This was beyond a joke.

He clicked the mouse, taking the screen back to the Google home screen, clearing the rubbish from his view. The chair creaked as he sat back and placed his hands behind his head with a loud sigh.

He gazed out of the window at the mountain beyond and thought he may just take another hike. Get the hell out of this room.

You can't go back to the cabin again, he'll get uneasy.

Saul chuckled, his thoughts drawn to Mac. The other night had been interesting. Mac's expertise and view of the mind could seriously help Ezzie, but Mac was also a mess. His wife's death was raw, and now the insinuation that she could have been the one at the cabin a few years ago?

He pushed out a breath as the clouds scurried across the sky. Low and heavy, like they would drop more snow at any moment.

That wouldn't be a good scenario for either of them, not at all.

The cursor blinked in the google search box and Saul found some inspiration.

Mac said that he taught. Saul didn't have a surname, but he knew a face. He only needed an image to find out who

Mac was. Wasn't there an accredited list of teachers, like there were doctors?

He typed Mac and then Teaching Mind Expert into the search bar. Then he hesitated.

Maybe he should search his field of expertise first. If Mac were a teacher of the mind, wouldn't that make him a neuroscientist of sorts?

If he held that title, there should be a register with his name on somewhere, shouldn't there?

But there wasn't a need for any of that he found, as his hand accidentally hit the enter button, and Mac's face appeared before him. Chubbier, and clean shaven, but definitely the same man.

He clicked the first image, and an article appeared.

'Mac Macauley - the mind guy - is there a science behind the teaching?'

As he scrolled, there were more images, more articles

'Mindful madness.'

'The mind guy does it again - sell out shows in Stockholm.'

Saul read through a few of the articles with amazement that this was the man sitting in a cabin a few miles down the loch. A man with much proven expertise, and very capable of being able to help Ezzie where Saul had failed. Mac's framework was much the same as psychology, a study of the mind, but with one dramatic difference which could be make or break for the eight-year-old. Saul had spent his whole life letting people talk and linking where their experiences in the past had dictated a response in the future. In reality, he thought, what did that give people, anyway? Nothing tangible to work with, but Mac's work looked forward. It focused on changing experiences through rigid focus on the future, designing the future as you see it, and dealing with the obstacles and objections the mind put in the way.

Saul read down an article where Mac had explained a little more of the framework.

The past, he read, was irrelevant. The only time we have is the present and what you can work toward in the future. The past is gone. You can't change it. Leave the memories alone, and work only on what you want to create. That is the way people have made some phenomenal changes using the framework. It's about learning to change neural pathways, banish old ones and make new ones.

The biggest obstacle to people following through was not inability, but fear, he said. Fear came in many forms - loss of credibility, loss of security, financial or otherwise, loss of face. But mostly fear of the unknown. In a survey conducted by Psyche Magazine, a whopping 98% of people said that they would drop everything to follow a dream if they were guaranteed success...

Mac, you dark horse, you.

Saul licked his lips and read down a few more articles until he came to the more recent ones.

'Is the mind guy losing his mind?'

Saul hinged on the most recent article where Mac looked a little more like the man he had met at the cabin. He clicked on the article and read through. It told how Mac had seemed to lose his way, had forgotten what to say halfway through speaking, had finished shows early sparking outrage after the fees people had paid to hear him talk. He had looked dishevelled and wild-eyed at his latest talk in London, the article said, and most of the show he had been incoherent.

I can confirm he's a mess, but he's a brilliant mess. One that may just be sent from heaven to help us here.

He read about Mac's wife Sula and how she had died of an aneurysm the year before, just as Mac had said, but there were no photographs, no other information.

Clicking back to google he typed Mac's full name into the search engine and added wife before pressing enter.

Several articles came up about Mac, so Saul clicked the images button and came face to face with the woman he had seen two years previously. His breath caught. The woman on screen had obviously been attending something formal. Mac was clean shaven, and wearing a dark suit, with a tie the exact colour of his wife's dress. The dress hugged her figure to the knee, before it flared down her calves to strappy heels. The neckline, and the back, shown in a different photograph, plunged almost to her waist, her full bosom the only thing seemingly holding the strapless number up. Her head tilted at the camera, her full lips red, deep brown eyes alluring, dark curls amassed around her shoulders. Next to her, Mac paled into insignificance.

She had been beautiful, Saul thought. She had also been to the cabin, posing as Nicky Devlin, not Sula Macauley. Quite possibly with Mac's brother.

Saul let out a long breath and tapped his fingers on the desk before him with a shake of his head.

'What's the matter?'

Saul turned to see Ezzie in the doorway, eight years of thin frame disappearing into her wheelchair, which seemed to eat her whole. The lively and spirited young girl, a dancer of epic talent and dry as any stand-up comedian with her stories, being eaten by nothing more than her own thoughts if the medical profession were to be believed. Just last year her deep drown eyes and dark skin had glowed with health and vitality, her tight dark curls glossy and full of bounce. He took in her reality since the ordeal that had been the last year.

Saul wouldn't know anything about that at the time. He had been busy in jail, but he wished he could have known, and he wished he had been there in Rome, too. He would have torn the bastard limb from limb before he had taken her a step.

'Frustration, Ezzie,' he replied. 'That's all. I'll be fine, sweetheart.'

Ezzie looked at him with deep, haunted eyes. Her smile only made the sadness of it worse.

'When I get frustrated, I scream into my pillow.' she said.

Saul looked at her, the doctor in him immediately jumping to the fore.

'Do you get frustrated often?'

The half-smile slipped from Ezzie's face, and she shrugged her little shoulders, the movement barely noticeable.

'Is it the chair?' he said, but she shook her head slowly. He found his frustration growing. If she would just admit it, he could help her. Why couldn't she just say?

'It must be hard, Ezzie. You were going to be a famous dancer, remember? It's okay to feel frustrated by that. Maybe... Maybe you can learn to dance together with the wheelchair? Invent a new style? Or maybe you can learn to dance again without it? Come over here.'

Ezzie wheeled herself over to him, keeping her gaze on the floor. Saul caught her hands. Cold, and so small they could have belonged to a child of four.

'Stand up,' he said, pushing the thought away.

She stared up at him.

'Stand up,' he said with a nod.

Ezula took her hands from his and pushed on the sides of the wheelchair half-heartedly, barely lifting her own thin frame, before flopping back into the seat.

'That's not it,' he said.

'I can't, I can't walk,' she said, eyes back down on the carpet.

'I didn't ask you to walk, Ezzie. I asked you to stand.'

'I can't,' she mumbled.

Saul swung his chair round to face hers. He took her hands and stood, forcing the child to stand with him.

'See?' he said, holding her upright. 'You can stand. The doctors say there is nothing wrong with you, Ezzie. You can do this, it's all in your head. You're the only one keeping yourself in the chair. If you want to dance, you can get out, you don't need to invent any new dances. You can walk. You can do this Ezzie, you can!'

Boyed by his own enthusiasm and the longing in her eyes, he encouraged her further. Maybe this was what Mac meant about the woman getting out of the wheelchair and walking again. Belief, she needed belief, and someone to believe in her.

'You've got this, Ezzie. I know you have. You can walk. There is no more need for this chair. You can do it.'

Ezzie nodded, and Saul let go of her hands. She fell immediately, plopping back into the chair like a rag doll.

Saul plopped back into his own chair, gritting his teeth with frustration. With a heavy sigh, he put a hand under her small chin, tilting her face to his and wiping the large ears that rolled down her cheeks.

'I can't,' she whispered.

'You can. I promise you, you absolutely can. There is no medical reason that you can't. None. When you decide you can walk, you will.'

She shook her head, trying to drop her gaze, but Saul held her chin firm, forcing her to look at him.

'Ezzie. I believe in you. You are going to be the greatest dancer the world has ever seen.'

Another tear fell down her cheek, and she hitched a sob that Saul could have matched with his own. He let go of her chin and ran a hand over her curly hair.

He thought of Mac. Mac had to be able to help her, he was the last hope. Saul didn't know how he was going to do it, but he had to convince Mac to come here and talk with Ezzie. Somehow, he had to get them together.

'I know someone who may be able to help.'

Ezzie snapped her head up to him, hope in her eyes.

'A doctor?'

Saul was about to ask why she put so much faith in doctors when they didn't seem to be any help - and then he stopped himself.

Faith. Wasn't that what Mac had said she needed? Faith.

He nodded slowly.

'A doctor, yes. But a mind doctor this time.'

'Like you?'

'No, Ezzie, he's better than me. He's the best mind doctor in the world and he will absolutely get you walking again. Guaranteed.'

Ezzie blinked up at him through her tears and he swallowed hard, fighting back his own tears that she should have had this ordeal and have to be fighting through this.

'Do you believe me?'

She nodded her head.

'Good, because it's true, he is the best in the world at teaching minds to-'

The phone buzzed on his desk. He looked at the screen and rolled his eyes.

'Okay, Ezzie, we'll finish up later. I have to take this - important business.'

Ezzie rolled her own eyes with more emotion than she had conveyed since she had been back home. Without a word, she turned and wheeled out of the room. Saul shut the door behind her before pressing to answer.

'Greg?'

'Take your fucking time.'

Saul bit back a retort. Patience had never been one of Greg's strong points, and for an ex-doctor, neither was empathy. It was a shame he had got out of the slammer on early release last week. Saul felt the peace of the last twelve months shatter.

'What's up?' he said.

He had a feeling that Greg was going to ask him to go to Poland and start a practice there, as he had suggested before. Keep their credentials illegally and start over, but he was taken by surprise.

'I've only gone and found the bastard,' he said.

Saul floundered for his meaning, and then it hit. He closed his eyes and lay his head back against the door.

CHAPTER FORTY-ONE

M AC STARED AT THE magnets, which sat in the same position they had been since he had put them there over five hours ago. He shivered on the cushion, his anger growing in the cold, until he decided to forget it and light the fire. He pushed the dog's head off his lap and stood, holding the table for support as he uncurled his legs and let the blood flow back down them to his toes.

Rolo stood and shook beside him, before walking to the door and waiting, as though it would magically open itself if he stared at it long enough.

'I'm coming, hang on.'

Mac shook his legs and turned away from the fridge. He let the dog out, leaving the door open a crack for him to return, and then he went to the fireplace, grabbing the last few logs and placing them into the burner, along with newspaper and firelighters.

'Funny how you're so desperate to talk, Sula, but when I give you an outlet, you can't be arsed to say anything. Don't come to me with your shitty dreams tonight and beg me to fucking talk. You talk. And while we're at it, you can tell me why the fuck you were at the cabin that time. If you were having an affair, so help me god, I'll...'

He broke off at his own sentiment.

You'll do what to a dead woman, Mac?

'I'll kill my brother. I know that much.'

Mac sighed as the flames began to spread and the heat warmed his hands and cheeks. Rolo appeared and came to sit by the fire too, leaving the door wide open behind him.

'What's this? Were you born in a barn?'

Rolo flopped onto his side unaffected as Mac rose and shut the door. The fridge caught his eye as he turned back.

He couldn't be sure, but he thought the letters had moved a little. They were still in a messy bunch, but the word in the middle was straight.

NO.

Mac wrinkled his nose. He may have missed the sentiment altogether before, he couldn't be sure now if the letters had always been arranged that way.

'No, what? Your great desire to talk amounts to *no*?' he said.

Or maybe no to your question about the affair?

Nice one Mac, make yourself feel better when you have no idea whether it was already there, anyway. Hell, all of this could be in your bloody mind.

'Well, Sula being out here, that wasn't in anyone's mind. I know it, Saul admitted that it may be her, and Tom said she had been here if not stayed. That's the bit that cuts, Sula. That's the bit that really hurts. Why didn't you tell me?'

The cabin remained silent, and he huffed a breath. Then he strode outside to fetch more logs from the wood store. The cloud was grey, the day was grey, and the flutter of more snow was in the air, not so much visible as tangible. He could almost smell it.

His feet crunched on frozen ground to the store, the birds squawked in the trees, a rustle came from the forest, and the lingering resonance of a pressed piano key came from the open cabin door.

Mac paused.

Upper D, he thought, and began to collect the logs to take back inside as Rolo came running back out.

CHAPTER FORTY-TWO

Saul packed a couple of hot chocolate sachets and the beer into his bag, then he stooped to take the small pie from the freezer.

'Make sure it's defrosted, and remember to cook it-'

'On one eighty for about twenty minutes,' Saul recounted with a smile.

'Or until it's piping hot,' his ma said, raising her eyebrows and pursing her lips in admonishment as Saul leaned to kiss the top of her head.

'Will do, thank you, Ma.'

'Take these, too. Your friend may be able to make use of them.'

She handed him two small home-cooked loaves of bread. Saul's mouth watered. If the bread made it to Mac's, it would be a miracle. Seeing the look on his face, she wrapped them in foil and motioned for the bag, where she packed them inside.

'Leave well alone,' she said, pulling the strings of the rucksack to close it. 'there's more here, and don't stay out too long this time, you have a career to sort. This isn't a boarding house, and I'm not your maid.'

'I'll be back in a few hours,' he shouted over his shoulder as he left through the back door. His boat was up by the gate where he had stowed it earlier, ready for the trip.

He dragged it through the gate and to the loch, throwing the bag inside and pushing off before jumping in himself.

A swirl of excitement rounded his gut. He already knew that Mac was the one to help Ezzie. After reading all he could consume about the man, he couldn't quite believe his good luck. Mac had dropped on his doorstep by divine guidance. He had run out of water that day in an act of perfect synchronicity. They had been destined to meet. Now he just had to get Mac to agree to come over. If he was lucky, the threat of more pie and beer may just do it.

He dipped the paddles into the water and pulled hard. The exertion felt good. He felt good, more positive he had been in a good while. Something was going his way for the first time in a good few years, and he knew the change was down to his new friend.

Frigid air filled his lungs, the smell of cold loch and earth running through his nose. His cheeks and nose felt frozen, but the rest of him was warm as he worked. He reached the bend within twenty minutes and turned to see the little cabin, just a speck on the horizon from here. Saul grinned as he kept the cabin in his sight and pulled hard toward it, the boat cutting through the water like silk, the trickle of the loch around the boat and the dip of the paddles the only noise right out here in the middle.

Within an hour he pulled up to the pier, using it to push himself forward gently, until the front of the boat hit land. Then he climbed onto the pier and down to the shore, to pull it high out of the water. He eyed Mac's kayak, which still sat as it had when he had been here a few days ago.

An uneasy feeling fluttered in Saul's chest. Had Mac really been sitting in doing nothing at all?

Don't be daft, he could have been hiking. He also had a ton of books on the shelves to read. Just because the kayak hasn't moved doesn't mean anything is wrong.

The feeling still sat uneasily in his chest.

He grabbed the rucksack and moved tentatively round to the cabin door, which only increased his unease.

It stood wide open - even in this cold.

A shudder ran through him.

What the hell is wrong here?

For a moment, he had the urge to turn back. To forget everything and leave. If Mac had been murdered in there, he had no desire to see the body.

But if he's hurt, then he may need help, the doctor in him said, and he knew he would have to go in - like it or not.

He reached the door and stared into the darkness of the cabin. It wasn't dark outside, just gloomy, but the small windows of the cabin let in so little light in winter that Mac would surely be using the lights even in daytime.

His eyes adjusting to the gloom, he scanned the area. No movement, and no sign of Mac or the dog.

'Mac?' he called.

There was no reply, but there was a strange scuttling from inside. Saul took a step backward, unsure. He bumped into something soft, and staggered to keep upright as the dog wound itself through his legs and stood looking at him with his tail swinging like a pendulum, the fur that dangled from it black with dirt. He grinned.

'What on earth have you been doing? You're filthy!'

The dog jumped to stretch his paws up to his shoulders and lick at his face, and the stench of something rotten flowed from his fur.

'Eww, Get down, you smell bloody rank,' he said, wrinkling his nose and pushing Rolo away.

'He's been digging up the vegetables. Tom will be furious.'

Saul looked to the doorway to see Mac, but his grin faded at the sight of the man before him. Pale and sallow, unkempt hair and dirty clothes that Saul would have put money on him having worn last time he was here, back when he had stayed over.

He found out about his wife.

A sinking feeling seemed to pull him into the ground with triple the gravity weighing on his shoulders.

'Are you okay?' he asked.

'Not really.' Mac said, no trace of humour on his face.

Saul put down the bag with a loud swallow.

'I'm so sorry, Mac. It sucks, it really does.'

Mac said nothing, his eyes were focused on Saul but there was no life in them.

'She's haunting me,' he said.

Saul nodded and stepped into psychologist mode.

'I'm not surprised,' he replied, and the light came on in Mac's eyes. Saul saw them flicker with hope.

'You know?' he said. 'You believe me?'

Saul nodded and picked up the bag.

'It's cold out here, Mac. Let's go in and get a hot drink. Have you got a fire going in there?'

Mac shook his head but turned to go inside with a flick of the hand, which Saul took to mean he was welcome to follow.

Saul showed Mac the hot chocolate and Mac had nodded his head with a small smile. Saul made the drinks as Mac got the fire going, and the small space gradually warmed to a temperature that felt above zero degrees. Even the dog was sitting by the fire, he noticed.

Saul took the cups over to Mac, who was sitting opposite the log burner, hands on his knees, staring into the flames.

'Here,' he said, handing a cup to Mac. Mac looked up with surprise, as though he'd forgotten Saul was there at all.

'Thanks,' he said, taking the cup and wrapping his hands around it.

Saul sat on the chair and took a sip of chocolate, letting the warmth sink all the way to his stomach before he started.

'So, what's going on, Mac?'

Mac wrinkled his nose and then sighed. He ran a hand over his dishevelled hair, trying to flatten it down. Saul smiled.

'Mac, it's just me. You don't need to spruce yourself up. I'm not after a date.'

Mac grinned, and Saul felt a little relief flooding in. Mac was having a bad day, that was for sure, but he wasn't as far down the rabbit hole as Saul had first thought.

'It's a good job. Look at the state of me.' Mac looked down at his own three-day-old jumper, pulling it out to show Saul.

'That's nothing, you should see the beard and the hair.'

Mac went back to flattening his hair as Saul chuckled, and then Mac grinned and started to laugh.

'I'm a bloody mess, aren't I?'

Saul nodded. 'Aye, but there's only us boys here. What gives?'

Mac's grin fell away, and he pushed out his lips with a sigh of air.

'I don't know. I don't even know what to think of this anymore.'

Saul felt his brow crease and his own smile faltered as Mac flapped a hand toward him. 'What do you mean this?' he said.

'You. I'm not sure why you're here. If I can be honest with you, can you be honest, too?'

Mac looked pained, like what he was about to say made him uncomfortable.

'Absolutely. I've never been less than honest with you.'

Mac ran a hand over his face and down his beard as he looked at Saul. Saul watched him, mindful that there was some sort of altercation here that was important, especially if Ezzie was to have any good come from their meeting. He waited.

'I spoke to my brother, as you said.'

'About your wife being here?'

Mac nodded his head, and Saul struggled to keep up with the problem. It wasn't as if *he* had come here with Mac's wife...

No, but his brother did. His brother who came with the lady who stayed in the cabin. His brother who shopped us to the police right there on my parents' drive.

'Yes, I spoke to him about that-'

Saul held up a hand to stop Mac. He had a horrible feeling he knew exactly what his brother would say about Mac meeting the criminal doctor in his own cabin. Mac cut off and stared warily at Saul, as though expecting him to jump up and pummel him to death.

'Okay, I think I know where this is going. There is a link between me and your brother. Do you know what that link is?'

Mac drew his brows together, clearly puzzled.

'Link? What? No.'

'Your brother didn't tell you anything about what happened when he was up here?'

Mac shook his head and frowned. 'At the cabin? You met him here, too?'

Saul put his own chocolate at his feet and leaned toward Mac, making sure to keep his gestures gentle and open. Whatever Tom had said to Mac, it had put him on edge, and whatever he had said wouldn't paint Saul in a good light. The last thing he needed was to lose Mac right now, and besides, he liked the man. He was the first decent chat he'd had for years. There was something of a kindred spirit about him.

'You know he wasn't here, Mac. I met him at the clinic when he brought your wife. Your wife was here. I saw her just a week or so later, alone.'

Mac's mouth dropped open. He seemed about to protest, but Saul held his hand up again. He wanted to get the information in first, Mac could process it afterward, and Saul would stay and answer as many questions as the man asked. Especially as he was about to crush his world.

It seemed Mac wasn't about to wait, though.

'No, I spoke to Tom. He said that Sula was only here to pick him and Josh up after their car broke down. That was the one and only time she had ever been. The lady you saw here must have been someone else, maybe a friend of Tom's.'

Saul licked at his dry lips and thought about the way he could tell Mac that he had researched who he was without sounding like a stalker or an untrustworthy friend.

'Right, and she just happened to drop her necklace by the loch in that short amount of time.'

Mac looked at Saul.

'Well, she must have. Tom swears it wasn't her staying here. What's the link?'

Saul blinked.

'Link?'

'Between you and my brother.'

Saul took in a large breath of warm air. 'I'll tell you what your brother said first, shall I? He said that I was a criminal, not to be trusted, that I would be out to get revenge. I suppose that would mean getting to him through you?'

Mac frowned and bit on his lip in thought.

'Right?' Saul said.

'Not in so many words, although yes, he did say to be careful, and that you weren't a friend. You were here for other reasons. We had a huge row, and I put the phone down on him, so I didn't get around to what those reasons were.'

'I'll tell you what those reasons are, although I will also promise you that none of that is true. I like you, Mac. I fell upon the cabin by mistake. I didn't know you would be here, and I didn't know that I would like the man inside as much as I do. This - us -' he gestured between himself and Mac. 'This is completely unrelated. I can promise you that.'

Mac nodded. 'Okay, I hear you. Go ahead.'

Saul kept his eyes on Mac's; trust of utmost importance for what he was about to say about Mac's brother. No matter how they disliked their family, people would always defend them above everyone else, and Mac hadn't said that he disliked his brother at all. This could easily swing Tom's way, not Saul's.

'Two years ago, I went somewhere I thought I'd never end up, for unethical practices, and yes, some of what we did was illegal, although I will say, there was a lot more came out when Greg talked and his office was raided, than ever came out of mine. But I was guilty. I did some things to help people that I shouldn't have done, and had I known where I would end up, I would never have done them. However, we worked from my parents' house, in the middle of nowhere, in the back and beyond of the highlands. I had no such fear of being caught at all, and so, I was unashamedly doing what I shouldn't.'

'You went to jail, I know,' Mac said.

Saul nodded his head.

'I did, but just before I went to jail, a posh English couple made an appointment at the clinic and came up just a week later to be seen by my partner, Greg.'

Mac shook his head. 'Saul, I just don't see what this-'

'Please, hear me out. I want to be as fully honest as I can be. You asked for honesty. That means I have to start at the beginning.'

Mac shut his mouth with a nod and sat back in the chair, crossing his legs.

Toward me, which is a good sign, Saul thought.

'The English couple came up. Tom and Nicky Devlin, only the lady had an accent if I remember rightly. She looked and sounded European, maybe Italian, right?' Saul waited for Mac to get it. He did instantly, uncrossing his legs and leaning into Saul, his eyes showing both trepidation and interest. 'They made their way into my partner's room, were seen, and then sent on their way. A week later, I get a call to come out here. At that point, Mrs Devlin was alone, but three days later we had a lull in patients. Greg made his way into my office, and we began to discuss an earlier case, one I'm not too proud of. I won't go into details, but I deserved what I got in her case. As we discussed it, Greg joked about some other cases, and as you've probably guessed, Mr Devlin was in the doorway with a query about the medication and the visit to his wife three days earlier.'

'My wife.'

Saul opened his mouth to object, but Mac cut him off.

'I know it was. You described her perfectly the other day, described Tom perfectly. And you just said that she was Italian.'

Mac looked crestfallen, but Saul already knew that what he deduced was right. He had confirmed it in his research. Saul shrugged noncommittally, but Mac nodded.

'It was her. I know it was. I feel it in my gut. Tom lied, didn't he?'

'Wait a minute,' Saul said. 'Let me finish the story and then you can share yours. We'll see what we come up with together.'

Mac motioned for him to finish. He was a shade paler than when Saul had first arrived and honestly looked around ten years older. Saul felt guilty for putting this on a grieving man, but Mac had asked. He wanted to know.

'So, an argument ensued. I don't argue, I try to discuss and placate, but Greg just winds up and up. Finally, there was a full shouting match about our ethics, and what kind of establishment we were running. I knew it was heading for trouble when Mr Devlin - Tom - didn't argue too much. He listened to Greg rant himself into a corner and then he said that he would be phoning the police to see what they thought of our practice.' Saul pursed his lips and shook his head. 'Within three days we were shut down and being investigated while awaiting trial.'

Mac closed his eyes with a nod.

'Sounds exactly like something Tom would do. He gets on his high horse about many things. He doesn't stop to think of the consequences, or just doesn't care, I don't know. But then, I don't know what you were discussing, do I?'

'I can't tell you that, Mac. I will tell you I'm not proud of it. I did my time and now I want to put it behind me and start over. It's that simple. I don't need revenge, I don't seek it, I just want to live my life with no more trouble. If I never see your brother again, it will be too soon, but I'm certainly not out to get him. Or you.'

Mac chewed it over with a sigh as he stared into the flames of the log burner.

'Do you believe me?'

'Well, you're either telling the truth or you can produce a story that matches what I know of Tom's so far extremely well. Tom mentioned that you may want to hurt me, to get revenge, I think he said. I would say you have something to get revenge for, but obviously there's Sula too, and what you know of her that may be making him uneasy.'

'If it's her,' Saul said, playing it low key, allowing Mac to slot together what he already knew.

'It is.' Mac looked at Saul and nodded.

'Can you tell me... please?'

Saul hesitated. Mac was already on shaky ground, the information about the clinic may just tip him over the edge.

'Please.' Mac said. 'I don't care what it is. I want to take the information to Tom and gauge his response about why you would tell me the truth when you apparently want to hurt me. She was here, I'm sure of that, but why?'

Saul shook his head.

'Mac, however much you think you're prepared for that information; I'm going to tell you right now that you're not. It will open up a whole wormhole. I don't want to hurt you, really, you're already grieving, but that is one sure-fire way to hit you where it hurts.'

Mac seemed to pale further, and Saul saw his Adam's apple bob.

'It's that bad?'

Saul looked down at his hands with a sigh.

'Yes. In my opinion, it's that bad.'

CHAPTER FORTY-THREE

Tom went into the large garden of his home and began to walk as far away from the house as he could. He heard the door crash behind him and grit his teeth in frustration.

'Dad! Where are you going? It's getting dark, and you said you'd sink some hoops with me.' Josh said behind him, his breath coming in jagged puffs as he jogged behind him.

The door opened again, and Meg crashed out. 'Josh? Leave your father be. He has to check the pond's pump. The koi will die. Come back inside.'

'I'll look too,' he said, matching Tom's pace.

'No,' Tom said, stopping and turning to his son, 'Go back inside. I won't be long, then I'll come and sink some hoops.'

'It'll be too dark by then,' Josh pouted.

'So be it. Better basketball tomorrow than dead koi. Do you know how much those carp were?'

Josh rolled his eyes, and Tom noticed the dark smudges on his lips in the half light.

'Are you wearing lipstick?' he said.

'It's black,' Josh replied, as if that made perfect sense. Tom watched his son's back for a moment as he walked back to his mother at the door. She coddled him inside and shut the door behind them with a small wave. Tom sighed heavily and pulled his phone from his pocket as he continued down to the pond.

Finding the silent caller's number, he pressed to dial. The last three days he had left messages on the number's answerphone but, as yet, no one had got back to him.

His heart thumped as the number rang and he kicked at the dead leaves that were still hanging around the bottom of the lawn. His hands shook, the inside of his lip began to bleed where he chewed too hard, and he felt an instant headache erupting at the front of his skull. In all honesty, he could have sat down and cried with the pressure of it all - and he wasn't a crying man.

The ringing stopped, along with Tom's heart.

Please be the answerphone. I'll just tell Meg I got the answerphone again...

There was silence, and Tom's pulse rate slowed as he waited for the woman's voice to tell him to leave a message.

'Hello, Tom.'

Tom's heart jumped up toward his throat, blocking off his breath. For a moment, he couldn't breathe, let alone speak. The wind ruffled through his hair; its coolness causing him to shudder. The person on the other end of the phone waited patiently until Tom felt he would have to speak, or they would stay in a silence stand-off.

'H... H... Hi,' He managed, kicking himself for allowing the weakness to show through quite so soon. He had thought maybe after a couple of calls, but not the first. 'Hello.' He said more firmly, straightening his back.

Pretend you're at work. This is just a client.

'I've had this number call me a couple of times. I just wondered who this is, please?'

There was a deep, slow laugh that resonated through his body, and the hair stood up at the back of his neck.

'Who is this?' the voice said. Tom tried to decipher whether he had heard the accent before, but the man sounded like a million and one other Englishmen he spoke to every day. He had expected a Scotsman. One doctor had been English - the loudmouth - but it hadn't been his practice. The Scottish doctor had held the majority of the shares. Tom hesitated, and the man spoke again.

'The question is - who is this?'

Tom opened his mouth to speak and shut it again almost instantly, the question catching him completely off guard.

'Who is this?'

The man gave a deep, low chuckle, completely unhurried.

'What a wonderful game this is. I'm so glad you called, Tom. Who is this?'

Tom ran a hand over his mouth. He was beginning to sweat out here in the cool of the evening and it was leaving him cold.

'Who are you?' he said.

'Who are you, Tom?' the voice replied.

Tom frowned and huffed a breath.

'Listen, I don't know who the hell this is, or what you want-'

'What I want?' the man said calmly, cutting him off. 'You rang *me*, remember. Who is this, and what do *you* want?'

'You know damn well who this is!' Tom said, fear and anger merging in his chest. What kind of game was this man playing?

'I do. I just wondered if you knew who you were.'

'What? Why the hell would I not know who I am?'

'Well, Tom Macauley, it seems last time we met that your real name had slipped your mind. Does Tom Devlin ring any bells?'

A shudder ran through Tom, and he found the little bench by the pond, sitting down on it before his legs gave out from underneath him.

'Well, which is it to be? Tom Devlin or Tom Macauley? Maybe it doesn't matter at all because they're both you anyway, right?'

Tom's mouth was as dry as a barren desert, his breath caught in his throat, making a clicking sound.

'Are you still there, Tom?'

'I am. What do you want from me?'

'Well now, there's a lot to think about before I determine what you can possibly do for me in return for the little favour you did for me and my good friend two years ago. I think we need to meet and discuss it, like big grown-up men.'

The breath left Tom's lungs.

'N... No!' he stammered, 'I won't meet you, just tell me how much you want. You can have it. Name your amount.'

There was a sound like a breath hissed between teeth, and then a low chuckle.

'I'm not sure there can be an amount put on a criminal record, can there?'

'Any price.' Tom said, wiping sweat from his brow, the phone clammy under his hand. His heart pounded in his ears. 'Name it.'

There was a pause, like a consideration, and then the man was back.

'No, I don't think so. Meet me at the Horse and Jockey on Sherborne Street tomorrow night at eight. If you're lucky, I'll let you buy me a drink while we discuss business.'

'Eight? Eight. No, that won't work-'

'I'm afraid there's no choice, Tom. Tomorrow, or the consequences will be severe for you, your business, and your lovely little family. How many children was it? Three, yes. Nearly grown now, eh? Two girls and a boy - although he looks like he may bat for the other side. And, of course, your lovely wife. What a Celtic beauty she is. Fiery too!'

How the hell would he know that? How long has he been watching us? And what else does he know? Fuck!

Tom felt his heart slam in his chest. The phone tapped periodically against his head as his hand shook.

'Are we on the same page, Tom?'

'Yes,' he whispered.

'Good, until tomorrow.'

The phone went dead, and Tom was left frozen and scared on the pond bench. He stared at the phone's screen, willing it to ring, and for it all to have been a silly prank.

SURPRISE!!

It didn't.

Tom rose from the bench and looked up toward the house.

A figure in black stood at the opposite end of the small pond. Tom felt his stomach do a complete three-hundred-and-sixty-degree spin as his legs buckled and he sat down hard on the bench behind him.

This is it, Tom, you're toast in your own back garden.

And then the figure spoke.

'Who was that dad? And why were you offering them money?'

CHAPTER FORTY-FOUR

'SO, YOU'RE GENUINELY NOT out to get revenge, or to hurt me to get back at Tom, or blah-de-blah, but this Greg may be?' Mac said, beginning to relax. Tom could say what he liked about Saul, and maybe Mac was a bad judge of character, but he liked this guy. There was a very genuine air about him. If he was wrong and he was murdered, so be it, but for now, he would trust him.

He wanted to trust him, and he wanted to believe he had Mac's best interests at heart when he said that he didn't want to go into Sula's care. Speak to Tom about it, he had said. If Tom told him, he would tell the rest from a doctor's point of view, but he wouldn't be the one to tell him.

'No, not you. He has no clue about you. He only said that he'd found him. I presume he meant Tom. As far as I know, Greg has never hurt a soul. A few bar fights, nothing serious, but his temper can be serious, and he can certainly hold a grudge. If he's after payback of any kind, he will pursue it doggedly.'

'Didn't you ask him?'

'No, by asking questions, I want in. Get me? He's like a dog with a bone, and then I'll almost certainly be dragged in, too. To be honest, what we spoke about before? I'm thinking that this whole thing blew up to allow me an outlet to get away from working with him. Now that the break is there, I don't want to fall back in with him again. I'll just make my plan and move forward alone.'

Mac grinned and felt the rush of pleasure that always filled him when people not only understood and took on board what he said, but really processed and acted on it.

'Said with true positivity and faith. You'll be fine, Saul. You really will.'

Saul grinned back. 'So will you, Mac.'

Mac looked back at the fire, his smile slipping.

'I'm not sure about that. I don't know why everyone lied, Sula included, and I don't know that I can handle what's on my plate now, without the dessert that's to come. I'm already cracking under the pressure. Any more and I may just split wide open and end up in psychiatric care.'

Imagine that, the mind guy in the looney bin! What a hoot!

Saul sat forward and reached across to pat his arm, his lips pursed. Then he reached into his coat pocket, pulled out a packet and offered Mac a cigarette.

'Shall we go outside?'

Mac smiled gratefully. 'Nah, fuck outside, just don't burn the cabin down. I've been frozen inside for the best part of the day.'

'To be fair, you did have the door wide open when I turned up.'

'I lost it. I had a nightmare about Sula last night. I guess I just couldn't get it off my mind.'

'A nightmare? Not a good dream then.'

'Hell no! Sula in the bathtub naked sounds like an awesome dream, right? But this Sula was a demon, I'm sure, and she was bathing in blood, left it all over the floor.'

Saul sat back with a start, a small frown passing over his face. Mac joined in his frown.

'What is it?'

Saul shook himself, his face returning to normal, smile back in place.

'Nothing, someone walked over my grave, that's all.'

'Probably Sula.' Mac said, with no trace of humour. 'Anyway, all I could smell when I woke up was her perfume. I just wanted it gone.'

'Hence the door,' Saul said, lighting his cigarette and passing the pack and lighter to Mac. Mac shrugged as he lit his own. He took a long, deep drag, relishing the taste. He had run out of his own over five days ago now. He had thought he may just cold turkey give up - there was no choice, really. But now it appeared there was a choice, and it seemed he didn't want to.

He handed the pack to Saul, but Saul waved it back at him.

'Keep them. You'll run out way before me. I can get to the shop. That reminds me, if you ever need anything, let me know.'

'Thanks.' Mac said. 'I appreciate that. And these bad boys are the one thing I have run out of.'

They smoked in comfortable silence for a while. Mac watched the dog stretched out in front of the fire, and then he broke the quiet.

'How have you been, Saul? Making that plan?'

Saul wrinkled his nose and got up to fetch a plate for the cigarette ash. He placed it on the floor between himself and Mac.

'I'm trying. I just get side-tracked, you know. There's a certain little girl who I worry about a lot. She tends to take up most of my mind space at home. Just today I got her to stand, as I try to do every day, but she just plops right back down again. I keep hoping that one day it will click that she's supporting herself. I get so frustrated.'

'Whether she clicks depends on what is blocking her progress. The mind is a formidable opponent, you know that.'

'I know, I wish I understood more. I just wish there was something I could do for her.'

Mac felt the familiar surge of responsibility. Saul may not be able to help her, but maybe he could with his different approach. The man had been more than kind to him, and still may yet tell him what Tom wouldn't about his wife.

'I could come over and see her,' he said.

He knew he had made the right decision when Saul broke into a wide smile.

'Would you? Mac, that would be amazing, thank you. Thank you so much. I didn't want to ask, but I hoped you'd offer. You're about our only hope left. Are you sure you don't mind? Oh, I can't believe you'll see her. I can't thank you enough!'

Saul brushed a tear from his cheek and pressed a thumb and forefinger into his eyes as he looked away from Mac.

'No, I don't mind. It will get me away from here for a while,' he said.

And god knows I could do with that.

'I just can't thank you enough Mac. Really.' Saul croaked. He dropped to his knees in front of Mac, forcing Rolo to jump quickly out of the way, the emotion almost bringing Mac to tears with him.

'Get up you daft sod, of course I'll help. It'll do me good to get out of here for a few hours. But listen, I'm not a miracle worker, and I may make no difference at all, but if I can help, I will.'

Saul nodded, got up off his knees, and sat back down, blowing out a breath.

'Whew,' he said wiping his eyes, 'Sorry Mac, I guess I didn't realise just how much she was playing on my mind.'

Mac grinned. 'Well, I know how that one goes.'

CHAPTER FORTY-FIVE

M AC TRIED TO RING Tom that afternoon after Saul left, just as the light was dimming in the sky and the rain drizzled down relentlessly. Finally, he left a message, called Rolo indoors, and made a hot drink. They had only had two beers today, but even so, Mac wasn't going to bed on any alcohol after last night's sleep trip to the bathroom. Tonight, he would be very much sober when he fell into bed.

He stoked the fire and pulled a book he had yet to read from the shelf. Not a fan of any unfamiliar noises in the cabin, he set the speaker and pressed his phone to play some classical chill-out tunes in the background.

Outside the wind battered the windows, but in here for once, Mac was warm and cosy. The cabin bordered on hot, and Mac had stripped to t-shirt and jogging bottoms in front of the roaring crackle of the fire.

As the day lost the light completely, Mac lost himself in the book, his brain making new connections as both new and old theories poured over him. He hit on one bit in particular that may help the child when he met her tomorrow and grabbed a pen and paper to scribble notes. As those notes flowed, other ideas and parts of his framework came back until he had three pages of ideas and things to try. Each mind was unique. It depended entirely on the girl which way it would go. Normally, he would preach to his audience and let them go on their way, but this was a different scenario, working one on one, and especially with a child. An hour later, though, he felt prepared and ready.

He made another drink and curled back up with the book until he felt himself drifting off. When his nose hit the pages for the third time, he took himself to bed and, for the first time in a long time, slept soundly until daylight.

Next morning, refreshed and energised, he dressed in clean clothes and tried Tom again as he made his breakfast. He had purpose today, and it felt good. For the first time in a long time, he wanted to work. He wanted to help this child if he could, and without the pressure of everyday life, he knew that he could take the time to assess if what he was doing was working for her. It was nice to be able to have that one-on-one connection, too.

You'll see more than one living person today, Mac. How's that for socialising?

Mac wasn't sure he could even remember how to socialise with anyone other than himself and Saul. He wondered if he had descended into grubby male grunt language without even knowing it. He supposed Saul would have picked him up on it, but then if Saul was like him, maybe they were both using grunty man language, unaware of each other's.

Mac combed back his hair, which was getting longer now, almost flopping into his eyes at the front, collar length behind, flecks of grey following it down amongst the brown.

'It's only been four bloody months,' he said to his reflection in the window. He didn't want to use the bathroom mirror. Didn't like to use the bathroom at all if he could help it.

He took it easy until 9.30am, listened to a voicemail from Tom saying that he would be in touch later, and then decided to set out in the boat with Rolo. Saul said that he would meet him at an inlet on the loch at 11ish. He just had to keep looking right, and he would wave. Mac flustered about the time. In his old world, time mattered enormously. There was always a schedule, a plane to catch, or to miss. Saul didn't seem to mind, though. He was laid back. He would be there when Mac arrived, he said, whatever time that was.

Mac could only deduce that his house must be right on the loch.

'Come on then, buddy,' he said to Rolo, who was rolling on the mat, having a good scratch. Mac waited as the dog wreathed, and then he finally gave up watching.

'Rolo!' he yelled.

The dog spun to his feet, his front legs splayed as he looked at Mac from under his hairy eyebrows.

'Come on.' Mac motioned out the door, but Rolo only lunged sideways with a bark.

Mac rolled his eyes and put his hands on his hips. 'It's not play time. It's boat time, come on.'

He motioned outside and the dog eyed him, waiting for a movement that said Mac was up for a game. Mac went to the kitchen to fetch a dog biscuit instead.

'Here,' he said, 'we have to...'

Mac paused as he caught sight of the front of the fridge. The magnets had moved, all but three had been pushed to the side and the 'no' that had appeared a few days ago was gone.

'You been playing with the magnets again?' Mac said, throwing the treat to Rolo, who caught it deftly in his teeth and crunched it loudly, spilling bits onto the wooden floor. Mac looked back at the fridge. In daylight, the writing didn't seem so ominous, especially as he was going to be out for a good portion of the day. He studied the word.

ZUL

'Zul. Zal, Sal?' He said, cocking his head to the right. 'Sool. Sool? like zuul? Ghostbusters! I get it, baby. I am the gatekeeper, or am I the key master? Either way, I've got to go. I'll think on it.'

It was only on the boat that it hit him what the fridge may have been trying to say.

Sula.

Shit. It really is you, isn't it? But I don't believe in ghosts. Please leave me alone, baby. If I know you're actually in there, I'll never be able to sleep again.

'Are you listening Sula?' he said aloud, just in case she couldn't read his mind. 'Please leave me alone. I don't need to live with a ghost. If you have a message, spit it out. Why you were here would be nice, and then just go. I can't deal with you anymore.'

And I don't have to for a few hours, he thought as the sun shone down on the boat for the first time in weeks. It was cold, but cold and sunny he would take. He grinned as he paddled the boat away from the claustrophobic cabin.

Maybe things were finally looking up.

CHAPTER FORTY-SIX

MAC ROUNDED THE BEND and continued along the centre line of the loch as it thinned to what looked like a wide river rather than the loch it resembled from the cabin. His strokes were steady, the boat smooth on the water, and it felt enormously good to be away from the cabin again.

You should have come out earlier. There's been many days you could have come out in the boat. It hasn't been too bad.

Mac grimaced at the realisation that he had sunk so low into what was going on in the cabin and Sula that he just hadn't seen a way out.

Perception. Should have just opened the door, he thought ironically. How many people honestly thought they were stuck in a situation they said there was just no way out of, and Mac had always told them there was a way. Always a way.

There is, but it took a while for me to find it.

Let's not slip back down there again, Mac. I didn't like it.

He pulled at the paddles harder, enjoying the exertion and the endorphins that had been absent for too long now. Then he saw something in the bush line ahead. A few more strokes, and he saw Saul waving his arms on the shore. Rolo barked and raised himself up onto the front of the boat majestically. Mac raised a hand and turned the boat toward Saul, half sorry that he had been so near, and the journey hadn't taken him another half hour onward.

You can come up this way any time. Maybe you should.

He vowed that he would explore the loch to its far reaches before he left the cabin if he could. A plan, he thought with glee. A plan and a goal, you're finally going forward, getting focused. He reached Saul, who strode into the water to help Mac pull up the boat.

'Hi! Hi!' he said as Mac disembarked. Together, they pulled the boat up into the shelter of the trees as Rolo jumped out and sniffed about. 'How was the journey?'

Mac grinned at his friend. 'Great,' he said, 'I should have done that long before now. I've been sitting in that damn cabin.'

'The boat was there the whole time,' Saul said clapping him on the back with a laugh.

'I know, couldn't see the woods for the trees, but I feel refreshed now, so much better.'

'Cleaned out, Ma would say. Come on, they're all excited to meet you.'

Mac forced a grin.

'Who's they? I thought this would be us and Ezzie?'

'Well, you know after I told Ma and Da they were excited to meet you, and Ezzie's mother, of course. That's everyone though, I promise.'

Mac raised his eyebrows. 'Excited to meet me?'

Saul reddened. 'Well, they're excited to see what you can do for Ezzie... you know.'

'Why do you look a little guilty, Saul?' Mac said, standing his ground as the man turned to walk away from the water.

Saul looked back, lips pursed, his eyes flicked to the sky, and he rubbed his nose. The gestures didn't escape Mac's attention.

'Saul?'

'They're excited to meet Mac Macauley, the mind guy.'

Mac felt lead settle in his chest.

'How long have you known?'

'Just a few days. It's only the family that knows, that's all. We don't see anyone else up here. They all know to keep it secret.'

'They'd better or my cabin days will be over long before they're supposed to be. No-one was to know.'

Saul came back down to Mac, who was still standing by the boat.

'Mac, I promise you. They won't say a word. My family are completely trustworthy.'

'I really hope so.'

Saul turned away, and Mac grabbed his arm.

'Saul, you know this doesn't change anything, right? I don't normally help people this way. It still may not work. I will try my best, of course, but no promises.'

'I know that,' Saul said, 'and I've told them that, too. Don't worry.'

Mac nodded, and they started up a path that seemed vaguely familiar.

'What made you hunt me down?'

Saul laughed.

'I wasn't hunting Mac, I promise. I was trying to find any connection between you and the lady who was in the cabin. I knew what she looked like, and I knew you taught mind science, so I typed in Mac teaches the mind or something of the sort and...'

'Loads came up, eh?'

'It blew my mind. I had no idea, really. You looked a little better scrubbed up back then, I must admit.'

'Thanks.'

Saul grinned. 'But it confirmed that the lady from the cabin was your wife. There were a number of pictures of you together and that was definitely her, I'm sorry.'

Mac shrugged. He didn't want his mood to fall before he got to the little girl that today was all about. He looked behind and called Rolo, who was lagging behind to sniff new smells.

'I kind of knew, don't worry about it. Tom is ringing me this afternoon. I'll confront him with it. I need to know what the hell was going on.'

'You absolutely do... but be prepared before you ask.'

'I will.'

They reached a stone wall lined with trees and a small wooden gate, which Saul opened. They walked through and déjà vu fell over Mac. He looked at the trees. Apple.

'You live here?' Mac said.

'Aye, all my life. Me, my little sister, ma, and da. In this big, cold, rambling old stone house. Too many rooms, that's why we based the clinic here and paid the olds rent for the rooms. Helped them out and they helped us out.'

They continued over the grass as the house and the outbuildings came into view over the sweeping lawn.

'I've been here before,' Mac said. 'I didn't recognise the inlet or the path now winter has properly set in.'

Saul looked at him sidelong.

'You've been here before?'

'Yeah, not too long ago, maybe a couple of months? I was out on the boat and pulled into the inlet.'

He left out the fact that he was chasing fire after human company like some weirdo.

Saul began to chuckle. 'Thank god for that. I thought you were going to tell me you'd visited the clinic too. More skeletons in the closet!'

'None in mine,' Mac huffed.

Before them, a blonde woman waved an arm and jogged across the grass toward them. No skirt today, Mac thought. Jeans and a blue jumper with wellies. No bun today either; her hair was loose, trailing behind her as she approached them with a grin that stretched from ear to ear.

'That's my sister-'

'Maddie, yes.' Mac cut in. 'We've met.'

Saul swung his head to Mac, whose grin was matching Maddie's own. Rolo ran ahead to greet her like an old friend. She stopped to fuss him and then continued on with him bounding at her heels like a star-struck lover.

'You met? Where?' Saul said.

But now Maddie was already calling.

'Hi! Mr Macauley! It's a pleasure to-'

She cut off with a frown as she reached them. Saul eyeballed them both as they all came to a stop in the middle of the lawn, house looming above them.

'Meet you?' Mac finished for her.

She swiped his arm with a gentle tap.

'Mac! I knew I knew this dog. Why didn't you call or text? I've had apples stored for you for months. I kept them aside, so that Ma didn't use them.'

Mac flushed and shrugged an apology.

'Saul was keeping me in apples,' he said, shifting responsibility to her brother, who held his hands up.

'I have no idea what the hell you're talking about.'

'Apples.' Maddie and Mac said simultaneously.

Mac looked at Maddie with a grin, only to find her grinning back, sunlight dappling a golden halo around her head. Her eyes full of amusement.

'Well, thanks for letting me know my role was taken. We could have talked travel. Saul doesn't know much about that one.'

Mac huffed a laugh. 'I'd still like to talk travel.'

'Then message or call, dumbo.' She said, linking her arms between him and Saul as they started toward the house. 'So, how much has Saul told you about Ezula.'

Mac stopped as though hit by a physical wall, the hair on the back of his neck standing straight up. Both Maddie and Saul looked at him questioningly.

'Sula?' he said.

'No, Ezula? My daughter, the girl you're here to see?'

'Oh!' Mac spluttered 'Of course, I... erm...'

Saul was quick to save him the embarrassment. 'I've only ever called her Ezzie. His late wife was called Sula. Pretty freaky, huh?'

Mac began to chuckle as Maddie placed a hand over her mouth. 'Oh, God, Mac. I'm so sorry.'

'For what? Giving your daughter a beautiful name? Besides, it only sounds the same. It just threw me there for a second, that's all. It's fine.'

'Ezzie, we always call her that, anyway. Let's stick with Ezzie.'

'Okay,' Mac said. He paused before asking where the name originated.

Please don't say Italy.

'She's half African. Her father insisted on the name, it was in his family. It is a pretty name, though. I didn't mind.'

Mac felt himself relax a little as they reached the back door of the large house, painted an immaculate slate grey. It opened into a tiled boot room that was larger than the entire cabin, and further into a dining country kitchen with an island that had the square footage of the cabin grounds. Mac felt a little overwhelmed at the vast space after being cooped up for so long and was glad that for once Rolo was fairly clean and dry.

There was a bark from the hallway and two black Labradors bounded in, taking a little notice of Mac, who fussed their ears, before finding Rolo and engaging in a game around the kitchen island.

'Rolo!' Mac said, conscious of the cleanliness of the space.

'Leave him,' Maddie said, going on ahead into the hall. 'They'll be fine.'

'But everything is so...'

'Clean?' Saul said. 'That's for your benefit. It's normally filthy from the dogs, especially at this time of year. Ma always says she can't be bothered to clean their paw marks more than once a week, it would drive her insane, so we have a clean 'hour' on Saturday morning, where the dogs are taken out so ma can clean - then they come back and wreck the joint.'

Mac laughed, and took a glance back at Rolo, who was sniffing at one lab's backside, his tail wagging furiously.

'Guess he hasn't seen another dog for some time, either. It'll do him good.'

'It will. What will you have to drink? I'll bring it down.'

'Gin and tonic would go down nicely right now.'

Saul grinned. 'Coffee then. Don't worry, the olds are great, if a little eccentric. You'll be fine.'

He nodded to the doorway, and Mac stepped out into the hall. To his left Maddie smiled and beckoned him down to her. Mac walked down the tartan carpet, eyeing the three deer heads mounted on plaques. Maddie ushered him in through a doorway and Mac stepped into a cosy living room with a roaring fire. High corniced ceilings and three heavily draped large sash windows faced out across a sprawling driveway, and more lawns. A further two deer heads and crossed silver swords adorned the walls, along with many framed pictures of the family, canvas paintings of the mountains and another canvas that bore a calling stag. The stone fireplace was almost as tall as Mac and bore an engraving that could have been Latin, or Gaelic, just under the mantle.

'Come and sit down,' Maddie said. 'Ma will be down in a minute. Da is staying with Ezzie until we've filled you in. You must have questions.'

'Lots.' Mac said. 'I could do with a complete breakdown of what happened, what she was like before, what's different now. I pretty much need a full picture before I work with her. I don't want to have her answering questions she doesn't need to, which may interfere with the mood, or the way things are going.'

Mac broke off as Maddie stared at him.

'I know it will be hard,' he said.

Maddie blinked out of her reverie.

'Not at all. Anything to get her better.'

'I hope I can do that for you, and for her.'

'I hope so too.'

The air felt tense, and Mac smiled.

'So, you're her mother, eh? You left that little nugget out last time we met.'

Maddie's gaze sharpened and she jut her chin at him.

'It didn't come up. Why so shocked? Just because I travelled doesn't mean I can't have a child, does it?'

Mac laughed at Maddie's forceful defensiveness and hurt stare.

'No, no. You have it all wrong. When Saul spoke of Ezula at the cabin, I naturally presumed she was his. He gave me no indication to say otherwise, and obviously I didn't know he was your brother at the time. So, try to imagine if you will. I believe Ezula is his. I pull up to the same inlet as before and we walk toward your house where he promptly introduces you as his *sister*... and the child's *mother*. I mean-'

Mac shrugged his hands up to the air.

Maddie cut him off with a wretching noise and threw a cushion at him.

'As if!' she said. 'You are really gross!'

'Imagine it from my point of view, just now.'

Maddie grinned, and then she was laughing. Mac laughed with her.

'If you really believed that, Mac, then I just don't know what to make of you.'

Mac shook his head through his grin. 'I didn't. I really didn't. I was just trying to break the tension.'

He laughed, and she visibly relaxed, her shoulders dropping three inches.

The door to the living room opened and two older people walked in. The Man strode ahead, heavyset, and tall up close, almost formidable. A grey woollen coat matched his trousers, his grey hair wild at the edges, flat on top as though he had just removed a hat or cap. His blue eyes twinkled, and a smile played on his lips in a perfect imitation of Maddie's. The lady was more reserved, her long tartan dress and shawl almost a nod to older times but fitting for the lady in front of him. Her face was just as friendly, blonde hair cropped short, fixed smile, but there was an air of sadness about her.

Her eyes, Mac thought. The smile doesn't reach her eyes.

Maddie introduced them as Ma and Da, and the man - the same one Mac had seen with the fire, he was sure - rolled his eyes.

'There's a fine introduction, Madeline. Christ up a tree he doesnae want to be calling us Ma and Da, and we didnae have more children for precisely the same reason.' He strode to Mac and held out a hand. Mac grabbed it and shook firmly. 'I'm Walter. You may call me Walt. This is Hester,' he said, pulling his wife forward from the elbow as he left go of Mac's hand.

'You may call me Hester,' she said with a warm smile and held out her hand to shake his.

Mac had never kissed a woman's hand, and he had no idea what made him do it now. Maybe it was the appreciation of the pie, or the fact that she looked like she belonged in another time.

'Lovely to meet you, Hester,' he said, 'and such wonderful apple pies. Saul and I are a good stone heavier since he's been bringing those pies to the cabin. Thank you, they were much appreciated.'

Hester's hand flew to her neck, and she visibly reddened as she flapped her other hand his way.

'It was nothing. I'm always making pie. If I'd have known it was for a celebrity, I'd have-'

'I'm not a celebrity, Hester. I'm just a man who wants to help people. This is the way I chose to do it, although Maddie has been telling me what a rubbish way to live it is, so I suppose I have to change my entire show now.'

Hester swung to Maddie, who grinned at her mother.

'Travelled all around the world and not seen a bit of it, Ma. What do you make of that?'

Hester looked back to study Mac.

'I'd say that's an awful shame.' She nodded as she looked at him. 'Maddie will sort that out for you, I'm afraid, Mr Macauley, whether you want her to or not.'

'Oh, call me Mac, please.'

Maddie grinned at Mac, and he couldn't help but grin back. He thought maybe he would like her to.

'You're very welcome to have the pies, Mac,' Hester said. 'In fact, I'll bring some mince pies through while you chat with Maddie. I presume there will be things you want to know about little Ezzie before you see her.'

'Yes, I don't want to have to ask her anything about it. I work moving forward, not looking back, but to have the background will be imperative for me in this case.'

Hester dipped her head and placed a hand on Mac's arm.

'I hope you can help her. The wee thing is horribly stuck. She just can't get herself around it. The doctors have said there's nothing physically wrong, she's had every test going, I'm sure she's positively radioactive she's had so many scans and x-rays-'

'Ma,' Maddie said, pulling her mother's arm, 'I'll do it. You get the mince pies. Where is Saul?'

The sadness that had crept back into Hester dissipated, but it was Walt that answered.

'He's with Ezzie while we came in to introduce ourselves. I'll send him in, Hester, come away now. It was nice to meet you, Mac. It'll be nice to have another face around the place for a while too. Make yourself at home, while you're here, anything you want or need.'

'Thank you, that's very kind,' Mac said, touched by their generosity.

Maddie grinned at her mother, who was shaking her head in wonder as she looked at Mac.

'Grab the wine to go with the mince pies, Ma,' she said.

Hester looked at her daughter with a frown. 'I don't think this should be a booze fest when Mac has to work with Ezzie afterward.'

'I'm fine,' Mac said, 'really.'

'Well, I'd like a drink,' Maddie said with a pointed look. Hester nodded and stepped forward to put a hand to her daughter's face.

'Okay dear, I'll bring the bottle of Pinot.'

'That would be great,' Maddie said. 'Thank you.'

Walt and Hester left the room, shutting the door behind them, and Mac looked at Maddie. When she looked back at him, her eyes held the same sadness as her mother's had when she entered the room. He put a hand on her arm and squeezed in a gesture of comfort. It was clear this little girl affected the whole family. There was a lot of love here. It made Mac pine for his own mother, who had died nine years ago. Her love had been filled with Sula's after she had gone. Now that Sula had gone too, he felt the emptiness of his own void, even as he felt the fullness of theirs.

'Shall we sit down?' Maddie said with a sniff.

'Wherever you prefer to be.' Mac said softly.

She led him to three-seater fabric sofa where they sat like bookends, knees turned in together as they faced each other. Mac waited for Maddie to start. He wanted to take her hand, but not really understanding the feeling, or its appropriateness, he kept his hands curled in his lap.

Maddie began right at the beginning, back when Ezula had been born. Maddie and the child's father had been travelling together for the best part of a year when Maddie found out she was pregnant. They were both thrilled and fully intended to continue to travel with the child as much as they could. However, after Ezula was born, Maddie had been struck with postnatal depression and they had returned to this house for the best part of two years.

'Ma and Da didn't like him much,' she said. 'I thought it was because he was black. I had no idea what he had done, or what he was capable of back then. Of course, neither did Ma and Da. Da just said he couldn't take to him. Ma said she didn't like his aura. It was two years of hell to be honest with you, not only trying to deal with Ezzie, but their reactions to a man I thought was my soul mate back then.'

Maddie sighed and broke off as Hester brought the wine and mince pies through, Saul coming in behind her. He pulled the coffee table closer as Hester left, and then pulled a chair up close to Maddie's side, and clasped her hand in his. She smiled and patted the top of his hand with her free one.

Mac felt a twist of...

Jealousy? Are you seriously going to start getting jealous now, Mac?

He shook the thought away as he and Saul helped themselves to mince pies. Mac placed one on a plate for

Maddie and opened the bottle of wine, filling the glass halfway. She smiled gratefully as he pushed them her way.

'Thank you, Mac.'

The jealousy eked off a little - *he's her goddamn brother, you idiot* - and he motioned for her to carry on her story as he ate.

When Ezzie had been just under three, they had taken off again, as much to get away from here as to continue the journey. Ezzie made it much more difficult, however, and her father couldn't cope with travelling with a small child, and not being able to do everything he wanted to. It could have finished them, but in the end, he had a phone call and told Maddie that he had been called home to help with the farm as his father had been taken ill.

'Of course, I let him go,' Maddie said around mouthfuls of mince pie. She swallowed and rinsed with wine. 'I had no other choice, but he wasn't pleased when I said that I would continue and we could catch up later, when things had been sorted.'

Mac raised his eyebrows.

'I thought you said he was your soul mate?'

'It wasn't like that,' she said. 'I was absolutely terrified of his father. We had stayed there, at his family's farm for a month, early on in the relationship. He's the only man who has ever scared me to the point that I couldn't be in the same room as him. Forever messing with his guns, very loose fingered with them. Shot any animal that wandered across the driveway, and once a man who wandered down it. His mother wasn't much better.'

She shuddered. 'Turned out the apple didn't fall so far from the tree, if you'll excuse the pun.'

Mac smiled.

'So, did you ever meet up again?'

'Briefly. He joined us in Vietnam four years later, when Ezzie was seven. He told me he had met someone else and that he was taking Ezzie home for a stable upbringing with his wife and baby. No more of this travelling around for his baby girl.'

Mac raised an eyebrow.

'What did you say to that?'

'I told him he could whistle. He got angry, threatening, we argued, and one night, while he slept in a separate hostel room, Ezzie and I left. I heard nothing more from him as we travelled back through India, where we caught a flight to Turkey, followed by a flight to Rome. That was the mistake. We stayed by the airport in Rome for two whole days while we waited for a flight back to Glasgow. We should have moved. I was so adept at travelling we could have flown from Germany or France instead, but I was anxious. I knew he'd be after us. Not hearing from him was worse. On the road felt more dangerous, so I waited. It was the first time I had ever questioned what he was capable of, given his parents and his upbringing. I didn't know how far he would go.'

Maddie took a large swig of wine, finishing the glass, and immediately poured more. Mac saw her hands shake and wished that he didn't have to do this to her, but without the knowledge of what happened, he couldn't move forward with Ezula.

'I'm sorry, Maddie,' he said.

She shook her head as she took another gulp of wine.

'If it helps Ezzie, I'll do anything.'

Mac sucked in a vast sigh.

I hope to god you can help this girl, Mac.

'What happened in Italy?'

'We were at a small shop by a cafe the next day. I wanted to buy some bread and cake to eat in our hotel room.

I didn't want to go out. I didn't want anyone to see us, but I couldn't leave Ezzie hungry. The problem was I also couldn't leave Ezzie alone in the room, and room service was out of the question when I had used almost all I had on flights back. I kept Ezzie by my side, held her hand the whole way. The only time I let her go was to buy the cake and bread...'

Maddie broke off with a choke and heaved some long breaths.

'You're okay, Maddie, it's over now,' Saul said, rubbing his hand over hers.

Maddie's cheeks were flushed when she looked back at Mac. He wasn't sure whether it was shame or embarrassment. It shouldn't have been either. He reached to touch her arm.

'Take your time,' he said. Saul gave him a sad smile from over her shoulder.

'I brought the bread,' She continued. 'It was the only time I let her go. The *only* time. He must have been following us for some time because, in that second, I looked back to find her gone. No sound, no scuffle, no bother from the people around us, although there were only two others and the shop lady. It was like she had vanished. I looked around that shop for an hour, telling the staff that she must be there, there was nowhere else she could be. Where the hell else could she be?'

Maddie's voice rose close to panic, and Mac touched her arm again. She broke off and took another slug of wine. A large tear ran down her cheek, the horror etched in her eyes. Mac could only imagine what it would be like to lose a child. He had never had one, probably never would now. She wiped the tear away with an apologetic smile.

'I'm sorry. I thought I'd be okay talking about this now. I know how the story ends, right?'

'I know how the Green Mile movie ends. I still sob every damn time. I even cry *before* the sad bit because I know it's coming,' Mac said.

Maddie spluttered and laughed.

'You're such a sop.'

'Got me sussed in one conversation,' he said with a grin. She grinned back, pulling herself together, took some more breaths and finished the story.

'So, her father and another man literally whisked her off her feet, gave her no option to say anything as far as we can get out of her. He told her he had a surprise outside the shop. By the time she was getting scared, they had her in a truck and were tearing across the country, heading for a boat back to Africa.'

'I was going out of my mind... I stayed in Italy for another week, pleading with him to send her back. Ma and Da were telling me to come home so they could help, and then Saul was released from-'

She stopped short and looked at her older brother with horror. Saul only smiled.

'He already knows I was in jail,' he said.

Maddie looked from Mac to Saul and back again, before nodding.

'So, Saul convinced me to come back. We tried everything to get her home. Police, government, the embassy. It was the absolute worst few months of my life, and we were getting nowhere. With so many countries in between, no one seemed to want to help or take responsibility for her. She was with her father, therefore there was no issue. She had gone without a scream; therefore, she had gone willingly...'

Maddie placed her head in her hands.

'I get the picture,' Mac said. 'Skip to the bit where you get her home.'

Maddie blew out a breath.

'That was a fluke. One of her father's friends called me to say how unhappy she was and that she was pleading to come home. He risked his life both to get my number, and then to call me. It was a big deal for him. So big. Ezzie's state concerned him so much he said that he would bring her to Rome airport so that I could get her straight home. I don't know why Rome, and the thought of going back there made me physically sick, but I did it. Three weeks later, he met me at the airport, Ezzie in his arms. I got a flight back to Glasgow within the hour, and Da picked us up and brought us back here.'

'But her father knows you're here, surely. How safe does that make you both?'

'I did worry about that for a while, but three months later, I heard from the man who brought her back to me. After he got back to Africa, Ezzie's father was waiting for him. They fought. He was shot three times, but luckily not anywhere that caused major injury. Ezzie's father was accidentally shot by another member of the group. He died at the scene.'

She licked her lips and dipped her head.

'I... I felt nothing but relief. Nothing.'

Mac nodded, feeling the relief slide off him too. Saul picked her hand up to kiss it.

'It's perfectly natural. We went over this.'

She looked up at Saul with a smile. 'I know, it still doesn't sit right morally, that's all. That doesn't mean I dwell on it.'

'I should hope not,' Mac said. 'So, how has Ezula changed? What has she told you about the months with her father?'

Maddie put her glass of wine down. Saul picked up the bottle to place the rest in her glass, but she shook her head.

'Other than the wheelchair, it's just her personality that's suffered. Not that she's different, just quieter, not so full of life. Like Ezzie, but with the batteries run low. She was always bouncing around, always chatty, always had things to do. She was going to be a ballet dancer.'

'So, what's with the wheelchair now? Saul says there's nothing wrong physically with her.'

Maddie shook her head.

'She's as healthy as any other eight-year-old. The doctors say there is no reason she can't walk, and yet the man that brought her to me carried her, I had to carry her onto the plane in Rome, and off again in Glasgow. She hasn't walked since.'

Maddie shrugged her shoulders, and Mac frowned in thought.

'Have you ever asked her why?'

Maddie and Saul both nodded their heads, and Saul squeezed Maddie's shoulder, indicating he would take over.

'She won't say,' Saul said. 'I have asked her in every which roundabout way I can. I've tried gently, more forcefully. I've asked her outright. She clams up. That's when we decided to concentrate on the fact that she could walk, rather than focusing on something that distressed her.'

'Right,' Mac said. 'And she was okay in herself, other than the batteries.'

Maddie smiled at him.

'She was so pleased to be home, and happy to be with Ma and Da and Saul. She said as much, but...'

Maddie trailed off with a frown, and Saul finished for her.

'It didn't seem to come through with emotion, you know? It was just words. She was almost apathetic. She said that she hated her father with just as much emotion, and that seemed to be the problem at first. Getting her to *feel* anything.

'She did come round, though, eventually. She was a lot more lively than she had been, a lot more giggly and loving. I just thought that given time she would naturally get up and walk, much like she has started to come back little by little. But she seems to have hit a wall lately, it's like she won't try to go any further. She's at the peak of her laughter, which is only around forty percent of her old laughter. She doesn't smile quite as much as she used to, you know.'

Mac bit his lip. This could well be out of his hands. It sounded to him like there was something much deeper at work in Ezula's brain.

'Have either of you managed to get anything out of her about her time with her father?'

'Nothing at all,' Maddie said. Saul shook his head, too. 'I didn't want her to relive anything she didn't have to, so I didn't push after a while.'

Mac nodded.

'Okay, he said, 'So Ezula has been through a very traumatic experience, even just been taken from her mother, but whatever went on in Africa may well be the key to getting her to walk.'

'I can't get through to her, Mac,' Saul said, 'and you said you work forwards...'

He trailed off as Mac nodded his head. 'I do. I'm not sure-'

Maddie swung to him, grabbing his arms with both of her hands. The pressure told Mac just how important this was to her.

'Please, Mac, don't tell me you can't. You have to try. Please! You must have worked with many people with blocks before, surely!'

'Yes, but they were adults, well aware of their blocks, and with a little motivation to move through them. Ezula doesn't sound like she's ready to address this yet. If she's not ready, nothing I say will change her mind. Mind work is highly personal. She's the only one who can change the situation for herself, and for all of you.'

Maddie's hands were still on Mac's arms. She looked devastated as another tear rolled down her face.

'Mac, please.' She begged.

Mac nodded. He had no choice. Maddie was desperate. He knew that the outcome probably wouldn't be in his favour, but at least he would still be in Maddie's favour for trying.

'Okay,' he said.

The relief visibly slid off both Maddie and Saul's shoulders as they both broke into huge grins.

Maddie flung herself onto Mac and kissed his cheek, then she grabbed his face with both of her hands and leaned in close.

'You don't know how much this means to me. Thank you so, so much. I know you'll get her better again. I just know you will.'

Mac felt his stomach drop with the realisation of the sheer faith she had in him, but it was a job he wasn't sure he was the best person for.

'I'll go get Ezzie. She's dying to meet you!'

Maddie jumped up and ran from the room. Mac gave Saul an uncertain look.

'Don't say it, Mac. Don't. Meet her, see what you can do. Give it some time. If you can't... then say it. But for now, please, don't say anything.'

Mac pursed his lips and gave a nod.

'I'll do my best. I promise you that.'

'That's good enough for me,' Saul said with a grateful smile. 'I appreciate this more than you know, and if you need paying come to me. I won't have the olds footing the bill, and Maddie can't pay. I have savings.'

Mac started to grin, and then he realised Saul was deadly serious. His grin fell away.

'The only payment I'll take is a mince pie or two, and your company at the cabin with a beer once in a while,' he said.

'I'm serious.' Saul said, his mouth a straight line.

'So am I.'

CHAPTER FORTY-SEVEN

THE NEXT FEW HOURS left Mac feeling twitchy and frustrated. Offering a plan of action to five hundred grown adults who had paid to listen to him was a whole heap easier than offering it to one eight-year-old girl who had no intention of listening to him. Ezula was a sweet girl, extremely polite, with wide brown eyes and a mop of dark curls. Sula and Ezula had lots more in common than just their names, and Mac must admit that it had started him off on the wrong foot with her. Timid and faltering. She had immediately lost interest in the bumbling fool in front of her and had disengaged.

Now, an hour and a half later, she sat in her chair, twiddling her thumbs, and staring out of the window. As luck would have it, the family had stepped out to let Mac perform his magic, which was good, as it was failing miserably.

He held his notes in his hand, outlines of the framework he had tried to explain to the child in simple terms, but she had looked bored within the first minute. Thirty-five minutes later, he had lost her completely.

I don't think you're going to get away with treating this like a show, Mac. She's a child. Try a different tactic?

But what? He had never had to teach this stuff any other way. Exercises in gratitude, mindset shifts, goal cards, power speeches from your future self, and meditation were taken for granted at his events. Here, the child hadn't asked for any of them, couldn't see the point, and wasn't interested.

Mac stared out of the window with her as the silence in the room lengthened. He was going to have to go over old ground to break her through to new, which was something he had no expertise in, and no real wish to do.

He was at the point of calling the family in to suggest a psychotherapist, although that wouldn't do his friendship with Saul much good, when inspiration struck him.

If Saul hadn't got through to her as a psychologist with twenty years' training, then this last forty minutes certainly didn't mean that Mac couldn't get through either yet.

This needs more time.

He frowned as his instincts kicked in. He glanced at Ezula, large, haunted eyes staring sadly out to the lawn and realised that she reminded him of his nephew, Josh. What would you do with Josh in this kind of situation? He had an idea.

'Do you have anything else to do today, Ezula? Something you wish to be getting on with? We should probably call it a day. This is going nowhere.'

The child looked at him almost crestfallen. The disappointment in her eyes clear. 'I thought you were going to help me?' she said.

Mac pursed his lips and shook his head sagely as he stared past her out of the window. 'I can't help you, sweetheart.'

The girl's mouth dropped open, and her bottom lip quivered. 'But I... Uncle Saul said you were the world's greatest, and that you were the one to help. I don't understand.'

Thanks Uncle Saul...

'Ezula, I can't help because your brain won't let you help yourself. I can't make you understand how important this stuff is. It's futile, because you have to do the work. If you're not listening, I can't help you.'

'I am listening. I am.'

Ezula's eyes filled with tears and Mac lay a hand on the child's arm, the jumper with embellished snowman on the front was so thick that he could barely feel her arm through the wool.

'You are, but only partially. That's not how this works. I need you fully engaged and ready to work. Brain work is hard, Ezula, possibly the hardest work you'll ever do, and nobody can do it for you. Not any little bit of it. You have to be the one to change this yourself. You.'

He squeezed his hand on the jumper, hoping that she could feel the contact. He still wasn't sure where her arm was, her hand seemed to be attached only to the cornflower blue wool.

Same colour as her mothers, he thought.

Ezula was looking at him now, holding his gaze. He didn't need to see the fear in her eyes. He felt it radiate from her. With a concealed sigh, he looked outside and spied something that may help on the far side of the lawn.

'I've got an idea,' he said. 'Do you want to get out of here?'

Ezula's eyes held question marks. 'Where to?'

'I'm not going to tell you until we get there. But I can tell you that you can't bring the chair.'

Ezula collapsed back into the seat, mouth turned down at the corners.

'I have to bring the chair.'

'Why's that?'

She looked at him a little like he had an alien perched on top of his head.

'Because I can't walk?' She said, phrasing the statement as a question and gesturing to the wheelchair underneath her. 'That's why I'm in here, duh. I'm not sitting here for my health.'

'Well, I think that's exactly why many people have wheelchairs - for their health. Except that you're as healthy as a fresh blueberry.'

The alien was back on his head, and Mac concealed a smile.

'A blueberry?' She said, disgust on her lips. 'I hate blueberries.'

'A blueberry is a superfood. It is full of nutritious stuff and vitamins, full of health.'

'So?' She said, no attitude now, only plain curiosity.

'So are you. Can I ask you a question, Ezula?'

'Call me Ezzie,' she said. 'No one calls me Ezula anymore.'

Mac let the statement slide - he could bring that one up later.

'Okay, Ezzie, I get the feeling that you love that chair. That's why you don't want to walk again.'

'I hate this chair,' she said with not quite enough venom to be convincing.

'Oh? You do? Well then, let's ditch it and go.'

Ezula was looking at him like he had a dozen screws loose.

'I can't just get up and walk. If it were that easy, I'd have done it by now.'

'Why do you keep talking yourself out of it?'

'Out of what?'

'Getting out of the chair? Do you want to come or not?'

Ezula folded her arms across her chest with a frown.

'I am *not* talking myself out of it!'

'You are,' Mac said.

'Am not.'

'Let's go then.'

Ezula looked confused.

'I don't understand. How can I get where you're taking me without this chair?'

'Ah, now you're asking a much better question. *How* can you, indeed? There are plenty of ways to travel without your wheels. Don't automatically jump to the default 'I can't'. Think about it first.'

Ezula looked down at the wheelchair and back up to him, bemused. 'My wheels? I like that,' she said with a laugh.

'Don't get too used to it. By the time I'm done travelling around with you, they'll seem positively boring. When was the last time you went to a park or climbed a tree?'

Ezula now slumped in her chair and rolled her eyes.

'I'm starting to think you're deaf, mister Mac,' she said, then she giggled as he looked aghast.

'Mister Mac? I'll have you know it's Doctor Mac. And I'll let you into a secret, shall I?'

She leaned forward, head bobbing eagerly.

Why do kids love a secret so much?

He looked around to make sure they were alone in the room. Ezula leaned closer to him, and a flash of inspiration hit him.

Now I have her attention. That's what it takes, huh? Maybe I have to show her this stuff, not teach her.

'I'm the best mind doctor in the world. The entire world. If anyone can get rid of those wheels, I can.'

'I know!' Ezula exploded. 'Uncle Saul told me that! I thought he was pulling my leg. It's really true?'

Thank you, Uncle Saul. I'll have to have words with you later.

'It's true. Now, are we going or what?'

It was as miraculous as it was sad.

Ezzie was so convinced in that particular moment that she actually tried to get out of the wheelchair and stand on legs that hadn't been stood on for a year or more. She fell back to her seat with frustration. Mac slid in quickly.

'You big dope. How will you walk over there if you can't walk?'

Ezula's head snapped up and Mac laughed. It worked like a charm as her frown fell away and she laughed with him.

'I thought you meant I'd have to walk,' she said.

'Of course you can't walk yet. You will, but right now I said there are other ways to travel. Ezzie, they're so fun that you won't want to walk by the end of my time here. It will seem way too boring. But neither will you be in that chair - that will be in your grandfather's bonfire.'

Ezula's face lit up. 'Really? Can we?'

'What?' Mac said. 'Put that horrible old thing in the fire? Hell, yes. We'll watch it burn together.'

'Grandpa won't normally let me near the fire.'

'I promise you he'll be there watching with us. It'll be like a party!'

Ezula's eyes lit up, and she began to grin.

'Can we do it, Doctor Mac? Can we?'

'It depends how much you hate the chair, I suppose. You have to get out of it first.'

'I hate this chair,' she said with passion. 'I want a party. I want to see it burn as I dance. It spoils all my fun.'

Mac gave an internal whoop of joy.

'Right then, so we have some fun work to do, and some hard work too. Are you ready to start operation burning chair?'

'Hell yes!' she said with a shout.

'Let's go then,' Mac said, crouching in front of the chair, his back to her. She needed no further explanation. She leapt onto his back, wrapping her arms around his neck - and her apparently useless legs around his waist.

That's my girl, he thought, standing up easily. He piggy backed her outside and down the lawn to an old an old swing and slide set next to an abandoned bench.

CHAPTER FORTY-EIGHT

T OM ZIPPED HIS PADDED jacket against the cool darkness as he walked down Francis Street, crossed the traffic lights at Oaktree Lane, and turned left onto Sherborne Street. In just the four streets he had walked, the houses changed from large detached executive homes to older, smaller rows of terraced, four-storey, town housing that stretched across this half of town and into the city. Cars lined the street, leaving a central passageway down the middle. A gang of youths crowded the steps to a basement flat, inhaling aerosols and laughing like hyenas. He tucked his head down into his jacket, averting his eyes and covering his mouth against the cool wind.

Across the road, a front door flew open, and a lady screamed insults that spilled out into the street as he passed. He tried to keep his head down as she stumbled down the steps, and spun round. She threw something at a man in the doorway, whose belly overhung his trousers, his white t-shirt stained with something brown under the orange streetlight - at least Tom thought it was brown. The man didn't flinch as the shoe hit his protruding stomach, but he did take the cigarette out of his mouth to glare at Tom.

'Whatcha looking at?'

Tom shook his head and kept going, his eyes focused on the pavement.

'Got a light, mister?' another voice said beside him. He glanced down to see a child of no more than ten, plunging velvet top that was supposed to enhance a cleavage that she had yet to gain. Her face was caked with makeup, a cigarette hanging from her lips.

'No,' he mumbled, tuning out her response and keeping his stride all the way to the other end of the road.

A road that ended in wasteland, where more kids were tearing around on motorbikes in the rubble, shouting and swearing accompanying the roar of their engines. A road that housed the Horse and Jockey, and a small car park that was littered with so much glass, he wondered if anyone ever parked on it. His feet crunched to faded brown doors with half-length windows. Horse was painted in gold leaf on one door, although the R and S were missing to leave HOE. Some bright spark had painted an apostrophe S with white paint. Jockey was still intact on the other door, although the same genius has painted another apostrophe S on this door too. The whole welcome now said Hoe's and Jockey's.

Tom put his hand on a tarnished brass handle and pulled the door open.

The smell of stale beer and cigarette smoke hit him first, his feet sticking to the carpet hit him second. He swallowed his revulsion and made his way inside.

He crossed to the bar, feeling the room go quiet and the eyes on his back. He wasn't a regular here, and for good reason, but this pub rarely got anyone new, being stuck at the end of Sherborne Street. Tom was amazed that it was still here at all, that it hadn't been shut down like so many others across the city as main roads were replaced with bypasses, and passing trade became less and less.

He kept his gaze on the bar woman, who wore a mask of makeup and a top similar to the girl he had seen down the street, although this time she had ample to fill it. So much so that he wished whatever the old man at the bar had whispered about Tom hadn't made her laugh. The whole lot threatened to spill out at any moment.

He reached the bar, and the breasts jiggled in his face, heavy creases folded down the middle.

'Up here, darlin',' she said, looking him up and down as his eyes rose to meet hers. Older than she had appeared from the doorway, he surmised sixties, although the makeup was so thick and heavy, at least some of the wrinkles were surely hidden. Maybe she was more like eighty.

'What can I git ya?'

Tom studied the row of spirits behind. Most of the bottles were empty, the only one half full was Bell's whiskey. Not one he liked. He searched the pumps instead and came up with Stella. A safe bet.

'Stella please. Pint.' He said, digging in his pocket for his wallet.

'Not from around here, are ya?' The man sat at the bar said.

'No, I'm here on business,' he said, turning to look at the man, whose wrinkles pulled down his face drawing deep crevices. Jowls wobbled below his chin as he spoke, lank and flat on his thin frame, pulling his mouth down with them, and greasy long grey hair fell to his shoulders, a portion combed over on top in an attempt to hide a bald patch with its streaks.

'No one does business in this pub that's legal,' the man said, letting out a large belch and taking a gulp of beer that looked like dishwater.

'I do,' Tom said with a smile that felt more like a grimace. The bar lady raised her eyebrows as the man chuckled at his own joke.

'Ignore him, three-eighty,' she said, placing the same yellow looking dishwater in front of him. Some of the liquid slopped over the top and onto the bar.

Tom pulled out a ten-pound note and waited for change.

'I'm supposed to meet someone here-' he began.

'Over there,' she said, pointing across the pub to a table in the corner where a large blonde man sat nursing the paper and a beer. He looked up at Tom with a wink and a smile.

'Right. Thank you,' Tom said, picking up his glass.

'Hope business goes well,' the man at the bar said with another guffaw. This time the bar lady joined him with a high, tinny laugh of her own. Tom left the sound of them behind and hurried through the tables. Far too many people for a Tuesday night, he thought, and most of them smoking, although smoking had been banned in public establishments for the last twenty years.

He reached the blonde man, who looked him slowly up and down.

Tom barely recognised him, could have been at the wrong table, he supposed, but then he spoke.

'Tom Macauley. I've waited a long time for this day. A very long time indeed. What an absolute pleasure this is.'

CHAPTER FORTY-NINE

TOM PLACED HIS PINT down on the table and pulled out the chair opposite the man. He sat down and immediately took a large gulp of beer that he wasn't ready for. Not only did it look like dishwater, but it tasted like it too. A pint of fairy washing up liquid may have gone down better. He held the liquid in his mouth, gagged, and spluttered it back into the glass.

The man watched him with a smile and sipped at his own glass of what looked like whiskey. Probably Bell's.

'I wondered why it was so bloody cheap. Half the price of The Princeton.' Tom blurted.

'The Princeton would have been far more interested in our business than this lot. Should have had the whiskey. Bottled. Who knows what shit they put into that. It's probably piss.'

Tom felt his stomach roll over and pushed the glass away from him. It stuck on a spot of something sticky on the table and the glass tipped, almost spilling. He grabbed it quickly with a clatter and looked around to see who was watching. The whole pub had seen the show, apparently. Even the bar lady had her arms folded under her breasts, pushing them up further as she watched. Tom raised a hand with a small sorry. Some of the patrons went back to their drinks, some watched without humour.

'Could you make any more of a scene? We are already intruders here. Outcasts. Let's not draw any more attention to ourselves, eh?'

'Sorry,' Tom said again, and then caught hold of himself.

Why the hell do you keep apologising? Let's get this over with and get the hell home.

He had transferred three million into his current account this morning so that he could transfer the money instantly. This man could watch it transfer over if he wanted. Meg had been insistent that he offer two.

The man will expect one, she had said. You ruined his life, so he thinks. Offer him two, blow him out of the park. Give it to him there and then and get your backside home as soon as possible. I don't like the thought of you out there on that side of town.

He had put up no protest. He wanted the man off his back as well.

The blonde man slugged his whiskey and watched Tom gather himself. He wanted a drink but wouldn't subject himself to a drop more of that pint. He glanced back at the bar. Luckily, the focus was off them again now, suitably settled as to become invisible.

'You look twitchy.' The man said, shrugging off his leather jacket to reveal a black jumper. He rolled up the sleeves to reveal faded tattoos and placed his arms on the table.

Tom swung back to him. 'I am twitchy. I want to know what the hell you want, and then I want to get out of here, go back home, and have nothing more to do with you again.'

'Take your coat off, Tom. You could at least look as though you're staying.'

'I don't want to, all I want-'

The hand shot across the table so fast Tom wasn't sure a video camera would have caught the swift action. It clamped on his wrist, pinning it to the table with brute like strength. The smile never wavered from the man's face.

'I said, take your coat off, Tom.'

Tom took his coat off and placed it over the back of his chair.

'Go and get another drink. I'd recommend the whiskey. More body than the beer.'

Feeling this was more an order than a question of whether he would like to, Tom hesitated only a second before rising to his feet.

'Yes please, mate,' the man said, 'make mine a double.'

The man held his glass up with a wink and a smile. Tom brought two double Bell's and took them back to the table. He sat down and took a big gulp, feeling the whiskey hit and burn the back of his throat as it went down.

'Okay,' Tom said, 'We've played nicely, happy mates and all that. I'm going to make you an offer, and then I want you out of my life for good.'

The man sat back and folded his arms with a frown.

'Interesting. What's the offer?'

Tom looked both ways to make sure no one was listening, but no-one was interested now, they were part of the furniture. The man looked bemused.

'I'm going to transfer two million into your account right now. I'll even wait while it goes through, and then we walk away, and you never contact me again. Do we have a deal?'

The man sucked a breath through his teeth and narrowed his eyes.

'It's so easy for you, Tom, isn't it? Offer the man a little money and shoo him away. Do you know who I am yet?'

Tom's mouth flapped. He hadn't expected so quick a rejection, but he had the other million to play with yet.

'I do. You're the doctor from the Scottish practice where Su... my wife and I came for treatment.'

The man smiled.

'The fuck she was your wife. She was your bit on the side. Why the hell else does a posh couple come up to Scotland from London simply for a backstreet abortion? There must be more clinics around here than in the whole of the highlands. So much effort.' He said with a frown and a shake of his head.

Tom swallowed and licked his lips.

'I was her husband,' he said, unsure why he was arguing the toss anyway.

'Bullshit.' The man said. 'In a practice like that, you see it all, from the streets to the millionaires, all of human nature is the same shit show. You were fucking her, she got pregnant, poor husband couldn't know, so you whisk her away for a small holiday, pretending, what? She's away with friends? That's it, isn't it, Tom?'

'I don't owe you an explanation,' Tom said, feeling the heat rise up his neck and into his cheeks.

'Yes, I suspect so. Poor husband, eh? Who was it you did the dirty on? Did you know him? Were you friends? They usually are.'

Tom grit his teeth, getting flustered. Why would this man not just take the money and go? What the hell could he possibly want?

'This is none of your business. Tell me what you want so I can leave. Three million, you've got it. Right now.'

'Tempting, Tom, but... no.'

'No?'

'No.'

'Then what?'

'You ruined my life in so many ways, Tom. Let me count them.'

He drank a gulp of whiskey and sat back into his chair, counting on his fingers.

'You took my career, you took my job, you took my home, you took my living, you took my friend, you took two years of my life, you took my dignity, you took my ability to work as a doctor again, you took my freedom, you took my record as a decent human being. That's ten. Need I go on?'

'Please don't,' Tom said, finishing his whiskey, and forcing himself not to add that at least four of those things were one and the same.

'Okay, I think we'll take an even fifteen and call it quits, then.'

Tom looked at him, the man looked back.

'Well?'

Tom shook his head, completely lost. 'Well, what?'

'Fifteen. Million. One for each of the things you took from me.'

Tom gasped out a breath.

'Fifteen? You must be kidding? I don't have fifteen.'

'Oh dear. How much do you have?'

Tom floundered. 'I don't know, possibly four and a half - six with the house and the business. There are a few investments...'

The man thread his fingers together and pushed out his lips.

'Well, then we have a problem, don't we, Tom?'

Tom gaped. Meg had made it sound so easy. Just offer him two and get the hell home.

Nice one Meg, what if the guy wants fifteen and we have nowhere near that figure? In any form.

'What can I do?' he said, his heart thudding wildly. Never had he been in a situation he couldn't talk himself out of, or buy himself out of.

The man shrugged, keeping his eyes on Tom. Thoughts raced through his head, pictures of his home, his car, his family. Mac. Out there all alone in the cabin, where the other doctor was keeping an eye on him. He forced back a horrified sob.

'Please. I'll do anything, I just don't have the money...'

The man leaned back with a smile and pulled a piece of paper from his pocket. He took his time as he unfolded it carefully and looked at it, before putting it down on the table, smoothing it out for Tom to see.

It was a picture of Sula and Mac, together, at some awards show or other. Tom felt the room spin. He ran a hand over his mouth.

'Recognise this lady, Tom? I'll give you a clue, she's not your wife, she's your brother's wife.' He shook his head and sucked a breath between his teeth again, Tom sat silent, horrified.

Not Mac. Don't bring Mac into this.

But you don't have the money, Tom.

Mac is out there all alone.

Where can I get the money?

'Hit a nerve, Tom? You've been a real shit to your brother, haven't you? He'll find out just how much, but first I already know where you can top up the rest of the money.' He tapped a finger over Mac's smiling face.

Tom shook his head.

'I can't just take ten million from my brother. I don't think he even has that much. He's not working now, and you know that because no doubt your little doctor friend has informed you how they're having little tete to tete's up in the cabin in Scotland. Oh, this all works out so very well for you, doesn't it?'

The man laughed long and loud.

'Even if he's not working, he has money. You can take his wife, but you can't take his money? This is a little fucked up, isn't it, Tom? I wouldn't want you to take only ten million from him, anyway. No, you see, because the price just went up. If you could get that much from him, then you may as well take fifteen. If you need help from the magical non-working, cabin holidaying Mac Macauley, then the price just went up to twenty Million.'

Tom stammered and paled.

'I just told you I can't get fifteen, and now you want twenty?'

'You need to buy me a new life, Tom. What price do you put on that? I need to start everything fresh. Everything. What could I buy with twenty Million? Hmm.'

Tom put his head in his hands on the table as a horrible thought came over him.

'If I had twenty million you wouldn't take it, would you? You'd up the amount.'

'Whatever makes you say that?'

'Just a feeling,' Tom mumbled into the table.

'You'd be right,' The man said, and Tom lift his gaze to a hard and serious face.

'Why? Why can't you just take my offer and leave my family alone? All of us. I'm sorry for what I did. If I could take it back and not make the call, I would, but I can't. Why do you have to do this?'

'Because you ruined my life, Tom, and now I'm out to ruin yours. Do you think I'm going to make it easy? I'm homeless, penniless, have no vocation, no pedigree - that's all down to you and your meddling bullshit. I have a hell of a lot of time on my hands, right now, and a whole stack of motivation to fuck with your life until it's as bad as mine. I think I'll start with your brother Mac at the cabin. What do you think, Tom?'

'No!' Tom shouted. The pub went quiet, and eyes turned to the outcasts in the corner again. Tom waited for them to turn away. 'No. Leave Mac out of it. He's done nothing, he's suffered enough. Please. You won't do anything, will you?'

The man said nothing. He finished his whiskey with a gulp, and rose, grabbing his coat.

'Wait,' Tom said, the plea so evident he wanted to cringe. 'Where are you going?'

'We're done. The game has begun. Good luck Tom.'

'I'll call the police,' Tom said.

The man shrugged into his coat and smiled.

'You won't.'

Tom stood too, grabbing his own jacket. 'I will, as soon as I leave this pub,' he hissed.

'And what will you tell them about who I am and where to find me?'

Tom frowned and stammered. 'I... I can find out. I can give them the phone number.'

'And I can dump the phone. I already know your number; I'll get a new one. Also, there's a saying that karma always comes back around to bite you in the butt, Tom. If you call the police, then I shall too. Seems you're up to no good in that little clinic of yours, doesn't it? Takes a crook to know one. I'm glad my time is done. It was the worst two years of my life, Tom. I hope you enjoy yours.'

Tom blinked and sat back down in the chair as his legs buckled. He jabbed a thumb and forefinger in his eyes, trying to ease the pain brewing behind his skull.

It was over. All over.

'Good night, Tom. I'll be in touch.'

The man strode away, leaving the pub door to bang shut behind him. Tom stared after him for a while, and then he pulled out his phone and dialled Mac. He got the answer Machine and left a message. After that, there was nothing more he could do. He grabbed his whiskey with a shaking hand and gulped the last mouthful in one. The man at the bar watched as Tom banged the glass on the table, rose, and walked to the door.

'Told you no business in here would be legal. Didn't I tell Ya?' he shouted to Tom with a slur, he leaned back with a laugh, and then there was a shout as he dropped to the floor backward off his stool with a thump. The door banged shut behind Tom and the noise of the neighbourhood engulfed him.

CHAPTER FIFTY

T HE FIRE THAWED THE last of the chill from Mac's bones as he watched the crackle and pop of the wood, and sipped at a coffee. It had dropped bitter outside and the trip back in the dark had been something he never wanted to experience again. In the daylight, the loch seemed tranquil and placid as he rowed; in the dark it was sinister and foreboding, with eyes watching from the dark trees, and unseen monsters lurking under the surface of the water. Even the cabin had seemed to watch him accusingly as he arrived back at the pier, and Rolo had hung back behind his legs only entering the cabin after he did, which further put Mac's nerves on edge.

He settled only when the door was locked, the lights were on, and he had checked that there was no further disturbance on the fridge, in the bathroom, or in the corridor. Then he fed Rolo, lit the fire, made a toasted sandwich, grabbed a coffee, and sat down. Rolo was at his heels the whole time, only settling down when Mac did.

It was late; after nine-thirty when he arrived back, and tiredness was creeping over him as he recounted the day. Ezula had done well. They had chatted a lot. He had pushed her on the swing, slid her down the slide, and finally sat her on the bench to talk. No pressure, just small talk. Just a small getting to know you before the real work started tomorrow. They had chatted and laughed, and Mac had discovered an emotionally intelligent young lady, with a will that was strong. Mac didn't know if he could do anything about her walking, but he thought he had a chance at changing her perspective about what she was capable of. She had gone back to the house gushing about her time on the swing and the slide, the feel of the wind in her hair. Not just the wind, but wind she had created by moving faster than she had since the time with her father. She gushed about getting rid of the chair, about Doctor Mac, and how much fun he was. The family had been delighted with the results and Mac hadn't the heart to tell them that she would revert back to herself within a few hours. All he had done was take her to some play equipment. She had accomplished nothing herself yet, but he hoped that time would come. He hoped to see her walk at some point.

He sipped his coffee and thought of Little Ezula, almost the image of his Sula. She had darker skin and tighter curls, but the large, wide set brown eyes, and strong will, emulated his wife perfectly. He had a strange feeling in that moment; a knowing, an intensity, a feeling that he was meant to be here. This was more than a coincidence, he was certain. Everything had happened here for a reason. Saul had stopped by his door to lead him to Ezula, whom he was destined to help. He felt lightheaded with both responsibility and the sensing of the shifts of a great power at work behind the scenes. A force - a vibration, a frequency - which set things in motion that were meant for him.

Maybe Ezula had been sent to him just as he doubted himself to prove that he was right. Maybe she was to prove to him that there was another way. Maybe she was to teach him to think outside the box and find other ways to teach what he knew.

Every problem was an opportunity, he used to say to his audience. An opportunity to thrive, to change, to teach, to learn, to grow. If you looked for it, every problem or catastrophe, no matter how big or small, was sent for a reason. He saw it now, really saw it. Sula's death was a learning opportunity. He had got complacent, knew his stuff inside out, thought he had a winning formula and needed to do no more work. It failed on himself after her death. Maybe Ezula was also a learning opportunity, to teach him there was more to it, new ideas and alternative ways to access the mind, to reach more people through a different way of teaching.

Mac picked up a pen and pad of paper from the bookshelf, and began to write all of the different ways that he could teach his fundamental formula's through practical activity, not just theory. Was it any wonder that only five percent of his audience ever went away and achieved anything? Practice would always embed knowledge better than theory, by *showing* how it was done, not teaching it.

Mac chewed the end of the pen and narrowed his eyes.

How can I show Ezula the things she needs to master to overcome this chair? What does the chair represent to her that it is both a comfort and a friend? But also, why is she afraid of it? Or afraid of not being with it? Maybe both?

He wrote the question down and mind mapped the thoughts that came to him from every different angle.

He then wrote down the steps within his framework and began to plan activities, thinking of ways to show, not tell.

He wrote for a solid hour before running out of ideas, but instead of being tired, he was buzzing, awake and energised, his mind awash with innovative ideas and insights. He placed the pen and pad at the side of him, staring at the fire, swigging the last of his coffee, and jotting down any new thought that came to him in the quiet.

Focus. It was quite something at work.

Ask and you shall receive the answer. How could he teach that one to Ezula?

Jeez Mac, one step at a time!

He chuckled, and Rolo shifted at his feet. His phone buzzed on the arm of the chair, and he stretched across to pick it up, stirring a grunt from the lump on his feet.

He swiped the phone to find a message from Tom.

Shit.

Tom was supposed to call, he'd forgotten all about him in the day's busy-ness. Mac sat up and opened the message.

Have you listened to my message yet, Mac? I need to speak with you urgently, if I don't hear from you tonight, I will call first thing in the morning. Please answer.

Mac frowned and closed the message. Another notification at the top of the screen told him he had five missed calls and one voicemail. He slapped a hand to his head; he had silenced the phone earlier to enable him to concentrate on Ezula with no interruptions. Now he tapped the button to turn the sound back on.

He pressed to listen to the message, a sense of trepidation growing in his gut. He stared at the three pages of notes he had written and was suddenly glad that he had done those beforehand.

As Tom's voice came over the phone, he reinforced that decision. Tom sounded flustered, a little nervous and low, as though he were speaking in hushed tones. Mac felt a chill settle over him as the message played out. It wasn't so much what Tom said, as the way he said it, but the end hit Mac the hardest. The end he wanted to scrub away and never listen to again. He had listened to the message motionless, let it run on into the lady, who asked him continuously if he wanted to listen to the message again, delete the message, save the message for later...

What in holy hell have I just heard? It's not true. It can't be. I won't believe it!

Mac wanted to erase it from his brain, instead he pressed to listen to it again.

'Mac?'

There was a scuffle and a huff of breath.

'Mac, I need you to listen to me very carefully. Very carefully. I know what you think you know, and I know what I know. I need you to know that this time, I know better. Trust me. I wish it wasn't so but...'

He broke off and there was another scuffle.

'Mac, there's been some trouble. You need to be incredibly careful of the doctor you've befriended up there. I know what you're going to say, I can hear you right now, but I'm very serious. I mean it Mac. There was some trouble up at the cabin a few years back, some trouble with a clinic I had a hand in shutting down. They were suspect people, very untrustworthy, and very immoral in the way they worked, they deserved what they got.'

There was an audible swallow.

'The thing with criminals is that they come back to get you. I'm in a little trouble, and I don't want you to worry about me, I have this side handled, but these guys are working together I'm sure of it. They worked together for many years beforehand, there's no reason to think they're not in touch now. I'm not sure what they're planning, but I'm pretty sure it's to catch you unawares to get back at me. The doctor up there has befriended you for a reason, the other one is down here tailing me. This is no coincidence, Mac, surely you can see that?'

There was a sigh of breath and a pause before Tom started again.

'There's some information that may come your way from the doctor that I want to tell you before he does - if he hasn't already. The amoral don't have a conscience, he may well have already said I suppose, but I'm going to tell you the truth about what really happened.'

Another swallow, a long blow of breath. A pause.

'Mac. Sula was... um, she was at the cabin. Just like you said. She was there, you were right. She stayed for a couple of weeks over the summer. This was a... a couple of years back now, there was a problem. Um. Er, Sula came to me for help, and we booked her into a clinic up there, around ten miles west of where you are. The cabin seemed the perfect place to recuperate, and you were... er, you were away. I'm sorry, Mac...'

There was another pause.

'Mac, there's no easy way to tell you this. Sula had an abortion. She was pregnant. I had to pose as her husband so that she wasn't recognised. She didn't want any talk of it in the papers. I... um... I think she intended to tell you, I... well... anyway, that was the reason she was there, but the clinic was underhand, and I shopped them in. Now they're on my case. It's serious. Please be incredibly careful. I'm so sorry to dump this on you now, but it's imperative that you be on your guard. I don't know what lengths these guys will go to, but both of them know where you are. The one down here told me so, and told me he'd start with you first. As he's in London surely that can only be through the doctor up there. They are working together, however nice he seems, Mac. It's a guise, pretence to lure you in. Mac... '

Another huff of breath.

'Mac. I'm so sorry there was no other way to do this. I will speak to you as soon as possible. Please, I know you're hurting, just answer your phone when I call. I love you, little brother, I would never hurt you, please believe me. I'll speak to you soon. Bye.'

Mac let the phone drop from his hand into his lap and stared at the flames.

Sula was pregnant.

He thought that Sula had hurt him all she could simply by being here without his knowing.

Was it mine?

Two years ago, a year before she died.

Or someone else's?

She had intended to tell him, Tom said, and yet in the last year of her life she had said nothing. Pretence. If he wanted to talk about deceit there it was, from Sula and Tom. His wife and brother, laughing and smiling in his face as though nothing had happened.

She had a fucking abortion?

They were the liars, the cheats. Did they cheat on him? Together?

There was a fucking baby?

He let out a small noise, a whimper that set Rolo to his feet with his own whine. Ignoring the dog, he let the whimper turn into a moan, and then a howl, and finally a scream. He threw the phone across the room and sat back on the settee breathing hard.

Sula, my wife, had an abortion. Right here.

He panted hard, struggling for breath that seemed too thick for his constricted chest. Tears filled his eyes, and the room became a watery vision. His chest hurt. His *heart* hurt. He thought it had hurt after she died, but this deception was worse. The pain more than anything he had ever felt. Three words stuck on a loop in his mind as he sobbed, threatening to drive him crazy.

Was it mine?

Was it mine?

Was it mine?

Or was it his?

CHAPTER FIFTY-ONE

S AUL SCROLLED AIMLESSLY DOWN the job adverts, which was the only position he seemed to adopt these days. It was driving him mad that there was nothing out there. Nothing near, and nothing far. Nothing. He was already living on his savings, and he wasn't happy with that at all. That was house, marriage and babies stuff. If it ever came his way. Certainly house, either way, he couldn't live here forever. The problem was that they were plunging fast while he wasn't earning. It was good that Mac had said no to payment, because Saul didn't think he could have afforded more than a session of whatever the fee would have been.

He's a good man. A good friend.

He tore his eyes from the screen and looked into the darkness outside, wondering how Mac had fared getting home. There was no ice, but it would be cold. He had stayed way beyond his time, even dining with the family for tea, which had brought them all around the same table to eat for the first time in years. It had been nice. They had talked. Much of daily life here was passing each other in the cold corridors on their own path, but somehow Mac had brought them together for that evening. Saul vowed to press them into spending more evening meals together. It was good to talk.

There was a knock at his door, pulling Saul away from his thoughts and the dark view over the mountains.

'Come in,' he said.

Maddie poked her head around the door, mussed up knot of hair flopping on top of her head.

'Am I disturbing you?'

'No,' he said truthfully, 'come in.'

She entered the room with toast and marmalade and a cup of coffee for him. His stomach rumbled as she placed them on his desk.

'Gift from ma,' she said.

'Ah, thank you.'

He watched with amusement as she crossed to the window seat dressed in cream cotton pyjamas and a blanket, which she pulled around her shoulders.

'You realise it's only nine-thirty, right?'

She grinned at him.

'I'm cosy,' she said, hugging her arms around her legs. 'It's not like there's anywhere to go, is it?'

'I suppose not. Stuck in social isolation out here.'

'Unless you can get into a boat and find a friend who lives in a cabin, anyway.'

Saul laughed. 'There's always that. How is Ezzie after her session?'

'Asleep. She's chatted about Mac the whole time since he left. I'm sure I even heard her say his name in her sleep. Whatever he said and did with her really made a difference.'

Saul took a sip of coffee with a nod.

'He knows what he's doing. Don't expect too much too soon though, she may kick back tomorrow.'

Maddie smiled out of the window. 'I don't think so,' she said wistfully, 'he's done such a good job with her so far.'

Saul looked at her with a bemused frown. He placed the cup on the desk and swivelled his chair toward her.

'Maddie, he's done nothing but talk to her so far.'

'Right, and look how much brighter she is already.'

Saul rolled his eyes, took a bite of toast, and surveyed his sister.

'He's amazing,' Maddie mumbled.

Saul cocked an eyebrow.

'He's a mess,' he answered.

Maddie rest her chin on her hand as she looked out into the night with a small pout.

'He's not in a good place, Maddie. When he is, I'm sure he will be amazing, but right now, he has more than enough on his plate. Trust me.'

'I don't like him like that, Saul. I was just saying.'

'Sure.' Saul said swinging back to the screen as he chewed the toast and marmalade and took a swig of coffee.

'Are you giving him therapy?'

Saul stopped chewing and turned to stare at her.

'No...' he paused to think, and Maddie watched him from the window seat. 'We both offer each other alternative perspectives, I suppose. We've both had the rug pulled from under us. Maybe that's why we gel so well. I don't know. We're both a mess.'

Maddie grinned and padded over to muss his hair.

'You're not a mess. You're perfect. You and Mac are like peas in a pod. I bet you have brain discussions all evening, it must be so boring!'

She laughed as she left the room, shutting the door behind her. Saul smiled after her.

'If you only knew,' he murmured, taking another bite of his toast, and aimlessly scrolling down more jobs, before logging onto his bank.

His stomach clenched as he entered the password. He knew there wasn't a lot left, he also knew that his ma would let him live here for free if the worst came to be, but he didn't want to have to take advantage of that. Didn't want to get that far at all.

The savings popped onto the screen, and Saul gave a small groan. There was just over three thousand left. Peanuts.

Shit. There has to be a job out there other than a cashier in a supermarket or the local village shop thirty miles away, surely.

Shop. An idea came to him. Ma's apple pies? Maybe he could sell them, set up a shop here? With Mac Macauley endorsing them too, surely they'd be a hit?

And surely, you're an idiot.

The phone ringing gave him a welcome distraction until he saw that the number was Greg's again. He watched as the phone rang out, wondering whether to bother answering, or whether to let it ring off. With a sigh he finally pressed to answer.

'Greg,' he said.

'Saul. Are you home right now?'

Saul's stomach plummeted. He hoped his old friend didn't need a place to stay. He wouldn't have a great excuse to say no with all these rooms going free, and he didn't want to be put in a position to have to offer.

'Not right now, where are you?'

'London. But where I am isn't the point. Are you staying with your parents?'

'Hmmm,' he said non-committal.

'Fantastic! Saul, listen,' he said, 'I have an update. How do you fancy earning a fortune?'

Saul sipped his coffee with a frown, already wary. 'Honestly? I have no desire to do anything even remotely illegal again, ever in my life. So if that's what's coming, I'm not interested.'

'No, this is not illegal. I'm just offering you five million if you can help an old friend out.'

Saul sat back in his chair and laughed. 'Five million? You've pulled that from the air.'

'No. I have it on good authority. I have twenty million coming my way if I can pull this off. For your part, and because you've been such a good mate, I'll let you have five if you can help me out. It's not illegal. You don't have to do anything but give me directions. I need to get somewhere. If it all goes tits up, which it won't, you won't be incriminated, because you won't know anything. Frankly, that's the way I want it, it was you that let us down last time with your loose lips.'

Saul barely heard the insult. He felt a twinge of interest.

Five Million? He could set up any business he wanted with that amount of money. Do something on his own again, and let's face it, with anyone else there would be incredulity, but Greg did have a knack of getting his hands on money. He had produced most of the start-up costs to the clinic here, and there had never been any comeback on that.

That's not to say that it was legal.

Saul licked his dry lips, his hand gripping tight to the phone. His eyes drifted to his account balance on the screen.

Did that matter if he never knew?

'Directions?'

'That's it. That's all. I won't even tell you what for, it'll be over in five minutes, you don't even have to see me.'

'Where to?'

Greg began to laugh. 'So, we have a deal? you'll do it?'

Saul hesitated, he felt the familiar instinct that Greg was up to no good, he also had a feeling this may be to do with Mac's brother and a payback plan after his last call. But that man deserved it didn't he? Especially if he had done the dirty across Mac too.

Are you talking yourself into this?

Four measly numbers stared at him from his bank screen. £3,108. He tasted salt from his damp upper lip as he wiped a hand across his mouth and his heart began to thump.

The money would be nice, and Greg is usually as good as his word. There will be no comeback, I don't need to know anything, right?

'Okay,' he said, 'It's a deal. I'll do it,'

'Brilliant!' Greg said, a little too enthusiastically, 'I knew I could count on you. This is absolute fucking gold, mate. Gold. Here's where I need to be...'

CHAPTER FIFTY-TWO

SULA WAS IN THE bathroom. Mac knew it. Knew what he would see, knew what would happen, and still felt himself drawn down the corridor to the lit room at the end.

He stood at the door, which was open a notch, light spilling into the corridor from inside. He heard the slosh of water (*blood?*) and the squeak of flesh against the bathtub. She was up. The water sloshed over the tub in a torrent. He heard it first, and then he felt it gather around his feet under the doorway, warm and wet. He knew what he would see before he saw it.

Red.

The slap of a bare foot on tile, and Mac saw his hand stretch before him, felt the cold of the wood under his hand as he pushed lightly. The door creaked open.

There was red pooled everywhere, running out of the bath, onto the floor and out into the corridor. It felt like molasses tugging at his stockinged feet as he walked through the liquid toward her.

Sula.

Olive skin naked, blood streaked. Swollen breasts, but this time the thatch of hair below was obscured by her heavily pregnant belly, which protruded full and round before her. Sula looked at Mac and cupped her hands underneath it as she pressed her bottom lip between her teeth. The act may have been seductive in life, but right now Mac felt sick, there was a pressure around his head that was causing a high-pitched whine in his ears.

She moved toward him, her eyes never leaving his.

'Mac? Would you like to meet your worm?'

Mac felt his stomach roll over as the stench of blood and something else, nauseatingly sweet, rose from her.

'Is it my baby?' he said. His voice thick with revulsion.

Sula began to laugh, throwing her head back so that he wet curls flicked and streaked a splatter of red across his face. He gagged and wiped it with his hand, smearing blood across his cheek.

'Of course it's not your baby, Mac.' She said, her eyes back on his, with no trace of mirth left.

Of course not, Mac, it never was yours.

Mac felt like someone had stolen his soul, he was empty and desolate inside.

'No?' he said. He hitched a breath and gagged at the stench from her as she moved close. She smelled old and fetid. Rotten.

Sula grabbed his hands in hers and placed them to her skin. Her huge pregnant stomach pulsed and rolled under his touch, something huge was in there, something ready to be born. The sweet sickly smell reached his nostrils again, and he tugged his hands back with a moan.

'It's your worm. You made it like this. It's not my fault.'

She began to moan, and Mac moaned with her as she dropped to the floor, grabbing at her belly which looked like it would explode from the movement inside. Her skin stretching so thin he could see veins threading across it.

'It's mine?' He said.

Sula screamed and threw herself back against the tiles, hands clutching at her stomach, clawing and grabbing at her belly button until it gaped wide. Inside something passed the opening, and Mac wanted to shriek, but he found air was precious in here, and he could draw no more of it in to let any out. He stood in a silent scream as Sula clawed open her stomach, grabbed the wriggling thing and pulled it out.

Octopus' tentacles hung from its meaty body in place of arms and legs, and a beak replaced its mouth. The baby opened its beady eyes, looked right at Mac, and began to squawk. Small feeble, bird-like cries. Sula looked repulsed. She held the squawking thing aloft and brought each tentacle to her mouth chewing them off and swallowing them whole as Mac watched, pooled in sweat and blood, his stomach convulsing with revulsion.

Fresh black blood dripped down Sula's chin, coursed between her full breasts and down between her legs. Long dark pulsing streaks. The baby squawk-screamed as every tentacle was consumed and then Sula grinned and offered the baby to Mac.

'Here's your worm. Take it.'

Mac shook his head feverishly, finally backing out into the corridor. The thing landed at his feet with a wet splosh and tried to move pathetically toward him, beak still making weak noises, and pecking at his stockinged feet.

He shrieked and ran for the door as Sula laughed long and hard behind him. The baby-worm was gaining on him, which seemed impossible with no legs, but the corridor was too long, there was no escape. He turned to the lump of flesh as it leapt at him, forcing its beak into his face as he fell backward. Down, down, until he hit the ground with a thump.

The bang reverberated and pain exploded through his head as the sharp beak turned to soft wetness. Mac whimpered and opened his eyes to find Rolo above him. Pushing the dog backward he sat up and nursed the bump at the back of his head surveying his surroundings in the darkness.

Bloody hell, Mac, you fell out of bed again!

'I fell out of bed,' he laughed as Rolo's tongue tried to lick at his face again. 'I'm not in the bathroom, I fell out of bed!' Relief turned his legs to jelly, his bones to rubber as he tried to get up. 'I fell out of bed after a shitty dream. That's all. There's no Sula. No baby.'

He laughed and checked his watch - five thirty in the morning. And then the statement hit home.

But there was a baby.

Mac froze, hand halfway through flattening hair that was getting as wild as it was long. Ice settled in his stomach, but white-hot heat burned his heart. An ache spread across his chest.

'There was a baby,' he whispered, bringing a hand to Rolo's head. The dog cocked his head to listen, ever the ear for a hard conversation. 'Sula had an abortion, Rolo, that's what Tom said, she was having a baby. We wanted a baby, but she got rid of it. What does that say? What does it tell you?'

Rolo whined and cocked his head to the other side, his face serious.

'Yes, exactly,' he said. 'It means that either Tom is lying about why she was here, or that the baby wasn't mine.'

There was a click downstairs, and a small scrape. Mac was thinking so hard he barely heard it. Rolo turned his head to the stairs and then looked back at Mac.

'The fact that Tom is now admitting that she was here, and that his story corroborated with Saul's, means that it's likely to be the latter of the two, eh? Sula was pregnant, and she got rid of it because it wasn't mine. She had been having an affair with Tom, who brought her here and looked after her as she had treatment to get rid of the baby, so that they never had to tell me what they had done.'

Downstairs something banged in the bathroom. Rolo gave a whine and Mac let out a moan as his stomach churned and bile rose in his mouth.

Fuck you, Sula. I don't want to hear anymore.

He sank to his knees and pulled the small bin next to the bed toward him as the contents of his stomach gushed forth. He wretched and gagged until he thought his stomach would crack and his eyes would bleed from the pressure. Finally, he sat back on his heels, wiping sweat, tears, and vomit from his face with his t-shirt, which he took off and placed in the bin to be thrown out.

Cold air wrapped his body, and he leaned under the bed to grab a fresh t-shirt and hoodie from his bag. He paused, one hand on the bag, the other on the bed above. Pain gripped his stomach, his chest, his head, and tears blurred his vision. His stomach hitched and clenched as he sobbed loudly. He had thought that he had cried all of his tears for Sula, and maybe he had. These tears weren't only for Sula, they were for betrayal, rejection, and a lost child that had never been his.

Downstairs, there was a small screech of the shower curtain, and something turned on the taps to run the bath.

CHAPTER FIFTY-THREE

Mac woke a little after twelve, still half-dressed on the bed, to a banging on the door. His face felt puffy, his eyes half closed and there was the sour stench of vomit next to him from the bin.

He raised his head, which throbbed with each movement.

This is like having the hangover from hell, but without the drink.

He raised his stiff neck, and a whine settled in his ears as the pounding hit the door again, urgent and hard. Rolo began to bark downstairs as the handle of the door shook and rattled and the pounding began again.

'Open up!' A male voice said over the banging of a fist and Rolo's barks.

'For fuck's sake, I can't even cry over my unborn worm in peace,' he muttered, and pulled a new t-shirt and hoodie on over his jogging bottoms.

'Are you in there? Open up!' The voice shouted again, although Rolo's frenzied barking was almost drowning the man out. Mac's mind sludged through reasons that someone would be hammering his door in the middle of nowhere, and then he was on the stairs, running a hand through his hair. A shadow passed the side window of the living room, someone large and dressed in black. Mac hesitated.

Tom said to be careful. There were people after him.

Was this one of them?

There was a shadow at the side kitchen window now and a gloved hand at the glass. Whoever it was they had circled the cabin and were now looking inside. Mac stood still and silent at the top of the stairs, trying to get a glimpse of who the man was, but a black hood shrouded the face in shadow. He swallowed and glanced behind him for anything that could be used as a weapon and came up with nothing but a Nike trainer.

It will have to do.

He leaned back to grab it as the shadow disappeared and the banging recommenced on the door. Harder this time. Louder, rattling the hinges against the frame, alongside Rolo's volley of barks.

'Who is it?' Mac yelled, ashamed to find he was shaking a little at the violence and persistence of the visitor.

Probably Tom's little confession, too. Thanks, brother.

He reached the door as the pounding started up again; the noise sending a jolt of pain through his head. If he was going to be murdered, he decided, at least it may be more peaceful on the other side. He opened the door to the back of a large man who was stepping toward the truck. For a moment Mac wanted to bang the door shut while the intruder was moving on but then the man looked back.

'Saul?' Mac said.

Saul hesitated, and then he smiled.

'Mac, thank God. I thought something had happened to you.'

Mac shook his head puzzled as Rolo pushed past him to greet his new friend eagerly. A twinge of worry crossed his mind as he remembered that Tom said to be wary of the doctor. This was Saul though - doctor or not, he was his friend - wasn't he?

'Why would something have happened?' he said.

Saul moved to the door, relief on his features. That wouldn't be there if he were out to hurt him, would it? Mac stood his ground in the doorway.

'What's the matter?' Saul said, standing respectfully back, then he peered more closely at Mac. 'You look like hell, Mac, what on earth is going on?'

'I learned some news from my wonderful brother. I'm fine. Why the hell are you breaking my door down?'

Saul frowned at Mac.

'Why? I was worried about you. You were supposed to be at the house with Ezzie over three hours ago. We didn't have your number. I thought something had happened, maybe we'd better swap numbers, eh? It would save me a trip... especially to stand on a doorstep in the cold.'

Mac's mouth dropped open.

Ezzie. Ezula. Bugger.

His hand covered his mouth with a slap.

'I'm so sorry, Saul. I forgot. I had an awful night. I had this crazy voicemail from Tom, it was...'

'Bad?' Saul said.

Mac looked at him. Saul, his friend, worry in his face. Worry for Mac. Was there a way that Mac could check his credibility? If he repeated what Tom had said about Sula, then surely, he would know that Saul was genuine.

He nodded. 'Yeah, as bad as it gets.'

'You found out about Sula.' It was a statement, not a question.

Mac nodded.

'Shit Mac, I'm so sorry. I wish I could tell you why she did it. It was never our job to go into details in those situations, and obviously she seemed like a switched-on woman. She knew what she wanted, there was no doubt, and her so-called husband was with her. It all seemed above board, so Greg gave her the tablets to do the job.' He shrugged and Mac felt a pain stab at his chest.

'What were the pills for?' he said, pushing Saul further. Saul frowned.

'It was early in the pregnancy Mac, there was no procedure, pills can be given to abort. Your brother brought her here to the cabin for the pills to do their job. An abortion leads to a few weeks of heavy bleeding. I presume she wouldn't want you to be suspicious by going straight home.'

Honesty, with no hesitation. Mac nodded and stared at the log pile. Stock was dwindling, he would need to cut more soon.

'Mac? I'm sorry I didn't say, you understand why I didn't want you to hear it from me, right? It wasn't my place to tell you.'

Mac looked at Saul and pursed his lips.

'Yes. I know.'

Saul nodded and rubbed his arms, his breath coming in clouds in the freezing air.

'Okay, well. If you're alright. I mean...' he glanced to the loch, and Mac suddenly felt bad for the man in front of him, who was only here because he cared enough that Mac hadn't turned up. The man that he had sat and laughed with, cried with, slept with, for crying out loud. The man who had cried as he pleaded with him to help his niece.

He trusted Saul. He wanted to trust him, and he wanted to help Ezula too. Mac couldn't place Saul with the monster that Tom portrayed over the phone. Saul turned away and Mac decided he didn't want him to go.

'Saul! I'm sorry, I forgot myself. Come in, and I'll get a fire lit, you must be freezing.'

Saul turned back with a chuckle. 'I didn't want to say, but aye, freezing about covers it.'

Mac dragged his mouth into a smile and stepped aside to let Saul in, scanning the trees for... something. He didn't know what he just felt uneasy. Satisfied that there was no one else around he shut the door and found Saul staring at him from the stairs.

'Are you okay, Mac?'

Mac shook his head. 'Not really.'

He put the kettle on and threw Saul the box of matches to light the fire. Once they were sat with their drinks, fire warming their bones, colour coming back into Saul's blue lips, Mac decided to ask. He felt a sudden need to know everything there was to know about what had happened, and he had a feeling that Saul would tell him the truth as opposed to Tom's white lies to save his feelings.

'What happened?' he asked.

Saul needed no prompting. He knew what Mac was after.

'Well, as I told you, they posed as a married couple. They were seen together and left with the clinic's card and the pills that would abort the foetus. I honestly thought that would be the last we saw of them, but a week later I had a call from the lady, Nicky - well, Sula, - to say that she was haemorrhaging, and could Greg come out to her? As it happened, Greg wasn't working that day, he'd gone off into Inverness. When she explained the loss, I wasn't too worried, I got to know the bleeding abortion can cause. I would have left it for Greg the next day, but the lady was terrified. She thought she was dying, and so I cancelled my last two patients and followed her directions to the cabin. Here.'

Mac nodded his head, feeling numb. Emotionless.

'When I got here, she was in a mess. There was blood. A lot of blood, but again, she had brought no thick towels with her to catch the flow.'

Blood.

Mac felt his head spin.

'Towels?' he said, his voice seeming to come from somewhere far away.

'You know. Ladies towels, for the time of the month? Only she wouldn't have got away with regular towels unless she had a good few boxes. The problem was that she had none. At all. It struck me as weird that she hadn't had that forethought, but I had brought several boxes with me for her anyway in case she had only smaller ones, so I gave her those.'

'What did you do for her?' Mac said, sipping his tea as he stared at the fire.

'Do? There was nothing to do. She had to lose the baby, which is to bleed at her gestation. She just had to bleed for as long as it took. I told her to wear the big towels, if she soaked through in less than an hour to call me, then she may need hospital, but I wasn't overly concerned. I told her to clean up, and I helped clean this place before I left. She was happy enough after I had explained, and I didn't hear from her again until your brother brought her back two weeks later.'

Mac felt something jar.

'You helped her clean up what. Her...' he couldn't bring himself to say it.

Saul reddened and shook his head quickly. 'No. No. She cleaned herself in the bath, before putting a sanitary towel on. I waited until she was clean, but there was blood on the floor in a few places up toward the bathroom. She had been completely unprepared. It had flowed from her with nothing to soak it.'

'Puddles of blood.' Mac whispered, and swallowed hard.

'Literally. It wasn't pleasant. I can see why she panicked, but she was fine.'

'I wish I could have been here for her,' he said, but he didn't quite believe that himself. She had taken his brother to help at a time she when she would have been petrified. Why hadn't she told him?

There's only one reason I can think of.

That reason filled his stomach with swirls that made him want to vomit again. He shook the thought away and took some deep breaths.

'Aye, I know. I can't think what happened for things to pan out that way-'

'You can,' Mac cut in, squeezing his cup hard. 'So can I.'

Saul stopped and stared at him, then he looked away toward the fire.

'I'm sorry,' he said.

Mac sighed. ''s hardly your fault. Thank you for helping her when she needed it.'

'It was my job, Mac, I would have done it for anyone.'

'I know. Thank you anyway.'

Saul stared into his cup.

'Do you know whose it was?' Mac said, impulsively spewing the question forth.

Saul shook his head. 'No. I presumed it was his, as they said they were husband and wife, but equally it may not have been, that's speculation. There is no DNA test done in those situations. There's no way to tell whose it was.'

'So it could have been his.' Mac said, lip curling in disgust.

'It could have been yours.' Saul said. 'We'll never know whose it was now, and you shouldn't speculate her reasons, you'll drive yourself mad.'

'Maybe Tom will tell the truth for once, now I know.'

Saul raised his eyebrows.

'Aye, maybe,' he said softly. 'but I can't tell you any more than that. That's all I know. A couple of weeks after she had the pills, they came back to the clinic together. He was ranting about the crap she had been given and what a scare she had. He heard some stuff he shouldn't before he announced his presence, and next thing I knew the police were knocking on the door.'

'Sounds like my brother, on his high horse. She must have been pretty scared if he came back to have a go.'

'She was. Terrified. But it was only because she was unprepared. That's all. The whole abortion was pretty textbook, by the time she visited the clinic after two weeks, the bleeding was already significantly less.'

Mac nodded and heaved a sigh, closing his eyes for a few seconds. When he opened them, Saul was staring down at the contents of his cup. Mac took a moment to study him. He looked like Mac felt. Tired, sad, and pissed off. Like he was having a conversation he didn't want to have, and staying to have it, anyway.

God Mac, pull yourself together. This is it. It can't get any worse now. The bombshell has hit. If they had an affair so be it, what the hell can you do about it now? Both of them can go to hell, I won't get dragged back down the rabbit hole again.

'I'm sorry,' Mac said.

'Sorry for what?' Saul said looking up at him.

'For dragging you through this shit, for letting you and Maddie down, for letting Ezzie down.'

Saul shook his head with a frown. 'It doesn't matter. You take as long as you need. This isn't a small shock, it's life changing, and I know there are things you'll need to sort that may knock you off your feet again. I'll be here either way, and so will Ezzie. We have until next August, right?'

A glimmer of a smile played around Saul's lips and Mac felt a smile creep across his face too.

'I won't be knocked back down again. I'm through with the crap. Sula seems to be causing me more problems dead than she ever did alive. I need to buck my ideas up. I'm sorry for doubting you,' he said.

'Doubting me?'

'Something Tom said to me in the message last night. He's had a little trouble with your friend by the sound of it, Tom said to watch both of you because you were coming for me up here. For a second this morning, I didn't know what to think. I should have known better.'

Saul pursed his lips and looked back into his cup with a nod.

'Don't worry about it,' he said, looking at his watch. 'I'd better get back, will you be okay? You could come back with me. Stay a few days at the house?'

Mac shook his head.

'I'll be okay. I need to have a chat with Tom, get a few things sorted here. I'll be up tomorrow though, for Ezzie. Please give my apologies to Maddie and the family, tell them I won't let them down again.'

'You haven't let anyone down, Mac, you don't have to come tomorrow if you don't feel up to it. Listen, here's my number, message me if you need to cancel, and don't feel guilty about it.'

They exchanged numbers and Mac and Rolo waved Saul off the pier.

Good job you're going up there tomorrow, he won't be back here to mop up your tears again for a while.

How did you manage to walk into such a big pile of shit?

CHAPTER FIFTY-FOUR

Tom followed Meg to a booth that sat right in a corner of their favourite pub, The Princeton. It was a far cry from the pub he had been in last night, even the clink of the cutlery, the sounds of glasses on wooden tables, the laughter, and the chat seemed gentler in here. The air smelled cleaner, and as an added bonus he didn't stick to the floor.

There was also a Christmas tree in this pub, and lively, tasteful, decorations. Instrumental Christmas songs played on the radio providing a cosy and festive backdrop. Down on Sherborne Street there had been no signs of Christmas. It could have been any winter month at all.

As Mariah sang about all she wanted for Christmas, Tom felt that all he wanted was to get rid of the debt that was hanging around his neck.

Santa, if only you were real, buddy.

Meg threw her bag over to the far side of the booth and sat down.

'What do you want to drink?' Tom said, and Meg looked up with surprise.

'They'll come round and take our order, sit down, Tom.'

'I need a drink now,' he said.

Meg pursed her lips and gave him a look that said she was less than impressed. She held her tongue, however. Thank heavens for small mercies.

'I'll have a large merlot then, please.'

Tom fetched the drinks from a tastefully dressed lady at the bar and took them back to the table, taking a swig of Jack Daniel's along the way. Meg tutted as he reached the table.

'Really, Tom, you look like an alcoholic. You haven't even taken your bloody coat off and half your drink has gone.'

'Only a sip,' Tom said.

He sat in the booth and looked at his wife with trepidation, tapping his fingers on the side of the glass as she sipped at her wine and nodded in approval.

'It's a nice wine, whose was it?'

'House.' he said. 'I couldn't remember whose you usually have.'

She huffed a laugh.

'It hasn't been that bloody long since we've been out,' she said.

'I know.' he worked his jaw and exchanged tapping on the glass for tapping on the table so that he could take another swig of whiskey. He glanced around the pub with longing. There were only a handful of couples in here tonight being mid-week. All of them looked cosy, loved up and happy, chatting and laughing as though they hadn't a care in the world. Who knew, maybe they hadn't. It was almost Christmas after all, the time of good cheer.

A warm hand covered his, and he turned to see Meg watching him.

'Come on Tom. I'm sure whatever it was it's not that bad. We've worked through a whole load of shit since we've been married. I'm absolutely certain we can work through this. What is it? Hit me with it.'

Now that they finally had a moment to themselves to talk openly, Tom didn't know where to start, which was ridiculous because the whole meeting with the ex-doctor had lasted less than fifteen minutes, and he had heard nothing since. He clenched his jaw and swallowed hard before finishing the last of his whiskey.

'I don't know where to start.' he mumbled down into his empty glass.

Meg waved the waitress over and ordered him another whiskey. She pulled out her purse, but he told the waitress to put it on a tab. It wasn't like they had driven here. He may just drink himself silly before the hour was out.

Meg put her purse away as the waitress left.

'Well, I know he didn't accept the two million because the account still has just over three in it. I presume the extra was persuasion money that he didn't want either?'

Tom pushed out his lips and shook his head. 'He wouldn't take it.'

'So, if he doesn't want money, what does he want? I can't believe there's anything else you have that would be worth anything to him. All crooks want money, surely?'

Tom nodded his head and thanked the waitress as she placed the double Jack Daniels on the table in front of him and left.

'Yes, they certainly do,' he said.

'So he wants money? Okay. Well, we can work with that, can't we? Did you offer him any more?'

'We can't pay what he wants, Meg. We can't.'

'Of course we can. Name it. We can re-mortgage, get a business loan, get a personal loan if we have to-'

'No. That would get us get us six million at the most.'

Meg frowned. 'Well, how much does he want? We could possibly scrape ten. I know a few people who-'

'Twenty.' he said, cutting her off. Meg's mouth fell open opposite him. She snapped it shut with a flick of her eyebrows.

'He is a greedy little bastard, isn't he?'

'I don't think he's even bothered about the money. He just wants to see me on my knees, in whatever fashion or form it takes. He wants Mac to make up the rest of the money.' Tom tipped his glass and swallowed a large mouthful that burned on the way down.

The thought of Mac twist his stomach with an iron fist. He still hadn't answered any of Tom's calls and Tom knew that he not only had to stay away from the doctor up in Scotland, but that he had armed him with the information about Sula's pregnancy to deal with up there alone.

'Mac?' Meg said, her voice raising in surprise, 'What the hell does Mac have to do with this?'

'Nothing.' He looked up to meet his wife's eyes. 'Nothing at all, but I do think the pieces we put together before may be a forgone conclusion.'

Meg scanned the pub, presumably for eavesdroppers, before looking back at him. 'How do you mean?' she said.

'I think they're working together to get to Mac, so that they can get to me through him. In fact, I know they are because I threw it in his face that he knew Mac was at the cabin and he didn't seem the slightest-'

Megs hand gripped his wrist. 'You did what?' she hissed.

'He already knew. It was obvious.'

'You can't know that you bloody fool!'

'I could tell from his face. He wasn't even surprised, Meg.'

'He may have had an inkling. He may even have wondered if the doctor in Scotland had the same man. He may have suspected, but he may not have *known* until you told him.'

Tom swallowed hard and looked at Meg, her words ringing truth in his ears. He felt sick; he felt like he had been played, and if he had given that information willingly then he *had* been played, without a doubt.

'Well, he knows now,' he said.

'Too bloody right he does!'

Tom shushed her, glancing at the other people spread around the pub. No-one seemed to be listening to the couple up the corner either way.

'Meg, we thought this when Mac was having trouble before, they could have been planning this for weeks. He had a picture of Mac and Sula. He knew.'

'Why would he have a picture of Mac? He wasn't there and Sula is dead, Tom.'

'I know.' Tom licked his lips tasting the sweet whiskey residue. 'I know. He wants to ruin me,' he said. 'Like I ruined him.'

'Fantastic. Sounds better than a boat trip to the Bahamas. I still don't see what this has to do with Mac and why they're targeting him.'

'He put two and two together and worked out that Sula wasn't my wife, but Mac's.'

He waited for Meg to put the pieces together herself, but she simply stared at him with a small shrug of her shoulders.

'Sula was at the clinic for an abortion with a man posing to be her husband. He obviously thinks we were having an affair, and that the baby was... was mine.'

Tom stuttered and reddened at the thought as Meg scrutinised him.

'Well, it wasn't,' she said.

'No,' Tom said feeling the heat flush his neck and cheeks. 'That's not the point. No one will ever know now will they, which means that they can mess with Mac's mind to get to me. Drive a wedge between me and my only brother. Skin us for money and leave us at loggerheads for life. I think that's what he wants. Not the money. To see me suffer, to see me break.'

Meg was staring at him. She took a sip of wine, her eyes on his.

'The baby wasn't yours, was it, Tom?'

Tom frowned and slapped a hand on the table.

'Goddamn it Meg, you know it wasn't. Sula came to both of us for help, I wasn't the only one there.'

'No, but you were very eager to help.'

'As were you!' he said. 'We all agreed to the plan. Me, you, and Sula. Meg, please. You know that's not the case.'

Meg pursed her lips and looked down at her almost empty glass as he swallowed the last of his second.

'Meg,' he said, reaching across the table for her hand, she pulled it away. 'This is exactly what he wants, Meg. See it's starting already. I'm going to lose everything through this, aren't I?'

He placed his head in his hands, fingers in his hair as he stared at the table.

'I'm with you, Tom. Unless I ever find out that baby wasn't Mac's. If it wasn't, so help me god, I'll squeeze your balls until they go blue and pop, and all of your baby making days are over.'

Tom looked back up into his wife's blue eyes, now tinged with red in the white which meant that she was close to tears.

'It wasn't mine, Meg. It wasn't my baby. I promise you. I was helping her out, that was all.'

The waitress stopped by for the glasses, and they ordered another round.

'Either way, I suppose we have to tell Mac the reason she was at the clinic now, don't we? You already lied about her being at the cabin. Why did you lie to him, Tom? Why?'

'I didn't want to have to tell him the truth, but I left him a voicemail explaining what happened yesterday-'

'You told him over a voicemail?'

'I had no choice, the doctor threatened to tell him. I had to get in first, to tell Mac the truth.'

Meg closed her eyes and brushed her nose as the drinks came. They forced smiles and waited until she left again.

'You left him a voicemail telling him that Sula had an abortion? He's up there alone, Tom, his wife died little more than a year ago. He was a mess before he even got to the cabin. I'm starting to think I married an imbecile. How could you do that to him?'

'I had no choice. I told him I'd ring and explain.'

'And have you?'

'He won't answer,' Tom mumbled.

'No, of course he bloody won't! What else did you expect? Tomorrow you get in the car, haul your stupid ass to Scotland, sort this bloody mess out, and bring Mac home.'

'I... Tomorrow I-'

'I don't care. You don't do this to people. You can't treat him like this. You get gone in the morning, or I am gone in the afternoon, and believe me, I won't be back. This time, you're on your own.'

'I have a big meeting tomorrow. We're rushed off our feet. Give me until the weekend, please? Then I'll go up, I promise.'

Meg shrugged herself into her coat as she stood. Fury radiated from her, and Tom stood too, grabbing her hands across the table, oblivious to the onlookers from other tables.

'I promise, and I'll keep ringing tonight and tomorrow, all the way to the weekend if I have to. I'll speak to him as soon as I possibly can. In fact, I'll leave him another message explaining, and telling him to stay put, and that we'll be there to collect him on Saturday, okay?'

Meg clamped her teeth onto her bottom lip.

'I will. I promise. I'll make this right.'

'I know you will, you have no bloody choice.' Meg said, with a look that could have turned him to stone.

With that she picked up her bag, took a gulp of wine, placed the glass on the table, and walked out.

Twice he had been to a pub in the last two days, and twice people had stared his way as his drinking partner stormed off.

With a sigh, he swallowed his whiskey in one go, and got up to pay the bill.

Déjà vu.

CHAPTER FIFTY-FIVE

M AC SLEPT SO WELL last night that this morning, as he dressed and went downstairs, he felt like hell. On his phone were two voicemails and seventeen messages from Tom. He ignored every one of them. Today was about Ezula, not about him, or his secretive wife. Nor was it about a guilty brother trying to abscond his guilt by confessing all and asking for forgiveness he didn't think he would be able to provide.

The night had been quiet but that didn't mean that Sula hadn't been busy. Mac stopped at the kitchen area and stared at the fridge, blinking at the letters, their bright colours giving him a headache.

MAD

He pulled a hand down his face as he stared.

'Mad? You're mad? Because if that's what you're saying, Sula, I'd start to think a little differently. If you're saying I'm mad, you're right, I am. You should have just come to me in the first place. If this was so innocent, which I'm not inclined to believe from the way Tom is acting too, then there would be no problem, would there? You know what I think? I think you aborted someone else's baby, possibly my brothers, and that fucking hurts like hell, Sula. I hope to God I'm wrong, but I just don't think so.'

He pulled in ragged breaths of emotion as the M slipped and fell from the fridge onto the floor. Mac huffed a laugh as he picked it up.

'I'm also talking to a fucking fridge. How's that for mad? Take it whichever way you want, honey, but yes, I'm mad. Mad as hell.'

Feeling a little better for his outburst, he set some music to play on his phone, heated pancakes with bacon and maple syrup, and had three cups of coffee before he left, simply trying to tell his body that it didn't need a further three hours of sleep.

It was the fresh morning air that finally revived him. Out on the lake, oars dipping into freezing crystal-clear water under a grey sky that was full and heavy. With the temperature well below freezing, the only vapour they would let go of today would be snow.

He made it round the loch and into the inlet way too quickly. He was enjoying the quiet, the fresh air, the morning birdsong, and this morning he was also enjoying the freedom of a little detachment from his wife. He knew if she had been alive that the abortion would have torn him apart - hell, it had torn him apart anyway, but the fact that she was long gone meant that there was little he could do, and on top of the lies she had already told, he was starting to feel a small stain begin to taint his marriage.

Not so perfect after all.

He had thought it was until her death. There had been no major arguments, no big confrontations that couldn't be solved, and there could be none now either. It would be what it was. It was up to Mac to pick up what was left of his life either way.

He pulled the boat up into the trees, and pulled out his notes, giving them a skim through before walking to the gate, while Rolo ran around his feet with excitement at seeing his new friends again.

It was Maddie that met him, just up the lawn as he walked down to the house.

'Hi!' she said with a wave, Mac raised a hand in greeting as she jogged toward him. Rolo ran ahead to beat him to fuss and hugs. Maddie scrubbed his head and threw him playfully to the side as she continued her approach.

'Hi,' she said again, grinning as she placed her hands on her hips and caught her breath.

'Hi,' he said, waiting for the reproach, the questions, but none came. There was no judgement on her face, just happiness and welcome. 'I'm sorry about yesterday, I had some bad news, it threw my day out. I just...' He broke off holding his hands out. What excuse could there possibly be that would have meant enough?

'Ah, don't worry,' she said with a smile, 'It meant that I could nip out and finish getting Ezzie's presents. I'm so late this year. I'm normally done by the time she breaks up from school. This year,' She threw her hands up, 'It all went out the window.'

'Is it her birthday?'

Maddie gave him a bemused look.

'No, Mac. It's Christmas. In a week.'

'Oh!' He hadn't given Christmas a thought this year. December had just been December. There had been no radio singing Christmas songs, no television to show him festive adverts every three minutes, no cards to write, no presents to get. 'Bloody hell, is it that time already?'

Maddie laughed. 'I wish I lived in your world, Mac. Is it really so isolated over there you don't even know what day it is? I need some of that.'

'You don't,' Mac smiled. 'It drives me insane most of the time. I'm getting better at dealing with it now, but it's been a rough ride.'

'You've had a rough ride, period, that's all. A cabin in the woods is romantic.'

It was Mac's turn to look bemused.

'It's only romantic with two people. There's no romance on your own, I can assure you. Just desolate isolation and craziness.' he looked sidelong at her with a frown. She was busy smiling wistfully (*beautifully*) down the lawn. He watched her a beat before she looked back at him with her own frown.

'What?'

'I was just wondering if you ever watch television.'

'Of *course* I do,' she wrinkled her nose at him.

'That film 'Cabin in the Woods'? That wasn't so romantic. Isolated cabins are nothing but horror infested shacks.'

I should know, my dead wife sleeps in mine.

He smiled as Maddie grinned. 'I haven't seen that one.'

'Don't,' he said, 'it will spoil your whole wonderful, innocent mind.'

'Innocent!' she laughed as she opened the back door into the boot room, and two black bullets flew out, nearly taking Mac's legs with them. The dogs barked as they tore off up the lawn.

'Rolo!' Mac shouted.

'Leave them. Da is out in the shed he'll bring them in with him later, they'll be fine. Come on.'

They were about to leave the kitchen when a man-made engine revved down the corridor. the noise of lips rasped together as the wheelchair spun into the doorway, pushed by Saul. Ezzie was laughing and screaming as she held onto the arms of the chair and came to a stop at Mac's feet.

'Doctor Mac!' she yelled, holding a hand high. He hit her palm with his own and he felt a smile cross his face at her enthusiasm for him being there. 'What are we doing today? You said something about exercises? They're not like school, are they? Because I'm on holiday and last time was a lot funner.'

'Woah, soldier,' Saul said. 'The man has barely walked in the door. Give him a chance.'

He rolled his eyes at Mac with a grin as Maddie laughed.

'She's been like this since you left last time. Whatever you did, it has her talking about you non-stop.'

'I didn't do much, we just had fun,' he said winking at Ezula.

'Coffee, Mac?' Saul asked. Mac nodded as Maddie turned to the girl.

'Ohh, Ezzie did you bring your gift down?'

Ezzie slapped both hands over her mouth.

'I forgot.'

'Oh Ezzie, really.' Saul said.

'I'll take her,' Maddie cut in, 'it'll be quicker, we'll be back in a jiffy.'

Maddie backed the chair out of the kitchen and disappeared up the corridor as Saul stirred water into the cups.

'How are you feeling?' he said, handing him a cup, and sipping a mouthful from his own.

'I'm okay. Better than yesterday and looking forward to working with Ezzie.'

'Good. Did you speak to your brother?'

Mac heaved a sigh. 'No. I decided I don't want to know yet. When I'm ready, I'll contact him. For now, I have a good many months of not having him turning up on my doorstep with that look of pity on his face. I'll get my head around it first. Thank you for telling me, though. I appreciate it.'

Saul pushed his lips forward and wrinkled his nose, not looking much different from Maddie on the lawn. This wasn't a jibing look though. It was a serious 'I have some shit to tell you' look. Mac gave an internal sigh.

'What is it?' he said.

'There's something you should know.' Saul stepped around him, checked the corridor, and shut the kitchen door with a quiet click. 'The other thing your brother mentioned? About Greg? He was right. Greg is after revenge, and after money. He's figured that you have more than Tom, and given that you're alone up here, he can kill two birds with one stone. Revenge on Tom and money to start over.'

'Right,' Mac said. This Greg didn't worry him too much, there was no way anyone was getting down that boggy track to the cabin or past the fallen tree at the end, never mind the trees that had fallen further up too if any had. Getting to him would be as much a nightmare, as it would be for Mac to get out.

Unless someone helps him from this side, anyway.

'Greg rang me a couple of days ago asking for directions to the cabin in return for a good chunk of money.' Saul continued.

Mac felt the floor shift under his feet.

'So, he knows–'

'Of course not. I'm broke, Mac, but I'm not disloyal, or stupid. As soon as he said where he needed to be, I told him I wouldn't help. We argued, and I don't think he'll be calling again for a while, put it that way. He was pretty desperate, Mac. He was mad, real mad, that I wouldn't help.'

Mad. As Sula had said this morning, Mac thought with a shiver.

'Thank you for not saying.'

'I wouldn't put you in any danger. He went off like he had a spanner loose. I don't know what he's planning, and he was never really a thug, just underhand, but yeah, like Tom says, just be careful who you open the door to. And if he turns up, call me. I'll speak to him. I know him well. He won't do anything stupid if I can talk him round. Okay?'

Mac nodded his head. 'Thank you, Saul. Sounds like I owe you one.'

Saul shook his head. 'No, I told you I want nothing to do with him anyway. Prison was a break free moment that I won't be going back on.'

Mac sipped his coffee.

'How much did you turn down?'

'Five million.'

Mac gaped, 'If he offered you five how much is he going for?'

'Twenty.'

Mac spluttered his drink and began to cough.

'Twenty? And you say he's not serious?'

'I didn't say he wasn't serious, I said he's never been dangerous. I didn't say he couldn't change - he's never gone off at me like that before either.'

'Well, he can come for twenty, but I don't have it. It doesn't matter whether he pulls each finger off one by one with a pair of tweezers, I still don't have it, and neither does Tom.'

'He knows Tom doesn't, that's why he pulled you into it.'

'Okay. Well... Okay.' Mac said.

'I don't want to worry you. Forewarned is best, though. He may find the cabin's address from someone else, but it certainly won't come from here. I can promise you that.'

Mac nodded. He may find the address, it still didn't mean that he would get through. He decided there was already enough to think about, he would worry about Greg if he ever appeared. There was noise from the corridor. Saul opened the door as Maddie and Ezzie came back down the hallway, Ezzie waving something in the air. It was a picture of herself and Mac, standing by the loch, stone skimming, she said.

'Ah,' Mac said, hope and delight lighting his face at the grin on hers, 'Does this mean we're going to get rid of that chair?'

'Not today,' she said, 'but eventually, I will stand and skim stones with you from the shore. That's my first goal.'

Mac smiled, pleased that she had taken on board what he had said about setting goals. Ezzie smiled back, and from the corner of his eye, Mac saw Saul put a hand around Maddie's shoulders.

'That's a fantastic goal, well done, it sounds wonderful.' Mac said, folding the picture and placing it into this pocket. 'There is one problem.'

'I know, I know, I have to get out of this chair first,' she said, pulling her mouth back into a grimace.

'Well, no, I know you'll do that. The problem is, that I can't skim a stone for toffee.'

CHAPTER FIFTY-SIX

M AC HAD INTENDED TO work inside with Ezzie today, he wanted to get a feel for the chair, her relationship with it, and what it represented for her, but she wouldn't have any of it.

'I want to go outside, Doctor Mac. Let's go out, pleeeeease.'

'Ezzie, Mac isn't here to cater to your every whim, he's here to help you, which means doing as he says,' Maddie chastised.

Mac looked out at the swollen sky. It was holding its contents at the moment, it would be cold, but he thought they could manage outside for a while.

'We can go out.' he said. 'The exercises can be done anywhere you like. It's cold though, so not for long and then we come in and carry on by a warm fire, deal?'

'Deal!' she said, grin widening. Maddie shrugged her shoulders at Mac from the island of the kitchen and he shook his head at her - *it's all right*.

'I'll bring you a hot drink out,' she said as she disappeared into the hall and reappeared with boots, coat, hat, scarf, and gloves for Ezula. 'I don't know how far you'll get on the damp grass though, the chair really sinks into the ground. I'm not sure this is a good idea, Ezzie.' Maddie said, watching her daughter pull on purple fur-lined boots and tie her scarf around her neck.

'We don't need the chair anyway,' she said, now pulling on her coat. Mac watched as the layers piled on and wondered if she'd fit on his back with his layers, too. He may end up carrying her forwards this time, but she was right, they didn't need the chair. He wouldn't go back on that, now.

Maddie pursed her lips, tightening Ezzie's scarf around her neck. 'Where are you intending on taking, Mac?'

'Only to the garden behind the wall. It's pretty, and sheltered, and old.'

Maddie cocked her chin. 'It's also winter. There's not much in there now. Summer, I'd agree with you.'

'But it's been so long. You always tell me we can't get there with the chair. I haven't been in months. I want to see the garden.'

Maddie looked up at Mac from her position stooped by the chair.

'It's not far, just behind the outbuildings. Try pulling her backwards-'

Mac nodded, that wasn't as far as the swing was the other day. They'd be fine.

'The chair isn't coming, ma,' Ezzie said, tapping Maddie's arm.

'Ezzie, stop being ridiculous-'

'The chair isn't coming,' Mac said, stopping Maddie in her tracks. She looked up in disbelief, and he shrugged with a smile. 'The chair is banned from our sessions.'

'Banned?' Maddie said as Ezzie giggled in the chair.

'Banned!' Ezzie repeated, 'It's far too boring.'

Maddie looked from her daughter to Mac, trying to get a joke that Mac knew she would never catch on to. Ezzie was loving having the secret from her mother. Her eyes were alight, and it was a joy to see.

'Lowers the tone,' he added. 'Never bring a wheelchair to a session.'

Maddie and Saul were both looking puzzled now, as Mac winked at Ezzie and lowered himself in front of her.

There was a shout from Maddie as Ezzie launched onto his back. He signalled that she was okay and assessed her position. Higher than two days ago, definite leg usage in the thrust. He noted it, but kept it to himself. No need to worry about the winter padding, the child was as light as a feather. He stood easily, Ezzie's arms around his neck. He grabbed her legs at the knees.

'Ready?' he said.

'Be careful, Mac, if you need a hand carrying her back, Saul can do it.'

Saul was nodding at the sink where he was re-filling the kettle.

'Are you implying that I'm old and unfit?' Mac said.

Ezzie giggled as Maddie floundered, the vibration from her laughter rumbled through his back pleasantly. He grinned.

'Of course not! I don't want you injuring yourself by...' she broke off at the look on Mac's face. 'Never mind. I'll bring you that drink out when it's done.' She said, cheeks reddening to the shade of her crimson cardigan.

'Let's go, Doctor Mac!' Ezzie's booted feet kicked at his sides as though she were sitting on a mule. He held onto her legs to keep her from kicking at his nether region, where her boots conveniently hung. 'Commencing operation burning chair!'

'Operation what?' Maddie said.

Uh-oh.

Mac pretended he hadn't heard and ducked out of the back door.

'Which way, navigator?' he said.

'Over there,' she yelled with another kick, stretching her arm to point at the apple sheds.

Nursing the hot tea and a hot chocolate that Maddie had brought over a few minutes ago, Mac and Ezzie sat side by side on a bench next to a large, wooden-framed greenhouse that ran the length of the garden. The outer wall served as one side of the enormous lean to, inside was almost bare save for a few mature potted plants - as were the gardens ahead of them. Gravel paths crisscrossed raised beds of soil, culminating at a large sundial at the centre of the walled area. The wall was old, the bricks and mortar crumbling in places. Four large wooden doors led from each wall, surrounded by elaborate stone arches, one of which Mac had carried Ezzie through. Trellising sat empty against walls, and a large trellis archway, which would be shaped like a cross from above Mac supposed, held the sundial central in its focus from any wall of the garden.

Mac took a sip of tea with a nod.

'Well, it's old, and sheltered, like you said. The pretty... I suppose I have to imagine?'

Ezzie pointed to their right where a few small trees sat centrally on earthy beds.

'It's split into four areas. Up there is the fruit area. Those trees are apple, pear, and plum. Around them are lots of different fruit bushes and plants. In the greenhouse we have lemons, oranges, and banana's too. Over there is the veg patch,' she said, pointing far right. 'The fruit and veg come down almost to the middle and then the garden starts this end.'

She pointed to their left.

'This end is mostly plants so colourful that your eyes burn. I told Mr Gabriel to mix the plants so that there's colour all round, but he says he likes thing separate. That way he only has to be in one area.'

'A good plan for him, but not so good visually, eh?'

'No, it sucks. I told grandpa that I would take over the garden when I'm old enough. I could plant it better than Mr Gabriel. I know some plants... but then I suppose... well, now I can't, anyway.'

Mac turned to frown at her, 'Why ever not?'

'They won't let me in here, especially in winter. Too much hassle. Stupid chair.'

Mac's gaze fell to the gravelled pathway. No, it wouldn't be ideal for a wheelchair, but an off-road chair would be perfect if she had been seriously wheelchair bound. The question here was why was she selling herself out when the chair wasn't permanent? Especially when doctors had told her that she was more than capable of walking. She was eight, not four. Surely, she understood what the doctors were saying?

'I know a lady in a wheelchair who manages to do her own garden very well back in England. There are ways around everything. You have your whole life ahead of you, you can do anything you want with it, so why not be a gardener? I think you would do a grand job out here.'

'How do you know?' Ezzie kicked at the gravel with her boot, which happened to house her not so useless legs. Mac wondered just how much she could bear weight on them if she tried. Movement and grip certainly weren't an issue. In fact, for someone who had been in a wheelchair for above a year, there would be an expectation of some muscle wastage, but Ezzie looked like she could rise and perform a highland jig right here on the gravel at any point.

'I've seen your drawing, remember, you obviously have a talent for colour, and what works well together on a blank canvas.'

Ezzie shrugged. 'Doesn't matter anyway.' she said.

'It will. When we've burned the chair, there will be nothing left to stop you, eh?'

Ezzie half smiled up at him.

'I'm not sure, Doctor Mac. Maybe I just have to let it go. If I don't get out of the chair, I'll just end up disappointed and stuck again.'

'Does that mean you don't try? Just because you may fail first time?'

'I could fail every time.' Ezzie frowned out at the garden.

Mac nodded. 'Yes, you could, but the thing is Ezzie, I know for certain that you can absolutely get out of that chair. There is no shred of doubt in my mind at all. So why would you start with not trying?'

'I can't do it,' she said staring down at her not so hot Chocolate. All the comradery and bravery of the other day gone.

'What makes you say that?'

'I know.'

'Because you keep yourself in there?'

'What?'

'If you won't try, then you most certainly do know that you won't get out. That's a fact. If you don't try, nothing will ever change.'

Ezzie pushed out her full lips into a pout and kicked the gravel harder, some of it spat across the ground in front of them. Mac watched it fly.

'You know what I'm wondering?' he said.

'What?' she cocked her head to the side as she looked up at him, fixing him with brown eyes full of... fear? Wariness?

Mac noted but said nothing. There was definitely something under this whole chair. She wasn't physically unable to walk, but she was certainly afraid to let it go.

'I'm wondering why you're in the chair at all. Your family don't seem to know what happened. Your mother said when they finally brought you home you just couldn't stand, but right now you're using your legs just fine. What happened Ezzie?'

Ezula's face darkened, her legs stilled, and her mouth curled downward as she picked chocolate off the edge of the cup.

Hit a nerve. Raw and open, right there.

Mac decided to back off, now he knew there was an issue he could approach it another way later.

'That's okay, if you don't want to say, let's play a-'

'You know what I'm wondering?' she said cutting him off.

Mac frowned, wondering for a second if she was going to ask why he was such a dick.

'What?' he said.

'I'm wondering why you're so sad. You could be happy if you wanted to. You're keeping yourself sad because you want to be.'

Mac blew out a breath.

Jeez, right between the balls.

He knew that she was cleverly deflecting, batting away a question she didn't want to answer with an equally hurtful one of her own, and using his own words against him.

'Okay, yes. You're right, it's much the same thing. The thing with emotions is that they have to be let out and expressed. You can't brush them under the rug and sit on them hoping they'll go away. Eventually they grow and turn in raging monsters that devour you whole.'

'So, you're sad because you have to be?'

'Sort of... it's complicated, Ezzie. I wasn't feeling so sad last time I saw you but something else happened, and when you're only just starting to feel happier, it can knock you back down to the sad side of the meter pretty quickly.'

'Right. Sorry,' she said.

Mac smiled at the sudden regret of her bolshiness. 'It's not a problem, Ezzie, but I think we both have issues that need to be resolved before we can move on. Not just you, me too. If we realise that, then we're on to a winner. I know my issues Ezzie, I want to go forward. I want to be happy. What about you?'

Ezzie swallowed thickly. She said nothing, but she slipped her gloved hand into his.

'Don't you want to walk? Don't you want to be happier? Come in here whenever you want to, and dance like your uncle Saul said you used to?'

There was no reaction from the girl, and Mac turned to see large tears rolling down her cheeks. She blinked at the garden, more falling from her eyes.

'Ezzie?' He said softly. 'What's the matter?'

She turned to him with eyes so full of pain and fear that he could have cried with her. Instead, he placed an arm around her shoulders, and she folded into his embrace, clinging to him as only a child can, as her tears came thick and fast.

'I'm scared, Doctor Mac, I'm so scared. Please help me.'

She dissolved into sobs that wracked her little body. Pain that no child that should ever have to express.

CHAPTER FIFTY-SEVEN

MAC TWIRLED THE PHONE between his fingers as he sank a beer before the log burner, his thoughts fully on Ezzie and what she had said. It was how these things went. He had a framework that was fast going out of the window because it wasn't what the child needed. In fact, Mac thought, probably she mostly needed an ear. If she was open enough to be able to tell someone what scared her so much, then a lot of the fear may dissipate of its own accord. The rest, an adult could help her to work through.

Except that she's been through a hell of a lot. It may not be that simple.

Mac took a cold swig of beer and thought it out, focusing on Ezzie and her nature. She didn't want to hurt her family, that much was clear, and some of the big smiles were certainly for their benefit. She was an intelligent girl, mentally and emotionally, to be able to put her finger on the fact that she was thoroughly scared, and that may have something to do with the chair and not walking.

She was also holding something back.

Mac walked to the kitchen area of the cabin, picked up the packet of cigarettes and the notepad and pen from the little table, and returned to the settee. He had written a few things down this afternoon when he had got back, now he wanted to go over them, and see if he could find any puzzle pieces that fit together. He sat back down, and Rolo jumped up next to him, curling at his side. Mac lit a cigarette and scrubbed the dog's head as he went back over the entire three hours he had spent with Ezula today.

After the breakdown in the garden, they had chatted some more about Mac's work and what made him so sad. He had explained a little about Sula, had told Ezzie her name, and she had commented on how spooky it was without prompting from Mac. Then they had retreated inside, out of the cold, and had played some games in the front room. Mostly question-and-answer games. What would you do if...? And similar things. They had chatted more about Sula. He tried to turn her attention to what she could see herself doing without the chair, but again she turned inward and quiet.

It wasn't as though she couldn't see herself without the chair, but more that she didn't want to think of herself without it. When asked to think that far ahead, she shut the game down. Mac wondered how in the hell she had ever drawn the picture in his pocket of them skimming stones, when the mention of it in the garden had produced such a strong reaction.

Or maybe that's how strong her want is to make her mother happy?

She had said that Maddie had prompted the drawing. She may have done it only for that reason.

The phone pinged, and Mac glanced at the screen to another message from Tom. Twenty-four over the course of the day. He hadn't opened or listened to any of the messages. He was quite happy engrossing himself in Ezula, he didn't need reminding of the crap in his life.

As a young girl in a garden said just today - you get to be happy if you want to be.

Turns out that he did want to be.

There was no way of solving this whole mess with Sula now, anyway. He would never have her word unless she wrote it on the refrigerator with magnetic letters, and so far, she had stuck to one-word sentences. Tom's word meant little now, and Saul couldn't tell him any more than the facts he knew. There was no-one else he could go to for the truth.

Except maybe Meg?

Mac toyed with that idea. It sat far more comfortably than speaking to Tom. But how much did Meg know?

Mac twirled the phone between his fingers again and stared into the fire.

Do you want to know, Mac? Do you want to know the whole story and the whole can of worms it may open?

His stomach clenched.

'Well,' he said aloud, stirring Rolo from his snooze, 'Do you want to know, Mac? Yes or no. Decide. Go with the decision and put this to bed. One way or another.'

I don't want to know, he thought. But if I don't know, it will catch me unawares like it has just now, possibly forever. Here I am working through Ezula's problem and up it pops to blast me in the face with no warning.

So, if you can't speak to Tom, talk to Meg.

His fingers stopped their manic twirl, and he stared at the dark screen of his phone. He lit the screen to check the time, 7.35pm. If he called now Tom may be around, although Christmas was also a busy time of year for the clinic, and Tom did work over a lot toward Christmas. It had caused many an argument between him and Meg over the years. Some of the only arguments between Tom and Meg were over the business and how it ate at his time. Mac was in no position to judge. He had been the same just a year ago.

Cut from the same cloth.

An eye for the same women?

No, he thought. I would never go for Meg. But Sula had flirted with Tom, as she did with most people. What if he had taken it further?

What if *she* had taken it further, lured him in?

His chest constricted, and he struggled to breathe around the lump in his throat.

'Sula?' He whispered. 'My Sula. Would she do that? Did you do that? Or was it him?'

The cabin was quiet tonight, as it had been yesterday, and Mac frowned.

'Running scared now the secret is coming out?'

Silence. Mac looked back at his phone, unlocked the screen, and typed a message.

I need to talk. Are you alone?

He sent the message to Meg, instantly regretting the ball he had set rolling, but also eager to get to the truth, whatever that may look like. At least it would stop him sitting here thinking about his dead wife's secrets.

The phone pinged. Mac was still reading the message as the phone rang.

Yes. I'll call.

It was short and sharp from Meg, but he figured she knew what was going on, and knew that Mac wasn't taking Tom's calls. He answered quickly before he changed his mind, his heart beating like a drum in his chest.

'Hi,' He managed before his voice caught in his throat. Meg was on him so fast he didn't think she would even notice.

'Mac! Sweetheart, I can't tell you how good it is to hear from you. I've been so worried. Are you okay?'

'Well, that depends on what okay means. Am I physically well, brushing my teeth, getting dressed, feeding myself? If that's what you mean, then yes, I'm fine. Mentally? Well, I suppose that part is a mess.'

'Thanks to my tactless husband, aye, I can imagine. I completely understand why you wouldn't want to speak to Tom, Mac, but we've been so worried about you. I wish you would.'

'I couldn't speak to him. Can't speak to him. That's why I asked if you were alone. I don't even want to hear his voice in the background, Meg, or I'll hang up. The thought of him...' Mac trailed off and took a few calming breaths. Getting worked up wouldn't achieve anything.

'To be honest, Mac, I feel exactly the same right now. I don't want to look at him, either. The way he's handled this is just... well. You know, you got the tail end of it.'

'I got the bit I didn't want or need.'

'I know, sweetheart. Luckily for us he's not here, not due back until something past eleven probably, as is usual this time of year. I didn't even ask him. I told him not to wake me when he came in.'

'I'm sorry, Meg.'

'I'm not. He shouldn't have told you this way. He panicked. I don't know why he had to panic and blurt everything to you over a message. Why he couldn't panic and sort this end first? I just don't know. He's like a different man at the moment.'

'He mentioned a man-'

'Aye. Someone was watching him, and they contacted. The same man whose clinic he had shut down, I believe. That's one thing that does worry me a lot, Mac. He says you've met the other partner of that clinic up there. He seems to believe they're working together. I didn't see this man. I don't know what was discussed, but that's why Tom panicked and made the call.'

'I know what he thinks, but I know the man here is legit. I've been careful, and he's been nothing but honest. He's genuine, Meg. There's a mutual benefit to the relationship. I know that he wouldn't muck up what I'm doing for his niece.'

'But Mac, you've only-'

'And he's told me that this Greg has contacted him and asked for directions to the cabin.'

He heard Meg's intake of breath from the other end of the phone.

'But,' he continued, 'he also said that he wouldn't help him, wanted nothing more to do with him, and he told me to be careful and gave me advice what to do if he arrives.'

'Oh, Mac, but-'

'He also told me what went on with Sula here at the cabin. Exactly as Tom said over the message. With no prompting, no force, and no information from me first. He told me his version, anyway. He obviously couldn't tell me *what* happened, just what happened following the termination, from his visit to the cabin, and then their return to the clinic and Tom's call to the police.'

'Mac,' she said with a sigh.

'I'm certain, Meg. I can't be a hundred percent, no. I don't know the family very well, obviously. I am well within the nineties, though. He's safe, I promise you. There is no way Greg is getting to me through him.'

'Greg. Is that the man's name?'

'The one down in London, yes. I presume the one who has spoken to Tom. Saul, the doctor at this end, says that Greg wants twenty million between us, and to make Tom's life a misery in the process, which is why he's targeting me. The fact I'm out here alone is just a bonus to him.'

'Right.' Meg said quietly.

'What do you know of it so far? What has Tom told you?'

'Pretty much the same, Mac. I'm surprised the man up there has revealed so much—'

'He's not involved, Meg. Trust me.'

Meg sighed and Mac doodled absently on the pad in front of him.

'Okay.' She said, 'he does seem to be acting like he's on your side. That may be half of the lure though, Mac.'

'It's not. He has a wheelchair bound niece who I'm helping to walk.'

Silence.

'Are you bloody Jesus now, Mac? How in the hell do you help someone wheelchair bound to walk?'

'It's a long story, but she is able to walk. It's all in her mind.'

'Ah, what you do best,' she said, and Mac's heart warmed at the fondness in her voice. Meg was a good egg. Now that he had been honest with her, he hoped that she would do the same for him.

'He loves the little girl to death, Meg. He wants her better, and to that end, he will protect me, not hurt me. I know human nature well enough to know that much.'

'You should also know it well enough to be cautious.'

'I am being. I asked him for his side of Sula's story before I revealed any of what Tom had said. There was no hesitation, and no difference in the turn of events.'

'Okay. If you really believe that, Mac, then I feel better. Stay on your guard, though, never let it fully down until we've worked out what to do with this man. Please.'

'I won't. What are you planning to do about him? Have you called the police?'

'No. Tom won't.'

'What?' Mac sat upright in the chair, a frown creasing his brow. 'Surely Tom is the one playing games with a dangerous man, not me.'

'I told him so. He says he doesn't know who the man is or where to find him.'

'Not by name maybe, but he knows damn well the police know who he is!'

'Tom wants to give him what he wants, pay him the money, and they both walk away. The end.'

'I don't think it often works like that, Meg.'

'I know. I know. There's something else, and I just wonder...'

She trailed off and Mac stuck the end of the pen in his mouth. That only brought an urge that made him fetch a cigarette from the table and light it.

'What else?' he said.

'The clinic. Let's just say Tom's not being so above board in his practices either. I wonder if the man knows and has threatened him.'

Mac blew smoke.

'What do you mean? Tom has always been ethical, always above board. That's who he is. It's like he has the righteous pole stuck up his arse.'

'I thought so too, Mac. I did, but when I found this out, I wondered, you know?'

'What is he doing, Meg?'

'Much the same as the practice, he shut down. Abortions excluded, of course. He's provided prescription medication to a minor in the past, we both know that, but it was supposed to be a one off. He's still doing it, by the bucket-load. Medication that could not only be harmful, but hasn't been prescribed by their doctor. In fact, their doctor, and probably their parents, know nothing of it. Opiates, narcotics. Drugs, Mac. He was trying to get kids away from drugs, not dish them out by the spoonful. I just don't understand.'

'How on earth did you-?'

'I saw some paperwork. Just the other week. I wasn't sure at first, so I read it through three times just to make sure I had it right. They're dealing with a company abroad to ship medication in. Lots of it. Hardly legitimate, is it?'

'He's also not a doctor. He can't prescribe, so how in the hell is he still getting his hands on it? I thought he'd quit that a long time ago.'

'I don't know. I didn't recognise the signature. I haven't told him I saw it, but I have told him I know what he's up to. I told him I want him to quit. I told him to shut the clinic down, but I'm not sure he will.'

Mac ran a hand over his mouth and tried to shake the fog from his mind.

'Meg, are you sure? This doesn't sound like Tom at all.'

'It doesn't, but I am sure. I told him if he doesn't shut up shop, I'll take the kids and go, but Mac, I'm not sure he will. I think I may have to do it.'

Mac shook his head in the cabin's living area, as though Meg could see him over seven hundred miles away from her own living room.

'No. No. He loves you. There's no way he would let you leave, especially if he knows you are serious. Not a chance.'

'I thought so, but I think maybe he loves the job and the lifestyle more than me. I'm the mother of his children. The cleaner, the cook. That's it.'

'No, Meg. You're wrong. Tom loves you, you're the tightest couple I know! I know that for a fact.'

'What about the baby, Mac?'

Mac was stunned into silence. It took him a beat to remember where the baby fit into all of this. His heart clicked up ten gears and goosebumps broke out on his arms.

'The baby?' He said, putting off what he knew was coming.

'Whose was the baby?'

Mac blinked and swallowed hard.

'I don't know about the baby, do I? I never did, Meg.'

'No, Mac, did you wonder over the last few days exactly why that was? Why were you never told?'

Mac shuddered next to the warm fire.

'I don't even know the story, Meg. I want to know what happened, and yes, of course I want to know why I was never told.'

Mac closed his eyes, he was shaking now, and this wasn't a minor shake. It was a full body kind of shake that he couldn't seem to control. His insides seemed to have turned to stone, cold and hard, while the skin over them tremored and shook.

'I'll tell you what I know Mac. I'll tell you, but you must promise me that you will call if you ever feel upset, or down, or even just lonely. I don't like you up there alone with this news. You will talk to me before you get to the point where you do something stupid, won't you?'

A tear slipped from Mac's left eye and rolled down his cheek. He swiped it away angrily.

No more tears for Sula. None for a liar and a cheat.

'I promise,' he whispered.

'It is true that Sula approached both me and Tom about the pregnancy. She had taken the test while you were away and found she was six weeks. She was a mess. Terribly upset, crying and mumbling how she didn't want it, couldn't do it.'

'But we were trying for a family-'

'I know. Just listen, Mac. So, we discussed it. She said that you weren't ready to be a father - how you were always dashing off some place or other, never home, never contactable, emotionally unavailable-'

'That's bullshit!' Mac said, rising to a stand.

'Listen.'

'I'm listening,' he said, throwing the cigarette into the fire and beginning to pace the small floor. 'Sorry, go on.'

'She said that she had to get rid of it. She wouldn't be able to cope alone, and that she had begged you to slow down for some time but that you wouldn't-'

'I would have for a fucking baby! For my family. There was no baby when she was asking me these things. I-'

'Mac.' Meg said, her voice sharp. Mac snapped off and held his tongue. After a beat of silence, she carried on.

'She said to get rid of it was the only way. I told her to speak with you. There were a lot of ways we could help out, but she was adamant. It had to be an abortion, and would we help her? I wasn't so keen, she didn't seem to be thinking rationally, Tom was more obliging. He found the name of the clinic that same day, and it just so happened to be next to the little cabin. Perfect. See, together they formulated the little plot, right in front of my own eyes.

She would have to change her name so that they, and the public, wouldn't link her to you. Tom suggested the fake marriage, chose the names, and phoned the clinic to book her in. They were to leave next week, and she would need a couple of weeks to recuperate, but that posed a big problem - by then you would be back home.'

Mac clenched his jaw and kicked at a log as he passed the hearth, sending it scattering across the floor. Rolo eyed him warily.

'She quickly said that she would say she was going away with a friend and called you there and then.'

'She made that call to me, with you?'

'Yes, in our kitchen, propped up the work top. I can see her now as though it was yesterday. It was all so mechanical, so fluid. I almost felt like I wasn't in the room. They worked through it all together within two hours. Before I knew what was happening, they were gone. On their way up to Scotland as Mr and Mrs bloody Devlin.'

'Tom and Nicky Devlin.' Mac said.

'Aye. She should have taken more time, should have thought it through, should have discussed it with you first to see what you could work out. That's what I thought at the time, and then I thought no more of it. I was sworn to secrecy, and that was the last we spoke of it. Any of us. Until now.'

'And now?' Mac said, sitting heavily back down on the settee and putting his head into his hand.

'I trusted Tom implicitly at the time, but with all that has been going on, and all that I've found out, it just has me wondering. Why didn't they tell you? Why was it to be such a secret? Why was he so willing to help out? Why the marriage thing?'

'Was it his?' Mac said, more of a statement than a question.

'That has crossed my mind too, yes. In fact, the more I think about how that day panned out, coupled with the lies he's been telling us about the business and the things he's been doing? I wouldn't put it past him. I don't think he's the man I married, Mac. I don't even think he's the man I want to be married to anymore.'

Mac nodded. He got it. Completely.

'I don't think I want to be his brother anymore, either. I know you can't be certain, Meg, but how likely do you think it is that you're right?'

'I can't be certain. That's the truth. But I'm certain he's not running the kind of business he set out to run, or the one he makes out that he runs, and in that vein, he could well not be the man I thought I'd married. Did they have an affair? Did they run off together to abort their illegitimate baby? I don't know, but it's more than possible, isn't it?'

She heaved a sigh on the other end of the phone. Mac knew Meg was a tough woman, solid and dependable, but he also knew that this new knowledge hurt beyond measure, not only the business, but the possibility of her husband sleeping with his brother's wife.

'I've thought it too,' he said. 'That's why I messaged. I had to be certain that I was being silly. Maybe not so much, eh?'

'I'm so sorry, Mac,' Meg said with a sob. 'I'm sorry for both of us. I suppose you never really know another person... until you know them.'

'I'm sorry too,' Mac said. Tears dripped onto the denim of his jeans, darkening the material. 'Meg, the same goes for you. You have a family, and many questions to sort. If you ever need to chat, whatever time of the day or night, I'm here. Call me.'

'I will,' she said with a sniff. 'If he did this, he's an absolute bastard, and I'm not sure I'd believe he *didn't* do it right now.'

'They were both to blame. If anything happened at all, I'm pretty sure she would have encouraged it the way she carried on. It wasn't all Tom's fault, half was Sula's.'

'How did we end up in this mess, Mac? Why, oh, why didn't Tom keep his meddling nose out of other people's business? What a bloody mess we're in!'

'We'll get through it together, Meg. We will. Right now, I have to think about all of this shit and put it into some kind of context.'

'Okay, I'll message you tomorrow to make sure you're all right. You take care, Mac. You didn't deserve any of this. I'm so sorry.'

'It's not your fault. You take care too. I'll speak to you tomorrow.'

He ended the call only a second before the pain engulfed his chest and he broke down, sobbing not only for Sula this time, but for himself. For being led and being lied to without even knowing. Here was the mind man, psychology expert, taken for a whopper of a ride.

What a fucking ride, Mac. Didn't even see the drop coming, did you? And this one goes all the way down, right down underground.

CHAPTER FIFTY-EIGHT

Aside from checking on Meg, Mac focused wholly on Ezula for the next two days, arriving first thing in the morning and not leaving until dark. The snow had begun to fall again, and a small covering had settled over the ground, making a pleasant change from mud to white, although the mud still got into the cabin anyway, hidden beneath the pure cleanliness of the snow.

This morning Mac had woken to a tune. At least, he thought he had. It may have been a dream, only the resonance of the tone lingering into his wakeful state. The same D he had heard before, the one that didn't work. Although when the piano had played a few days ago, it hadn't had a problem with the D. In fact, the whole thing seemed a little bizarre looking back. He wondered if he had imagined the tune.

He also awoke to a fridge message - if you could call it that - it simply said:

YOU

He had blinked at it for a good many moments before ignoring it and leaving to get in the boat.

Outside he had crunched through three inches that had been dumped from the sky overnight and with more forecast later in the day, he wondered if he would get back at all, but Ezula was doing well opening up to him so far and the crux of the matter was definitely close now. The child could walk. That was immediately obvious after the tests he did around her legs as well as her mind. She could walk and she knew it, he was sure, but she wouldn't. She didn't want to, and this was the part of her mind that Mac had to crack. They still hadn't gone into what Ezzie was scared of. She skirted the issue with expert skill, at one point denying that she had said anything at all. He pulled the boat onto the lake, called Rolo inside, and set off.

Four hours later Mac and Ezula were sitting in the large living room in front of a roaring fire, with a tray of juice, tea, and sandwiches which Hester had brought through when they hadn't emerged at lunch time.

Mac had done some exercises, testing her leg strength again, which was good. He had told her to practice the exercises every day, as many times as she could. To his knowledge, she had been doing so. This morning he had her standing, holding her from behind as he had over the last few days. Today, though, he had moved his hands gently away. She had stood for a good many seconds before he revealed he had let her go, but instead of the shocked jubilation he had expected, she had plopped back into her chair with a pout, like the rag doll she wanted everyone to believe she was.

Mac frowned. The only way this child was going to walk was if she confronted her issues. She was more than a good way to walking anyway, she just didn't want anyone to believe she could.

This was a whole different ball game.

This isn't about Ezzie not believing she can walk. This is about a child knowing she can – and choosing not to. For reasons she's not only scared of, but scared to admit.

'Okay, let's break,' Mac said, taking a sip of tea and picking up a cheese and onion sandwich. He stared into the fire, pretending to watch the flames as Ezzie tentatively picked up her own sandwich and began to nibble at the crust, sneaking furtive glances at him. Mac ignored her, knowing the lack of pressure would entice her to speak first. Eventually, she did.

'Doctor Mac?'

'Uh-hmm,' he said through a mouthful of sandwich, deliberately not making eye contact, appearing unbothered.

'Do you have any secrets?'

Mac drew his brows together. 'Do I have any secrets? Depends on what you mean by secrets. I have many secrets from you, and from your mother, for instance, but from my brother? He knows most of my life story. Not many from him.'

'Yes, but do you have any secret secrets, ones just you know?'

Mac thought about what he had experienced at the cabin over the last few months and nodded. 'A couple,' he said. 'There are a couple of things I wouldn't really want other people to know. Everyone has those sorts of secrets, I think. They're not bad, just a little squirmy, you know. Do you have any?'

Ezzie focused on her sandwich, and Mac's heart tried to force its way out from behind his ribs.

Give her time, let her come forward, don't force the issue.

Mac ate the rest of his sandwich and sipped more of his tea, swallowing harder than usual.

'Ezzie?' He pressed finally.

She nodded her head, still looking down at her food, which sat untouched in her hand.

'You *do* have a secret?' he said.

She looked up at him, eyes wide.

Careful, don't lose her.

'Yes.'

'Okay,' he smiled. 'A secret only you know?'

'No,' she whispered, shaking her head. 'You know it, too. I know you do.'

Mac looked into her eyes, and saw the fear that sat behind them.

'You won't tell them, will you?' she said. 'I don't want anyone else to know.'

Mac felt as though he had dropped into this moment, this room, from an alternate universe. He was almost certain of what Ezzie was going to say, but before she said it, he couldn't know for sure. He felt like Neil Armstrong about to step foot on the moon for the first time.

If she said what he thought she would, he wasn't sure how to play it from there.

'I can't tell what I don't know, Ezzie. Who am I to keep the secret from?'

'Ma, Uncle Saul, Grandpa, Grandma.'

Mac wondered if she wanted him to confirm what she was getting at not. He decided to play it safe. He knew nothing until she spelled it out.

'Right, well, I can't say anything about something I don't know about. So, your secret is safe with me.'

He smiled, but she pushed.

'You *do* know, I've seen it in your eyes.'

'I do?'

'Yes.'

Mac looked at her. The force of her willing him to say it out loud was almost tangible. She wouldn't say it, but she wanted him to. Maybe there was safety in him saying it instead. Whatever she was scared of hiding down another path, this was a detour it didn't know about. It couldn't lurk and wait to pounce here.

'You can walk?' he said.

Ezula's large brown eyes filled with tears as she nodded her head. She reached for his hand, and he took it, squeezing it gently. A small reassurance that she would be alright for admitting it.

'How long have you known?' he said, reaching for his tea.

'Always.'

Mac paused with his cup halfway to his mouth. He lowered it again.

'You've never believed you couldn't?'

She shook her head, no. Her breathing accelerated to a pant, and he put his cup down to calm her.

'Deep breaths, Ezzie. I promise you, this is good. The pain won't last, it never does, it's fleeting if we don't focus on it. Fear too.'

He felt her hands shake in his as she moved from her chair to sit next to him on the settee, her bottom lip beginning to quiver. It was only a step, but it didn't escape his attention how easily she moved.

'You're scared, Ezzie. I know, and I know it feels very real to you.'

A tear slipped down her cheek, quickly followed by several more.

'You have to promise me that you won't tell anyone, Doctor Mac. *Anyone*! I'm scared you'll tell them.'

Mac swallowed.

'Ezzie. I have a job to do, sweetheart. Your family has asked me to help you walk. If we both sit on the fact that you already can, then where does this end? I can't keep coming round here for the rest of our lives. So, I'd have to admit that I couldn't help you and walk away.'

Ezzie nodded quickly. 'Yes.'

'I can't do that, Ezzie.'

'W... why?' She stuttered, face aghast. 'Ma will be mad at me, please!'

Mac frowned.

'Why on earth would she be mad?'

'I know she worries about me. She always smiles and laughs and makes jokes, but I hear her crying at night, Doctor Mac. If she knows that I knew I could have stopped it all, she'll be mad.'

Mac felt a twinge in his heart at the thought of Maddie crying night after night. It seemed they were more kindred spirits than he thought. She wasn't so carefree after all. How could she be?

'She won't Ezzie, she'll be more overjoyed that you're walking-'

'No!' Ezula wailed, throwing herself into his shoulder.

The living room door opened, and Hester made it three paces inside before she noticed Ezzie sobbing and made eye contact with Mac. Mac wondered what the hell it looked like with them locked in an embrace on a sofa, although clearly the child was upset. He waved a hand at Hester signalling to give them 5 minutes. Whatever the woman thought, she nodded her head without a word and backed away, shutting the door with a worried look.

If that's worry that I'm doing something I shouldn't, I'll be hauled out of here within the next sixty seconds.

He prayed to god that Hester would trust him. They were so close now. If he could get Ezzie to talk, he could begin to work with her to change her perception. Something he could do with his eyes closed. If he got that far, he was almost certain that he could get her out of the chair.

So close. So far.

Mac prized Ezzie from his shoulder so that he could see her face.

'Ez, listen. There's a way we can do this without them knowing anything about what you just said. No secrets revealed. We can lock that up tight, both of us, right? It never comes out, but we get you out of the chair. Sound good?'

Ezula frowned, small hands coming to her face with the sigh of someone much older than her years. Her breath hitched, and she wiped away her tears.

'No, Doctor Mac, there's no way. I can't walk.'

'But you can. You just said.'

'No, it was stupid. I was testing you. I can't walk.'

Mac sat back, regarding her. She deftly avoided his gaze.

'I don't understand, Ez. You drew me a beautiful picture. I thought you wanted to get out of the chair, stand by the loch and skim stones with me, remember?'

Ezula nodded.

'I had no choice. I had to draw it. Ma thinks I'm okay if I do things like that. If I'm sad, she gets really sad and worried. I don't want her to worry, so I drew a picture that makes her happy.'

'But do you think that really makes her happy? Don't you think she's worried about you all the time? Every doctor in the world has told her you can walk, and yet you insist on being in this chair. Ez, if I know you can walk, and you know that you can walk, we can just say you could do it from today. The past has no bearing, and everyone stops worrying. Including your ma.'

Ezzie swallowed hard. Mac took her hand.

'I know this is hard, sweetheart, believe me. Remember what I said about confronting the issues, not sweeping emotion under the rug?'

Ezzie stared into the fire, making no acknowledgement that she had heard him. He nudged her arm lightly. 'Hey?'

She dipped her head.

'I don't have emotions to sweep under the rug, Doctor Mac. I can't walk.'

'You do have emotion, Ezzie, very strong emotion. I know you're scared. I don't want you to sit on that.'

'So what if I do? What's it to you?'

Mac took the dig, although it hurt. When you had spent a number of consecutive days with someone, however big or small, the whole relationship was amplified. Mac was already as fond of Ezzie as he was of his nieces and nephews. He enjoyed both her company and her humour. It was refreshing to see the world through a child's eyes, and she already knew more about his problems now than most, opening up to her as he had tried to get her to open up to him. He only hoped that she felt the same connection now, or she wouldn't take the bait.

'I like you a lot, Ez,' he said, 'I think you're an intelligent, charming, funny, and caring young lady. I think you'll go on to do great things, and I'd like to see you achieve them, but if we can't get past this, you're not going to move forward. Not only that, but I have to tell your family that I can't help you, and I have to leave.'

Ezula picked at her lip with thumb and forefinger, her face downcast.

'What do you mean, leave?'

'I'll have to carry on living my life, as will you. I can't keep coming over here for no reason.'

'You're friends with Uncle Saul and Ma. I can still see you, Doctor Mac.'

'No.' He shook his head. 'It doesn't work like that. I will only visit maybe once a month or so until I leave the cabin, and then maybe not for a year or so at a time. I live a long way from here.'

A pain crossed his heart at having to leave this family, who he had come to care about a whole lot, but he also knew it was the truth. After Christmas it was January, from there it wouldn't take long to get to Easter, and then August, and he would have to leave. Tom would want his holiday cabin back again by then.

'No, you can move in here. We have space! Please don't leave me!'

'I have to, Ez. There's no choice. I live in England.'

Ezzie looked at him, wild-eyed.

'Doctor Mac, you're my best friend. I haven't had this much fun in ages. Please stay. What do I have to do? I don't want you to go.'

Mac grabbed her shoulders with a look of serious contemplation. She stared back at him.

'You know what you have to do, Ez. We have to work through this.'

'You'll stay with me, even when it's over?'

'When it's all over, you won't need me to stay. I promise.'

'I don't want you to go.'

'Then we have to talk about this chair. Seriously. Like I said, we don't need to reveal the whole secret, but we do need to get rid of the chair. It's detrimental to you and your family to keep up this pretence. I just don't understand. Why? Why would you put yourself through this? Why would you put your ma, and your family, through this?'

Ezzie fought with her own turmoil, her face contorting as she looked from him, to the fire, to her hands, and back to him.

'I'm scared,' she whispered, before lapsing into fraught silence, which dissolved into more sobs.

'Do you like being scared?' Mac asked gently.

Ezzie shook her head. Brown curls, so much like Sula's, bouncing around her face.

'Do you like pretending you have to be in the chair?'

'No,' she said. 'It's hard.'

Mac nodded as she looked up at him.

'I should imagine it is. How you've kept this up for an entire year without anyone suspecting is beyond me.'

'I have to. He'll come for me if I don't.'

Mac felt his heart give a jolt.

'Who will?'

'I can't say.'

Mac suddenly had a horrible feeling this tied into Saul's unethical partner, but Ezzie hadn't really known Greg at all, had she? She hadn't been around when he was here. They had been travelling.

'Is this about a man named Greg?' he said.

Ezzie frowned, her tears subsiding. 'Who's Greg?' she said.

'No-one,' Mac said with a shake of his own head. 'I was putting two and two together and getting five, that's all.

Ez, if you don't want me to have to leave, we need to be honest with each other. I need you to tell me who this person is.'

Ezzie shook her head from side to side, and Mac nodded his head in front of her.

'Or I have to go,' he said.

'It has to be a secret,' she finally whispered.

'I'm good at secrets. I promise whatever you say from here on in will be just between you and me, okay?'

'Pinky promise?'

'Pinky promise,' Mac said, linking little fingers with the girl.

'It's my da,' Ezula said, catching Mac off guard.

'Sorry?' he said.

'My da will come for me.'

'I need to speak to her,' Maddie said. Her hair was back in the messy bun that Mac decided he liked a lot, much like the lady wearing it. Tendrils of blonde pulled around her freckled face in the wind. She tucked them back behind her ears, but the wind pulled them out again.

Without thinking, Mac leaned forward to tuck the hair back for her.

He realised what he was doing mid flow and stopped, hand almost at her face. She watched him without moving. It seemed as if time had stood still around them.

I've started so I'll finish, he thought, tucking the hair back gently. Maddie looked down at her feet with a shy smile, folding her arms across her chest.

'It's been a long time since anyone has tucked my hair back,' she said as she looked back up at him with a smile.

He smiled back with no answer. He didn't know what the hell had made him do it, either. They gazed at each other caught in a timeless moment, and then Mac remembered what they were talking about, and the fact that they were waiting for Saul and Ezzie to come back with another present for him.

Ezzie, Christ Mac, mind on the job. She'll be here soon.

'You can't,' he said, looking back toward the house where he wondered if anyone had been watching them. He stepped back a little, feeling self-conscious.

'Can't what?' Maddie said, smile slipping.

'Speak to Ezzie. This isn't something I should be discussing with you. It's a secret.'

'Are you serious?'

'Deadly,' he said, his own smile gone. 'Maddie, if she knows I've spoken to you, she will close up again completely. She made me promise not to say. I just wanted to be sure I was getting the facts right. Her father is dead, right?'

'Yes, he was shot.'

'You're certain?'

Maddie pushed out her full lips with a slow nod. 'As much as I can be, yes. I would set my source at one hundred percent reliable. The only reason I can't be *absolutely* certain is because I didn't see it myself. The lack of contact is very telling though, especially as she was literally smuggled back out from under him. He's dead, Mac. I know it. I *feel* it.'

'Okay,' he said. 'Don't say a word to her. I'll pick it back up tomorrow. Promise me.'

'I promise, Mac. If this is what it takes, then I'll keep out. She's never mentioned her father since she's been back, so she's obviously opened up to you far more than us. I have to trust that, don't I?'

'Please.' Mac said with a nod. 'It's imperative. You could knock everything back, and don't mention it to anyone else either. Keep it to yourself for now.'

'Okay,' she said. She faltered, licking her lips before looking back up at him. 'Mac, do you think she'll walk again? Tell me honestly.'

Mac grinned. This one he didn't have to lie and keep secrets about, the answer was as obvious to him as to whether the moon would rise again tonight.

'Absolutely, one hundred percent,' he said. Maddie's mouth dropped open as she gasped a laugh.

'Really? You're that certain?'

'The only thing stopping her from walking is her fear. I've tested her legs in many ways over the last few days without her knowing. They're strong. She kicked me like a mule when she was on my back. Those legs are far from useless, she's just scared.'

Maddie laughed.

'I'm sorry. She can be - or used to be - a little overzealous. Not so much now, but then, if you're getting that side of her, that's good! What is she scared of, though?'

Mac thought of Ezzie's confession earlier: *ma cries every night. I hear her.* The last thing Mac wanted was to exacerbate her worry.

'I don't know, but I promise you I'll get to the bottom of it. Don't worry about her, she'll be fine.'

Maddie stepped into his arms and hugged him hard, only surprise stopping him from responding straight away. He folded his arms around her more gently, inhaling the scent of her hair. Feeling her warmth so close made him giddy with desire he didn't want to admit, even to himself, but he couldn't be the one to let go first. If they were here, then he would take it for as long as it lasted.

'Thank you so much Mac.' She said into his jacket. 'Just... thank you. I can't thank you enough.'

'It's my pleasure. She's a great kid,' he said over her head, looking at the apple shed to restrain himself from placing a kiss on top of her head.

That crosses the appropriateness of the moment, Mac. She's grateful, not desperate.

Maddie pulled out of his arms and glanced out toward the house before looking back at him.

'I mean it. Thank you. I know you have such a lot to deal with right now, helping Ezzie means the world to me, but you do know I understand if you ever need time... a break, if you have other things to do or sort. I don't expect this, don't ever think that I do. I'm grateful for every moment that you're here.'

Mac knew Saul had told her much more than he may have done himself, but he realised he felt more comfortable with that than he had thought he may be. At least she knew the truth. Lies and secrets could spoil the very fabric of a relationship before it had begun. Mac had a feeling this was a woman he didn't want to spoil anything with.

And tread over poor Sula like she meant nothing?

Mac tried to hide the wince with a smile. Nothing could happen with Maddie anyway. Sula ruled his every day.

'I do have a lot going on. That's the truth. But I'm in a cabin, miles from anywhere, with more time than I know what to do with. Ezzie is helping me to keep focused, too.

I can't keep thinking around the same old shit each day. I'll go insane.'

Maddie looked at him, concern in her eyes.

'Saul hasn't gone into detail with the situation, but he says you're a mess, Mac.'

'I am.'

'Then being out there alone won't help. Why don't you stay here?'

Mac looked at Maddie. He longed for a life so simple that he could take in how utterly beautiful she was without feeling like such a shit.

Sula may have cheated on you, remember?

You don't know that.

'I can't,' he replied. 'I have to look after my brother's cabin.'

'What's going to happen to it?'

'All of my stuff is there.'

Maddie grinned.

'I suppose the deer may steal it. I saw a deer around here just last week with walking boots on.'

She raised her eyebrows, and Mac felt his lips stretch into a smile.

'They were mine,' he said. 'When you see that deer again, tackle him to the ground. I need them back.'

Maddie smiled and stepped forward to place a hand on his cheek.

'I will. Mac, you have my number if you ever need to talk, you can call or message, anytime. You do still have it, don't you?'

Mac nodded. His cheek tingled with the warmth of her touch, intensifying as she rubbed a thumb over his cheekbone.

'Mac?' She said softly.

'Hmm.'

'Get a shave.'

She grinned, and he slapped her hand away playfully as Saul and Ezzie turned the corner of the patio.

'Here it is,' Ezzie shouted, waving the cap at him.

This time Mac did smile as she handed him the cap. Saul leaned his arms on the back of the wheelchair, panting hard.

'Honestly, Ezzie, you need to get the hell out of this chair because I'll need it if you carry on making me push you like we're in a formula one race.'

Maddie laughed, and she and Ezzie high-fived one another.

'We'll get him fit yet,' Maddie said.

'And Doctor Mac too, but mind fit, not body fit.'

Mac grinned and high-fived her other hand.

'I'm off,' he said as he looked at the sky, which was growing dark. 'Take care, promise me you'll do your exercises, Ez, and I'll see you in the morning.'

'Ez!' she said with a giggle. 'I've liked that, Doctor Mac. No one calls me Ez. That can be our special name.'

He winked at Ezula. 'Sounds good to me, on one condition. Drop the doctor, just call me Mac.'

'Deal, Mac.' Ezzie said with an exaggerated wink.

'Thanks for this,' he said waving the cap at her before turning to walk away with a wave.

'I'll walk down with you,' Maddie said.

'So that leaves me taking the driver back inside, eh?'

Ezzie giggled as Saul revved the engine.

'Bye, Doctor Mac.' Ezzie shouted as Saul turned her toward the house.

'Yeah, bye Doctor Mac, thank you for coming again. I'll bring some goodies your way in a couple of days. We'll have another lads' night!' Saul echoed. He turned to Mac with a grin and mouthed thank you again, before turning to wheel the child inside.

Mac and Maddie walked through the lengthening shadows across the lawn down to the gate at the back of the wall in comfortable silence, Rolo jogging alongside. Maddie opened the latch, swinging the gate wide, and walking down to the loch with them.

She watched as Mac called Rolo, pushed the boat into the water and jumped inside, using the oars to push off the ground at the edge.

'That looks fun,' she shouted, 'it's one of the few things I've never tried, canoeing.'

'Kayaking,' Mac corrected with a smile, 'I'll teach you one day.'

She grinned and clasped her hands to her chest in excitement. Her abundant excitement of everything was a quality that made his own chest constrict.

'I'll hold you to it. Thank you for coming, Mac. It means the world to all of us.'

Mac nodded his head. 'It's no problem. She's a sweet girl. If I can help, I will do. I'll see you soon.'

Still a bit freaky that she looks a little like Sula and her name is Ezula, but we'll let that one slide.

Maddie crossed her arms.

'See you soon, Mac, and remember we're always here if you need anything. Please. You're doing so much for Ezzie, let us help you, too.'

Mac smiled and held up an oar.

'I will,' he said, spinning the boat around and paddling out into deeper water.

'Promise?' she shouted from the shore.

'Promise,' he yelled, looking back over his shoulder.

She held her hand up in a wave and disappeared back up into the foliage.

Mac wondered if he had made the book of records for the most amount of promises made in one short day.

He also wondered if he had made the record for shitting on his dead wife's memory the most times in one day. He thought maybe he had, and then he felt like more of a shit as he rowed back to the cabin.

CHAPTER FIFTY-NINE

THE STARK LIGHT FROM the central fluorescent strip was giving Tom a bigger headache than what he was seeing on the paper. Granted, supply had increased, but not to this extent. After the secretary had left them in the crap, he had lost control of the incomings and outgoings. She had tied all the ends up without him having to dot every 'I' and cross every 'T'.

There is more here than there should be.

He placed the sheets down and rubbed a hand over his eyes and down to his mouth, thinking about Meg and her altercation.

Finish up and shut it down.

Had she seen this?

The paper had been on the desk when they had spoken about Mac. Paper was bloody everywhere since she had left them in the shit, and he still couldn't find a useful, trustworthy replacement for the girl.

More to the point, the man had indicated he knew about this, too. How had he got information? Who was providing him with it?

How is this all going to shit, Tom? It's all unwinding, coming unravelled. You should never have let the clinic get involved, especially when others began working here.

Secrets, the clinic hinged on secrets and prescriptions that should never be. And now one of the main people in the web had left, stringing the secret to wherever she wanted, no longer bound.

Had she said something?

His eyes drifted above his computer screen. Leaflets littered the wall above his desk, pinned to the board where he could see and assess them before doing large advertisement drives which had started by leaflet dropping in his neighbourhood and had now extended nationwide.

Drug abuse: The facts.

Don't get high, get help.

Are the drugs using you?

Need a drink? Need a crutch.

There's always an easier way down.

Know what you're taking tonight?

The campaigns were edgy with punchy explanations, and pictures of pills, and children with haunted eyes and grey pallor. They geared them toward the children themselves, and they were effective thanks to a marketing whizz - a friend of Sula's - who worked in an advertising agency by day, and was so moved by his dedication to helping youngsters, that she had offered her time and resources for free most evenings.

Well, free wasn't really the word - he had offered her payment of sorts, the kind they had both enjoyed for a while before it had mutually ended. She stuck around regardless over the years to help, though, which he appreciated. Without her, the clinic may still have been the small backstreet unit it had started out as.

In the beginning, the odd youngster came to the clinic of their own accord, desperate and anxious, and waving leaflets in his face. Dropping in with whispered tales of things being out of control, and how they longed for the hold of the addiction to stop. These were kids at their wits' end, sometimes parents at their wits' end with kids. Tom spent hours with these kids and their families, helping them through the vital first months, advising them to go to the doctor when medication was needed to temper cravings. This was usually where he hit a wall.

They rarely asked anyone for medical help. Telling him had been hard enough, it taken all of their courage. Going to tell a doctor too? Not a chance. They trusted Tom, trusted that he would help them through cold turkey, which he never could. No one was prepared for the battle that brought - not the kids, and not the parents. And that was where the battle was usually lost, and the addiction won.

Just one more hit, to make me feel a little better - then I'll quit.

It was always just one more hit. Mac had been the same, and ultimately it was the desperation of Mac's situation that had fuelled Tom's drive to source the medication himself. He was a psychologist - he couldn't legally prescribe. He could have taken the extra training to become a psychiatrist sure, but these kids needed him *now*, Mac needed him *now*, and with the help of a friend who had gone on to become a psychiatrist he managed to get his hands on the medication needed, mainly opioids such as methadone and buprenorphine which helped suppress withdrawal symptoms and relieve cravings. Sometimes, if he could get the detoxication far enough, naltrexone, which was useful for alcohol abuse too. These kids rarely came with one set of problems, but it was the whole tangled web that he had loved to sit and un-weave with them. It was the therapist role that he loved.

As the success of the clinic grew, more organisations, doctors and even the NHS were referring kids with problems his way, not knowing that his success hinged on not only therapy, but fake credentials and getting hold of medication illegal in his trade. That was when the clinic had exploded, and he had taken on paid staff. He chose carefully, making sure they knew what they were getting into and why. He chose passionate people, not by the book people. His sources were guaranteed, his lines secure, his credentials had never been questioned yet. They were doing this for the good of the kids. Getting them instant help that would take months with referrals. Saving lives.

By this time, he wasn't able to go as far as he had with the kids that came to his door. He wasn't able to get to know all of them personally, and have the time to tailor a plan, with time for emergency slip backs too. In the end, burnt out and frustrated, he had to choose. Manage the clinic and the staff, or hand it over, let go of the reins, and become the counsellor he wanted to be.

Money had spoken, illegal drugs had spoken, and he'd had no choice but to take a backseat. The clinic thrived, and he managed with just a handful of good, trustworthy, staff, but it didn't take away the frustration of not having the contact himself.

Tom sighed and got up, taking his cup to the coffee machine, and hitting the button. The Machine buzzed and crunched.

If I could go back, I would never make the call. I would never get the medication involved. If I had known that I would eventually take myself out of the loop, out of the contact, the part I love? I would never have done it. Why did I do it?

Hindsight. Glorious. Useless. Mocking.

The cup filled with thick brown liquid

The truth was, he had done it for Mac.

The last person he had expected to walk into his clinic was his younger brother, but one day that's exactly what had happened, and without the medication, Tom was powerless to help him. Without methadone, Mac would never have kicked his heroin addiction. Three years later, at twenty-two, depression and smoking had been the last remaining problems for Mac, which had worried Tom, as that was exactly how it had all started. Depression and smoking had led to more, and then more, until Mac had tried most illegal substances and was addicted to heroin on a steep downward spiral. Tom knew at that point the needle could fall on either side of the dial, and he didn't know how much more he could do for his brother, but with a strong will to pick himself up, and with some therapy, research, and fantastic mentors, Mac had turned his life one-hundred-and-eighty degrees and catapulted to the place he was now.

Funny how Mac was the addict, and yet he got the acclaim, while Tom had done nothing but help addicts, and was still working his butt off for pennies.

Tom took a sip of thick, gloopy coffee, and yawned. The clock said that it was eleven fifteen, far too late to be at work, but Meg would be in bed now anyway, and if he could find a way to solve this mess, alongside the mess with the doctor, it would be worth the late nights for a few days while the clinic had shut for Christmas.

In fact, before Christmas put the kibosh on everything.

He sat back at his desk and picked up the paper, it's rattle concealing the small squeak behind him. He took another sip of coffee and then pain exploded through the back of his head. Coffee spurt from his mouth onto the paper before him, his cup slid off the table onto the floor and smashed.

He tried to turn. More pain bolted through the side of his head and the world went black.

CHAPTER SIXTY

Ezula had an art class with Hester the next afternoon so after a morning chatting about yesterday's revelation and treading around the way they would progress, with a few laughs for good measure - no tears today - Mac found himself with an afternoon free.

After waving Ezzie off as Hester drove the car down their long driveway, he sighed and folded his arms.

It was a nice afternoon. The snow had settled; the earth glistening white and the sky a bright winter blue. The last place he wanted to go was the cabin.

His mood took a downturn as he realised that was exactly where he may have to go. Saul was out this morning, getting some Christmas shopping before the big day, which was in just five days apparently, although Mac had no idea. If Maddie and Saul hadn't entered his life, Christmas would have passed him by without the lifting of an eyebrow. The day no different to any other.

Although Sula may have wished him merry Christmas on the fridge, he supposed, or left him blood on the floor, or played him a piano piece for his entertainment.

It's white over too.

The first white Christmas he had seen in years - as long as it stuck around for the next five days that was. Typical. Romantic it may be, but never with your dead wife's ghost in a cabin in the middle of the forest. That was as unromantic as it got.

He huffed a laugh at the now empty driveway.

'What's so funny?' Maddie said, knocking his arm with hers.

He smiled down at her, her blonde hair loose again today, blowing gently in the breeze.

'Just thinking what a lovely white Christmas we'll have... except I'll be on my own in that damn cabin with no tree and no one to share it with.'

'You can come here,' Maddie said immediately. 'In fact, you *must* come here. You shouldn't have to spend Christmas alone. Although, I'll admit, a cabin in the woods surrounded by snow sounds like a perfect Christmas to me.'

'Well, we'll see. I can't intrude on your family. It wouldn't be right. I'll be fine out there. I can play Christmas tunes on the phone, string the three lamps up in the trees outside, wrap myself a tin of beans...'

He trailed off with a grin. Today was a good day, one of the best he'd had in a long time. He felt at ease with himself and the world, and if that was Christmas, so be it.

'Oh Jeez, that's scraping the barrel,' Maddie said, stuffing her hands into her jeans pockets as she turned to him.

'The beans? Well, I could wrap myself a log for the fire instead. It's pine, pine smells like Christmas, right?'

'Pine smells like forest - all the year round here.'

'Don't ruin the vision. I've even got a tin of spam, some frozen sprouts and a tin of potatoes for dinner.'

'Aye, perfect, and I'll wrap you an apple for pudding.'

'That *would* be perfect, actually. I'm easily pleased.'

Maddie laughed. 'I'd think you were joking, but I know how far you'll go for an apple.'

Mac chuckled as something occurred to him.

He was free, Maddie was free, the kayak was free. The day was bright and the loch calm.

But can you ask her?

'Maddie, I was-' he started.

'Mac, I was thinking-' she said at the same time. They broke off laughing at each other.

'Ladies first,' he said.

Maddie grinned and dipped her head before looking up at him, her cheeks flushed. Mac felt his stomach turn over and fill with those cliched butterflies. The first time he had felt anything like it since he had developed feelings for his passionate Italian piano teacher. Right now, he wanted nothing more than to fold his arms around Maddie like he had yesterday. Only this time with more time to savour the feeling.

'I wondered if you fancied the boat, um, kayak. It's such a lovely day and Ezzie won't be back for hours. The art club is in Inverness...' She trailed off as Mac nodded at her.

'Jinx, I was actually going to say the same,' he said.

'Really? That would be amazing. It's a rare free day from Ezzie's care for me. It only comes once a month. I'd like to spend it with you, away from here. I never seem to be able to get away from here,' she tilted her head, 'If you want to, that is.'

'Well, I've nowhere else more pressing to be.'

'Mac!' she chastised as he grinned.

'I want to,' he said. 'Grab your coat. Let's get out of here.'

Less than five minutes later, they were out on the loch, Mac at the back paddling gently so there was barely a ripple in the loch's glassy surface. Maddie sat in front of him. Rolo took the front seat, his front paws hanging over the edge in his usual fashion, back end squashed against her legs.

'Rolo! You should have got in the back, you daft dog, you're squashing Maddie. God, I'm sorry you have to share the kayak with this hairy oaf.'

'Oh, don't worry, I like you Mac,' she said with a laugh. 'Rolo is fine too, aren't you, boy?'

Rolo cocked an eyebrow back at Mac and laughed, tongue hanging out. She scrubbed his head, and Mac couldn't help but flick a bit of freezing loch water her way, enticing a shrill scream into the quiet wilderness.

'Oh! You bugger! Oh, that's so cold.'

'Never make fun of the paddler,' he said with a grin that she couldn't see.

As the minutes grew into an hour, Mac fell quiet and listened to Maddie as she stared out across the water, pointing out the different mountains, and identifying birds around them, most of which she knew by call. They saw a herd of deer up on the mountain he had walked up all that time ago, back when he had spoken to Tom, and the ground had been solid underfoot, not mush and mud.

He couldn't make out half of what she was pointing at, or how the hell she identified a single bird amongst the hundreds that seemed out today, but he enjoyed listening to her anyway. He took in the scenery, the quiet, the lilt of her accent, softness of her voice, gold of her hair, soft padding of her dusky pink jacket, her cream and pink bobble hat, and couldn't stop smiling behind her.

Perfect.

It was so perfect, he almost wished he could stop time and stay in this moment forever.

'Ooh, look, is that the cabin?' she said, shaking him from his reverie.

'The very one,' he said, feeling the foreboding as they edged closer.

'Can we go, Mac? Please?'

'If you want to,' he said begrudgingly.

None of your shit this afternoon, Sula, or we will really fall out, especially after what you did to me.

'I do. It's so quaint,' she said, turning to look at him with a grin. He smiled back.

Not quite the word I'd use.

'Yeah, it's okay,' he said.

She lapsed into silence, and Mac tried to keep his spirits up as they paddled toward the pier. Five minutes maximum, they'd be inside. Mac wondered what they'd find. He also wondered if he'd left any dirty clothes on the floor or dishes in the sink.

Too late now.

The pier loomed next to them, and Mac pulled the kayak up next to it.

In the cabin Mac lit the log burner, collected a few clothes that were hanging around, and cleared the books from the settee so that Maddie could sit down. In the kitchen he glanced at the fridge as he made them both coffee - nothing new there, and glanced at the corridor to the bathroom on the way back over to the chairs, nothing there either.

Small mercies.

He handed the drink to Maddie, and was denied the choice of seats by Rolo, who had spread himself on the settee next to her, legs pressed against the arm of the chair, head on her lap. She scratched his ears affectionately as his eyes dropped closed.

'Thanks,' she said. 'This is such a lovely little place, Mac.'

'It's all right,' he said, 'Not mine, though. My brother's, he lives in London, but uses this place as a complete getaway a few times a year.'

Or a shag palace as the mood takes him.

'A holiday home. It's a perfect place to get away from the city.' She took a sip of coffee, eyeing him over the top of the cup. 'But you've not been on holiday all this time, have you?'

'Well, it was a sort of holiday. More respite, really.'

'From the mess?'

'I am the mess, Maddie. To sort out the mess and get back on my feet, I suppose.'

'Ah.'

She asked no more, but Mac gave it anyway. Saul knew everything. If she wanted to find out, Mac was almost certain Saul would tell her at least a little of it, although he would probably do it diplomatically.

'My wife died last year. I pushed too hard trying to be okay, burned myself out, got slated by the media and ended up here, away from everything and everyone.'

Maddie pursed her lips.

'I'm sorry,' she said. 'That's a pretty shit deal.'

Mac shrugged, giving her a small smile. 'We all have them. At least mine was in the realms of normality. What you've been through with Ezzie would seem like an unbelievable plot, even in a Peter Jackson film.'

'Well, at least the end has the potential to be fantastic if she walks again. You really think she will?'

Mac nodded. The one thing he was confident about was that Ezzie could walk. She had told him so herself, he only had to get her mind out of the chair and release her from the clutches of fear and she would be right as rain.

'I know she can, and she will, one way or another. I just have to find out what's scaring her about getting out.'

'You still think it's something to do with her father?'

'That's definitely at the centre of it.'

'She must not have processed his death very well. I did kind of skim over it. I asked her if she was all right, but because I didn't really care about him after what he'd done, I suppose I didn't think that she would either.'

'He was still her father, and maybe at three or four you could have got away with that, but at seven and eight children are coming into their own. Developing their own opinions and thoughts regardless of parents, although they're still not ready to argue with you like a teenager. That takes a few more years.'

'I'm a dope,' she said, wrinkling her nose at him with a smile, the pain in her eyes giving away the shame and embarrassment she felt.

'You're not. We're only human. Ezzie hides her pain and fear very well. Even I've had to dig around to find what's holding her back. I'm usually good at reading people and reading between the lines. Ezzie has been difficult to crack, and even so, that's all it is at the moment. A crack. She could seal it up as easily as it could break open right now. I've seen it go both ways a good many times. You can never call it.'

Maddie gazed at him, and then dropped her eyes and smiled down into her cup.

'Remember when we first met, Mac?'

She looked back up at him, and he raised his eyebrows.

'In the apple tree.'

'Or out of it,' she said, reminding him how he had fallen. He chuckled. 'Anyway, you said you were an events speaker. An *events speaker*, remember? You said nothing about being well known across the world for changing people's lives. You said nothing about being a mind and brain expert. You said you travelled the world as a speaker, not that you were Mac Macauley.'

Mac shifted in his seat. 'Does it make a difference?'

'No, of course not. I just think it's funny that you're such a big personality out there and you never said.'

'You didn't recognise me, and neither did Saul. Do you know how often that happens? It was a godsend just to be plain old Mac.'

'I wouldn't have recognised you either way. It's only been since I googled you that I know about you at all. Saul had heard of you. Your name has been batted round in his field... not all good though, as anything a bit airy fairy is.'

'Airy fairy?' Mac said, amused.

'You know psychologists. They're very serious,' she said, lowering her voice with a frown. 'Everything has to be worked back, extracting with precision like a surgeon performing brain surgery. They like to make the links, to give the feedback on what is wrong with you. Like telling you will change it, but really, it's only information, isn't it? Then they just leave you to it, maybe give you a few more sessions to talk it through and extract some more, then some pills, then-'

'No pills,' Mac said. Maddie stared at him, her mouth dropping open.

'No pills?'

'Psychologists can't prescribe. They talk, and extract, as you said. Then they possibly refer you for pills.'

'Ah.'

He saw the fleeting frown, the confusion which flit across her face at some connection she was trying to put together. Unlike her daughter, Maddie was a refreshingly easy read.

'That's part of what Saul and Greg were done for, yes.'

'Right. He told you? Okay. Anyway, that's by the by. So, from what I can tell, you take things from the point of extraction and help people to change the things that are holding them back by understanding how the mind works both for and against itself. You give them practical things to help change mindset and paradigms - the programming that hold us back?'

'Said just like Wikipedia.'

She grinned and flushed. 'I did read that too, sorry.'

'Don't be. You're mostly right, in a nutshell. I'm all for understanding how we're programmed, and how to use the mind to work alongside us, not against us. See, up until around seven years old our brain waves sit in a Theta state – a type of hypnosis, if you like, which allows us to download what's around us and give us tools to understand how to survive. But no one child's upbringing is the same as another, and all children will be given the programming from their earlier generations, from parents, grandparents, etc. The problem is that these generations are already 'out of date' and those ideas, rules, and skills are no longer applicable. So if you imagine the programming like a thermostat for your heating, it will constantly - and more importantly subconsciously - correct your course as you grow to keep you on track with your program. Most people think this track is the right one, and the only way, they don't even know the thermostat can be set to anything, and anywhere, you want – there are no limits. The people who do understand that still have trouble resetting the temperature to one they want – subconscious is a tricky beast, and that's where the work is done. People are stuck, they're ignorant, I help with that.'

'Ignorant? That seems harsh.'

'Not if you understand that the meaning of ignorance is simply not knowing. The solution to being ignorant of anything is to study it. Most fears start and end with ignorance, and most fears are life blockers. It's a real problem.'

'Even my fear of spiders?' Maddie said. There was no grin, no malice, just curiosity. Mac liked that. Open-minded meant she was a lot less ignorant than most of the population, who didn't want to listen to how their fear of spiders had a butterfly effect on the rest of their life. Or how that fear could help with other fears.

'Okay,' Mac said, putting his tea down on the floor. 'Fear of spiders is fear of...' he trailed off and let her lead. She shuddered.

'Legs, fangs, and, oh god, they move too fast, they're just vile.'

Mac grinned.

'Have you ever studied the spider in all of its varieties and forms? Do you know why it has eight legs? Why it's hairy? Why it runs fast? Why it spins webs, jumps, has many eyes, lives underground, lives in the trees?'

'No!' Maddie said, disgust on her face. 'Why would I?'

'Because it scares you. If you research enough, read enough about the varied species and how they've adapted to their own environments, you'd realise just how amazing they are. How amazing the whole of the natural world is, but spiders do get a bad rap, so we'll stay there.'

'That's great. I'm not sure I'd like them in my bedroom any more than I do now.'

Mac laughed.

'No, the point is, whether you knew it or not, the more research you did, the more respect you'd have for them and the less impulse to stomp on them and scream. You may not like them in your room, but outside you may even just study one a little closer. If you kept up that research each day for a year, you'd find the fear drop away. You'd know which ones bit, and which were harmless, which moved slowly, and which moved fast.'

'Okay.' Maddie said, looking at him dubiously.

'You'd be a little less ignorant, more confident. Less fearful. You'd understand them enough to get a cup and paper and let them loose outside without a meltdown. The opposite of fear is faith. We have more faith in what we know, what we understand, and that is the purpose of study. Not to like something more, but to understand it more. Get it?'

Maddie nodded. Her eyes fixed on him.

'Right,' she said, 'so for Ezzie, she doesn't understand what happened to her father. He may have said something to her before she left - before he died - that has triggered a fear that he will do something if she walks again?'

'As stupid as that sounds, you've probably hit the nail on the head.'

'And it sounds stupid to us because we understand the situation and what it ultimately means. There's no way he can do anything from beyond the grave.'

Mac blinked. He would have believed the same a few short months ago, now he wasn't so sure.

'Well, that's another fear, isn't it? Death and the afterlife. But yes, you're right, as far as we are aware, or as far as our ignorance takes us, we understand that it can't happen, so to us the fear is irrelevant.'

'But to Ezzie it's very real.'

'Exactly. Not only real, but life-alteringly real. This is how powerfully the mind can trap someone in a prison of their own making. It doesn't have to be as extreme as Ezzie's situation. It can be as simple as not walking on the cracks in the pavement. I've known someone change their whole behaviour, the streets they walked, people they visited, places they went, just because they thought it was bad luck to step on a crack in the pavement.'

'But that's OCD-'

'That's fear. Fear drives OCD. What will happen if...' Mac said. 'A lot of people are afraid of a lot of things, and they mostly aren't big scary monsters or spiders. The life altering ones are simple. I can't leave this job to be a musician because I'll be broke. I have a mortgage to pay, bills, a car to run. How will I do that as an unknown musician? I have a decent job, it pays well, I'm better off where I am. How many people who think like that ever get to even play or sing their own music at a gig?'

'None?'

'None, because they're scared. They have no faith. Their dreams are dashed before they even explore them. If they thought about it, you don't have to give up work to write and sing songs, to play pubs in the evenings, to build a brand for yourself. You only give up the job when the security is enough to squash some of that fear. Most people discard their dreams before they even take one small step. Mindset, with a side helping of society's expectations and judgement... it's a dream stealer, and we only have one life. We should be living our own path.'

'That's what you help with.'

'Life blockers. The Who once sang about nothing being as simple as reaching the highest high - and that's true, but they also got the rest bang on. If you listen to the lyrics, The Messiah points to the door, telling them there's better out there, that's where the high is - but not one follower had the guts to leave the security of their temple and leader. To leave behind what they knew... even for the promise of something better.'

Maddie seemed to turn this over with a frown, and then her eyebrows shot up.

'Oh, yes! 'I'm Free' I remember that song. I didn't take any notice of what was being said, but you're right, even though they're being shown the way to a better place, they don't go.'

'Safer inside than out. Better the life blocks we know than the success we don't. How the hell would we cope? Comfort. Our mind loves it, but it's outside the comfort zone that the magic happens. We need to get comfortable with being uncomfortable, but that's a whole different story.'

'I feel like a whole new person just listening to you.'

Mac chuckled and picked up his tea to take a lukewarm sip.

'It all depends on what you do with the information. It's proven, it's science, it's been written about for hundreds of years. There's a science to success that is little known, but if you look, it's right out there in plain sight. All you have to do is take note and follow the path. And people get this wrong. It's not a generic road map, a one for all - there are no maps like that, but there are parts of our journey that people have travelled before us that we can use. It's a path, but it's individual. You chart your own path, using other people's discoveries. Someone has already achieved whatever it is you desire. How did they get there? What was their route?'

'I feel like I need to do more.'

'You're already pretty good at it, Maddie. You're what's known in the industry as an unconscious competent. You travelled the world for years with no means to get around, no job, no money. That would put most people in a tailspin. You already have a lot of faith in yourself, faith that things will come your way when you need them, but we can all learn. Learning never stops.'

'I want to learn. Tell me more,' Maddie said, twiddling the fur on Rolo's ear.

'I normally charge £250 an hour.'

Maddie's jaw dropped open.

'Are you for fuck- sorry, are you for real?'

Mac shrugged.

'I'd give it away for free, but for some reason, people want to pay. I'm just a normal man, nothing special, but everyone wants to put me on a pedestal. That's why I fell so hard, and so publicly when Sula died. That's why I'm here, out of the way. I couldn't grieve in peace when everyone thought I had enough control to keep it all together. I had the magic pill, I could override silly emotion, right? I'm the mind guy, for god's sake!'

'Catch twenty-two.'

'You said it. More coffee?' Mac said, holding up his cup. Maddie nodded with a grin.

For the next hour, Mac turned his attention to Maddie. He asked her about travel, where she had been, and the things that she thought Mac should see. She gushed about the culture's she had experienced, places she had slept, worked, the people she had met. He listened attentively, enjoying the sound of her voice, the passion and enthusiasm which were the obvious kick-starters for such an adventure. They touched on the future and what they wanted - Maddie wanted to travel, although not so completely as she had. This time she wanted to take it easier, do it from a base. A home. She loved to make jewellery and wanted to set up her own shop, maybe somewhere on the coast. Some stability for Ezzie now that she was growing up. Mac said that he would always work in his field - he loved helping people too much to quit, but one of his first future dates with himself would be thinking of new ways to spread the word of his work without spreading himself too thin. He had spent one half of his life working every hour, and he would spend the next half enjoying the freedom that had brought, and appreciating what he had. He wanted to travel properly this time - around his work, instead of for it - and maybe Maddie could join him when she wasn't too busy, show him some of the sights? Maddie had immediately agreed and thrown out a list of places that they must see and why.

Mac hadn't enjoyed himself so much for quite possibly the last five years. Even before Sula had died, he hadn't had such a stimulating and fun conversation with someone who listened as much as they talked. Sula had quit listening when he hadn't slowed down after she'd asked him to, and if he was honest, the last few years of marriage had been a strain. Right now, Mac didn't think anything about Maddie could ever be a strain. She was equally tough but delicate, hardy but fragile, intelligent but childlike, serious but fun, and to top it off, she told a damn good story. He hadn't laughed so much in what felt like decades.

That was until she noticed the bulk under the mezzanine floor that he had tried so hard to ignore.

'Mac! Is that a piano? Oh wow, do you play?'

And his heart sank through the floor.

CHAPTER SIXTY-ONE

WHEN TOM WOKE, IT was dark, and he was lying on something hard and cold. There was a roar underneath him that was familiar, but the fuzz in his head wouldn't place it for him. He tried to move his hands to feel the part of his head where a throb persisted, but they held firm, bound, stuck behind his back as though they had been super-glued.

He tugged again and recognised rope.

Rope?

He was bound at the wrists. He tried to move his feet and got more of the same, pain shooting through his leg at the tightness of the rope around his ankles.

What the fuck?

Stomach strong from swimming, the adrenaline was enough to shoot him up to a sitting position. His shoes banged off wood that sounded hollow, and he almost lost his balance, along with his consciousness, as his throbbing head tried to catch up with the movement.

He sat awhile, blinking into the darkness, letting the small *room?* Come into focus. And then the floor shifted, and he was over again, bouncing his head off the floor as the roar got louder, and suddenly, he knew exactly where he was.

A vehicle. Most probably a van.

Adrenaline surged him upright again, his heart thumping in his ears as he tugged at the solid binds on his wrists. Someone knew how to tie a good knot because Tom couldn't shift his wrists more than an inch.

And then he remembered. He had been at the office, and there had been a figure. A figure that had swung something at his head. Someone who had now bound his hands and feet and was taking him who knew where. Was this to do with the doctor? He squinted, and then shut his eyes tight as he remembered the invoices, and all of the illegal medication ordered through his company, far too much. Was this something to do with that? What the hell was going on?

His mind began to race. Who the hell knew he had been at the office? It wouldn't be one of the staff surely, and he only knew of one person that had been stalking him over the last couple of weeks.

Fuck!

The van swayed again, shifting to the left, and swaying Tom to the right. He fought to hold himself upright but swung over onto his right side, managing to avoid another bump to the head, but feeling a new pain where something hard dug into his hip. His phone.

His heart surged. His phone was zipped into the pocket of his fleece, and it looked like whoever had done this hadn't thought to check his pockets and take it out.

Tom scuffled his fingers along the soft jacket, but his hands were bound the wrong way for the job. He tugged the material with his knuckles, shifting onto his front when it snagged under the weight of his body. Swaying with the motion of the van, Tom felt a bead of sweat run down his cheek and into his mouth. He tasted salt as he edged the material slowly up, feeling the weight of the phone as it lifted off the floor. His knuckles complained, and the jacket slipped. He grabbed it again, pain shooting through his hands and wrists. More sweat trickled into his mouth, and then into his eye.

He clamped it shut with a curse, trying to wipe it with his shoulder to no avail. Letting go of the material, he swung himself upright again and shuffled his feet closer to his backside until he could use his knee to relieve the sting instead.

Panting, he lay back on the cold floor and blinked into the darkness. Everything hurt - his head, his hands, his legs, his back, and now his stomach. It was impossible.

You'll just have to wait. Wait and see where you end up.

His stomach didn't like that idea. It churned, sending his lunch from what seemed like eons ago spinning over. His mind screamed at him too, screamed at him to *do something*, to get the damn phone.

It won't do you any good with no hands, anyway. You have to wait, bide your time.

Feeling like he may throw up, he closed his eyes as the van turned a heavy left, rolling on its axles, before slowing to a stop.

Tom heard music as the engine cut. The radio playing Alice Cooper's Poison, and then the music cut too, and the van rocked as the door opened and someone got out.

The door slammed shut. Tom moaned and finally lost his lunch.

CHAPTER SIXTY-TWO

'P LAY SOMETHING FOR ME,' Maddie said, firelight dancing in her eyes.

'No, I need to get you back.' Mac stood and stretched, and peered out of the window, more for effect than to see. The snow was falling again, although he knew the loch wouldn't freeze over for a good couple of hours yet, if it was going to.

'Spoilsport,' she teased and when he looked back, she had made her way around to the stool and lifted the keyboard cover. She plonked on the keys, a rudimentary tune that made Mac smile in its simplicity and childlike tone.

She smiled over her shoulder at him. 'Can't you play? Or is getting me back home just a way of getting out of it?'

Mac shrugged 'No, I play... I just. Well, I haven't played since... since...'

'Sula.' Maddie said sadly. Mac nodded, grateful that he didn't have to explain himself further.

'Well, does it count if you help someone else? You can teach me to play! We have a piano at home, but no-one ever plays but ma. Think of the surprise on her birthday if I suddenly pop up and play her a song.'

Mac smiled. That was easy to get out of.

'I could, but some of the notes don't seem to work. I don't know where the piano came from or how old it is.'

He thought of the tune that had played when he had been out on the pier.

Supernatural tunes don't count, Mac.

'It seems to be in perfect tune but some of the keys just don't play,' he added.

Maddie's face fell, and Mac moved around the settee to join her. He pressed the upper D that liked to play itself, but had never worked under his finger, and was surprised when a perfect tone rang out across the cabin.

'Oh. Well, that was one that didn't work before.'

He shifted Maddie across and performed a quick chromatic scale from one end of the piano to the other with a frown.

Perfect working order. How strange.

Maddie watched him. 'It seems to work,' she said uncertainly, as if she wasn't sure whether to push the issue, and suddenly Mac knew if he said no, she would accept it and move on with no judgement. She plinked the low keys next to him lightly and in a flush of gratitude for her tact, Mac felt himself begin to grin. He liked Hester a lot. She had done much for him, from the way she had accepted him up at the house, to even just sending down food and drink to the cabin. It wouldn't hurt to teach Maddie a tune, and he thought he had an idea, if she could do it in the timescale.

'When is her birthday?'

Maddie stopped plinking keys. '20th Feb,' she said, 'around five weeks?'

Mac sucked a breath between his teeth, and Maddie frowned with a grin.

'What?'

'I'm just wondering whether you can hack it. I won't be able to teach you the music - I don't have it - just the song.'

Maddie's eyes lit up. 'You'll do it? You'll teach me a song for her?'

Mac nodded and then he staggered back, laughing as Maddie launched into him, enclosing him in a hug. Mac closed his arms around her, smelling the coconut of her hair, the flowery perfume, light and airy, so different to Sula's heavy scent.

'Thank you so much, Mac,' she said into his jumper, 'ma will love you forever!' She squeezed hard and let him go far too quickly. 'What shall we play, any ideas?'

Mac had the perfect idea, one she would hate, but would hopefully break the tension between him and the piano first. He hadn't played anything in a while, but this song he had always played to wind up Sula, who hated it. It was morbid and boring; she had said. Getting one up on Sula may be the only thing that drove him to sit at the piano stool right now.

Hope you like it, baby.

He lay his fingers on the cool keys and felt a rush of emotion that he hadn't felt for a long time. A longing for the keys under his fingers, for their tones and the melody as they worked together harmoniously. His fingers tingled and he stared at his hands, the same hands that used to play, and yet different.

Home, he thought. The feeling of being one with the instrument rose back up to meet him like an old friend with a warm hug. He clenched his jaw to halt the tears that welled like a wave and swallowed around the large boulder that seemed to be stuck in his throat.

'Mac?' Maddie whispered beside him.

'Yes,' he said, snapping out of the reverie and forcing back the emotion with a knowing smile. 'So, I was thinking this one.'

He caressed the keys. The tune pouring from under his fingers like a soothing balm, and even after all this time the tune came perfectly, seemingly with no help from him, filling the small room, caressing every nerve and fibre in his body, the music lifting him even as he thought of Sula's annoyance. He imagined her in the bathroom, hands over her ears, screeching at him to stop.

He played on, all the way to the end, leaving the last note to resonate through the space as Sula seemed to have done to him with a broken D most mornings.

He stuck an imaginary finger up at Sula and turned to Maddie with a smile.

'Well?' he asked.

Maddie shut her mouth with a snap, a look of horror on her face. Mac tried to hide his smile

'The first part is really slow. It'll give you time to think as you play.'

Maddie stared at him.

'It's quite easy, this bit,' he said, biting back his grin and looking back down at the keys to hide his face as he replayed a small part of the song. He'd never been good at keeping a poker face, never been good at lying. Unlike his late wife.

Stop it, Mac.

'Do you even know what that's called?' Maddie said, crossing her arms over her chest.

Mac knew the official name, but he also knew Maddie was referring to its more well-known name.

'Of course, it's Chopin's funeral march?'

Maddie's mouth fell open. 'You're going to have me play the death march at ma's birthday? I think not-'

'Funeral march,' he corrected. 'It's timeless.'

Maddie ranted and Mac began to laugh until he received a cushion around the back of his head and fell forward with an 'oof'.

'Okay, okay,' he said, holding his hands up against more cushion violence. 'I was only joking. Let's try another.'

Mac tried a couple of the more well-known easy classical pieces, but each time Maddie was unsure.

'They're beautiful Mac, but I don't really know them myself! I mean, we're not really a classical household. Do you have any Queen?'

'Queen?'

Maddie wrinkled her nose with a shrug, and Mac turned back to the piano.

'I'm insulted. The greats of their time composed these songs. They're moody, feisty, orchestral, monumental. Bloody Queen?' He shook his head and began a rendition of Bohemian Rhapsody without pause. When he finished, Maddie looked awestruck.

'Mac, that was absolutely amazing. You're so talented. Ma would be thrilled. She loves Queen!' She said, 'but... I'll never be able to play that.'

Mac resisted the urge to reach up and touch her hand, so close to his. 'You will,' he said, 'Apart from the crossover, it's really easy, mostly octaves. We'll just cover a section, not the whole piece.'

Maddie gave him a lopsided grin. 'You have a lot of faith in me.'

'I always have faith in people,' he said. 'I know what they're capable of.'

She held his gaze, a slight smile on her face, and his heart turned over in his chest. He swallowed and looked away, getting up from the stool.

'Come and sit,' he said.

Maddie sat, and Mac propped his backside up the back of the settee as he showed her what an octave was, and where to place her fingers.

'First, we'll get the touch right, then we'll learn the song.'

'The touch,' Maddie said matter-of-factly, hands on the keys.

'Place your hands over the keys lightly. Never rest them down. If they're there, they're ready to play, and that means poised ready for movement. Wrists higher, let the hands kind of hang, or you'll trip over the keys when playing.'

Maddie lifted her wrists until they were parallel with her straight fingers.

'Like this?'

Mac pushed the settee back a little, enabling him to move behind her. He reached around her, placing his fingers gently under her wrists, lifting them higher. 'There.'

She nodded as he moved back to her side.

'Now when you play a key, press it gently, caress the note, don't just plonk your finger down.'

Maddie plonked her fingers down and Mac began to wonder if this may be too much after all.

'Not like that. Look. Don't move your fingers, let me move them.'

He moved back behind her and placed his hands over the top of hers. The touch of her soft skin, warm and delicate, made his hands tingle as much as the piano keys had. Mac closed his eyes for a second, trying to stop the spin of his mind.

He pressed the keys, lightly at first, and then steadily with more force until she could hear the difference in the tone and volume of the keys. If he was honest, he went on a little too long, enjoying the feel of her between his arms, the smell of her, the softness of her skin, the warmth of her body. If she noticed, she never said.

'Okay?'

She nodded without a word, and he began to teach her the notes to play. She was quick to learn. Long fingers and dexterous hands helped enormously, but even after an hour and a half it was clear that this would take an enormous amount of practice.

'I'm not going to be able to do this, Mac,' she groaned after another choppy run though of the first eight bars.

'You only started playing an hour ago. Don't be so hard on yourself. It'll take practice.'

'I can't practice at home. Ma will hear me.'

'Okay, well then, we'll have to get you out here as much as we can around Ezzie.'

'Is it going to be enough?'

'That only depends on you, and how quickly Ezzie can break her barriers.'

'Five weeks isn't long.'

'No. But it can be done.'

Mac looked at the lengthening shadows outside. The sun was lowering fast. They had to get back to the house or it would be dark.

'Maddie...' he started.

'I know. Time flies when you're having fun.'

He grinned. 'I'm glad you've had fun, and if it didn't take so long to get you back, we'd have more time, too.'

Maddie sighed and grinned up at him from the piano stool.

'Until next time,' she said, closing the keyboard cover and pushing the stool under. Mac followed her out of the small space, and they grabbed their coats, gloves, and hats. Rolo jumped from the chair, bemused by the sudden activity, and began running in mad circles from the kitchen to the living area.

'Rolo! Bloody hell. Quit. Get outside!'

Maddie laughed as Mac opened the door, and the dog tore round to the pier. They had followed him to the boat before Mac realised he had left his phone on the table.

'Oh, wait. I just have to get my phone. I don't want to run into trouble out here without it.'

'Unlike me, who never gave mine a second thought when I left.'

Mac grinned. 'You're with me, not alone.'

He jogged back inside and grabbed the phone from the small table, the fridge magnets catching his eye as he pocketed it. He stopped short and his heart thumped.

MAD.

It sat central, the rest of the magnets now on the floor. Mac felt anger rise from the pit of his stomach.

'Yeah, well, you don't get to be fucking mad, Sula. After all you've put me through up here? Leave me alone.'

In the bathroom, something dropped and rolled across the floor. Mac ignored it and went back out to where Maddie, Rolo and the boat were waiting on the pier.

CHAPTER SIXTY-THREE

THE BACK DOOR OPENED and orange light flooded into the back of the panel van. The bulky form of a man stood in the doorway, his face in shadow in the dimming light of the day. Tom blinked, letting his eyes adjust, assessed it must be around five or six o'clock, and quickly took in his surroundings.

The boarded van was completely empty, aside from the puddle of vomit next to him. He wrinkled his nose. Outside, he could make out a hedge to the passenger side of the van, pulled up tight. Through the doorway was a vast car park, a few parked cars, and the glow of streetlamps. From the constant drone of the traffic, Tom deduced that they were at a motorway service station.

'Where are we?' He croaked and cleared his throat.

'Nowhere you need to be bothered about. It's where we're going that's important.'

The man. It was the doctor.

Even with his features in shadow, Tom would recognise his voice anywhere.

That rules out the medication theory.

For an insane moment Tom felt relief trickle through him - the business was safe, his staff were loyal. This was the crazy man whose business he had shopped a couple of years ago - and to that end, he was crazy. That's why Tom was here.

Kidnapped.

Fear rammed through him as the man sat on the tailgate entrance and calmly lit a cigarette, the van dipping under his weight. Tom swallowed hard, trying to stay silent, trying to judge his next move, but the intensity of the man's statement ate him up.

'Where are we going?' he said.

'Somewhere only we know,' the man sang. His voice was an insult to the soft melody of Lily Allen's voice. He chuckled and blew out smoke into the wintry night air.

Tom tried to inch away from his vomit. The sour smell sending his stomach rolling again as it drifted to his nostrils on the breeze.

The man turned, face still in shadow, but Tom knew it anyway, could see the outline of his eyebrows as they raised.

'Somewhere far away, somewhere you're going to help me get to. First, I'm going to get some grub.'

He flicked the cigarette out onto the tarmac and stepped into the van. Tom rolled, crushing his hands in the attempt to get away from a kicking that never came. There was the rustle of a bag and when Tom looked back to the man, he was pulling on medical gloves. He pulled out a cloth and some spray and in one fell swoop gathered the vomit on a cloth, threw the cloth out of the door into the bushes and spray cleaned the area thoroughly.

Tom blinked.

'I fucking hate mess, Tom. May I call you Tom?' the man said as he sprayed and scrubbed. 'I especially hate mess in my van. If you had your hands free, I'd make you clean the whole of the back right now. As it stands, you're a lucky bastard, Tom. Your hands are tied and we're in a public place. I can't take that chance until we're in agreement.'

Tom licked his lips as two more cloths followed the vomit-stained rag into the bushes, the gloves following closely behind. The man packed the cleaning spray away, surveyed his work with a nod, and stepped out of the van.

'Don't get into trouble now. I'll be back shortly.'

The door shut with a bang that reverberated around Tom's head. He winced as the door opened again.

'Just so you know, we're not on the main car park. There's no one here, and a car alarm going off at the service station won't make much of a difference to the people here right now. It would be nice if we could collaborate, Tom, but if you want, I can make your life a fucking misery instead. The result for me will be the same. I win. Whichever way you want to play it.'

The door slammed again, and there was silence.

Tom listened hard. There were no tell-tale footsteps leaving the van, but then the man could be wearing trainers. The door stayed shut. Tom took his chance.

'Help!' He screamed, 'Help me! I've been kidnapped! HELP!'

He spun on his back, aiming his feet toward the side of the van, and kicked them as hard as he could at the side panel with a thud. He kicked again and again, yelling frantic words that sounded ludicrous to his own ears.

Kidnapped! How the hell does a grown man get kidnapped?

He yelled anyway, for lack of any other way to put it. That's what had happened after all, wasn't it?

Each thud of his feet sent waves of pain up his legs and into his back, and within a minute he was gasping for breath, his teeth clenched in pain, the bleach smell of the cleaning product burning the back of his throat. He looked around him. There wasn't a single shred of light in here. The panel van had a bulkhead which concealed the cabin. He thought the back had been empty, and yet the man had opened a bag which he must have stowed up by the roof.

Tom swung his legs back around and forced himself onto his front. His knees crunched underneath his weight as he kept them bent before him, cheek mashed to the floor, ass in the air, like he was praying to Mecca.

He wondered if he was facing East. Wondered if he should be praying to God.

Come on Tom, get your thoughts together. You don't have much time.

With a grunt, he pushed up onto his knees. His feet were crossed, as were his hands. If he could get them next to each other, he should be able to stand. He pushed his right toes onto the floor, taking the weight as he tried to manoeuvre his left foot over the top of his heel.

Pain raged through his ankles as the rope snagged tighter, tighter, and then gave a little. His foot snapped over his heel, shifting his weight to the left unexpectedly. He fell back to the floor with a hollow clunk, his head bouncing off the floor, sending another bolt of pain through it.

'Fuck! Fuck! Fuck!' he said through clenched teeth, banging his feet down onto the floor and cursing as he crushed his hands further under him.

It was then that he noticed his feet were on the floor. Feet that met. Side by side, ankles touching.

'Shit! Yes!' he whispered, a bolt of adrenaline shooting through his chest. He rolled back onto his hands and, using his hands, stomach, and legs, thrust himself forward and up into a crouch. A crouch that would have toppled him forward if the side of the van hadn't been there to catch the fall with his face.

He eased backward. Wobbled, and slowly rose. Legs shaking with the strain of trying to keep him upright, thighs and calves burning with effort, and then he was past the pain point and up. Standing fully. He laughed, remembered his predicament, and shuffled like a demented penguin to the corner of the van that the cleaning stuff had come from. He used his shoulder against the bulkhead to keep himself steady while he used his face and nose to 'feel' into the darkness.

Just up ahead he felt a bag, plastic but hard. He rubbed a cheek against the side. Woven plastic. Like canvas. It would be hard to feel what was in there as he was. He almost left it.

What if there's a knife? If I can get the bag down, I can tip it whilst sitting... somehow. If the van starts moving, I'll have no chance up here.

There's probably no knife.

But what if there is?

He wants to collaborate. Maybe you should play ball.

He's a crook, he'd kill you as look twice at you.

Tom shoved the voices from his head, put the back of his head under the bag, and lifted. On his tiptoes, shoulder taking the strain the bag gave, and a few items dropped over his neck and back and clattered to the floor. He couldn't see them from up here. He would need his phone light.

Standing where he was, he used his knuckles to pull at his jacket. Now that it wasn't caught under him, it moved easily until he had the zip, but he couldn't get the material taut enough to open the pocket. With a grunt of frustration, he lowered himself down the bulkhead to his knees, relieving the pain from his ankles which had been mashed together. He rolled onto his side, placing his hands toward the fallen items. He was blind anyway in here, so he would do this by feel.

His hands scrabbled, knocking small items out of his reach before clasping a small cylindrical object. Manoeuvring his hands under the rope, he managed to get his fingers facing each other. The strain on his shoulders was telling, but if he could identify a knife or anything to get him the upper hand, it would be worth it. His tongue flicked to the top of his salty lip as he passed the small object between his fingers, feeling as a blind person would have to. It was plastic and felt like a pen, although not as long.

A small pen?

There was a cap at one end that he struggled to remove with the closeness of his hands. It finally gave with a pop and there was a sharp sting on the pad of his finger. He hissed in a breath as he pulled the sting out and felt his heartbeat double.

A syringe.

Full of what?

You haven't injected yourself; it stabbed you.

Needlestick. Needlestick injury. His brain screamed instructions from long ago when he had worked in the hospital. Squeeze, make it bleed, get it under water, flush it out.

Tom could do none of those things stuck in this van. He couldn't even see the syringe to see what he had stuck himself with.

He knew it could have been new - empty, sterile and unopened - but his brain presented images of the youths in London who'd once had a fad of stabbing unsuspecting clubbers with needles infected with HIV.

What if I've injected something lethal? What if?

His heart banged as he gasped for breath, cool sweat lying clammy on his t-shirt under the fleece. His brain spun, the floor spun, the van spun beneath him. He gasped for breath one last time, and then the already dark world slowly switched off.

CHAPTER SIXTY-FOUR

THE LIGHT WAS FADING fast, the sun lowering into a sky with a hue of pink as they pushed off the pier and headed back to the house. Mac stuck to the middle of the loch, not sure if he was more comfortable taking his chances with the shadows in the trees at the water's edge, or the monsters that lurked in the darkness below him. After Sula's message, he was on edge, erratically wondering if she was so mad that she could sink him out here and feed him to the wildlife.

His eyes skittered along the bank as Maddie sighed before him.

'It's so beautiful out here at this time of night,' she said, blowing breath onto her gloved hands for warmth in the crisp chill of the air.

Is it fuck. It's creepy as hell, and I have to row back alone in an hour or so.

'Hmm.' Mac answered aloud.

'Look at the trees. The snow is hardening already. There'll be ice tonight.'

'I should think so,' he said, wishing he had left the fire lit so that the cabin was warm on his return. He wondered why no-one ever bothered about fires being alight when they were at home, but when they were gone, the fire goblins would surely send out a spark to burn the place down.

'What if you can't get to us tomorrow?'

'Then I'll message and have a day in the cabin.' She turned to him, and he caught the eye roll with a laugh. 'What the hell else would I do?'

'We'll miss you,' she said softly.

'I'll miss you too,' he said, bemused, but the warmth in his stomach told him he meant it. He had come to enjoy his days at the house a lot, and after today was sure he enjoyed being with Maddie a whole lot, too.

He smiled as she turned away with a smile of her own.

They were well past the bend now, and Mac kept his eyes on the shore, looking for the small inlet that led to the back of the house. He assessed every rustle of foliage, every creak of wood, every snap and squawk.

And then his heart almost had a de-coke as Maddie suddenly yelled. 'Mac, look! A Grey Heron, it's fishing!'

The boat rocked alarmingly as she swung to him, and Rolo, having eyed the same bird, leapt from the boat as the bird took off gracefully into the sky at the commotion. Maddie laughed, holding onto the sides of the boat.

'Christ, Rolo!' Mac shouted, falling onto his knees in the small space behind Maddie, and grabbing for his collar, leg, tail, anything – and missing anyway.

There was a loud splash and Rolo swam toward the bank in the freezing water. Maddie turned to Mac with a grin, and for a second they were almost nose to nose as he leaned, hands on his thighs, watching the dog.

'He's crazy,' Mac said, shaking his head.

'Aye, he's a mad dog,' she said with a laugh, turning back toward the front. 'He must have a damned good fur coat, that's all I'll say.'

She leaned back toward him, and before he could check his own actions he had instinctively wrapped his arms around her waist from behind. He wondered how he could be so callous, and yet how it could feel so good to feel the heat of her warming him, her body against his in the cold air.

'The dog has issues,' he said next to her ear.

'Like his owner,' Maddie said with a laugh, lowering her head back onto his shoulder, and reaching a gloved hand backward up to his face.

'Thanks. You're not wrong.'

The sun was low over the loch, casting a bright red/orange glow across the darkening sky, picture perfect over the dark glass of the water stretching before them. Snow had settled on the mountains, the ground, and the trees, which glittered in the low light like diamonds.

'If only I had a camera right now,' she said, her head still on his shoulder, the coconut of her shampoo in his nostrils. Reluctantly, Mac pushed her gently off him and pulled an arm free to fetch the phone from his pocket for her to use. He took the cigarettes from his other pocket. If she was going to take pictures, he would warm up with a smoke.

Maddie sat forward to snap off a few shots as Mac pulled his other arm away to light the cigarette. At the click of the lighter, Maddie twisted sideways on the tiny seat, staring at him.

'What?' he said, the unlit white stick hanging from his mouth.

'In all the hours you've spent at the house, you've never smoked. I don't think you need that, Mac. It's a crutch.'

Her pale eyes and freckled face were lit from behind by an orangey golden glow that made her look like an angel. Albeit an angel with a woolly hat, not a halo. Her cheeks were a flushed pink, her lips...

Mac caught himself. He was staring. Not only was he staring, but she was staring right back. She reached up a hand to the cigarette hanging from his lips, took it from him gently, and threw it into the loch, her eyes still locked on his. His heart thumped. Nowhere to go in here, nowhere to run. Trapped. Gloriously, horrifyingly, trapped. Nowhere he'd rather be; and wanting to be anywhere but here.

His palms were sweating inside his gloves. He took them off for something - anything - to take his attention from Maddie.

Your wife hasn't long gone, Mac. What will the world say about this?

'It's bad for you, Mac,' Maddie murmured. 'You don't need it.'

Mac brought his eyes back to her pale blue gaze, so close. Red cheeks, freckled nose, full pink lips, no smile on them now.

'Right.' he whispered back. It was all he could manage. He found himself reaching to touch the rubber name of her coat, just below the shoulder, and then his hand found its way into her hair, feeling its silky softness, like spun gold. His fingers tingled, and his body ached with the longing to hold her. She wasn't Sula. She was vastly different, and she was so very right, but she had been through as much as he had. He had to get over his wife as much as she had a child to concentrate on, and besides, he still loved Sula, didn't he?

'Mac? Are you okay?' she said softly, her head now tilted, a slight smile back on her face. She removed a glove and brought a hand to his face; soft, warm, and gentle, and he found himself drawn toward her.

'I don't know. I think *you* may be bad for me,' he whispered, leaning to press his lips to hers before he could think it through any further. She let her lips linger against his momentarily, and then she pulled away, and he was left with a longing so deep he could have cried.

'Oh, I'*m* bad for *you*?' she said with a laugh, her hand still on his face. Then her smile disappeared, and her thumb traced the line of beard on his cheek. 'You're the one making a rash decision right now, and as much as I want you to make it, it wouldn't be right. Think it through, Mac, think about the mess.'

Mac nodded, his heart crestfallen that she hadn't let him carry on, but his head eternally grateful that she had stopped him before he had crossed the line. She dropped her hand and dipped her head to put her glove back on.

'Sorry,' he said, 'I just... I forget the mess when I'm with you. You're right I should have thought about what I was doing.'

Her head came up and she stared at him, processing his words, before breaking into a huge, beautiful grin. A grin he would like to be able to put on her face every day, starting with Ezzie and that damn chair. She leaned to place her forehead against his, hands on his face. So close he could hardly breathe.

'You don't have to apologise, it was harder to pull away than you know. You are an angel, Mac, and I hope that we can pick it up sometime. Either way I hope that you're in mine and Ezzie's lives for a very long time.' she whispered, warm breath in his face.

Mac nodded. She was still close, seemingly reluctant to pull away, and just as he thought he would go crazy with desire and kiss her anyway, despite what his head said, Rolo splashed back to the boat, throwing freezing water over them, and breaking the moment entirely.

'Woah! Christ, Rolo. You sure know how to break up a party,' Mac said, as Maddie turned and shooed Rolo back to shore with a laugh. Mac sat back on his seat, picking up the paddles and followed the dog to the small inlet.

He made Maddie stay on the boat, jumping into the water to pull it higher and then offering his hand so that she could get out without wetting her shoes. His eyes scanned the foliage, dark, silent, and pensive around them. It seemed to Mac to be denser than when he had left this morning. Things hiding, watching, waiting.

'Want me to walk back down with you?' he said as Maddie jumped onto the path.

'Nah. I'm fine, been doing it all my life. You should get back before darkness really sets in.'

'Okay,' he said with a nod. 'Well, I guess we'll see you tomorrow.'

'Fingers crossed.' she said, crossing her fingers in front of her face.

Mac smiled. 'Thank you for a lovely afternoon. It really took my mind off things.'

'Well, I suppose that's good.'

Mac nodded. 'It is. It put my mind on things I didn't expect, too. I can only apologise. It won't happen again.'

It was just light enough to see the frown flit across Maddie's face.

'It's okay. Don't apologise. My mind has been there for a while,' she said with a small smile, 'but I get it, Mac, you don't have to explain any further, really.'

Mac had fully intended to get back into the boat, go back to the cabin and think about what had already passed between them before anything further happened. There was Sula to think about, and his emotions to sort out. Maddie would understand that.

But as she stood on the shore next to him, fully understanding what he was saying without him saying anything, even reaching a hand to touch his arm, he felt something give. It was an emotion so raw he was close to crying. Instead, he grabbed her hand and pulled her close, feeling her arms close around him as he held her. He stood for a while, feeling her, smelling her, enjoying how she fit against him, causing a stirring he hadn't felt for a long time. She said nothing, there were no words needed, she simply held onto him as he held her.

Eventually he pulled back, keeping his arms around her, and kissed her forehead lightly.

Do the right thing, Mac. The right thing.

'I don't want to hurt you,' he whispered, a lead weight dragging through his chest as Maddie looked at him, eyes wet with what could only be her own tears.

'It's okay, I get it,' she said, swallowing hard.

He rubbed the tears from her face with his thumbs gently. 'No, you don't. I *really* don't want to hurt you. I have huge issues to sort. You're right, it's not a good time, at all.'

'I know.'

He pulled her closer anyway, wanting to feel her in his arms again, not wanting to lose the moment. She didn't resist. She placed one hand on his face with a sad smile, the other around his waist. He leaned into her, unable to help himself.

'Mac?' she whispered as their noses touched.

He felt himself shake. His heart thumped, wanting to pull back, wanting to draw her closer, wanting to do the right thing, but helpless against the pull of desire. He closed his eyes and when her lips met his he felt himself respond anyway, pulling her closer, and deepening the kiss. She responded with a fervour that took him by surprise, igniting a passion and desire he thought he would never feel again.

'Christ, Maddie...,' he murmured when they broke away. Maddie grabbed his gloved hands with her own.

'Mac, that wasn't a good idea. I should have stopped you. I just...' She dipped her head, looking at their intertwined gloved hands, and then looked back up to him. '...no one has ever made me feel the way you do. I really hope I haven't added to the mess, because that's the last thing I ever wanted to do.'

'No...' Mac began.

She dropped his hands and turned to look at the wooden gate. 'I should go, Mac, it's getting dark. I'll see you tomorrow.'

He nodded, unable to respond, his body reeling with emotions, but she didn't need a response. She smiled, said a small 'bye' and then she was gone, through the gatepost before he had even caught his breath.

Back on the boat, Mac paddled furiously.

What did you do, Mac? Why didn't you stop? Why didn't you damn well control yourself? Do the right thing?

Right thing or not, he hadn't wanted to stop. He liked Maddie a lot. He had wanted that kiss more than anything, and he had enjoyed every second. If she were offering another right now, he would take it.

But Sula...

'Fuck Sula,' he said into the night. 'She was having my brother's baby. Tom's baby. She was obviously putting it around, having fun. When do I get some fun, huh?'

His heart gave a painful jolt, and he knew he was close to sobbing again. Sobbing with heartache, sobbing with relief, sobbing with joy, and sobbing with not knowing which the right path was. He knew he should take more time. It had only been twelve months, but Maddie had hit him square on from the moment he had seen her. He had been dubious of his own feelings, but now he knew for sure.

Can you love two women at the same time? Even when one wasn't faithful and didn't deserve it, anyway? Even when she's dead?

Mac bit down on his lip, tasting a trace of lip-gloss. His heart hurt again for completely different reasons. Maddie had been mortified, he knew that, and he hoped he hadn't ruined everything with her. This may be the end of the path either way if she felt strongly enough.

He felt his chest constrict as he paddled hard, confused. He paddled so hard that even Rolo had curled up inside the boat instead of draping over the front in his usual stance.

In his pocket, his phone started to ring. He almost left it, but the thought that it may be Maddie ensured that he stopped paddling to check.

It wasn't Maddie. It was Meg. Mac frowned. He knew she was struggling, but for the last few days, all she had sent were messages. If she was calling, it must be important.

'Meg?' he said, answering the phone. 'How are you?'

'Mac? I'm okay, I think. Have you heard from Tom?'

Mac frowned. He hadn't heard from Tom in a good many days, although he had been getting voicemails and messages from his brother until yesterday.

'No,' he said. 'I haven't spoken to him in ages. To be honest, I never pick up his calls or answer his messages. I'm not able to speak to him yet.'

'No, that's understandable. I feel the same, to be quite honest with you. Has he messaged you at all today?'

Mac frowned, checked his phone for messages, and put it back to his ear.

'He hasn't today. He did around ten yesterday morning. I think that was the last time.'

Aware of the blackness of the surrounding sky, the twinkling of the stars above, and the little cabin sitting in the distance, Mac put the phone on speaker and continued to paddle back. The loch was serene, still, and spookily quiet at night. Pensive, as though waiting to jump out and swallow you whole when you least expected it. It unnerved him more than he would like to admit.

'I haven't heard a thing from him,' Meg was saying over the speaker. 'I'd normally not worry, but this is so unlike him.'

'Maybe he's at work? You know he always likes to check things twice at Christmas, a bit like Santa.'

Meg didn't laugh, and Mac felt a tug of anxiety. Meg was worried, really worried.

'Yes, but he hasn't called. I can't remember the last time he slept over at work, and never without telling me where he is.'

'He slept over last year, didn't he?'

'Yes, but he told me. I've heard nothing, Mac. Nothing since yesterday morning.'

'Well, were you... you know, arguing? I know you're ready to leave him, and I don't blame you. I just wondered whether you were speaking to each other?'

Meg heaved a long sigh.

'Not really, no. But even so, I wouldn't expect this. It's been over twenty-four hours.'

'I'd never have expected what he did, or a fight like this between the two of you, either. Maybe expectations aren't to be trusted.'

'I hear you, Mac, but my gut says something isn't right.'

'Have you tried calling him at work?'

'Of course I have, both his phone and the office phone go to answerphone. The office phone says they're shut for Christmas.'

'Well, that's nothing. He's probably working in the peace. Have you been there to check?'

'I went this morning at around half nine after dropping Beth at her friends. He wasn't there, but the door wasn't locked and there was a broken coffee cup. The pieces were in the bin, so he can't have been far. It placated me at the time, but I still haven't heard anything more.'

'Right, he must be somewhere about then. Have you been back since?'

'No. I'm just getting annoyed with him now. Well, Flitting between annoyed and out of my mind with worry.'

'Yeah, I get it,' he said and immediately thought of Maddie, which made him think of the kiss, and wonder if he'd screwed everything up with her. He pushed the thought aside. 'I'll call him, or message. I'm sure he'll answer me. He seems so keen to explain what happened. I can put up with that for you. Hell, maybe I actually need it, anyway.'

'Oh, would you, Mac?' she gushed, the utter relief in Meg's voice evident. 'I'd be so grateful. I don't even want to know where he is. If he doesn't want to speak to me, just let me know that he's okay. Then I'll rest.'

'Yeah, okay. I'm almost back at the cabin now. I'll call when I get in and let you know the response.'

'Thank you, Mac, you're a sweetheart. I can't tell you the dressing down he's going to get when he does make it home.'

'Try not to worry, he's probably lost in invoices. Speak to you soon,' Mac said as the pier drew closer.

There was a sound emanating from the cabin. Music. The hair stood up at the back of his neck.

Fabulous. Looks like I'm in for an evening of ghostly music for entertainment.

'Bye, Mac.' Meg said and the phone call immediately cut off. Mac put the phone back in his pocket.

The tune got louder as he pulled up to the pier, and he recognised the frantic melody. One that in this situation, out here in a secluded cabin on the loch, left him colder than the winter night air. The piece, Totentanz by Franz Liszt, was more commonly referred to as the dance of the dead. Mac tried to ignore the insinuation.

The piece was ferocious and hard, and inside the cabin the unknown player was going for gold, literally pounding the melody on the piano keys. Mac tried to ignore the wild thump of his heart as he pulled the kayak high and moved to the door of the cabin. Rolo whined behind him, his tail clamped between his legs.

'No chance of you going in first then,' he murmured.

As his hand touched the door handle, the music stopped instantly.

Mac entered to the strong smell of musk. With a hand over his mouth and nose, he turned on the light and looked around. Only the thrum of the piano remained, and even that didn't last long. Nothing was out of place except the keyboard cover on the piano, which was raised, although he was sure that Maddie had shut it before they left. He leaned over the chair to place it down again and then stood listening to the silence with unease. When the smell of musk began to dissipate, he tugged off his hat and gloves, putting them on the kitchen table as he flicked the kettle on and unzipped his coat.

It was then that he noticed the word on the fridge. It was still in the middle, the other letters still scattered on the floor from this afternoon's message. Only the word was different.

DIE

Mac's breath caught as he stared, and a shudder ran through him.

'I may put these letters back in the store, Sula,' he murmured. 'I'm not sure I'm liking our chats so much anymore.'

The E dropped from the fridge onto the floor with a small tap. Mac blew out a breath and turned away calmly, trying to block his rising panic before it sent him running from the cabin screaming.

CHAPTER SIXTY-FIVE

When Tom came to, light was shafting into the van from the open door. There was a blurry figure, small, unmoving, haloed by the light. From his solid build, Tom would have said male.

Rescue? Help? His heart leapt.

'Where am I?' he croaked, straining his head toward the light. His body felt heavy and laden. He coughed and swallowed, trying to lubricate his throat.

The figure tilted his head. In the silhouette of his form, Tom could see his chin moving as though he were talking. Tom felt his heart rate rise.

Why can't I hear?

'Hello?' he shouted. 'I can't hear you. I think there's something wrong with my hearing. I've been injected with something. I don't know what it was, but it took me straight out. Help me, please!'

'Chill out,' the man said, clear as day, and the relief that Tom felt at being able to hear was quickly replaced by understanding that this was the man who had taken him. The doctor.

'Number one,' the doctor said, holding up a finger to the light. 'You're in the same place you were ten minutes ago when I left to get my grub.'

He held up some sort of food in the half light, possibly a burger, and took a bite, his chin moving as he chewed and swallowed.

Eating, Tom. He was eating; you jerk.

Lost your fucking hearing, what a joke! Ha ha.

The man swallowed and held up two fingers to Tom.

'Number two, you weren't injected with anything-'

'I was,' Tom said, cutting him off. He scrabbled around the empty van on his side, kicking his bound legs and arms for motion like some kind of demented fish. The van was empty, nothing on the floor.

'It was here, the injection. They were all here on the floor.'

'I know that. Another mess in my van. Quite the unruly passenger, aren't we? You weren't injected with anything.'

Tom huffed a breath, his anger rising.

'Okay. I injected myself.'

'That was pretty stupid for a couple of reasons. One, you didn't know the needle was clean, two, you didn't know what was inside. It could have been fatal. You would think a stint in the local hospital would have taught you the dangers of sharps injuries or were you hoping that it was fatal? Get you out of a few dilemmas now, wouldn't it?'

'I didn't do it on purpose,' Tom hissed as the doctor took another bite of his food. 'I was trying to feel what it was when it stuck me.'

The man shook his head with a sharp intake of breath.

'Foolish, Tom. Silly mistakes will get you into trouble.'

They already fucking have, Tom thought as he worked his jaw. The binds at his wrists were the most troublesome now. Each movement of his hands produced a burning sensation that could only be from an open flesh wound. He tried to stay still, but they throbbed regardless.

'What on earth were you doing in my things anyway?' the man said, throwing the packaging from his food - a McDonald's paper bag - into the bush with the cloths, gloves, and vomit.

'Nothing. The bag fell. I just wondered what it was. It's dark in here with the door shut. I couldn't see.'

'Hmm.' The man picked up a drink and slurped noisily through the straw. Tom felt his dry mouth constrict and realised he was thirsty on another level. Another side effect of whatever he had stuck himself with? 'Funny that. For all the bumps and sharp turns this van has taken, never has my bag fell from its fastenings. But sitting stationary here, in this dismal excuse for a service station, it jumps from its hook and showers you with the contents. Interesting.'

'It must have worked its way loose-' Tom started, wincing at the pain in his wrists.

'Or you must be some sort of warlock because the bag is clamped on a snap lock, which is why it didn't fall when you pushed it, it simply spilled.'

'I didn't push it,' Tom muttered.

The doctor laughed calmly. 'Of course you did, probably thinking I'm idiot enough to leave a knife in there to get yourself free.'

Tom clenched his jaw and closed his eyes. The van rocked, and Tom opened his eyes to see the doctor kneeling beside him.

'I never got to number three, Tom.' he held three fingers up in front of Tom's face.

Tom tried to shuffle further away, but his wrists screamed. Shaking and sweating, he looked up at the doctor, his features more readily available now that the streetlight could enter the van.

'What's three?' he said, licking his dry lips as the man stood to retrieve something from the bag. He stooped back down, holding the needle up to the light.

'Three. The needles you spilled were brand new and empty. Aren't you a lucky boy? If you had got the boxed batch, you could have stuck yourself with a good few milligrams of methadone. Shame.'

Tom felt himself reel with relief. 'Empty? It was new? Clean?'

'All of the above. While you were out cold thinking you were dying of whatever drug you had poisoned yourself with, you had actually fainted. Funny.'

Tom swallowed.

Fainted. You goddamn idiot.

'What's even funnier, Tom, is that I was going to see if you wanted to help, free your hands and legs a little, get you a little more comfortable. Now you've messed with my stuff, I kind of have to make you pay.'

Tom felt his heart jolt.

'What? No! No, I won't do it again. I won't touch anything else. I promise. Talk to me. I want to help you. I will, I'll do it.'

'I've been told that before. I can't risk you not following through.'

The doctor rose above him.

'What are you doing?' Tom said just before the heel of the doctor's shoe met his stomach. Tom blew out what little moisture he had in his mouth with a hard oof.

'Wait!' he said, as the foot connected again, and pain disturbed a bunch of angry bees in his stomach.

'One more for luck,' the doctor said, and his boot collided with Tom's chest. There was an almighty crack and pain flared hot and white up his right side. Tom screamed as his vision wavered.

'Right.' The doctor said, rising again. Tom whimpered and tried to shuffle back, the pain trying to send the world black. 'That should do it. So, the plan, Tom. Let's go over the plan. It's really remarkably simple. Only one step, even you should be able to manage it. And then we really need to get on the road. We have a long way to go.'

The plan *was* simple, Tom thought as he lay on the floor of the van. Especially now that it was in its final stages, after being planned for many months before. The doctor had been patient, silently planning and waiting; biding his time. The calls and the meetup were simply a way to get to an end point. It ended here - well not here, Scotland. At the cabin, where it all began.

Tom couldn't decide if he was crying for his sheer foolishness, or from the broken rib. It was dark in here, and his body was a mass of pain as the van rocked and rolled up country, leaving him time to think of nothing but the pain, and what would happen now.

The doctor wanted the cabin. Wanted Mac. Wanted his twenty million. Tom was not only bait - Mac wouldn't know the doctor was a threat initially, Tom was to pass him off as a friend - but directions too.

If he didn't comply?

The doctor would shut down Tom's life and take everything he could, anyway. He had his ex-practice partner and friend on standby to dispose of Mac at any time he gave the signal. By dispose, Tom could only think he meant dead, which made his blood run cold. Hadn't he warned Mac against the man? Why the hell hadn't he listened? Now the doctor had him over a barrel because Mac trusted the friend. Completely. Together, they had played a clever game, getting Mac hooked into doing whatever they wanted through trust.

As if that wasn't enough, the doctor also knew that Meg was at breaking point over the extra illegal drugs at work, which had only been a fluke addition that had worked in the doctor's favour. The doctor himself had ordered the extra medication. By breaking in and forging Tom's signature he had managed to order and process huge quantities that he had intercepted and stored ready to place in the clinic premises at any moment before inducing a police raid. This time would be much worse for Tom as files, invoices, treatment plans, even patients had been forged over the months after the doctor had found he could slip the unit's security lock with just a credit card.

Months, Tom thought. This has been going on for months! Meticulous, savage planning. No mistakes, no get of jail free cards.

Tom listened as the doctor went over just what they would find at the unit should the police get involved. He would go down for much more than supply, and much longer than the doctor ever had. Not only that, but he made sure that some of his unsuspecting staff would go down with Tom, too. How was that for genius?

Tom had sat listening, kicking himself for not having installed an alarm, or for fitting good quality locks. In fifteen years, they had never had a break in. Not one. Until now. Now had to be the time that Tom became aware of how easy it was to enter the building. The doctor would simply force back the lock with the card, hold it open with a small clamp until he had finished, then he shut the door and slid the card out, relocking the door.

Neat. Shit!

Incidentally, the methadone and syringes in the back here with Tom were part of the intercepted supply. When the doctor had ordered the supplies, he had known the unit was shut for Christmas, and running short of time, he had chosen the only daytime delivery he had ever chanced. The unit was concealed on a private trading estate, all he had to do was open the roller garage door, take delivery, sign, transfer it to the van and leave the way he came in. From the outside, it looked legit, and security was low.

Fortunately, or unfortunately for Tom, the delivery that day had contained an extra surprise as the closed unit had contained Tom, busy pondering the invoices that had been left on his desk. They were supposed to be a threat that the doctor had never got to make. Now he was in the unit anyway, and that had given the doctor a stunning idea.

He had knocked Tom out, taken delivery, put the items and Tom into the van and left as though nothing had happened.

The doctor had told Tom to take until the next stop at the Scottish border to make up his mind whether he would help willingly or by force. As he rolled in pain and the van took a sharp turn, Tom imagined the entrance to Gretna Green Services. Tom knew what his answer would be, he could have given it straight away.

As the doctor had said, he would win. Whatever Tom's choice.

Tom knew there was no choice. To save Mac, and hopefully himself, he would have to help.

CHAPTER SIXTY-SIX

MAC HAD TO ADMIT he was a little worried as he rowed over to the house for Ezzie's session the next morning. He had tried Tom three times with no joy both last night and this morning, and Meg hadn't had any further contact either. She had been to the unit office to find it in the same state as it had been the day before. Tom had not been back. No, there were no signs of a break in, no signs of a struggle other than the smashed coffee cup in the bin. She had gone on to call some of Tom's employees with no joy. None of them had heard from him either.

Mac had been able to do nothing more than try to console Meg and tell her he would try again today. Past that point, it may be wise to inform the police of his disappearance. Meg hadn't liked the finality of that statement, but Mac didn't know what else to do, and although he was at odds with his brother right now, he also wouldn't want to see him hurt. The one thing left unspoken between Mac and Meg was the man. The doctor who had threatened Tom. Neither of them had spoken of their fear that something had happened to Tom, as if that would make it a reality.

At the house, Maddie had let Mac in as she was getting ready to go out. She was warm and welcoming, as usual, asking how he was and chatting freely with no awkwardness, no judgement, no expectations. Mac had been grateful. He enjoyed the presence around her, and gravitated to her cheerful company. She made him a drink and told him he could go through to the lounge if he wanted. Ezzie would be in shortly, she was still getting washed, school holidays style. Mac had thanked her and stayed in the kitchen, anyway. Lingering to watch her as she pulled on her boots to take the dogs up into the hills – including Rolo if he wanted to come?

Mac had said sure, and Maddie had continued to chat as she wrapped up against the cold, but all too quickly she was giving him a fierce hug and leaving via the back door with a yell that she would be back soon. The kitchen became quiet; effervescence fading with her as the three dogs ran rings around her legs up the lawn. For a moment Mac had wanted nothing more than to go with her, and then Ezula had called him from the hallway.

'Doctor Mac?'

Mac turned from the window with a smile.

'Mac,' he said. 'How are you after yesterday's art class? Should Picasso be worried?'

'He's dead. And I'm ready,' she said with an unusually timid smile. Mac felt his eyebrows twitch together.

'Ready?' he said.

'I want to walk, Mac, I want to burn this damn chair, and my damn fear,' she said.

Mac grinned and nodded.

'Then let's get to it.'

'What prompted this, Ez?' Mac asked as he sat himself on the settee in the lounge. Ezzie rolled herself to him, not quite getting fully in front because of the angle of the coffee table.

'This.' She huffed, spreading her arms wide. 'All I want to do is sit by you properly, not have to look at you from wherever I can get the chair. This house is wheelchair friendly now, so you can imagine the problems everywhere else. It's annoying.'

Mac cocked his head.

'Art class made this decision?'

Ezzie looked down at her hands, together in her lap.

'I got stuck,' she murmured. 'I pulled over an easel that had a ladies' painting on. It was ruined. She said it was okay, but I could see it wasn't. I'm not stupid. You know the thing that made me most upset?'

'What?'

'I knew that I could get out and walk. Save all the issues of everyone pretending to be extra nice, and moving things for me, adjusting the heights of the easels, moving their chairs and stands so that I could get around. It was like I was seeing all the extra work all for me for the first time. It felt wrong. I felt stupid, Mac, I felt like an idiot. For the first time I saw how people treated me, and that it was different to how people who walk are treated. More than that, I cared that it was wrong. I felt like I was being unfair to the people who have to deal with me and sort me out when I can do these things myself. I'm pretending to be like my friends at school, but I'm not like them. I have a choice. They don't. Understand?'

Mac nodded.

'I do. I think you're growing up fast. I also think you're right. So, what do we need to do?'

Ezzie wrinkled her snub nose and scratched above her eyebrow.

'I don't know. You're the doctor. I'm just a kid. I thought you would tell me?'

'You know where you want to start, Ez.'

She shook her head, frizzy ponytail a blast of curls under the white scrunchie on top of her head. 'No worries' was emblazoned across her white fluffy jumper. Leggings adorned her legs today, pink and white stripes all the way down to black Dr Martin boots.

'You do,' he said. 'Listen to your heart. Take a moment and tell me what it says.'

Ezzie took a moment and then looked up at him.

'I don't want to start there,' she whispered.

He altered himself on the chair and took her hands.

'It will all be hard, and all of it will take courage. If your intuition tells you to start there, maybe it's better to get it out of the way? Once things are out in the open, the fear and hurt have a tendency to go away.'

Ezula stared at him, brown eyes large and wide. Her hands shook in his, but she squeezed his fingers hard. Finally, she gave a slow nod of acceptance.

'So where are we starting?'

'Africa, with my da.'

Mac stopped himself from physically letting out a sigh of relief. This was good. This was exactly where they needed to be. Everything up to this moment was child's play and earning trust. The real work began now.

'I'm listening. Take as much time as you need.'

But Ezula began to cry and shake instead. 'I can't.'

'That's okay, Ezzie. How about we find a bit that you can talk about? There must have been good memories with your father, yes?'

'Before.' She said, hitching a breath. 'When we... we were travelling. That was good.'

'Did you like travelling?'

Now Ezzie smiled and her face lit up under the tears.

'So much! I loved seeing all the different places. It was like the whole world was my home. People talked funny, ate funny things, did funny things, but everyone was nice. Everyone was my family. I played with loads of children, I walked lots of beaches and hills, I saw some really cool things. Now I'm stuck, stuck here... and stuck here!' she kicked the chair with a boot. It rocked, but the brake held it in place on the carpet. 'I can only just remember half of the things we did. I feel like that happened to another Ezzie, not me.'

Mac nodded and squeezed her hands. 'So, what happened?'

Ezzie shook her head.

'Dig deep, Ez. I know it's hard, but nothing here can hurt you now.'

'There is. My da...' she whispered, breaking off and breaking eye contact.

'Ezzie, he's gone, sweetheart. He died. You are aware of that, aren't you?'

'Yes. He was shot. Ma told me. But that doesn't matter.'

'I don't understand,' Mac said, completely lost on why a child should fear her dead father, and be scared enough for it to trap her like this.

'He cursed me. In Africa. The only way I get to have a normal life now is to not walk. I must be in this chair or bad things will happen to me. Very bad things. I could die.'

Her voice shook and her lower lip wobbled. Mac had no idea what to say.

'I've cheated, though,' she whispered. 'I've cheated and I think the impundulu knows.'

'The what?'

Mac heard Ezzie swallow, and a tear rolled down her cheek.

'I'm scared,' she said. 'I'm scared to speak his name in case he hears me.'

'Ezzie, whatever this thing is? Together we can fight it, we can figure it out, but you need to tell me.'

'Can you stop it, Mac? Do you know about curses?'

Mac thought about his answer.

'A fair bit. They mostly attack the mind, just like they have with you. I can probably work it out, but not if I don't know what it is.' he half-lied. He knew nothing about curses, but they were probably mostly rooted in the superstitious brain after all.

'It... it's a bird,' Ezzie said. 'A lightning bird as big as a person. He sends storms mostly, but he can work with witch doctors to curse, and he can shape shift into a human. My da had me cursed when we went to Africa. I was to stay with him on the farm at all times. Forever. No matter how much I missed ma, I wasn't to contact. If I ran more than a metre down the track, the curse would take my legs, and I wouldn't be able to walk ever again.'

'But you *can* walk,' Mac said.

'The witch doctor said the Impundulu would be watching. If I were to ever walk again, if the feeling came back? The curse would unleash tenfold and the Impundulu would send storms for me *and* ma all my life. If I didn't die, I would wish to be dead.'

Mac stared at Ezzie.

Fuck! Who the hell says that to a little girl?

A scared father. A father out for some sort of revenge. But his problem was with Maddie, not Ezzie. To say such a thing to a child was unacceptable. Keeping her there beyond her will.

Mac thought hard. How could he get around this?

'I don't want to die, Mac, I want to live, but sometimes stuck here I don't want to. Sometimes I think I'll get out and if the storms kill me, it will be better than being in here. Then I get scared. I don't want bad things to happen to me and ma. Ma doesn't deserve the bad things. She did nothing wrong. I wanted to be home. I hated Africa, hated the house, and my grandparents. There was too much fighting. I wanted to be here. I wanted to come home, that's why I asked the man to help me. The nice one. I had to come home, even if I couldn't walk.'

Ezzie was somehow screaming and crying at the same time. Frustration taking over her fear for the moment. Mac let her vent. She needed it. He was also formulating a small plan.

'And you are home. It worked. Now we just have to get rid of the Imudan...' he shook his head, 'the bird,' he finished.

'You can't,' she sobbed. 'Only a witch doctor can remove a curse. I can't go back to see him, Mac. Please don't take me back. I'm too frightened. I don't want to go back there! Please!'

'You don't have to go back there, I promise. I know someone who may be able to help here.'

Ezzie stopped wailing, sniffed, and looked up at him with hope filled eyes.

'You know a witch doctor? From Africa?'

Mac shook his head. 'Not from Africa, but a witch doctor, yes. Expert in removing African curses. Like I said, I know a little about these things.'

Ezzie's tears came fast, her relief palpable. She launched herself from the chair and threw herself onto Mac, not dissimilar to the way Maddie had launched at him a few weeks earlier on this very couch.

The apple doesn't fall far from the tree, he thought, and Ezzie just took a step right in front of me.

He held the crying child in his arms and smiled.

All he had to do now was a little research, speak to a few people, and within the next few days, with a little planning, Ezzie would be free of her curse.

After a pleasant lunch prepared by Hester and Maddie, Mac had spent a few hours with Ezzie and the family, enjoying their warmth and hospitality. Walt was a funny man who would have plied Mac with dram after dram of the finest whiskey, if Mac could have handled it without his eyes nearly popping out of his head. Smoke, earth, and peat seemed to linger at the back of his nose and throat long after he had swallowed. Mac didn't know what it was, but he had never tasted anything like it. They talked, and played one of Ezzie's favourite games - Sussed, where you have to suss out what someone else would do in a given situation. As the sky had dropped darker, Mac had reluctantly said his goodbyes.

Maddie had walked with him to the edge of the patio where she had hugged him and thanked him again, not only for helping Ezzie, but for the pleasure of his company, and for a fantastic afternoon with the family. Mac had held her too long, placed a kiss on her cheek, and made his way to the kayak as if he was walking on air.

If that was family life, he'd take it. Every day. Over everything he had.

The only person that had been missing from the afternoon was Saul, but Mac found him now, sitting on the edge of his kayak. Waiting. He lifted his head as Mac approached and rose to stand. Mac grinned.

'Saul. Good to see you! What the hell are you doing out here?'

Saul pursed his lips but didn't smile.

'I can't let you go, Mac,' he said.

Mac swallowed, confused. Saul looked on edge, eyes flitting to the undergrowth around them.

'What are you talking about?' Mac said with a nervous, half laugh.

And then Saul pulled out the gun, and suddenly Mac wasn't smiling anymore.

CHAPTER SIXTY-SEVEN

T HE BACK DOOR OPENED to a dark form and orange light like this was groundhog hour - except that this hour hurt far more than the last one had. Tom wished for nothing more than to have his hands untied so that he could nurse his ribs. He was shaking with pain, drenched with sweat, and bone cold. The fleece not holding its warmth with cool sweat underneath and no heating in the back of the van.

'We're officially in Scotland,' the doctor said. 'I know the cabin is near the house, so that gives us around five to six hours' drive. We should make it by...' he looked at his watch, twisting his wrist into the light, 'say nine o'clock? Just in time for an evening tipple and chat. I hope Mac has some booze in and doesn't mind surprise visitors. Have you made your decision, Tom?'

'Yes. Yes. I'll help, just please. I need my hands. My ribs, oh god my ribs!'

The doctor cocked his head on one side, seeming to contemplate his plea.

'I can't let you go free Tom, that would be foolish. As you're so willing, I will re-tie your hands at the front if you wish. I also have some pain relief if-'

'Oh God. Yes,' he breathed, and his rib sang out. 'Ow, fuck. Please. I'll do anything.'

'I know you will. Now listen, because this is what is going to happen. I'll re-tie your hands and get you the paracetamol. Your legs will have to stay tied, I'm afraid, at least until we get nearer the cabin. You can ride up in the cab with me, but be warned, I have a syringe or two of methadone up front - enough to kill. I keep it there for emergencies. I won't hesitate to use it in one. Get my drift?'

'Yes.' Tom whispered. 'Yes. I won't be any trouble, I promise.'

'I like to have a backup, and you have been unruly enough already. However, I do you need you comfortable and coherent for the next part. After that, well, we'll see.'

The doctor stepped into the van and untied his hands roughly before bringing them to the front and retying them just as tight. Tom bit down on his lip to stop himself from screaming with the pain. Any thoughts of escape right now out of the window, he would cross that bridge later.

Next, the doctor gave him two paracetamol and a bottle of water, which Tom managed to take by himself, although the blackness nearly took him twice. He swallowed the pills and glugged the water, pain clamping his chest like a vice.

The doctor watched in silence.

'Christ!' Tom said. 'Haven't you got anything stronger? I feel like I want to black out each time I move.'

'Of course,' the doctor said, and Tom nearly passed out with relief. 'But you will stick with paracetamol. It will take the edge off the pain in twenty minutes or so. I can't have you being too comfortable, Tom. No saying what little scheme you will hatch if the pain is completely gone.'

'I won't-'

'We're wasting time. Get in the front.'

Tom shuffled on his backside, numb from the pain shooting through every single fibre, from his head to his toes.

I hope that paracetamol gets to work quickly, or I may go insane from pain.

At the edge of the van, the doctor checked their surroundings and helped Tom down with a little more vigour than Tom would have used, but what the hell? Everything hurt anyway. What was a bit more of a pinch here and there?

Tom shuffled to the passenger side, and the man opened the door.

'You'll need helping up, I suppose,' he said. He squat behind Tom and in one fluid motion, shoulder under his butt, he heaved Tom inside face first.

Tom screamed, long and loud, as the man shoved his legs to the side and shut the door. Then he was at the driver's side, getting inside.

'Good job I parked away from the public, eh? You've got a great set of lungs, Tom. Would you mind belting up? We have to go.'

'Uggghh.' Tom managed, still face down on the seat, his knees on the floor, the pain a single entity that encompassed him whole.

The doctor huffed and leaned across to pull Tom onto the seat.

'NO!' Tom screamed, 'No! I can do it. Give me a chance, please.'

'There's no time.'

Tom moved onto the seat as fast as he could and the doctor did up the seatbelt, crushing his rib in the process.

'Fuck! Stop, please! It fucking hurts!'

'I know. I had broken ribs once. Hurts like a mother. It's no fun, I can tell you.'

'I don't need telling,' Tom said through clenched teeth, trying his hardest to stay still and not breathe. 'Why does it seem like you're enjoying this way too much?'

'Because I am. We're going to have some real fun, the four of us in the cabin. A veritable party.'

'Four?' Tom breathed, and his face contorted in pain.

'You and I, your brother Mac, and our mutual friend, doctor Montgomery.'

'The other doctor?' Tom said as the man turned on the engine.

'The very one. He has Mac. I have directions from the both of you, and I have to swing by the house, so no point trying to get me lost, Tom. Tonight, we party. Fun, huh?'

Tom grit his teeth and looked out of the window.

'I didn't need to help you? So what am I doing here? You're planning to kill me out there, aren't you?'

'Really, Tom. How little you think of me! The party just wouldn't be the same without the dick who made the call that put me in the slammer now, would it?'

CHAPTER SIXTY-EIGHT

M AC STARED AT THE gun and raised his hands slowly into the air.

'Saul. I don't want any beef with you. Think about your path. Remember what you told me in the cabin?'

'I had to do it, Mac. I had no choice. I had to help him. I need the money. Who the hell turns down five million after all? You'd have to be stupid, wouldn't you?'

Mac kept his eyes trained on the gun while trying to assess how volatile Saul was. He had read a million people, could tell on the spot whether they were serious or not. If he could keep calm, he may be able to catch Saul off guard and take the gun. There may be a fight, but Mac thought he could hold the bigger man off, maybe even beat him back to the safety of the house.

'That would depend on what the deal was, and whether it would put me back where I didn't want to go.' Mac said.

Saul flicked the gun at him, and Rolo finally began to sense something amiss and began to bark. Saul turned the gun to the dog. Mac's heart leapt into his throat.

'No!' he yelled, lurching to the dog, but Saul had the gun trained back on him in less than a second.

'Then shut the dog up, Mac. Greg says there'll be no trace back to me. I'm not going back there. I have no choice, you understand.'

Mac shushed the dog, who sat whining behind his legs. The gun was shaking in Saul's grip, but the look in his eyes was hard and cold, his stance solid. Mac broke out into a cold sweat. Did this man, who had seemed like a thoroughly decent guy back at the cabin, really want to shoot him? Especially when he had been so adamant that he hadn't wanted to go back to jail? This was money talking, surely. Easy money. Mac knew that it derailed many a good man, but he was determined that this man would not go back down that route. If not for himself, or Mac, then at least for the family who didn't deserve the pain of a son in jail again.

'Saul, whatever the plan is, you do have a choice. Don't do it. If not for me, for Ezzie. She needs you - she can walk!'

Mac cut off as Saul began to laugh.

'Ezzie? You're bringing my niece into this? For real? Like you know my family so well?'

'She needs you,' Mac said. A trickle of sweat dribbled down his cheek, causing a phenomenal urge to scratch, but he didn't dare move.

Think Mac, how the hell do you get out of this stalemate without being shot?

The pressure caused a pain in his right temple as his heart thud.

'Okay. I think I can make this work for both of us,' he said. 'Let me go, Saul. If you told Greg, so be it. I can handle it from the cabin if that's where he's going. You can take the five million. I won't say a word. Hell, he'll probably kill me, anyway. Job done. Your name will truly be clear. Just let me get in the kayak and you'll never see me again.'

Saul frowned, and the gun wavered. Mac noted the inconsistencies. This wasn't a man ready to shoot. Should he just get into the kayak, anyway? He edged left, keeping Rolo behind him.

'Stay where you are!' Saul shouted.

The gun straightened. Saul now aiming with two hands, and Mac raised his own hands.

Why doesn't he shoot? Do I need to be alive?

That could be your get out of jail free, Mac.

Do I take the chance?

Mac stopped, forcing himself to speak calmly while his body was firmly in 'flight' mode, legs screaming at him to run. It was harder for a gun to hit a moving target than one standing still, even at point blank range. The odds were better for running. FUCKING RUN!

'Saul, listen, it's–'

'No.' Saul said firmly, seeming to regain some of his composure and hardness. 'You listen to me. I don't need you at the cabin. I need you here, back at the house.'

Mac reeled. 'The house? But your family...'

'We're going back to the house... both of us. To wait.'

Mac thought of Maddie, Ezzie, Hester and Walt. His heart was pounding with uncertainty. He couldn't go back there and expose them all to this terror. Especially not with a small child there who had certainly been through enough for one lifetime.

'No,' Mac said. 'I'm going to the cabin. Shoot me if you must. I can't expose your family to this.'

Saul clicked off the safety with a small grin.

'My family are already exposed. They know. We're going back.'

Mac felt the breath leave his lungs with the force of a punch.

Maddie. Ezzie.

'What have you done with them?' he said, 'Saul, what the fuck have you-'

Saul laughed.

'You think I'd really hurt my family? After all they've done for me?'

'I don't understand? They know?'

'You're not very quick, Mac. I thought the pieces would have come together by now.'

Mac felt the world fragment around him. No. They weren't involved. They couldn't be. Could they? Had this been an elaborate plan all along? Entice him in and fleece him?

Maddie? Pain flashed across his chest. It was all fake? She wouldn't do that, would she?

Do you really know her? Really? Really know any of them?

'No,' Mac whispered.

'Yes.' Saul said. 'They know. You're going back to the house.'

'Ezzie...' Mac breathed. Surely the child couldn't be involved.

Saul swallowed.

'As you said, she can walk.'

Mac sank to his knees, his legs giving out under him.

Ezzie could walk... of course she could.

'You got me,' he whispered. 'All of you.'

'Hook, line, and sinker,' Saul said with a nod. He waved the gun at the small gateway.

'Go,' he said.

Mac swallowed as he got to his feet, his head swimming.

All of them. Five against one. In their domain?

Run for it, Mac.

RUN!

RUN FOR YOUR FUCKING LIFE!

His eyes shifted left - the dark trees at the edge of the path that he hated so much may just be the perfect cover right now. Heart threatening to pound right out of his chest, he turned on his heel and ran.

The shot reverberated through the forest, echoing off the mountains, vibrating through the trees, and sending wildlife skittering with squeals and squawk's for many miles around.

CHAPTER SIXTY-NINE

THE PARACETAMOL KICKING IN, combined with quenched thirst and warmth, was starting to make Tom drowsy. It had been too long since he had slept. He sat back against the seat, staring from the side window, his eyes dropping, until he winced at the occasional pain that shot through his chest.

'Not long now.' The doctor shouted over the music, which he insisted on having at eardrum shattering level, and singing a few decibels higher, off key. Tom wasn't so sure that it wasn't purely for his discomfort. He'd heard the music in the back before, but unless the bulkhead was insulated, which he doubted, the sound had been only half this level, he was sure.

Without moving his chest, Tom turned his head to the front and saw Loch Ness beside them, moon shimmering in the black surface to the driver's side. A sign for Drumnadrochit came into view on the left, lit by the headlights of the van, and his heart sank. They were close. Forty minutes at most after a left turn at the town, taking them through Cannich and into the wilderness of lochs and mountains and single-track roads.

The doctor signalled left and turned onto the small A road, leaving Loch Ness behind them as they travelled toward the towering snowy mountains, just visible against the clear dark sky. It was a cold night up here, and snow had fallen, although not recently as the road was clear. With a bit of luck, the van wouldn't make the latter, less tended roads at all, and they would have to return.

'Right,' The doctor said, turning to Tom. 'Obviously I know where the clinic is - as do you. What I need to know is where the track is for the cabin. Saul said it was before the turn for the house by a fair way but he was uncertain exactly. You signal when we're near, right?'

Tom nodded his head.

'I'm not sure this van will make it down the track,' he said.

'What?' The doctor shouted and turned the music down.

'I said I'm not sure the van will make it,' Tom said. Talking hurt his ribs, he said no more.

'No problem,' the man said, turning the music up louder. 'I'm not stupid. I worked at the clinic for many years. This baby is a four-wheeler, and I have snow chains. We'll get there.'

Tom turned back to the window, thinking how excited he would normally be by now as the dark, but familiar landscape passed by. The cabin approaching. Solitude. Isolation. Time alone with Josh if he was with him. They would be discussing what they would do first, right now. Tom would usually be left with the luggage while Josh took a swim or marched off into the woods to take in the magnificent views.

Tom felt a tear slide down his cheek. He would give anything to be home with his family now. Comfortable, eating at the table with the usual family banter - and no broken ribs. He blinked his eyes, dispersing the tears, the one that had fallen drying on his cheek. He wished he could call Meg, let her know he was okay, and to tell her to call for help. She must be going out of her mind.

She told you not to come back last time you spoke. She could think you've done just that. Left.

Tom's eyes closed. The pain was returning, and he didn't want to think about the fact that Meg thought he had left her, or even that she hadn't called someone for help yet. She was a smart woman. Surely she must have put two and two together by now?

And she may not. Maybe you're out here and nobody is looking. And when we get to the cabin, Mac will be trapped too. Both of you with no one thinking to look, no one thinking anything is wrong.

Tom's thoughts slid to Mac. It had been so long since he had spoken to his little brother. He had no idea what Mac was thinking about Sula and the abortion. Had no idea if he was still angry. Although he surely would have called if he wasn't.

That was something the doctor hadn't factored into his little quest. Whether the brothers actually got on at all, and whether the happy little reunion would seem out of place. Tom knew that Mac would immediately be on his guard, and maybe that was a good thing. He would act more quickly than Tom with his broken ribs.

The road had narrowed a while ago, passing places only. Trees huddled against the side of the road, bark shining white in the headlights like an army of ghosts. Tom knew there was a river to their right, not visible in the darkness.

When an icy line of frozen slush lined the middle of the road, Saul pulled up in an opening next to a gate.

'Do I have to bring you outside to put the chains on?'

Tom felt his stomach turn over at the thought.

'No, please. I won't move. The pills are wearing off. It hurts too much.'

The doctor left the door open. Freezing air circulated the cabin, making Tom's teeth chatter, as he heard the rattle of chains. Tom waited, not daring to move as the man applied them to the wheels, an aching pain winding through him from head to toe. He closed his eyes in the quiet, trying to keep shivering to a minimum. When the chains were on, the man entered the back of the van, causing it to rock on its suspension. Tom's eyes flew open, and he yelled, and then the man was back, shutting the driver's door behind him with a bang that rocked the van and made Tom hiss through his teeth.

They moved on. Music too loud for concentration on the treacherous strip of snowy tarmac, but the doctor knew the small road well and traversed the twists and turns with care. Finally, Tom recognised the small bridge ahead and knew the turn that would take them to the cabin was close.

'Nearly there,' he said, wishing he could let him sail straight by.

The doctor glanced at him, and the music was turned down again.

'What?'

'Here.' Tom grunted as the turn came into view. 'Next on the left, between the trees. Slower.'

The doctor slowed, and the snowy entrance to the track came into view. The doctor turned the van, and they began the bouncy, winding route down into the woods. Tom whimpered and moaned, the doctor having no care for his passenger with the broken ribs and no arms to balance himself from the jolts of the suspension or the cut of the seat belt across his chest.

He passed out twice, yelled more than once, but the music overthrew him for attention and then suddenly, around halfway through the forest, the van stopped. Tom could have cried with relief. His vision was blurry with pain, but he saw the doctor peer out of the windscreen.

'There's a car,' he said.

Tom tried to breathe. 'A pickup,' he managed, remembering that Mac had tried to leave and said he was stuck.

'No. A car, little red one blocking the track.'

Tom squinted out of the windscreen, and a blur of red came into view. 'I don't know whose that is.'

'Well, we can't get round. How far is it?'

'Just over halfway, maybe, around a mile or so to the cabin.'

'Guess we're ready to rock and roll then,' the man said, reaching over Tom into the glove box. Tom lay his head back against the headrest.

'There's no way I can walk that far.'

'Here.' The doctor placed a couple of objects in his pockets and then held a syringe out to Tom, who eyed it warily.

'Naproxen - for the pain,' he said, 'then I'll undo your feet.'

Tom eyed the syringe as the doctor pulled off the cap and injected his arm, even as he tried to protest. He very quickly became free of pain alright. His vision blurred further, and the van's cab began to spin slowly, then he lost consciousness.

CHAPTER SEVENTY

'DON'T MOVE!' SAUL YELLED and Mac felt himself halt.

Am I hit?

He didn't think so, but he hadn't made it any more than two steps. He hadn't thought Saul would shoot if he was honest, but he had. The gun had gone off, and that was a game changer for Mac. He didn't want to die. Out here seemed perfectly plausible - inside with an eight-year-old child? He didn't think it would get that far.

Plan B - Get inside and stick to Ezula like glue.

Mac turned with a nod. Rolo was gone, and for a second Mac thought he had been the one to get the bullet, but there was no furry body nearby. He thanked God for small mercies, and hoped he would find his way back to the cabin.

Saul was pointing the gun at him. No safety on now. Mac swallowed hard.

'Okay. I'm coming to the house. You don't have to point that thing at me. Please.'

Saul flicked the gun toward the gate and Mac walked down the lawn and to the imposing house that had this morning seemed friendly, but now seemed foreboding. He walked slowly, giving himself time to think, Saul behind, presumably with the gun pointed at him. Mac wasn't going to check.

At the patio, the back door opened, and a profoundly serious Walt motioned him inside. He went. Saul following behind.

The door shut behind them... and it was like the room breathed a sigh of relief.

Hester stepped forward to hug him, while Walt pat his son on the shoulder and chastised him for using the gun.

'I told you not to shoot it!' he said.

'He was running. I'm not daft. I shot it in the air like you do.'

'You don't know what the bloody hell you're doing. You could have killed Mac, or yourself. Where's the dog? Where's Rolo?'

Hester let Mac go and frowned. 'Yes, where's Rolo?' She said.

Mac looked from one to the other of the three people in the kitchen. People he thought he knew. People who were willing to drop him in it for money, and yet were still acting like they cared. Did they really think Saul hadn't said anything?

'Mac?' Hester said before him, concern on her face that couldn't possibly be genuine.

'What do you care? He ran when your son tried to shoot me.'

Saul and Walt answered together. Saul now removing his boots and coat.

'I didn't shoot you.'

'He wasn't supposed to shoot.'

Mac felt his anger rise. The situation was uncertain enough, and they were all still acting like they cared. His head spun with confusion.

'Well, I guess that makes everything hunky-dory then. Put the kettle on, and we'll sit and have a nice chat while we wait for the main man to arrive, eh? I suppose he decides who to shoot, and Saul can really be free of any crime. Clever.'

Saul smiled.

'Mac, you've got it all wrong, buddy. I was never going to shoot, but you scared me to death.'

Mac swung to him, lunging forward, and Saul stepped back until he hit the wall behind him. Mac stopped when his nose was inches from Saul's. He heard Hester gasp.

'I scared you to death?' he said, kicking hard at Saul's boots next to him to save from kicking the man himself. They flew into the door with a thud that rattled it on its hinges. 'I scared YOU to death. You're the one who shopped me in, you were the one waving a gun in MY face, you're the one who puts money - fucking money - before someone's life! I'd have given you the money myself if you'd just asked - all five million. I thought you were a decent man, Saul, but you're not. You're fucking scum, just like the other one.'

Saul stayed quiet as Mac ranted, but it was Walt who stopped the flow, placing a firm hand on Mac's shoulder, and pulling him back. Mac spun to him, pulling a fist back, adrenaline surging through his veins, but a look at Walt's kindly face and the man looking every bit his eighty years stopped him. He wasn't immoral. He could outrun this old man any day of the week.

It turned out he didn't have to. The man took his hand from Mac's shoulder.

'Mac, please. We need to explain. It appears that Saul has told you things that aren't true-'

'He was going back-' Saul tried. Walt gave his son a look, cutting him off.

'Things that need to be put right before you kick off. Hester, get a drink, we'll go to the living area.'

Hester reached out to squeeze Mac's arm with a sad smile. 'We want to protect you, Mac. You've done so much for this family.'

Mac wavered. He wanted to believe them; wanted to like this family, but he didn't know who or what to believe, right now. He turned to Saul.

'This had better be fucking good after you waved a gun in my face, and scared my dog away to god knows where.'

Saul nodded, but he was pale. 'It will be worth it, I promise you.'

Mac swallowed. Saul held his gaze, not wavering.

Finally, Walt turned to the hallway. 'Let's tell you what we know in comfort, eh?'

It was Saul that started it, he admitted, by offering to give the cabin's location away for money, albeit, he hadn't known that was the location when he agreed. He had managed to put Greg off, saying there was an emergency with Ezzie and he would get back to him as soon as possible, and cutting the call before he had given any directions. Feeling like an idiot, and at a loss what to do, he confided in his father.

'Saul told me that Greg was out for revenge, and the man who had shut the clinic was your brother, Mac. He also said that Greg had located the man and was planning to come up to the cabin, and that you had confirmed this with what your brother said in his calls to you.'

'Tom.' Mac said, 'My brother's name is Tom, and yes, he was probably more scared than I gave him credit for. I thought he was meddling in things out here, trying to keep control. There was my late wife's association with the clinic, and I really couldn't deal with speaking to him.

To be honest, neither myself nor his wife have heard from him for the last couple of days. I need to call the police. Something could have happened. I don't know why I didn't do this sooner.'

'We've already called the police. Don't worry about that,' Walt said, nodding for Saul to continue.

It turned out that Walt had told Saul to play it cool, call him back with the directions, and find out his plans. When Greg got to the cabin, the police would be waiting.

'But I didn't like that,' Saul said. 'I couldn't chance you being there when Greg arrived if the police were late. I didn't want you to get hurt, Mac, so da said to tell you, and you could stay here when Greg was putting his plan into action.'

'So, what was wrong with that variation?' Mac said, accepting the warm tea from Hester with thanks.

It only vaguely went through his mind that they could all still be acting, and the tea poisoned - and then he chastised himself. Hester had offered him the tray first, and all of the men took their tea the same, surely she wouldn't chance poisoning one of her own.

He shook the thought away, and took a sip.

'Well, that was the plan, but I have been on the phone to Greg throughout the day because a new development came up that I had to be sure of. I was going to grab you as you left, but you were with Maddie. I didn't want to... intrude.'

Mac reddened. He would have been a little pissed for sure, but this was also important. Time with Maddie could come afterward.

'So why the gun?'

'I panicked. I knew I had only minutes to convince you before you were on the boat. Greg bothers me. He's gone further than I ever thought he would. I don't know what his plans are. I didn't want to have to follow you to the cabin and risk us both being there while I explained. I was a little fired up - desperate I suppose, so da handed me the gun, just in case I needed to persuade you.'

'It was stupid,' Walt said, shaking his head. 'We both panicked, and from the way things turned out, my son is no good at persuasion.'

'Definitely not his strong point,' Mac said, thinking of how early in the conversation the gun had appeared. If Saul had just spoken first, there would have been no need. Mac trusted him. He would have understood and returned without the force - and without losing Rolo. His heart gave a twinge at the thought of the dog out there somewhere in the cold.

'So, what was the new development?' he said with a sigh.

'I heard sounds at first. I knew Greg was driving, so I dismissed it as road noise, however when I called again, I heard a voice. A man's voice. I asked who it was, fearing he was bringing someone with him to help with whatever he was intending to do at the cabin - he never told me what that was. First, he told me it was someone who needed to see, then he said he was enjoying the payback, and in a later call he spoke to Tom, calling him by name. I already had an inkling by then, but now I'm almost sure he has your brother with him.'

Mac's heart almost leapt out of his chest. 'Fuck! No, how the hell does that happen? How does a man kidnap a grown man? Was Tom so scared that he agreed to help? How the fuck does this happen?! I need to call Meg. I need to call the police!'

Mac pulled his phone from his pocket, and Walt placed a hand on his arm.

'Saul came to me, scared for the both of you and for how far Greg had gone. I called the police immediately with all of the details. They were on their way here. I told them to stop by the cabin first. They should be there soon, but Greg may be there first.'

'Greg will call me when he sees you're not there. I know he will,' Saul said. 'He will suspect foul play. I hope I can keep him on the phone by playing ignorant, mentioning the money a lot, and giving him places to look around the area until the police arrive. I can only hope this will keep Tom safe, too.'

Mac took a sip of his tea. It turned over in his stomach.

'The police are coming, thank you for that,' he said, 'I need to call Meg, let her know what's happening. Fuck! I wouldn't return his calls. If I had, maybe he would have told me how bad things were getting. I was so caught up in the damn baby. I'm an idiot.'

'You're not, my darling,' Hester said. 'No-one could have foreseen any of this. From the very start, Greg seemed such a nice man. The clinic was a surprise, as was jail. We gave Saul the benefit of the doubt when he said that he hadn't known what Greg was up to, although the jury disagreed, but it seems Greg was the bad seed after all.'

'I need to call Meg,' Mac said, fighting the urge to say that Saul had agreed to accomplice something he knew nothing about, and which was obviously illegal, when he said he would help for the money. He pushed the thought away. Right now, Saul had also possibly saved his life, despite the money he would now not get.

He pulled out his phone and swiped the screen. It lit to two calls, a voicemail, and three messages. A few were from Meg. The rest were Maddie.

Maddie?

He opened the message with a frown.

Ma said she will have Ezzie for a couple of hours. I thought maybe I could come over and tackle this piano for a bit? I tried ringing, but you're probably paddling by now. I'll drive round. I think I can find the track. Don't worry, no pressure at all. Hope you don't mind - say the word if you do, I can turn back. Xx

Mac felt the blood rushing from his body. He immediately pressed to call her but the phone went straight to voicemail. Ice slid down his spine as he listened to her own voicemail from earlier, his heart pounding.

'Hey Mac, guess what? I'm stuck!' she laughed at her own misfortune. 'I'll follow the track, but you may have to take me back via the loch. Da will get the car tomorrow. I'm so sorry, I shouldn't have come, now I'll have to put you out again.' She sighed. 'Oh well, can't be helped now. Be with you soon.'

The call clicked off and Mac squeezed his eyes closed. Oh, Maddie, I'd have put you up, you idiot, he thought, tears filling his eyes as pain filled his chest.

'What is it?' Walt said.

Mac looked up to see three pairs of eyes settled quietly on him.

'Maddie.' he said, holding up the phone and running his free hand over his face.

'She went for a drive not long after you left,' Hester said. 'Why? What's the matter?'

'She's on her way to the cabin,' Mac said quietly. 'And her phone is dead.'

He let the words sink in for only a beat before he was tearing out the back door toward the kayak, Saul close on his heels.

CHAPTER SEVENTY-ONE

THE BRIGHTNESS OF THE cabin was a welcome sight for Maddie after an hour's muddy stumble in the dark with only a phone light for company. She had almost fallen countless times and was feeling grateful that she still had every bone intact. In fact, she not only felt grateful, but invigorated.

When she had travelled there were many spur-of-the-moment adventures like this. Some for enjoyment, some to see a sight early morning or late night, some with a heart pounding need to get away from a situation - thankfully not too many of those.

I was usually dressed for the occasion before, though.

She stopped at the edge of the forest and looked down at her legs and snow boots, which now had an extra thermal layer of mud almost to the thigh on her right leg. Her hands were just as bad.

She grinned, and used snow from the wood store roof to clean herself up a little. When was the last time she had this much fun? Sneaking out to see a man and having an adventure through the woods to boot. For the first time since Ezzie came home, she felt fully alive. Not that it was Ezzie's fault and, of course she would do all she could for her little girl, but sometimes caring for her full time, and having no opportunity to go anywhere but home and school - which was a forty-minute drive both ways into the next village, up and down the same old unkempt road - was excruciating. There was no opportunity to deviate, to drive a new road - she felt tunnelled in, forced on one straight path that she sometimes felt herself kicking back against for no good reason. The situation couldn't change unless she moved. Carer's allowance didn't amount to much and her parents were letting them both live at the house for very little. She knew that they loved having them there, and Maddie appreciated it, but sometimes it was stifling - it drove her to the point of insanity.

Tonight, she had just wanted Mac's presence. Something different, somewhere different. The only thing bothering her now was his lack of response, and she regretted that he may think she was pushing for more, but she wasn't stupid. The kiss, as wonderful as it had been, and as much as she had wanted it, was a mistake that she couldn't let him repeat. It was too soon, and this was a relationship she didn't want to spoil. She would wait, as long as it took for him to know for sure it was what he wanted, and if it wasn't then she would take his friendship, however much that hurt.

Mac had been sent here as a gift for Ezzie, of that she was certain. All Maddie knew was that she wanted him in their lives. She had known it from the moment he fell from the tree in the garden, like some fictional angel thrown down from heaven. He wasn't her usual type; older and wiser for sure, but also clever, calm, warm, funny, charming, and even with his insurmountable problems and grief, he had been nothing but kind and generous. Maddie couldn't thank him or repay him enough for all he had done with her daughter, who was changing in small ways on a daily basis. Maddie had no doubt he would get her walking. Maybe that was foolish on her part, or maybe that was instinct and faith - just as Mac had said he had faith in her playing when she had never touched a keyboard.

Whatever it was, and whatever happened between them, she was willing to wait, to listen, to learn, and to let him heal. What was meant to be, would be.

Maddie shivered and became aware of the piano playing in the cabin, a soft, skilful tune. One that she didn't know, but was played with such feeling that her arms littered with goosebumps. It drew her toward the door, and she half wondered whether to disturb him as he hadn't responded to her messages.

She chewed on her lip, looked back at the trees, and knew it was hopeless. Unless she walked home, there was no way the car was getting out of the mud on the track. She was kicking herself for being too presumptuous, when the tune finished, and another began to play. This one she knew.

Bohemian Rhapsody.

Maddie grinned and let out a breath. It was all the indication she needed. He must have seen her approach from the woods through the side window. She walked the last few paces to the door, gave it a knock for politeness, and turned the handle.

The music stopped instantly as the door swung inward. The cabin was cold and dark.

Maddie blinked, smile faltering on her face.

But the light was on. It led me the last part of the way through the woods.

'Mac?' She called.

Stuff the light, Maddie, the piano was playing. He's having a joke with you. He's behind the sofa.

She grinned and strode to the underneath of the mezzanine floor.

'Very funny,' she said as she looked behind the sofa. But the space by the piano was empty. The cabin was eerily silent.

'Mac? Where are you?'

She listened to the silence in the darkness. Then there was a small scrape from the kitchen area and relief fell over her. He was playing. He was in the kitchen.

I need a light. Where was the switch?

She crossed to the cabin door, pushed it shut to keep the cold out, and found the switch at its side. She Flicked it down, and yellow light filled the cabin. The cosy glow she had seen from the woods. Now she could see the kitchen area.

Empty.

A cup and a couple of plates lay in the sink, but otherwise the area was clean and tidy, and she could see straight under the table. Nowhere to hide.

Maddie looked around the cabin slowly. There was no sign of anyone. From here, she could see most of the corners from front to back. It was also freezing, her breath coming in clouds before her. Something wasn't right here, and if this was a game, it was one she didn't like too much.

'Mac? Please come out now. I don't like it. Let's give this up and get the fire going. Please? I'm cold, I'm muddy, and I'm tired from the walk. I really don't want to play anymore.'

She was met with silence, but it wasn't comfortable.

It felt eerie, like someone was lying in wait. Maddie swallowed hard.

Let's just check the entire place. This is getting you nowhere.

Maddie moved into action, starting with the upstairs, which was the only part she couldn't see. There were two beds, a muddle of clothes by a sports bag, a book, and a couple of pairs of shoes. Otherwise, the floor was empty, under the beds clear.

She moved back to the top of the staircase and heard the same scuffle from the kitchen that she had heard before.

The room was lit. She could see everything - see nothing – and she didn't want to go down.

Don't be ridiculous, it's obviously Mac. He's here somewhere, and I'm going to tear a bloody strip off him when he appears.

She moved quickly back downstairs, glancing behind the sofa, as she made her way to the kitchen.

There's nowhere here to hide! How would he be here and then not? I would have seen him move.

'Mac? I'm begging you now, please-'

She cut off as she saw the fridge magnets. Most were on the floor, only six on the fridge. One word, split into two to enable it to fit on the small door.

MAD

DIE

Maddie stared, a prickling working its way up and over her scalp.

This has to be Mac. He's here.

Unless he's playing with fridge magnets when he's alone?

It was an attempt at humour that left her cold. It didn't feel like Mac, it didn't feel right.

Stepping away from the fridge, she looked down the corridor. The shadows fell in rows - an exaggerated version of the stairs painted on the floor. She assessed the space, deciding two things instantly.

One, she didn't like the area - at all - especially the window at the end. And two, she didn't want to go down there.

She glanced around the ground floor again. No one here. No-one upstairs.

If anyone is in the cabin, they're down this corridor.

Heart drumming, she strode into the dark space and opened the door on the left. A storeroom, well stocked with food and supplies. Nobody hiding inside. Backing out, she shut the door and turned to the one opposite. The window bothered her. She didn't like being able to see out into the dark in this darkened, confined space.

Silly, but true.

She was tense, wound up like a spring, her muscles taut and ready for action against something she couldn't see.

She crossed the window quickly and opened the opposite door. A bathroom. She turned on the light.

A small sink and mirror to her left held simple cosmetics, toothbrush, shaving foam and razor. Not that she had ever seen Mac clean shaven - it was the only thing that seemed out of place.

Ahead of her the shower curtain was pulled across the bath and she thought she heard a breath, almost like a snigger that the owner was trying to hold back.

'Mac?'

Maddie hesitated, blood beating in her ears. Finally, she picked up the razor and moved to the curtain.

It ruckled softly before her, and the razor shook in Maddie's outstretched hand.

'Mac?' she whispered.

The curtain lay still again. The air pensive, and Maddie could have cried. Instead, she reached out her free hand and tore back the curtain with a shrill scream that send goosebumps skittering up her own arms.

Empty.

'Mac? Please come out,' she whimpered. 'I'm scared.'

She didn't like this room; it was like being inside a pressure cooker, and yet when she turned to leave, she didn't want to step through the doorway into the corridor either.

Then there was a small click, and the bathroom plunged into darkness. The door creaked.

Maddie didn't need any other cues. She was out of the bathroom and into the light of the cosy living area with a scream. Except that now it didn't feel so cosy. It felt alien and creepy. She stood in the middle of the room with the razor, holding her breath as her eyes scanned every crevice, and her ears listened for every small sound.

Mac wasn't that fast. He couldn't keep up a game like this. No-one could. It wasn't possible.

She glanced out of the window at the pier, and a flicker of hope spread through her.

The kayak. She knew what she was doing, she had seen Mac. She could go home.

With a sob she opened the cabin door and ran to the pier, but even out here, the theme of the evening was intent on mocking her with no give.

It was empty.

The water lapped at the shore and around the wooden posts of the structure. But there was no kayak.

Maddie let out a cry of fear and frustration, before another thought slammed home, knocking the breath from her lungs.

No kayak? No Mac.

He wasn't here. He hadn't come back... or something had happened.

Maddie clutched at her hat with both hands, squeezing the sides of her head.

But the light, the piano, the noises, the damn feeling.

Maddie looked back at the cabin, panting hard.

No car. No Kayak.

She swung her gaze to the mountain to her right. The house was just the other side, but she knew it was a good few miles, and Saul had said the going was hard. The foliage thick and dense in places.

She pulled the phone from her pocket to check the battery to see how long the light would last, and almost slammed her hand to her head with her own idiocy.

Mac, Da, Saul, Ma.

All of them had a phone. She could call!

You idiot, she thought with relief. She swiped the screen, but it remained dark, so she pressed the button on the side of the phone instead. The start screen loaded. Maddie shivered as she waited, eyes hooked to the screen. The home screen loaded, then the battery icon flashed in the corner and the screen went dead.

Maddie stared in disbelief.

She hadn't bothered about the phone charge coming here. Maybe Mac had a charger that fit. If not, she would be with him, anyway. No bother.

Now it was a bother. It was getting colder, and with no light, she couldn't walk.

She had to go back inside. There was no other way.

Every fibre of her being protested as she walked back to the cabin door and peered inside. The small space seemed colder inside than out. The pressure so intense that she felt the roof would have to blow to let it out.

Maddie shuddered and realised she was still in the doorway.

Maddie, get inside, light the fire, and look for a charger. It's the fastest and only way to leave, or you stay all night, and who knows when Mac will be back.

The plan made her feel better, gave her something to focus on. She stepped into the cabin.

The door slammed behind her, and the light flicked out.

'No!' she yelled. Flicking the switch and then flinging herself onto the door. It was stuck fast. She pulled and tugged as hard as she could, and then the urge to turn became stronger than the need to pull. She paused. Her scalp prickled, and she turned her head slowly to look behind her.

In the corridor was a dark form. Maddie stared as it slid toward her, revealing itself as a woman with wild curls that reminded Maddie of Ezzie's. The woman held a tiny baby, and when her eyes met Maddie's, they were pools of deep watery brown. Grief stricken and imploring.

Sorrow hit Maddie. So strong that she folded and began to sob.

'Don't cry,' the lady said. 'He's yours.'

Maddie cried anyway. Fear and despair rolling in to one. She no longer had the capacity to be afraid. It was like the fear meter had broken, it's needle flopping uselessly. Whatever happened now, Maddie would take it willingly, anything to not be here anymore.

She looked up at the lady, who seemed distraught, like she had seen all of the most heart-breaking things in the world, and bore the burden of them on her shoulders. Maddie felt all of it. Every bit of the lady's pain and heartache encompassed her on the floor until she thought the weight of it would break her heart. A tear slipped down the woman's olive cheek as she kissed the baby's head softly and held it toward Maddie.

'He's yours,' she said. 'Please take care of him.'

'No,' Maddie whimpered. The clean fresh smell of the new-born filling her nostrils.

And then the atmosphere changed. The smell became foul, like death and rot, and the woman above her turned dark, her face twisted and angry.

Maddie felt terror climb up her spine.

'Get out!' The lady roared, hair and clothes suddenly flying behind her as though a gale force wind had blast through the cabin. 'Now!' she raged.

Her face contorted and changed above Maddie, and then through the window at the back of the corridor, another shadow. This one pressed its hand to the glass. A face appeared. A man. Too big to be Mac or Saul.

A stranger.

Maddie's heartbeat trebled. The woman in front of her was gone. Heart in her mouth, she dashed for the stairs, taking them two at a time, before diving into Mac's bed as the door to the cabin slammed open.

CHAPTER SEVENTY-TWO

TOM CAME ROUND SLOWLY. It was pitch black. Everything ached. His head was fuzzy, and his mouth dry, but he was warm. He half wondered where he was and vaguely thought he should find out, but deciding the pain wasn't worth it, he lay his head back against the seat and closed his eyes.

What was I injected with?

Injected.

The word triggered a memory that began to surface from the depths. Tom lay with it a while, puzzled and intrigued by his own question, but not fully understanding, or wanting to right now. He drifted, saw the needle, saw it plunged into his arm, saw the man (*for the pain*), felt the sting.

He jolted awake, pain bouncing off his ribs.

Ribs. Injection.

And everything rushed back to greet him like an old friend.

The doctor. He was in the doctor's van. The doctor had broken his ribs, given him the injection, and left the van to go to the cabin. Alone.

Tom sat upright, and pain bolted through him in sharp stabs. As his body gasped for breath against his broken ribs, his mind was two steps ahead.

Mac! He had gone to the cabin for Mac.

Tom tried to throw the door open to follow, realised his hands and feet were still bound, and that his ribs hurt beyond measure, and sat back with a gasp.

No, there will be time to heal afterwards, Mac could be in trouble by now. How far would the doctor have got?

Tom realised that he had no idea what time it was, and not least what time the doctor had left the van, but he may have been out a fair while.

Not good. Not good at all.

Ignoring the pain in his ribs, he shook his wrists. The ropes seemed looser than they had around his back. His hands had more manoeuvrability, they weren't as squashed together, although the binds certainly weren't loose enough to slip off by any stretch of the imagination.

Clenching his teeth against the pain, Tom leaned forward and flipped down the glove box door. He rummaged through the contents to see if there was anything he could find to cut the rope. His hands moved through tissues, pens, paracetamol - he took these out and dry swallowed two - log books, old cd's, a syringe, a head torch - which he threw back onto his lap with a flick of his wrists - and a packet, which dropped to the floor.

Tom ignored it. There was nothing to cut the binds.

He steeled himself, took a short breath, and launched his feet up on the dashboard in front of him. He may have screamed out loud, he wouldn't know, the pain took his consciousness for a time. When he woke, his feet were still on the dash, and he was drenched in a pool of sweat.

Not good for winter outdoor pursuits, he thought.

Leaning his arms forward, he managed to reach the knot at his feet. His hands shook as he pulled and tugged at the rope, trying to get his fingers between a knot that was unbelievably tight. Each time his ribs protested too much, he stopped to rest, before frantically trying again.

Why isn't it coming loose? It didn't take the man long to redo my hands in the back of the van. There's no way it's this tight.

Finally, he forced himself to sit and look at the knot, the loop, the way the rope knit together, and could have kicked himself.

It was a simple bowline. He recognised it from his scouting days, and it was one he used all the time out here at the cabin to tie up various things, including his kayak to the pier. Bowlines were one of the easiest and strongest knots to tie, the advantage being they were also easy to untie by pushing the rope back onto itself.

It was still hard with both hands tied, but infinitely easier than what he had been doing - which was pulling the knot tighter. After a minute that felt like an hour, the knot gave, and the rope fell away. He moved his feet as his hands worked on the knot at his wrists. This was more awkward and took a little longer, but with the help of his teeth, the knot finally gave and then his hands were free.

The relief of being free of the binds overshadowed the pain in his upper body as he opened the van door and slipped out, the packet from the glove box coming with him to drop to the floor. He picked it up, looked inside, and thought an angel must be looking out for him. A full box of Methadose in 10mg tablets. The badass of chronic pain – butt-kicking, fast acting, and complete.

He had no idea if they would react with whatever the doctor had injected him with, or whether he would overdose, but he would have to take the chance. With the pain as it was, he would be getting nowhere fast out here.

He snapped open the pill packet and swallowed one dry before pocketing the rest and finding his phone.

The bloody phone! Idiot. I could have called Mac by now, at least fifteen minutes ago. If I get a signal.

He pressed the button and got worse. The battery icon. Dead.

Of course, what else?

Tom pocketed the phone, grabbed the head torch from the van, and on a whim took the syringe from the glove box. The doctor said that he had two for sedation in the van. One he had obviously given to Tom. This must be the other. As Tom had woken, he presumed the dose couldn't be as lethal as the doctor had said. This one may come in useful. He zipped the syringe into his fleece pocket, placed a hand on his chest, and began to walk, concentrating on placing one foot in front of the other, and staying as much as he could in the track's ruts where the ground was fairly level.

Ten minutes later the pain was easing. The Methadose was finally kicking in, which would give him around four hours pain free.

Tom upped his stride.

Hang on Mac, I'm coming. I'll sneak up on that bastard and break a few of his ribs in payment. Or maybe I'll just kill him and be done with it.

At that moment, Tom had never meant anything more in his life.

CHAPTER SEVENTY-THREE

'H ELLOOOO? ANYONE HOME?'

A man's singsong voice shouted around the cabin, and there was a flick of the light switch, but the light remained off. Maddie heard a curse, and then the door shut, and there were footsteps in the living area below her. She dragged the covers over her head. She was slight. If the man came upstairs, with the chaos of clothes on and around the bed, he may just miss her entirely. Or at least, she hoped.

She lay in the darkness, wondering if it was better or worse that she not only couldn't see, but she couldn't hear what was happening downstairs very well, either. She poked a hand down the side of the duvet, opening up a gap with which to hear more clearly, but one which could be closed easily and with little movement to someone coming up the stairs.

Better.

She lay spread flat against the sheet, cheek mashed to the mattress by the opening, the smell of Mac rising to meet her nostrils. He usually smelled fresh and clean, like cologne. This was similar, but musty, earthy, more natural. It was a comfort just the same, and she was glad she hadn't chosen the other bed in her haste.

Downstairs, the man was messing with Mac's things, and Maddie felt her hackles raise.

Who the hell is this person that has seen fit to waltz into someone else's property and look around? Cabin or not.

Maddie listened intently. The wood shifted next to the log burner, books were flicked through and dropped onto the floor and sofa, an ornament was picked up and inspected before being set back down with a thump.

'Helloo.' The man said again, 'There's nowhere to go. Where in the fuck are you?'

Maddie frowned as the footsteps retreated to the back of the cabin. She knew that voice – knew it, but couldn't place it. Downstairs, doors opened, and from the shuffles and bangs, he was looking through the store cupboard, followed by the bathroom.

Then the footsteps came back to the front of the cabin. A packet rattled, and then there was rhythmic crunching. Maddie swallowed her revulsion.

He's eating Mac's food? Does this man even know Mac?

The man ate his way through an entire packet of what sounded like crisps before she heard scrunching. Maddie didn't hear the bin, so who knew where that packet was now. She did hear the tap though. Heard the man drink a glass of water with huge gulps, and then go quiet.

'Ah!' he finally said.

Maddie frowned, trying to listen more closely, and then footsteps crossed the floor and started up the stairs.

She gasped, trying to control her breathing, as her heart threatened to pound out of her chest.

'Come out, come out, wherever you are.'

Maddie recognised the voice, just as the footsteps reached the top and the covers were snatched from the bed, exposing her whole. She gasped in shock and rolled off the bed, standing to face the man before her, who was bathed in moonlight from the skylight above.

Greg. Saul's partner. A man she'd had the displeasure of meeting for a couple of months between trips. He was in jail when the trouble with Ezzie had started. She hadn't laid eyes on him since, and Saul never mentioned him anymore. Maddie wasn't surprised after the blow up at the clinic.

So, what the hell is he doing here?

She realised she was gaping at him, shocked, and he gaped right back, mouth dropping open. Then he began to laugh.

'Well, fucking hell. What the fuck are you supposed to be, bait?'

Maddie frowned and shook her head.

'I don't know what you mean,' she said.

'Bait. You know. Get the target out of the way, and lure the bad guy in.' The look on his face was condescending and Maddie felt a flare of anger.

'I was actually visiting my friend. He just hasn't got back yet.'

'And you were waiting in his bed? Classy bitch. Could I be your friend? Pleeeaaaseee.'

Propelled by anger, Maddie stepped forward and slapped his face. The noise echoed around the small space.

'Don't ever speak to me like that, especially after what you put my family through. What the hell are you doing in Mac's cabin?'

Greg rubbed his face with a chuckle. She wondered if he had felt the slap at all and found some satisfaction at the slight reddening of his pale cheek in the moonlight.

'Sheesh, someone knows how to handle herself, doesn't she? Oh dear, little Maddie thinks she has it sussed, acting all big and tough. Funny, I've squashed stronger flies. This isn't Mac's cabin, by the way.'

'I know,' she said, anger still flooding her veins. She had never liked Greg's attitude before, and she wasn't liking it much now.

'It's Tom's.'

'I know,' she repeated.

'Then you know what I'm doing here, as if Saul hasn't already filled you in.'

Maddie faltered, her scalp prickling with uncertainty.

'What does Saul have to do with anything?'

Greg laughed again, long and hard, and then cut off abruptly.

'What does Saul have to do with anything?' he said. 'Saul set the whole fucking show up, darling. The whole party complete with time, date, RSVP, and party poppers. I hope he brings extra champagne as we seem to be including one more now.'

'What show?' Maddie said, nerves sending butterflies dancing in her stomach.

'This one,' Greg said, reaching to pinch her cheek like she was a small child who couldn't get the point.

Maddie shook him off, feeling the sting of his fingers.

'I have absolutely no idea what you're talking about.'

She moved around the bed toward the stairway, but Greg stepped sideways, blocking the way down, his hand on the top of the banister.

'Where are you off to?' he said.

'I came to see Mac. He's not here. Now I'm leaving. I'd say it's nice to see you again, but...'

'But what?' Greg said with a grin.

'It's not.'

'So, I suppose you're going to drive your little car right out of the mud pit?'

'I'll walk.'

Greg raised his eyebrows. 'Oh, all that way in the dark? I should just wait here for the party to start, darling. In fact, I insist.'

'No.' She said, trying to prise his fingers off the banister to allow her down.

Greg's smile stayed glued to his face.

'I said, I insist.'

Maddie stared at him, her heart thumping, stomach weighted with stone. She swallowed hard as the realisation hit that he wasn't going to let her go. Brute force would get her nowhere with Greg, she would need another tactic, more subtle.

She forced herself to stay calm. If Greg and Saul *were* still friends, then at least he shouldn't hurt her, but she trusted him as much as she trusted a fox around the hens. If she could get downstairs, she had a better opportunity to escape.

'I suppose we may as well wait in comfort, then. Shall we go downstairs?'

Greg smiled. 'No, I think up here is just fine. Smaller area, and heat rises. It's warmer up here, and I can see you wherever you go. That suits me better.'

A trickle of fear wound its way into the annoyance. Outwardly, she shrugged with fake nonchalance.

'So, who's coming?' she said.

'Saul, Mac. Tom was supposed to, but he's a little indisposed back up the track.' He smiled, and Maddie felt sick.

'Mac's brother, Tom? Indisposed?'

'Oh, he'll be all right, don't worry. He'll miss the show, but I intend to record it, anyway. It'll be just like being here. To be honest, I thought they'd be waiting for me. It's pretty fucking disrespectful, really, considering what I'm doing for your brother.'

Maddie worked her jaw. What in the hell had Saul done, and for what price?

Greg began to laugh again. 'Poor little Maddie, no clue have you, darling? No clue what a piece of shit friend your brother turned out to be. Poor Mac, I almost feel for him.'

Maddie felt the heat rise up her chest and into her neck.

'What have you done?'

'Me? Nothing. I told you, Saul arranged it. Call it a little payback party.' He winked and Maddie felt bile rise in her stomach.

'Payback,' she murmured, the gears in her mind clicking into motion.

'You know, for fucking up our business. Fucking up our lives.'

Maddie had been away when everything kicked off at the clinic - a few weeks earlier, and she would have seen the whole show. It was something her parents didn't like to talk about, so the whole affair had been hush-hush at home. She knew their Da had spoken to Saul lots in the beginning when he got home from prison; quiet conversations that Maddie had stayed clear of. It took her a moment to remember Mac's wife, which linked her to Tom. According to Saul, Tom had been the one to shop the clinic in, back when he was ruining the future Mac's life by helping his wife abort a child.

'No, Saul wouldn't do that,' Maddie said, shaking her head. 'He's not interested in payback, he wants to move on. He likes Mac, he thinks a lot of him.'

'Are you sure about that?' Greg said, pulling a packet of cigarettes from his pocket. He lit one, jovially offering Maddie one as though it were an actual party.

'No, thank you,' she said, folding her arms across her chest. 'Of course, I'm sure. I know my brother.'

'Not well enough, but then that's not hard considering you're never at home, anyway. Always off on your jollies. Saul's not innocent, Maddie. It wasn't all down to me.'

'Of course, but when Saul went to prison, he paid. He knows what he did and doesn't intend to cross that line again. He's a good man.'

'Really? Then why am I here?'

He smoked and grinned, clearly enjoying her discomfort as she struggled to understand the whole situation.

'I don't know why you're here.'

'Duh, Maddie, you're so slow. Do I have to go through the whole story?'

Maddie stayed quiet, a pain beginning to thump in her head. Where were Saul and Mac? Were they coming here at all, or was she alone with this?

Greg moved away from the stairs and began to pace.

'Well, long story short,' he said, 'by a weird stroke of luck I managed to leave prison and find the bastard who took my business and career living only a few miles from my new rented flat. We met up, had a few chats. He understood where I was coming from, and he agreed to let me have twenty million to start over as compensation.'

'He agreed to give you twenty million?' Maddie said in disbelief.

'With a little force, but he was pretty easy to talk round. The thing is, it turned out the bastard only had six. He offered to get the rest, and I'm a fair man, but I'm not getting any younger. I have a fucking life to build again Maddie, see?'

He finished the cigarette, dropped it to the floor, and scrubbed it out with his heel. Then he continued to pace. He was getting agitated, but that was good, it meant that he was pacing further and further from the stairway with each sentence. Maddie only had to bide her time, and she would be able to get downstairs.

'So, it turns out that he has this famous brother worth millions. What are the fucking chances? And then I speak to my old buddy Saul, who says he knows the guy and that he's staying alone on holiday in this cabin.' He stopped by the far bed, looking at Maddie for a reaction. She kept her face neutral, and he continued his walk. 'Well, as you can imagine, I've never felt so lucky in my fucking life! I knew what I had to do. The opportunity was clear. Saul willingly gave me Mac's location, and I offered him five million of the twenty for his trouble. Tom agreed to come along and see his brother...'

Maddie ran as he approached the far bed, his back still to her. She was halfway down the stairs when he came after her with a shout.

The air around her felt electrified as she lunged for the door, but Greg caught her coat, dragging her back.

'No!' she yelled, falling onto her backside with a thump. The zip from her coat gathered around her neck, digging under her chin as her head snapped up and pain shot through the bottom of her spine. Taking no notice of her shouts, Greg continued to drag her away from the door, and up the corridor.

'I knew you wouldn't play ball, Maddie, knew it was too good to be true. You're a real fucking party pooper, eh?'

He opened the storeroom door, and for a second she thought he was going to lock her inside, but he kept hold of her coat, the zip biting underneath her chin. Maddie's feet scrabbled underneath her as he pulled her in with him.

They stopped and Greg rummaged through the shelves above. She tried to twist up onto her feet, but the hold on her coat was tight, cocooning her like a straight-jacket, and the zip was surely drawing blood by now. Maddie grit her teeth against the pain, and then she had an idea.

The Zip.

Her fingers fumbling, she grabbed the top of the zip and pulled it quickly down, the instant relief on her neck was like a tonic, and then she was up on her feet, free, pulling the sleeves of the coat inside out as she rose.

'Oi!' Greg shouted beside her.

There was no time to think of her next move as Greg closed a hand around the back of her neck, swinging her round and slamming her against the shelves. She gasped with pain, winded, as items on the shelves jammed into her legs and stomach. Her cheek mashed painfully into another shelf as his grip tightened. Maddie whimpered and closed her eyes.

'Even after all I've told you,' he said calmly, 'you still think I'm someone to be fucked with? Now where did I see it? Ah, yes.'

Keeping a hand on her neck, he leaned down to get the rope and then grabbed her hands, forcing them tightly behind her back and typing the rope around her wrists.

'Ow, Greg, please, that hurts.'

'It's supposed to, darling. If it didn't, then you could concentrate on how to pull your shit again. As it is, you can concentrate on the pain instead.'

He pulled her from the storeroom and into the living area. Cold encircled her now that her coat was off, and she almost regretted the rash move. If she got outside now, she wouldn't last two minutes before hypothermia set in, and with each minute, it was looking increasingly likely inside, too.

He pulled a chair from the kitchen, faced it toward the living area, and told her to sit. She did as he asked, and he immediately untied the rope on her wrists and retied them around the chair.

'There now. And you'll get a front row view of the action too. Lucky girl.'

He pulled out his phone, pressed the screen, and waited.

Maddie began to shake with cold, her throbbing cheek the only bit of her that seemed warm.

'Greg, why are you doing this? Tom is your gripe. Leave me and Mac out of it, and Saul is your friend? What will he think when he knows you have me tied up? You're making this much worse for yourself. I don't understand why you don't just let me go home.'

Greg was pacing again, the living area this time. He stopped to look at her.

'Darling, you don't get to go home. I don't want to hurt you, but you're part of this now. I can't have anything fuck up my night. I've planned for this for so damn long. Dreamed of it, although I'll be honest, the dreams weren't quite so exciting as the reality is now. All I want is my money and I'm gone. Nobody will ever find me again. I'll disappear. Poof.'

He huffed with frustration and threw the phone down onto the settee.

'It should be so simple it's like baking cookies, but Saul can't seem to get anything right, and now I'm stuck here with you.'

He strode over to her, placing his hands on either side of the chair, leaning in so close she could smell cold air and sour breath. She leaned back so far that the chair dug into her spine. He put his mouth to her ear and whispered.

'So, we have a little time, it seems. What shall I do with you now you're at my mercy?'

'Leave me alone,' she said, breathing hard as every nerve stood on end and her heart thumped.

Not that. God, anything but that.

She sat rigid as he sniffed her hair, and then he flicked his tongue in her ear, and she lurched away, almost knocking over the chair. Only Greg saved it from tipping over completely.

'Steady there,' he said with a soft laugh, bringing his face back in front of her. She clamped her lips shut and closed her eyes 'I'm messing with you, darling, you're of no use to me, I don't like these.' He gave both breasts a rough squeeze and she clenched her jaw to stop from crying out in shock and pain. Her thin jumper no match for his big hands. 'Cock turns me on. Your brothers is particularly nice. Did you know he's gay?'

Maddie didn't, but she sure as hell wasn't going to let Greg wind her up. It didn't matter to her whether Saul was gay or not, but it made sense with the lack of girlfriends over the years, she supposed.

'Yes.' she said. 'I don't care. It's up to him.'

Greg was thrown off his stride, and Maddie grinned inwardly. He had expected the shock, thrived on it, she thought, but it didn't take long for his game face to return.

'You like men, though, Maddie,' he said.

She didn't reply.

'You must,' he said. 'You were lying in Mac's bed waiting when I arrived.'

'I was only up there because you came in. Mac and I are friends, nothing more.'

'That's a shame. A friendship destined not to last. Heart-breaking.'

'You know nothing about him.'

'No, darling, but I know what I'm planning. Are you able to mind read?'

Maddie felt her heart racing, the beat so fast and strong that she wondered if he could see it through her jumper. She dropped her gaze from his, conflicted in what seemed to be a circle of damned if you do, and damned if you don't. She wanted Mac to come back more than anything, but she felt just as strongly that she didn't want him to come anywhere near the cabin at all.

'Can't you just leave him out of it? Six million is a lot, Greg. Tom is the one who shopped the clinic. Mac has done nothing to you.'

Greg crouched before the chair and appeared to ponder the situation. Maddie knew it was only for her benefit, men who had already gone as far as Greg wouldn't give up. He couldn't, he was too far in. If Tom was back up the track – indisposed, as Greg as put it - and quite possibly freezing in the woods, Maddie was quite sure he hadn't come of his own free will.

That made Greg a dangerous man. The calmness he exuded just his style. She had seen it in the storeroom - felt the force of his hand, her cheek still throbbing from the pressure of the shelf. He could turn in an instant.

Greg smiled at her. Maddie was sure to an outsider it would look like a genuine, caring moment; him sitting at her feet with a smile on his face. Only her fear and the ropes would give anything away. It made her wary. She swallowed hard, half expecting another blow.

It didn't come.

'No.' he simply said, and rose. 'Not possible. You see, I have no prospects in the UK anymore, do I? And I'm already in a lot of trouble. The police are possibly scouring London for myself and Tom right now. If he has said anything to his wife, they'll have a good start on where I am. I need to get out of the country ASAP. I need to disappear and begin a new life with a new identity. Fortunately, I have some good friends. It's all in motion, all set up. I just need the money.'

Maddie stared at him. How could he admit all this so easily - so calmly?

'What if Mac just offers you the money? Then you could just leave us all alone, Tom too, and leave as you want to.'

Greg grinned again.

'Well now, where is the fun in that? I haven't gone to all this trouble just to walk away without a little fun. Saul and I may be due a little reunion before I leave, too. I can't ever see him again once I go. It's too risky.'

Maddie swallowed the bile in her throat.

'Saul could do with upping his taste. I thought he had more self-respect. You'll be no loss to him,' she said, lip curling.

The words were out of her mouth before she realised her mistake, and his fist connecting with her cheek was an unwelcome surprise. Pain rocketed around her neck and face as she gasped. In the flash of movement, she noticed his smile was gone.

You lucky thing, he chose opposite cheeks to punch and smash off shelves.

Her bottom lip quivered, and she tried not to let her tears go. She didn't ever want to show him that he'd broken her.

She tried to swallow the lump in her throat, but it stuck solid.

He raised his fist again above her, and Maddie recoiled, the chair scooting backwards under the force of her feet.

Greg laughed and came forward to lean on the chair again. 'So fucking easy to wind up, aren't we? Did we learn a little lesson there, darling? Don't fuck with me, you will come off worse.'

Maddie snapped as his condescending tone sent anger surging through her, she swung her leg up and back, knee to her chest underneath him, and in one quick movement kicked hard.

He hunched over, eyes bulging, and she knew she had hit her target.

'Don't fuck with me, either.' she whispered, hoping he hadn't heard.

Greg was doubled up, one hand on the chair, head bowed, when a vision appeared behind him.

There was a man standing silently in the doorway. Maddie didn't know when he had got there, or what he had seen, but the main thing was that he seemed to be on her side.

Another angel sent at just the right time.

He held a finger to his lips, motioning for her to remain quiet as Greg began to laugh again.

There was a moment of suspended time when Greg was laughing, the man was standing, and Maddie waited for whatever was to come. There was nothing more she could do. The air was tense with expectation.

And then Greg rose with a roar, put his hands on Maddie's arms and lift her and the chair into the air. Simultaneous with him slamming her back onto the ground, where she thought her bones would shake straight out of her body, the man approached. In a smooth motion, he lifted the log he had brought in with him, raised it above his head with both hands, and brought it down against the back of Greg's head with a loud crack.

'Get out of the way,' the man yelled as the log dropped, and he dropped to his knees, one hand to his chest.

Greg moaned and tipped forward as Maddie gasped, scuttling back in a hunched position to move away from his falling body. He fell to the floor with a thump, grasping his head.

'You will fucking pay for that,' he said, getting back onto his hands and knees.

'He's not knocked out,' Maddie yelled, a new light of fear igniting inside her. If he hadn't been mad before, he certainly would be now, and this new man, this new angel, looked to be in some sort of pain. Neither of them would be a match for Greg.

The man was calm, though. He fished in his pocket and brought out a syringe. Uncapping the end, he jabbed it into Greg's thigh, through his jeans, and without hesitation he emptied the entire syringe.

Within seconds Greg was out, hitting the ground from his knees almost gracefully, as if he had chosen to lie down.

CHAPTER SEVENTY-FOUR

MAC PULLED THE OARS hard behind Saul, the kayak gliding swiftly through the water as a fine rain fell like mist around them, chilling him to the bone in the frozen air. They hadn't said two words since they entered the kayak a mere thirty minutes ago, each taken with their own worries about what was going on down at the cabin.

Mac still wasn't certain of Saul's intentions, and he wasn't sure he wanted apology or explanation. There wasn't a word for what he was feeling right now. Panic and fear were top of the list, he supposed. He would sort the rest later.

'Mac?' Saul said in front of him. 'If we get there before Greg, we should just get Maddie and kayak back then-'

'You can kayak back. If we get there before Greg, I'm waiting for my brother. I can't leave him alone with a psycho.'

'Mac, the police will be coming...'

'I don't care, and I don't care what you think of him, or what he did to you all those years ago. I won't leave Tom in a monster's hands and simply kayak off into the sunset. If this fucker wants a fight, he'll damn well get one, and if he's laid a hand on Maddie, I'll rip his fucking head off. Thanks for only thinking of yourself... again.'

'No, I wasn't... that wasn't what I meant, Mac. Of course, I care what happens to Tom, I'm just... I'm scared. Maddie's my sister.' Saul said. He stopped rowing to turn in his seat.

'She is, and look at the trouble you got her into,' Mac hissed with undisguised contempt.

'I know that, and I intend to get her out of it. If she hadn't been so taken with you, she would never have driven to the cabin.'

'So, this is my fault?'

'I didn't say that,' Saul said with a frown. 'But let's face it, it was your brother who started all this by calling the police.'

'It was your partner who started it with his dodgy practices,' Mac spat back.

'It was your brother's fault for choosing the clinic in the first place,' Saul shouted.

'It was your fault for being so close to the cabin.'

'Your brother's fault for *buying* the damn cabin.'

Both men were breathing hard. They were almost nose to nose now, tensions riding high, the kayak bobbing in the water. Mac was trying to fight the urge to knock Saul around the head with the oar, but both men were anxious and afraid. Emotion as high as the tension.

'Your mother's fault the day you were born,' Mac said, sitting back in his seat and beginning to paddle. Saul stared at him. 'For fuck's sake, can we get to the damn cabin?'

Saul dropped his gaze, fight gone, and turned back to the front.

They pulled in unison; the boat cutting through the water quickly and efficiently, and Mac had to admit it was quicker with Saul than without, and the extra pair of hands would come in useful - if he didn't switch sides again, anyway. Either way, there was no going back now.

It was a good ten minutes before Saul spoke again.

'I'm sorry,' he said.

Mac stared at the back of Saul's jacket as he pulled, matching his partner's strokes row for row. He was too worried about Maddie and Tom to care.

'I'm sorry for everything, Mac, I've mucked it all up, haven't I?'

'I thought you were genuine,' Mac said between puffs of breath.

'I am. I don't know what I was thinking. If anything happens to Maddie now, it's my fault. I know that.'

'You're fucking right it is, and if anything happens to her, I'll...' Mac trailed off. There weren't words for what he'd do.

Saul nodded anyway.

'I'll kill myself before you get to me, Mac.' He said. His voice had a tell-tale wobble of emotion. 'I would never have put her in this position had I known. You must know that.'

Mac did know, and in here he also knew he was projecting his own fear. They both had the same goal now. What happened afterward could be discussed then. He was desperate to get to the cabin. Desperate to get to Maddie and Tom, and although they were paddling hard together, they still weren't going fast enough for Mac. The fear was driving him insane.

'I know,' Mac said softly, giving at the emotion in Saul's voice.

There was another beat of silence, and then they rounded the bend of the loch. Mac felt a sense of release at the cabin in the distance. From here, it would still take a good forty minutes at this pull, but with the cabin in sight, he felt better, like he was on the home run.

He focused and pulled the oars smoothly, a thought occurring to him.

'I'm sorry I snapped, too,' Mac puffed. 'I know you're as worried as I am. Saul, Maddie must have met Greg. How well did she know him? Do you think she could talk him down as you could?'

Saul shook his head. 'Not a chance. Maddie is a tough cookie, Mac, but I don't think she'll be able to handle Greg. She was only at the house for a brief period when the clinic was running, but they never really hit it off. He just liked to wind her up. She steered clear mostly. I wouldn't be so worried if I thought she would be okay. I know that's not what you wanted to hear, and it's not what I want to think about either. She's been through enough over the last couple of years. Ezzie too.'

Mac didn't reply, he had a feeling if he opened his mouth he would vomit. He refocused on the cabin and found that made him feel worse. The cabin and Maddie seemed to pull further away with each stroke. He gave a grunt of frustration and stabbed the water with the oar.

'Don't focus on it, Mac, it'll drive you insane, just concentrate on rowing.'

'I can't. I *am* going insane.'

'You can. Breathe. Focus. Pull.'

'I'm going to focus on breaking this oar over your back if you don't shut the hell up.'

'Then we'll get nowhere fast.'

'Sorry,' Mac said, immediately regretting his anger.

'I know how you feel. We're both wired, but we have a long way yet. We have to try to think of something else.'

Mac pulled his oars. He knew Saul was right, but he also knew he couldn't. He understood better than anyone the theory of focus and thought direction. The disease and rot of worry. It didn't help one iota sat here right now. Saul could spout it as much as he wanted.

'Mac, you said something before about Ezzie. It's been on my mind since this whole shit started, and since we're stuck in here, maybe you can tell me what you meant?'

Mac's thoughts, which were on the home straight to hysteria, were abruptly halted. Mac pictured them with question marks over their heads as they stood in confusion.

Huh?

Mac turned the gears of his mind to Ezzie. Ez, the charming little girl he had seen only hours ago, but which felt like weeks. He couldn't even remember what he had said to Saul about her. Couldn't focus with Maddie, and possibly Tom, in the cabin.

'I don't know what I meant,' he said. 'I can't remember what I said.'

'You said she could walk.'

It came rushing back, the moment at the kayak with the gun. The moment when he realised everyone was in on the game - even Ezzie.

'You know she can,' he said.

'I only said that because it swayed you to come to the house. Of course, I know she can in theory. That's nothing new. But what you said? It's played on my mind ever since.'

Mac screwed his eyes closed, struggling for clarity in his cluttered mind.

'So, you're saying you know, or you don't?'

'I know as much as I knew before. She is physically able to, but can't.'

'She can,' Mac said.

Saul stopped rowing to gape at him. 'She can?'

Mac gestured to his oar. 'Keep paddling or I don't talk. The cabin comes first.'

Saul turned back and began to pull hard. Mac matched him.

'So, what do you mean, she can?'

'She took a step earlier. She can walk. She's just frightened.'

As they paddled, Mac told Saul all that Ezzie had told him about the curse her father and the witch doctor had bestowed, and how much it scared her.

After a beat of silence, Saul spoke.

'Bloody hell,' was all he offered.

Mac knew the feeling.

'I offered to help, and she told me only a witch doctor can remove the curse. I told her I knew one. She was so ecstatic she took a step toward me of her own accord, stood up, right out of the chair.'

Now Saul did swing round, mouth open. Mac gestured, and Saul turned back to paddle.

'This is amazing work, Mac. Bloody brilliant! So do you?' he said.

'I know a lot of people... but no witch doctors. I was hoping you could help with that.'

'I don't know any either - what sort of circles do you think I hang around in?'

'Dodgy ones.' Mac couldn't help it.

Saul turned back to him, saw his face, and grinned.

'We don't have to know one though, Saul, just know someone who could play one. Just well enough to remove the curse.'

Saul was quiet for a moment.

'I may know someone, actually,' he said.

As they discussed helping Ezzie move forward, Mac took a sneaky glance at the cabin. It was finally beginning to get closer.

He thanked Saul silently, as the man continued to speak about his friend, who would make a perfect witch doctor.

He's better at implementing mind control than I am, Mac thought, with irony.

CHAPTER SEVENTY-FIVE

T OM HEARD THE SIRENS in some far-off universe. He thought he had imagined them until the girl asked if he heard them too.

'The police?' She said.

'The track is blocked,' Tom huffed, wiping the sweat off his head with his hand.

'I hope they'll walk. How long will Greg be out?'

Greg. A name for the face.

Tom fumbled with the knots on the chair in the cabin's low light, his ribs murder each time he moved. His hands shook, and sweat layered his face in a sheen that seemed permanently wet, even when he wiped his brow.

'I don't know. A long time. I hope.'

He knew something wasn't right. The pain in his chest seemed far worse than it had back in the van. As soon as the girl was loose, he would have another tablet. It had been but a couple of hours at most. He knew he would probably overdose, but paracetamol wasn't going to cut this kind of pain.

As he managed to loosen one knot, he thought of Meg.

Whenever he had been in pain, she had rolled her eyes and told him it couldn't possibly be as bad as childbirth. He had thought she was being dramatic, as women seemed to be about it - probably because men could never know. He realised now that any pain he had felt before this hadn't been pain at all - even his broken arm had been a mere niggle. He wondered if this compared to childbirth. If it did, Meg deserved a bloody medal or three for willingly putting herself through it.

He loosened the other knot, and the girl was free. She rose from the chair, rubbing her wrists and shaking her hands.

'Thank you,' she said. 'I was getting pretty worried there for a while. You came right on time. I'm Maddie.'

She looked at Tom; her face was swollen and bruised, but full of concern.

'Tom.' He muttered, swallowing hard. He could barely move from his crouch on the floor. Maddie moved to crouch beside him, stepping over the doctor's form.

'Tom. You must be Mac's brother. It's nice to meet you. What did Greg do to you? It looks like you may be worse off than me.'

'Broken ribs,' he panted. 'Can you help me up?'

'Sure.'

She clasped his arm but didn't pull, allowing him to lean on her at his own pace. After standing, he motioned to the settee. 'Over there.'

She held his arm as he shuffled like an eighty-year-old over to the large chair, and then helped him into it.

'You don't look so good, Tom. I'll see if there're some painkillers around here somewhere.'

Tom clasped her arm with as much strength as he could muster and shook his head.

'I just need water,' he said.

'Water?' She said with an incredulous frown.

He leaned an arm down to pull the Methadose from his pocket, shaking from the pain the movement induced.

Maddie took the box from him.

'Methadose? This is basically morphine in a box, isn't it? Where did you get this?'

'I'm a doctor,' he managed. Maddie looked to Greg, and then back to Tom. 'Please, I can't... take much more of this.'

Maddie pursed her lips and nodded. She fetched a coat from the storeroom -Tom vaguely wondered how it got there - got him water from the kitchen, and broke a tablet from the packet. Tom swallowed the tablet and drank the water greedily.

'Thank you,' he said.

'No problem. Is there anything else I can get for you?'

Tom shook his head and rest back against the chair, closing his eyes.

'Give me ten. The tablet will work quickly. I can't... I can't talk well.'

Maddie sat with him, perched on the arm of the settee, holding his hand for the entire time it took for the tablets to kick in. When the pain started to subside, he opened his eyes and took a breath, the first proper breath he had taken for a good while now. Possibly he was hurting something inside. For now, he was just glad the pain was receding to a bearable level.

'Thank you, Maddie, you're an angel.'

Maddie smiled, and then winced.

'I was thinking the same about you when you appeared in the doorway.'

'He got us both good, didn't he? I have some paracetamol if you need it, it's in the store.'

Maddie shook her head. 'You may need it. I'm fine, just a headache.'

Tom nodded lightly, trying not to move too much. 'Well, it's there if you need it, although you'll have to find it yourself, I'm afraid.'

She smiled back at him.

'That's fine. I'm sorry about Greg. He's an asshole.'

Tom laughed, winced, and laughed again.

'That's an understatement. You know him?'

'He was my brother's partner at the clinic.'

Tom grimaced. 'I'm sorry,' he said, wondering why on earth he was apologising.

'For what? He was a crook. He deserved it.'

'I couldn't agree more. I'm sure your brother was more... er...' Tom trailed off, looking for the right word, especially as he knew that the very man had helped Greg right to this point. Maddie touched his arm and shook her head.

'He wasn't innocent. How can he have been when they sent him down, too? He didn't know the extent of what had gone on, that was for sure, but he didn't act perfectly himself.'

'Mac said he knew your brother. I was worried he was like...' a sharp pain stabbed through his chest, and he hissed a breath. 'Like him,' he finished.

'Like Greg? Absolutely not. Saul knows he did wrong. Knows he paid for it. He's not out for revenge, I can assure you.'

'Then why did he help Greg? Mac was being framed by your brother.'

Maddie's face fell, and she shook her head.

'He wouldn't do that. Greg said the same, but I know Saul. He wouldn't. I don't understand - unless Greg had some sort of hold over him?'

'He was good at persuasion,' Tom said, pointing to his ribs.

Maddie smiled sadly.

'It goes further than that. They were lovers, apparently. If what Greg said is true, anyway. I didn't know that. Didn't suspect anything.'

'Ah, love is blind,' Tom said, shifting in his seat.

'Do you want a cushion? I think we have a wait until someone gets here now.'

Tom shook his head. 'I'm fine. I'll probably just have to keep shifting. So where is Mac?'

He was relieved to hear that he wasn't at the cabin and hadn't fallen foul to Greg, but now he was worried about where he was at all. Was he out there in the dark?

Maddie chewed on her lip. 'I don't know,' she said. 'He left the house just as it was going dark, say three-ish?'

'What house?' Tom said with a frown.

'The clinic, well old clinic, is my parent's home. You can kayak in a little over an hour to the back. Mac is helping my daughter with some,' she hesitated, 'issues. He is with the family most days. He should be back, should have been back long before now. I don't know where he is. My phone is out.'

Tom saw the worry on Maddie's face.

'Mine too,' Tom said.

Maddie didn't seem to be listening. She stared at the log burner, looking a little like she was the last girl left sitting on the bench at a dance.

'Greg said that Saul, my brother, helped him to set all of this up,' she said, turning back to him. 'That he told Greg how to get here?'

It was more of a statement than a question, and Tom knew she was struggling with it, but as he assessed her, something occurred to him. It was what he had been told too, but something wasn't right.

'It appears that way, although it obviously wasn't a fool proof plan, was it? Mac isn't here. Why isn't Mac here?'

Maddie narrowed her eyes, and then they widened.

'No, Mac isn't here. And the police are on their way.'

Tom saw where she was going. It was plausible. Risky, but plausible.

'Are they good friends? Mac and Saul?'

'Yes,' Maddie said. 'Saul was here a lot with Mac before he came to the house for Ezzie, my daughter. That's why I can't get my head around it. I'm certain Saul wouldn't do this, and yet,' She gestured to Greg, still on the floor unmoved. 'Here he is.'

'But Mac isn't. And the police are here. It sounds like Saul *was* helping, but to frame Greg, not help him. In a sense.'

'But I don't understand how they would frame him. And does Mac know? He never answered my messages earlier to stop me from coming here.'

'They may have known about me. Saul did. I know that for certain. I would hope my wife has noticed me gone by now, too.'

Maddie slapped a hand over her mouth.

'Of course! I'd forgotten about you. I'm so sorry,' she tittered.

'Good job they didn't,' he said with a smile. 'This smells like a set-up. If it is, I may have had your brother wrong myself.'

Maddie sighed. In relief, he supposed. Tom was relieved too, in this version Mac was safe, worrying about Mac had made him anxious, and anxious hurt his chest.

I hope we don't have it wrong.

'So how did you get to be here? You can't have been planned for.' Tom said

He saw her neck flush, cheeks reddened.

'No. I came over on a whim. Mac was helping me to play the piano for my ma's birthday. When the cabin was open, I decided to wait. I thought he couldn't be far. My car is stuck on the track.'

The car we got stuck behind.

Mac is playing the piano? Or at least helping Maddie. Maybe Meg didn't have it so wrong getting it here after all.

Tom looked at the girl in front of him. Petite, fair, pretty features when her face wasn't swollen, he presumed, but she had be ten years Mac's junior at least. Still, the house all day, and the cabin in the evening? That was a lot of time to be spending together. Did she know about Sula at all, or had he been coy?

'Mac's wife died last year,' Tom said.

Maddie showed no surprise. 'Yes, he's been quite a mess, by all accounts, although he seems to be doing a little better now.'

'Did he mention me?' Tom asked, wanting to find out how much she knew.

'Only to say you were fighting. I know something happened, and I know it involved Sula. I don't know any more than that.'

Tom felt himself relax, his fear that Mac was pretending to be on a holiday and was using the girl easing, along with the pain.

'Maddie, I need you to do me a favour. If you get out of here and I don't? I need you to pass a message to Mac.'

Her eyebrows flew up in surprise.

'Okay. But, Tom, you will get out of here. You'll be right as rain once you get to the hospital. You can tell him yourself.'

'I'd rather tell you first, while it doesn't hurt so much to talk. Just in case.'

He didn't tell her that he thought there was far more damage inside than he knew, and that his stomach was now rolling like he had taken far too much Methadose. He didn't want to admit it to himself, but he really may not make it through this.

If you get to the hospital fast enough... if.

Maddie bobbed her head at his side, still perched on the arm of the other settee. She grasped his hand.

'You will be able to tell him yourself, but if it makes you feel better, you have my word that I'll relay anything you say to Mac.'

'Good,' he said. 'Listen, I did something stupid two years ago. I brought Sula to the clinic - your brother's clinic - for an abortion.'

Maddie's mouth dropped open, but she collected herself fast and he appreciated being able to continue as she nodded her head again.

'That was a week of ruin for me. It was the week I called the police, thinking I was doing the right thing. Sula had problems here, I believe it was your brother, not Greg, who gave her the extra care. I thought he did wrong, and then I overheard a discussion at the clinic when I went back to tear a strip off them. I was angry, but Sula was fine after all.

'Anyway, long story short, you know who Mac really is, I presume, if he is working with your daughter?'

'Yes.' Maddie said.

'Well, as you can imagine, living in London, the media were always somewhere around snapping shots and overhearing conversations, as they do. Sula was adamant that Mac couldn't know about the baby. She came to me and my wife for help. The clinic up here with a new name seemed the most I could offer her, and this cabin for recuperation. It was simply luck that the two are fairly close-'

'Why didn't she want him to know?'

Tom hesitated and blew a breath through his lips.

Where to start on that one?

'Lots of reasons. The main one was him working too hard. She felt she would have to raise the child alone. She had asked him to slow down, as he was hardly ever at home at that point, but he had refused. I only found out later that they had been trying for a child anyway, and that Mac would have dropped the whole show for her and the baby if she had just spoken to him about it. She didn't. She came here to abort. Nothing changed at home until the day she died. Mac knew nothing.'

'Until he came here,' Maddie said, looking horrified.

'Right. After Sula died, the media tore Mac apart. There was no chance for him to grieve in peace. He carried on working, carried on making a very public hash of things. I suggested a year out here to get his head together. I had no idea he would find the clinic, meet your brother, and that the truth would come out.'

'I understand,' Maddie said.

'The problem is that things get skewed. I tried to protect Mac, so I lied. It's that simple. Your brother told him the truth. I dug myself into a hole. That's why he won't speak to me.'

Tom shifted again, trying to shift the cramp under his right ribs. Maddie waited.

'The thing is,' he continued, 'when your brother learns that you've taken his wife to have an abortion, that you faked being a married couple, and that you brought her to your cabin so that she can go through the abortion, recuperate, and he never finds out?'

Tom held his hands up, and Maddie raised an eyebrow.

'Sounds very dodgy, I've got to say.'

'I know. But it really wasn't. It wasn't my baby. She just needed a hand getting the abortion without the media getting wind. If they had found out, Mac would have found out. She loved him dearly. She certainly didn't want to break him, but she feared being left alone with such a responsibility. She panicked. That's the only reason. I know he thinks otherwise, or he would call me, speak to me. Maybe he even thinks the baby was mine, that we had an affair, and I regret that, because that wasn't it at all. The baby was Mac's. She was faithful. I was trying to protect both Sula and Mac. It backfired.'

Maddie stared at him. He held her gaze, imploring her to believe him. Finally, she nodded.

'You're a good man, Tom.' she said, 'I feel it, and I believe you. I'll tell Mac, but only if you really don't get a chance. It would be better coming from you.'

'I know, and I hope I get the opportunity. Thank you,' Tom said. He closed his eyes. He had never felt so sleepy, like he could lie right here and sleep for a whole week.

There was a thud at the back of the cabin, up by the storeroom and bathroom. Tom opened his eyes to see Maddie looking up that way, too.

'What was that?' he said, glancing back to see Greg still on the floor where they had left him, and cringing at the crunch in his chest cavity.

'I don't know,' she said. 'Maybe the police? I'll take a look.'

'Be careful.'

'I will.'

Tom wished he could be more help, but his eyes felt like lead weights hung on the lids. He closed them again as he heard Maddie walk up the corridor and open first one door, and then the other.

'Tom, is that you?' she said.

Tom frowned. He wondered if he had dreamed it. He wasn't moving anywhere.

Then she gave a yell.

'NO!'

Tom dragged his eyes open to see Greg coming around the chair. He tried to move, but couldn't get up fast enough before Greg was in front of his face. He was grinning, and Tom felt something warm at his stomach, but still in a methadone induced haze, he didn't feel anything, not even fear. Instead, he found he was mildly amused by the man standing above him.

'Piss off,' he mumbled, and closed his eyes again. He wanted to sleep, but then Maddie was screaming. He turned to her voice, saw Greg walking toward her up the corridor, saw the knife in his hand, and only vaguely registered the red dripping from the tip.

'Wait, don't hurt her,' he said, forcing himself from the chair and staggering to the stair rail. There was still pain in his ribs, and now there seemed to be a pain in his stomach, too. The pills, he thought, until he looked down and saw the red on his fleece, blooming like a flower.

Maddie yelled as Greg jabbed the knife at her, and Tom felt his legs give as she ducked under Greg's arm.

At that moment, the door banged open. Tom expected the police, but it was Mac and the other doctor, Saul. Maddie ran toward them, and Mac immediately pulled her behind him as Greg came down the corridor, the knife glinting.

'Well, well, boys, a little late but always time for a good party, eh? Saul, my friend, good to see you. You're looking really well.'

Saul didn't reply.

There was a loud bang, which reverberated through the cabin, and through the woodland beyond. Tom saw Mac flinch, and heard Maddie yell. He saw Saul, Maddie's brother, arms outright, gun held before him. Moving his weighty head on a neck that didn't want to hold it up, Tom Saw Greg put a hand to his chest, blood ran between his fingers, he held them up to his face, and then his legs buckled. He sank to the floor and lay still, blood pooling before him.

Tom smiled. 'Good shot, doc. Mac, thank god you're safe,' he mumbled and closed his eyes.

CHAPTER SEVENTY-SIX

There was a surreal moment when Mac thought that all the horrific dreams that he'd had in this cabin were combining into one big horror show. In the silence after the shot, no one moved. Mac stared at Greg's body, a puddle of blood growing on the floor of the corridor...

...just like the one he had mopped in almost exactly the same place.

Maddie broke the spell.

'You stupid idiot!' she yelled. 'The police must be almost here. You'll be going straight back to jail.'

Mac turned to see Saul, shock etched on his face, the gun still out in front of him.

'I only meant to stop him, not kill him. He was coming for you with a knife!' he said.

Mac looked back at Greg's body.

'We don't know he's dead yet,' he said, not feeling optimistic. The blood that now circled the mid-section of his body was vast and dark. Even if he was alive, he wouldn't last much longer.

'I'm okay,' Maddie said. 'Tom is the one hurt. We could have taken down Greg between the three of us. There was no need, Saul.'

'I'm fine,' a voice croaked from the stairs.

'You're not fine,' Maddie said.

Mac finally saw his older brother, slumped against the foot of the stairs. He didn't look fine. He looked pasty and tired, dark rings around his eyes, his lips had a blue tinge. There was also a large, dark red stain covering most of the left-hand side of his fleece.

'Fuck.' He felt the floor shift as he moved to Tom's side. 'You look like hell, Tom.'

'Good to see you too, buddy,' he breathed.

'Greg stabbed him right as you got here,' Maddie said, pulling down his fleece zip and checking the wound. 'Saul!'

Saul finally lowered the gun and looked at Tom.

'Saul! What do we do?' Maddie said.

'I'll grab some towels,' Mac said, but Tom grabbed his hand.

'No. I'm done for.' He nodded his head to Saul. 'Get the gun.'

Mac recoiled, and his heart began to thud.

'What? No way! I won't do it.'

He turned to Maddie, beautiful Maddie, one cheek swollen and bruised, a small cut on the other. 'Grab some towels,' he said, 'there are clean ones in the store.'

She nodded and ran up the corridor. Saul was still standing where he had been when he had fired the gun, staring at Greg on the floor.

Shock.

Tom pulled weakly on Mac's hand.

'Get the gun, Mac.'

'I'm not going to shoot you. Don't be so fucking stupid, Tom.'

Tom tried to laugh, wheezing. A trail of blood leaked from the side of his mouth and ran down his chin.

Mac's chest constricted. He wiped it clean with the sleeve of his coat. The blood on his fleece was bad enough, bad enough for Mac to understand he may not make it through. He couldn't take more blood. If he wiped it away, he could pretend it wasn't there.

Maddie came back with the towels, pressing one to the wound to stem the flow of blood.

'The police,' Tom whispered. He coughed, clearing his throat, and Mac's stomach turned over. Clearing it of blood. 'Put the gun. My hand.'

Mac looked at Saul, and back to Tom.

'What are you saying?'

'I won't make it. He saved... you.'

Mac glanced at Maddie, who looked back at Tom and wiped a tear from her face. 'He wants us to tell the police he shot Greg. To keep... to keep Saul out of trouble,' she said.

Mac looked back at Tom, who gave Maddie a small smile.

'Payback,' he whispered again. 'He saves you. I save him.'

Mac felt himself teetering on the edge of yet another dark precipice. A place he had fallen into more than once over the last year and a half.

'You are not going to die, Tom. You can't.'

Tom closed his eyes. The tinge to his lips was getting bluer, almost grey. In fact, his skin was almost grey.

'Get the gun,' he whispered.

'Maddie.' Mac said. He didn't even know what he wanted to say. He couldn't think clearly. 'I don't know what to do.'

'He wants the gun,' she said quietly.

'You think he'll...'

Mac trailed off as Maddie bowed her head and moved her hand to Mac's arm to give it a squeeze. 'I think maybe he will.'

'No.' Mac grabbed Tom, trying to lie him flat, he supposed. He didn't know. There had to be something to do.

'Mac,' Maddie said gently, 'He has broken ribs. You'll hurt him. Saul! We could do with some help here.'

Saul finally came out of his reverie and came to Tom's side.

'Sorry,' he said.

His face was ashen as he checked Tom over, timed his pulse, and checked the wound.

'Something isn't right. Why is he not in more pain? He has broken ribs, and he's been stabbed? Why is he so relaxed?'

Maddie searched his pocket for the box of tablets and handed them to Saul.

'How many has he had?'

'Only one here, I don't know about before, but he managed to walk a mile down the track. It was hard going even for me in the dark.'

Saul looked at Mac. Mac needed no words, but Saul said it anyway.

'His pulse is really weak, Mac, he's lost a lot of blood, and if he gets through that? I think he's overdosed.'

Mac felt an ache drag through his chest. He put his hands to his face.

'Well, what can we do? You're a fucking doctor, Saul. There must be something we can do.'

Saul shook his head lightly. 'Make him as comfortable as he can be.'

Tom opened his eyes. 'Give... me the gun,' he said, looking up at Saul.

Saul shook his head. 'No. I did it. I panicked.'

'I have... nothing to lose. I want to.'

'I can't let you do that,' he said.

'Thank you... saving Mac,' he breathed, trying to lift a hand and not quite managing. Mac grabbed it. It was ice cold. He closed his eyes and blew out a breath.

He was dying. Mac didn't want to tell himself it was true, but he was.

'There was no question of putting Mac in danger, Tom. I wanted to get Greg, to stop him from hurting you. To stop the whole ridiculous vendetta.'

Pain squeezed through Mac's chest. Pain that he had doubted Saul, Pain that Greg had got to Tom, Pain that Tom was hurt. Pain that Maddie had got caught in the crossfire and was also hurt.

'Let me... save you,' Tom wheezed now, and more blood trickled from his mouth. Mac squeezed his hand as a tear fell down his cheek. He didn't try to stop it. He couldn't. 'Please... the gun. Wipe it'

Maddie wiped her own tears as Saul stared at Tom. It was Mac who took the gun, used a towel to wipe the prints and placed it in Tom's hand.

'I don't deserve it,' Saul said as he broke down. Mac didn't think he could take much more before his own dam burst. Maddie was crying openly as women seemed able to do in these moments. She hugged him.

'You do, you stopped it, and you kept Mac safe,' she said.

'I let you walk into the trap.'

'You couldn't know.'

As they hugged hard, Saul sobbing on her shoulder, Mac felt his fingers squeezed lightly. He looked down at Tom and knew his time was close. He looked like death itself. His eyes sunken and lifeless, his lips fully grey. There was a yellow-grey tinge to his skin.

'She,' he whispered so quietly that Mac had to lean down to him. More blood oozed from his mouth. Mac wiped it away with a towel.

'What?' he said.

'She...loved you,' Tom said, closing his eyes.

Mac felt the fight about Sula was a million miles from over now. Nothing mattered more than his brother right now.

'I don't care, Tom. Whatever happened with Sula, it's done. It doesn't matter now.'

Tom swallowed.

'The baby... was yours.'

'It doesn't matter,' he said.

And then the words hit him. He would never have said four words could pack such a powerful punch, but these almost physically knocked Mac back. He looked at Tom, not breathing. Everything else gone aside from the two of them.

Tom gave a small nod, spluttered more blood, and tried to smile.

'Yours. Don't doubt. She... loved just you.'

Everything felt tight, constricted. Mac couldn't breathe with the pain of what he had thought of his wife, and his brother. What he had thought of the people he loved most.

'I should have spoken to you. Why did you lie? Why didn't she speak to me?' he said with a sob.

'Maddie,' Tom whispered.

'Maddie?' Mac said.

Maddie left Saul on the settee and came over.

'What is it?' She said softly, wiping her tears.

Mac gestured to Tom with a shrug. 'He was talking, then he called for you.'

Tom frowned lightly, heaved a breath, and spluttered more blood. Maddie wiped this bit off with a tenderness that touched Mac.

'Baby. Promise.' he said. His voice was a mere sliver of breath, as though he didn't have the energy to force the air through his voice box.

'I will. I'll tell the whole story. As you said it, you have my word.'

Mac frowned at Maddie as Tom closed his eyes. 'He told me earlier, in case... Mac, I think he knew he was taking too much.'

Tom coughed, bringing their attention back to him.

'Mac, I lied. Protect you.' he said, and his eyes slipped closed. He was so still that Mac thought he had gone. Panic began to knock at his chest. And then Tom heaved a breath and opened them again. 'Sorry. Love you.'

'I'm sorry I doubted you. I love you more than anything, Tom. Thank you for saving my life all those years ago. I owe you so much.'

Tom heaved something that Mac thought may be a laugh. More blood. A wince of pain.

'Stupid. kid,' he said.

Mac laughed through his tears.

'I was,' he said.

Then there was a harsh banging at the door.

'Police! Open up!'

Mac let go of Tom's hand to answer the door. It was the last time he saw his brother alive.

CHAPTER SEVENTY-SEVEN

SNOW FELL OUTSIDE THE window. Mac stared at it, lost in a world of swirling flakes which quietly covered the ground, hiding the debris and muck, covering it with a cloak of clean, pure freshness. Like all the bad had been washed away - except that it hadn't. It was underneath, just waiting for the moment when it would be exposed again.

All that glitters isn't gold, all that's white isn't pure.

The door to the living room opened, and Walt came in with a cheery hello, carrying a paper and a coffee. Mac thanked him with a smile, told him no he didn't need anything else.

Walt brought the paper every day, and Mac ignored it every day. It wasn't like they didn't fill him in on the news, anyway. All of them.

It had been barely three weeks since Greg had descended on the cabin. Christmas had come and gone. Maddie's face had healed, her two black eyes finally fading to a pale yellow, but all three of them had wounds that carried far deeper after the attack.

Maddie was tetchy and upset about the damage one man could inflict. She carried some guilt that she had let Tom take the tablet too. Mac told her to let it go, he would have died of blood loss either way.

Saul carried the guilt only someone who has taken a life can know. The fact that he hadn't intended to kill Greg was irrelevant. The man had died either way, and though it was self-defence, the thought ate at him. The psychologist was now seeing his own psychologist to try to get himself back on track. Whatever had passed between Mac and Saul had dispersed. They had become good friends. One Mac hoped would be a part of his life for a very long time.

Mac blamed himself for neglecting Tom at the time of his life he had obviously needed help the most. He had let assumption and accusation affect his relationship with his brother - and Sula for that matter. Not getting the facts could have cost him the relationship forever if they hadn't reached the cabin in time. He played both that, and the fact that Tom had slipped away without him, over and over.

He took a sip of coffee and placed the paper to the side, planning to leave it, but a picture caught his eye on the folded front page. A man, familiar and yet not. This man was no longer shiny and bright, no longer a star for the stage. This man seemed older, more rugged, his eyes tired. His hair was longer, and a beard covered the lower half of his face.

Mac opened the paper to reveal the full article. No longer a massive full-page spread, but still front page just the same, and continued on page five. His picture, and an idyllic picture of the cabin, sat side by side at the top of the article, and just for effect - to show just how far down the spiral he had gone - an old professional picture from a few years ago sat halfway down. Just close enough to be able to compare the two nicely.

He scanned his eyes over the words and shook his head.

Same old bullshit, embellished for drama.

Mac was still looking at the paper when Maddie came in, her cheeks rosy, a smell of earthy cold air and snow wafting in with her. She moved to the fire, warming her hands in front of the crackling flames.

'Ooh, that's better,' she said. 'How are you feeling today?'

He smiled. 'Not bad. Where have you been so early?'

'Out with the dogs. I couldn't sleep, and it still bothers me that Rolo is out there somewhere.'

Mac nodded. It bothered him too. There had been no sign of the dog since he had run off into the woods three weeks before. They had hunted and scoured the area daily ever since. None of them said it, but all of them were better with another focus. They were happier hunting for the dog than sitting with their thoughts.

The police had taken thorough statements over a week ago, but they were still advised to stay put, just in case they were needed again. It meant that Mac couldn't see Meg. Speaking to her daily had to suffice. There was no release for her or the children, as Tom's body was retained up here for autopsy and investigation. No release for Mac to be able to share his grief with someone who had known his brother as he had.

It sucked for them both.

That said, he couldn't have asked for better hosts, the media had no idea where he was staying, and the house was big enough that he was left alone when he needed it. Some days were better than others. Some days he sobbed for Tom, Sula, and the baby. Some days he turned the events over, playing different scenario's and 'what if's' until he was exhausted. Some days he felt more cheerful, joining Walt for a walk, Hester in the kitchen, or Ezzie for games in the front room. When there was a foot of snow on the ground, there wasn't much getting out in the wheelchair. Something that Saul would be helping to change soon, all being well.

Either way, there was a lot of talking between them. They were an incredibly open, very loving family, and Mac felt honoured to be able to stay with them. He had opened up about his own feelings a lot, something that he hadn't allowed when Sula died. Something that he had pushed to bury, to block out, was now being expressed in huge globs of emotion. Emotion that left him feeling fragile, spent, and sad, but peaceful.

Here he was allowed to just *be*, in all of his glorious rawness, with no judgment. He couldn't thank any of them enough.

Mac put the paper on the coffee table as Maddie came to the settee and sat down beside him.

'No sign of him then?' he said, already knowing the answer.

She shook her head. 'We'll find him. I'm determined to bring him home,' she said.

Mac reached for her hand, which was cool from the frigid air.

'He's probably long gone in this weather. I wish he hadn't run.' he said, placing his other hand over the top, creating a cocoon that warmed her hand with his own.

'I'll bring him home anyway,' she said, forcing her other hand inside to warm that too.

'I think you probably will, through sheer determination,' he said with a grateful smile. He rubbed her hands until his own cooled, and then he kissed each one, and let them go gently as Maddie laughed.

She laughed a lot; he found. Sometimes even through her tears. He envied her ability to see the positive, even when things had gone to shit. Mostly he envied her ability to let the tears go freely, whenever she felt the need, and her surrender to the love, care, and attention that came with being upset. She took their kind energy, used it to release, and came back stronger. She was doing better every day in leaps and bounds. Mac was doing better every day in tiny steps, sometimes even stepping backward.

'I'm nothing if not persistent,' she said, leaning over to the coffee table and the paper. 'Who's that guy?' she said, pointing to the professional picture.

'Very funny.'

She picked up the paper to scrutinise the photograph, scrunching her nose. 'You don't look like the same person, Mac.'

'I'm not. That's bullshit. This is real.'

She turned to study him. 'I like real better. You look too polished there.'

'I was, and what I didn't polish someone else would polish for me. That's how life went, all day every day, because I never knew who would be watching.'

'Did you care who was watching?'

'Too much.'

'Hmm,' she cocked her head to the side, and turned to page five, where the story continued - this time with a full page devoted. At the top was a picture of himself with Sula at some show, dressed too shiny, smiles too wide.

Fake, Mac thought. That happy scene was fake. We argued the entire way there, and then got out to loving smiles and a kiss for the cameras, the perfect couple.

What a ridiculous life the showbiz world was, and what a vicious circle of concealed moods and feelings. Always bright, always happy, always so grateful to be there. So lucky.

Bullshit.

Mac noticed Maddie had gone quiet. She was staring at the page but didn't appear to be reading.

'What's up?' he said.

When Maddie turned to him, she had paled a good three shades.

'What is it?'

'This was your wife, wasn't it?' she said.

'Sula, yes. She was Italian-'

'I saw her. This woman...' Maddie said, cutting him off, and then trailing off herself as she looked back at the picture.

'She was here at the clinic remember, maybe you recognise her from then?' Mac took a sip of coffee.

'I wasn't here then.'

'So, where have you seen her?'

'The cabin.'

'You just said you weren't around.'

Maddie shook her head.

'No, the night Greg came.'

Mac almost spat his coffee over the small table in front of them.

'I would have turned back. The only reason I was in the cabin was because I thought you were there.'

Mac almost held his breath as he turned to her. Sula had appeared to Maddie in the cabin?

I hope to God she looked more appropriate than the Sula in my dreams.

'You think I'm nutty, don't you?' she said.

Mac pursed his lips. 'No, as it happens, I don't. There was some strange shit at that cabin I would never tell a soul for fear of being taken away in a straitjacket. What happened?'

'I haven't really processed it myself yet. When I walked out of the woods, the cabin light was on, and the piano was playing. I thought it was you. The door was open, so I went inside.'

Mac felt his stomach disappear through the floor. He hadn't expected the piano, but he couldn't deny it had happened to him too; back when he was sat on the pier in the ice, refusing to go inside.

'There was no-one in there though,' she said. 'It was like everything stopped instantly the moment I opened the door. I know it sounds stupid. I can't explain it, it was weird.'

'Not so stupid,' Mac said. 'That happened to me too.'

'It did?'

'Yep. I remember asking Saul if he believed in ghosts.'

'I bet he said you were going crazy with grief.'

'Something to that effect if I remember rightly.'

'Well, I certainly wasn't, and if you'd have asked me, I'd have said I didn't believe either, but she scared the shit out of me scuffling around, writing my name on the fridge. And then she appeared, just before Greg got there. She told me to get out.'

'She appeared?'

'Fully, like she was real almost. I think she was trying to help me, to warn me Greg was there. Maybe.'

'And you're sure this wasn't someone else, somebody real?' he said thinly.

She had recognised the woman from the picture. Of course, it was Sula.

'It was her,' she said, pointing to the picture. 'No question.'

Mac looked to Sula on the photograph, smiling brightly at the camera, hand on his stomach where she had always put it for the media.

'She was sad, Mac, but she tried to give me the baby, told me to look after it.' She paused, and Mac raised an eyebrow. 'What do you think she meant?'

'I have no idea,' he shrugged.

The living room door opened, and Saul came in, rubbing snow out of his hair.

'That'll be news later today,' he said.

'What?' Maddie asked.

'The cabin is burning. Probably one of the paps cigarette ends or something. There's enough of the bastards out there.'

Mac was on his feet instantly.

'Burning? I need to take a look.'

'Don't take the kayak. They'll get pictures. It'll turn into a shit storm of you burned it yourself. Out the gate and left, there's a small track between the trees. You can just about see it in the snow. Climb the hill to the top and you'll have a view from there. Take you about twenty minutes if you're quick.'

'Right, see you both later.'

'Be careful,' Maddie said.

'I will.'

He pulled on his coat and boots and ran across the lawn and out the back gate. He gave up running at the steepness of the small track, the snow making the going difficult. He changed gears, walking as fast as he could cope with without having a heart attack.

Within half an hour, he had reached the top. There was a crop of craggy rock that he climbed onto to get a better view, careful to check where his feet were landing with the snow underfoot. At the top, he crouched. From here, he could see just above the tree line. He kicked himself for not bringing Walt's binoculars.

You can see enough. The fuckers have burned it.

Smoke engulfed the cabin, flames licking high into the sky. The photographers that had been there since the night of the notorious cabin murders were moving about, taking shots from every angle. One of the idiots was out in the loch up to his thighs just for a different view.

Not one of them was attempting to put the blaze out as far as he could see.

Pathetic.

Saul had said that the three-mile track was packed with cars that spilled out onto the road, and from the number of reporters and photographers there now it wouldn't surprise him.

He felt his heart tug at the fact that he would never sleep there again. As silly as it seemed looking back, he was sad that this would be the end of Sula too. She hadn't been at the London house, and he wasn't going back there, anyway. He would sell it. The only place she had ever appeared to him was in the cabin.

Now he knew that she had appeared to Maddie too, he wanted to speak to her, to let her write on the fridge again. To tell her he was sorry for doubting her, sorry for being such a shitty husband that she felt she had to abort their child without saying a word. Sorry for working too hard, sorry for not trying harder to stop them from drifting apart. Sorry for everything.

Tom told you about the baby at the cabin. Maddie told you more afterward. She knows Mac. She knows all of that.

He heard sirens and wondered how they would get through. By the time they got here, the cabin would be gone.

'Should have come by air and dumped water on the lot of them,' he said to himself.

Mac clenched his jaw as tears fell down his cheeks.

'Bye, Sula. I love you so much, baby. See you someday.'

Mac blew a kiss into the air, and then he frowned and pointed at the sky.

'Don't think that means you need to follow me around with your worm shit. I don't want to see or hear from you again until I get up there, got it?'

His heart constricted, and he wiped tears from his blurry vision with a smile.

For the first time since she had died, he felt better about letting her go. Okay to move on in his own time. At peace with his feelings for Maddie. If Sula had tried to warn Maddie of danger in the cabin, and Mac didn't doubt one bit of her story, then Sula must be okay with her, too. Tom was with her up there. They would no doubt spend their time criticising and laughing at him from above.

'Look after her, Tom. Love you, buddy.'

He felt a release in his chest, a lightness that he hadn't felt for well over a year.

The cabin burned, and the reporters floundered for the next photograph, the perfect shot. There was nothing more to see here.

Mac began to climb down from the outcrop, slowly and carefully.

There was noise below him and he peered down to see something small and brown move.

Shit! A wildcat?

Am I better up or down?

He was trying to decide when the animal hobbled into the track clearing and looked up at him with a small whine.

'Rolo?'

The dog whined, and his tail wagged slowly. Mac could see he was thin and almost black with dirt, but it was definitely his dog.

'Rolo!' He shouted, scudding the last few feet on his backside, and falling onto his knees by the dog.

Rolo whined and licked at his face once. He was half the dog he had been, dirty, shaking, and obviously lacking energy.

'Rolo,' Mac said stroking his ears, 'Where the hell have you been? We've been so worried. Where did you go? You silly dog.'

More tears fell as he hugged the dog that was now skin and bone.

'How are you even still here? Let's get you home, get you warm. Come on.'

Mac carried Rolo as far as he could, put him down for the rest of the steep track, allowing him to follow slowly, and then picked him up to carry him the rest of the way to the house across the lawn.

If it had been just a month earlier, Mac wouldn't have been able to carry him at all. Now he was light, all long bones and angles, and put up no resistance to being carried.

The back door flew open as he reached the patio, and Maddie flew out.

'Rolo!' She said, slowing to rub the dog's head gently. Mac felt Rolo's tail knock lightly at his back. 'You found him!'

'He was up on the hill,' he said with a grin. 'God knows where he's been. But I'm so glad he's back.'

'Oh, me too, Rolo, we've missed you!'

'Maddie, you left the door open,' Hester said appearing in the doorway, and then she stopped and put a hand to her chest.

'Is that Rolo? Poor thing, bring him in. He must be frozen and starving.'

They brought the dog inside and watched as he devoured a small amount of food. Not too much, Walt had said, or he'll end up with more problems than he already has.

Mac held on to Maddie's hand, shaking with emotion as they stood watching him eat, and then she plucked something from the shoulder of his coat.

'A Feather,' she said, holding a delicate white feather in her hand with a smile. 'That's lucky, Mac, someone up there is looking out for you.'

'It's about time,' he said, letting go of her hand to squeeze an arm around her shoulders with a smile, before kneeling next to the dog he had missed much more than he had let himself believe.

THE END

REVIEW

If you enjoyed this book it would be fantastic if you could leave a review.

Reviews help to bring my books to the attention of other readers who may enjoy them too.

Help spread the joy... or indeed, the fear!

Thank you!

DARKNESS. PARANOIA. ISOLATION.

What do you do when your dream home becomes your worst nightmare? Emmie Landers is about to find out!

Visit www.rebeccaguy.co.uk for more information.

TURN THE PAGE FOR A PEEK AT CHAPTER ONE.

CHAPTER ONE

Emmie Landers stamped on the brake and the Honda's tyres screeched on the cool tarmac. The seatbelt locked, throwing her back into her seat as the car came to a sliding stop.

She blinked, heart pumping.

Pulling her mouth back in an embarrassed grimace, she glanced into the rear-view mirror. The road behind her was empty.

She let out a breath, rolling her eyes.

Jeez Em, that's one way to get out of starting a new life, kill yourself first, cleans up all the mess in one go.

She cackled and pressed the button to lower the driver's window. Cold air poured into the car, lifting her dark fringe from deep blue eyes. Breath clouding before her, she leaned out of the window to look back at the small wooden sign, covered with stray branches stripped bare by winter. It hung lopsided, making this side only marginally clearer than the one she had just passed. She squinted at the weather faded writing in the growing dusk.

BRUADAIR.

That was the place.

Pushing the button to retract the window she jammed the car into reverse and backed up, stopping adjacent to the the sign. She peered into the gloom at a single track lane in bad repair. Large trees and overgrown hedges lined each side, and potholes were prevalent in the ageing tarmac. Grass poked its way through the cracked surface marking the central line of the lane with a patchy mohican.

Emmie checked the car's digital display – 3.34pm - which made her officially late to meet the estate agent..

She pursed her lips. Better late than never.

The car's headlights flicked on against the impending dusk as she turned onto the lane and steered her way up the narrow track, swerving to avoid the worst of the potholes and stray branches which reached from the hedges like arthritic hands. Emmie wrinkled her nose. She had an idea she may need an open mind for this viewing.

Rounding a bend, an old farmhouse came into view and her spirits rose at the signs of life within the lit windows. She slowed, peering into a dimly lit kitchen, trying to catch a glimpse of the occupants, curious as to the type of people who lived up a lane like this. She was still craning her head when the steering wheel wrenched from her grip, scraping through her hands as the car dipped sharply left. Fighting to control the vehicle before it railed into the hedge, she yelled as it bounced back out of the large hole with a thud.

'Christ, couldn't someone fix the damn road?'

Heart thudding, she passed the gated driveway and outbuildings and drove on with more caution, back into the murkiness of the darkening landscape.

Just as she was beginning to wonder how far up the lane this blessed house was, the road stopped abruptly. In front of her sat a small picket fence and gate in dire need of repair and a fresh coat of paint. To the right was a grass clearing where a small Ford sat parked neatly. Emmie raised her eyebrows. Driveway? Well, it was different. One point to the house.

Grinning, she pulled the Honda onto the grass beside the Ford and climbed out of the car, taking a moment to stretch her stiff joints after the long drive. The relief of stretching her legs fell away as she turned to look at the house she had come to view. Heaving a sigh, she felt the last of her optimism fade away under sagging shoulders.

Beyond the picket fence the path to the house was barely visible; hell, a machete might even be in order to get through the tangled mess of grass, brambles, gorse, and bracken.

What she could see of the house didn't fare much better. Light from inside illuminated parts of the wall revealing holes in the mortar, like missing teeth, between the grey stone. The stone porch looked precarious on its column legs and most of the guttering was broken, it hung limply down the house like tinsel on a neglected Christmas tree. Tiles were missing from the roof, one of the two chimney stacks had fallen, and there was a broken window thrown in to boot.

Pulling her wool coat around her against the cold air, Emmie blew out a long breath as she thought of Bryson Estate Agent's particulars.

Tired and rundown, they had stated. In need of restoration.

This house isn't tired, it's half dead, and what it needs is a demolition crew. Are desolate wrecks really all I can afford?

Emmie bit her lip fighting the urge to get back into the car, but she had driven eight hours to view this house, and despite whether it was worth it, she couldn't bear the thought of driving up here just to drive straight home again. Besides, her sister was right, it was time to move on. Three adults and five children squashed into Natalie's four-bed detached down in Surrey was never going to be a forever deal.

She looked back at the house.

Maybe I should just buy a tent.

'Ms Landers?'

A deep voice cut into her thoughts, and Emmie looked to see an elderly gentleman in a grey suit and heavy wool coat coming up the path. He stopped to un-pluck a bramble that had stuck itself to one trouser leg before continuing toward her.

'Ms Emelia Landers?' He enquired again.

Emmie froze, wondering erratically if she should say she was just passing by.

In limbo, and aware of how ridiculous her reaction was, especially given the that there was nowhere to 'pass by' to, she fought the urge to giggle.

'Hello?' The old man bellowed. The sound stretched and echoed. Emmie thought of the officer on the lifeboat after the Titanic sank in the film, Hello! Is there anyone alive out there?!

He was only missing a torch in the fading light.

This image enhanced the already suppressed laughter which erupted from her nose as a loud snort. Eyes watering, she quickly looked down into the collar of her coat, shoulders shaking as she searched for a tissue.

Christ, Em. What is wrong with you? Get a grip.

Blowing her nose, she struggled to choke back the next wave of laughter as she looked up at the man who had now stopped by the gate and was watching her bemused.

'Sorry, allergies.' She offered, getting herself back under control and making her way toward him.

In winter? Crap... well, it's said now.

His bushy eyebrows rose as he regarded her. She shrugged nonchalantly and smiled.

'Ms Landers?' He asked for the third time.

'Yes.' She said, accepting that she was going to have to look around this ramshackle and make the right noises even if she never intended to come here again.

'Mr Roberts, from Bryson Estate Agency. I'd just about given up, thought you'd seen the place and gone back the way you'd come.' He chuckled and offered his hand.

She shook it with a smile, his mild manner and slow Scottish dialect setting her at ease. For a moment she was transported back to her childhood when many family holidays had brought them to Scotland - touring in an old split screen camper van, pitching in the wilderness; sitting around campfires in the dark, telling stories, or singing along to her father's guitar.

It reinforced the fact that this was the right decision. Scotland seemed the most natural place in the world to choose to start over. It gave her a warm, excited feeling in the pit of her stomach, and it made her feel comfortingly close to her father, whose passion had been everything Scottish before he had died four years ago.

Looking at Mr Roberts' genuine smile, she felt foolish at her earlier behaviour.

'Come this way,' he said, holding back the offending trail of bramble that hung over the pathway. She skirted around it and followed him down the overgrown path.

The garden was huge, just over six acres wrapped itself around all four sides of the house which comprised its own stream, small woodland, orchard, and masses of grassland for the children to play. As they walked, Mr Roberts pointed out the boundary lines barely visible in the murky distance.

Bordering the property were miles of fields belonging to two farms, one of which was the farm she had passed down the road. To the right of the house rose the southern edge of a hill range that stretched out for many miles north. Bracken Cruach, the nearest craggy peak to the house, looked more like a mountain than a hill to Emmie, but research had told her it was indeed a hill and far from the highest peak in the range.

Emmie felt warmth swirl in her stomach.

Apples from the orchard, our own stream, picnics on the hill. The kids would love it here –

She broke off mid-thought as Mr Roberts turned their attention to the house and her heart plummeted.

She stalled, running her eyes over the dejected facade.

'Aye, There's much to be done, it's true,' said Mr Roberts, catching her hesitation, 'But it will be a superb little property with some time, love, and attention. The majority of the wounds are superficial according to the surveys.'

'It's always what you uncover when you scratch the surface though isn't it?'

Emmie's heart gave a jolt as she inadvertently recaptured one of Scott's favourite sayings from their house hunting days as newly-weds. She momentarily wished she could go back to those days and tell herself, then sixteen years younger, to scratch under the surface of the marriage too. 'Scratch harder Em, see what he's doing to you?'

Mr Robert's voice filtered into her thoughts, and she took a deep breath of cold air to steady herself as she turned to re-focus on him.

'... won't be without its problems, as all houses are,' he was saying, 'this one wears its heart on its sleeve; it's what it says on the tin - it's cheap, and it needs a lot of work. Other houses may look perfect but scrape under the surface, and they could end up costing as much to put right.'

Fully back in the present Emmie smiled. She could almost see the house beaming with pride.

Unfortunately, it didn't make it look any better.

'Let's go inside,' she said shivering as disappointment and a cool breeze wrapped itself around her.

RUIN IS AVAILABLE AT ALL MAJOR RETAILERS NOW!

SOMETIMES THEY COME BACK...

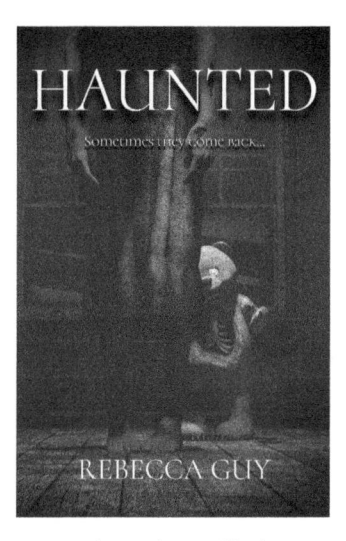

Sixteen years ago her sister died, now she's back. Haunted, terrified and alone, will the truth set Meredith free, or take her soul?

Visit www.rebeccaguy.co.uk for more information.

TURN THE PAGE TO GET THE FIRST SIX CHAPTERS FREE!

Want six free chapters of **HAUNTED?**

Sign up to my mailing list to read the first six chapters for FREE!

You also get access to exclusive behind the scenes content and extra's, and you'll be the first to hear about promotions, discounts, forthcoming titles and competitions!

Signing up is completely free and you will never receive spam from me.

To sign up visit - www.rebeccaguy.co.uk

You can opt out easily at any time.

DECEPTION. GREED. VENGEANCE. BETRAYAL.

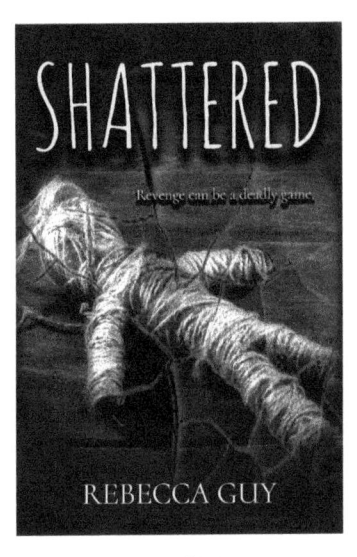

SHATTERED

Revenge can be a deadly game.

REBECCA GUY

A secret envelopes Fortwind House, years old, covered in dust and locked up tight. Rumours surround the formidable woman who lives there, rumours that terrify Charley, but it is the secret that will blow her life apart.

Visit www.rebeccaguy.co.uk for more information.

Lightning Source UK Ltd.
Milton Keynes UK
UKHW011823260123
416025UK00006B/450